in a hurry. Malone is a massive talent...' Luca Veste

'A disturbing and realistic portrayal of domestic noir with a twist. The humour and emotion laced within the darkness was just the right mix for a shocking yet compelling read' Mel Sherratt

'Malone's effortless writing style confirms him as a sharp new voice in crime fiction' Anya Lipska

'The plot is layered and intriguing, my attention never once wandered; it scared the heck out of me in places and kept me reading into the early hours. Overall it was an intense, emotive and beautifully honed piece of "gritty crime" fiction' Liz Loves Books

'A slick thriller with a killer punch' Douglas Skelton

'Funny and brutal, heartfelt and compelling. Highly recommended' Craig Robertson

'Tough, funny, dark and so in your face it hurts' Ken Bruen

'Malone writes beautifully' Chris Ewan

'Wow! What an emotionally powerful read' K. E. Cole

'Highly recommended' Thomas Enger

'It's difficult, unnerving, unputdownable, and simultaneously impossibly sad and also hopeful' Richard Fernandez

'An intriguing tale with a haunting, Gothic quality that compels you to keep reading till the end' Howard Linskey

'Unexpected and beautiful, the novel has all the gothic elements of classics like *Rebecca*, and the all the poetry and page-turning trickery you'd expect from Michael Malone' Louise Beech

'Utterly brilliant! Scary, captivating and beautifully written' Emma Clapperton

'An unsettling and upsetting story that kept me enthralled, horrified and quite often, in tears. Dark, disturbing and peppered with his trademark humour' S.J.I Holliday

'Unsettling, thought-provoking, and absolutely riveting' Love Reading

'Malone drives a compelling narrative with a plot that will twist your stomach and have you on the edge of your seat' Live and Deadly

'Malone has a superb talent for building up the narrative so subtly and carefully that it is only when you reach the end the reader realises that they have read a book which has completely blown their mind' Segnalibro

'Have you ever read a book that made you question your beliefs? Pulled at your emotions until you felt stripped bare and exposed? ... That is THIS book!!' Crime Book Junkie

'Undoubtedly absorbing and will get under your skin from the very first blow. It is stunning' Woman Reads Books

'A book that will leave you on the edge of your seat and take you on an emotional journey, gripped with worry, anger, tension and relief' Off The Shelf Books

'Dark, powerful and highly emotive' Bibliophile Book Club

'A fascinating book to read, chilling, difficult to put down and at times difficult to read' Steph's Book Blog

'Interesting, gripping and so real that you will not be able to put it down' Blog Loving

'The wow factor had me completely wrapped up in a twisted, addictive story of how one action can cause a life to spiral out of control, with severe consequences' Reviewed the Book

'This is a story of survival, in the toughest conditions. A domestic horror story' Northern Crime

'Malone's perfectly written prose is both profound and insightful' Postcard Reviews

'I couldn't put this down, was frantically page-turning and I feel thoroughly drained now after reading this!' Mrs Blogg's Books

'This is a novel full of twists, tension and gut-wrenching emotion' Chillers, Killers and Thrillers

'This was a really emotional read on so many levels' The Book Trail

'One of the finest novels within the domestic genre' The Misstery

'It was brutal and compelling. It was outstanding. This is a book that will stay with me for a very long time and one you certainly won't want to miss' Ampersand Book Reviews

'Michael has written an evocative, dark and emotional novel that also works as a compelling psychological thriller' Bloomin' Brilliant Books

'It will wrench your heart, challenge your perceptions, turn you upside down, inside out and spit you out, a mangled wreck, on the other side' Chapter in my Life

'What a story. Beautiful, like a string of fascinating words given new a meaning when put together. Skilled, like the sharp blade of a razor. Riveting, like an obsessive puzzle with missing pieces' Chocolate 'n' Waffles

'Fantastic characters, a gloriously mysterious house and a delightfully twisty plot. Highly recommended' Espresso Coco

'One of the better novels of this type that I have read this year' Steph's Book Blog

'An extraordinary story with a magical gothic setting in today's reality. An outstanding supernatural and psychological masterpiece. Just wow!' Books From Dusk Till Dawn

'All those topics wrapped up in one beautiful creeptastic package' The Pages in Between

'This novel rocked the gothic vibe very well ... the ending was amazing, in the most twisted and shocking way!' Keeper of Pages

'Well-developed and intentionally plotted – resulting in genuinely shocking and satisfying plot twists and sustained suspense from the book's first page to its last' Crime By the Book

'Michael J. Malone has created a haunting psychological thriller with so many interesting characters that you will ask for more!' Varietats

'A very original psychological thriller and one I would urge anyone and everyone to read just because it's such a powerful and beautifully haunting novel' The Book Review Café

'Malone had me hooked from the first page to the last in this exquisitely woven story of the past meeting the present' Emma the Little Bookworm

'An easy read that I sprinted through – just because it's so darn good – with page after page bringing a magnetic welcoming' Page Turner's Nook

'Equally haunting and frightening' Ronnie Turner

'Michael J. Malone took me on a journey, he filled my head with the unimaginable and made it come alive' It's All about the Books

'A creepy and atmospheric tale' The Crime Novel Reader

'It's a psychological thriller mixed with a gothic horror and I loved every single page of it' The Book Magnet

'With writing that is almost poetic in nature, this is a beautifully written book that keeps readers guessing throughout' The Quiet Knitter

'A fresh, remarkable read!' Novel Gossip

'A satisfyingly, chillingly, haunting and delightfully disturbing read, don't miss it!' Chapter in My Life

'The author truly shows off his diversity and displays a remarkable talent for storytelling' Novel Deelights

'A cracking read that combines a real mystery with a genuinely touching and emotionally affecting story' Mumbling About

ABOUT THE AUTHOR

Michael Malone is a prize-winning poet and author who was born and brought up in the heart of Burns' country, in Ayr. He has published over two hundred poems in literary magazines throughout the UK, including *New Writing Scotland*, *Poetry Scotland* and *Markings*. His career as a poet has also included a (very) brief stint as the poet-in-residence for an adult gift shop. *Blood Tears*, his bestselling debut novel won the Pitlochry Prize (judge: Alex Gray) from the Scottish Association of Writers. His other published work includes: *Carnegie's Call* (a non-fiction work about successful modern-day Scots); *A Taste for Malice*; *The Guillotine Choice*; *Beyond the Rage* and *The Bad Samaritan*. His psychological thriller, *A Suitable Lie*, was a number one bestseller on AU/UK ebook charts, and *House of Spines* soon followed suit. Michael is a regular reviewer for the hugely popular crime fiction website www.crimesquad.com. A former Regional Sales Manager for Faber & Faber he has also worked as an IFA and a bookseller.

Follow Michael on Twitter @michaeljmalone1; on Facebook: www.facebook.com/themichaeljmalonepage, and his website: www.mjmink.wordpress.com.

After He Died

MICHAEL J MALONE

ORENDA
BOOKS

Orenda Books
16 Carson Road
West Dulwich
London SE21 8HU
www.orendabooks.co.uk

First published in the UK in 2018 by Orenda Books
Copyright © Michael J. Malone, 2018

A catalogue record for this book is available from the British Library.

ISBN 978-1-912374-33-5
eISBN 978-1-912374-34-2

Typeset in Garamond by James Nunn
Printed and bound in Denmark by Nørhaven

For sales and distribution, please contact *info@orendabooks.co.uk*
or visit *www.orendabooks.co.uk*.

1

Through a medicated fog, Paula Gadd looked along the line of mourners waiting to greet her. It took her last scrap of energy not to tell them all to leave. Someone gripped her hand. A woman she didn't recognise; her face a twist of assumed empathy.

'I'm sorry for your loss,' the woman said.

Paula looked from the woman's surprisingly strong hand to the powdered lines around her mouth, caught a wave of her sickly perfume and managed a question:

'Who are you again?'

The woman gave a small nod, as if acknowledging that Paula's grief was making her momentarily senile, then moved on. The words *Minister for Business* nudged at her mind. Thomas knew all kinds of important people.

Thomas, her dead husband.

She was way too young to be a widow, wasn't she?

When she first met him he was Tommy, but his drive for success meant a return to the name on his birth certificate. You can't be informal, apparently, when you're aiming for the big bucks.

'I'm sorry for your loss,' the next person said. A man in a black suit. All these men in black suits were merging into one. Except, the bulb shape at the end of this guy's nose was threaded with veins; Paula couldn't take her eyes off them, following the lines as a blue one crossed a pink one.

Must be the drugs the doctor had given her, she thought. To be fair, the only way she could handle this service was through a haze. She took a breath in through her nose, as if sniffing for a reminder of the name of the drug printed on the small bottle. Whatever it was, she was immensely grateful.

'I'm sorry for your loss,' she aped the man. He cocked his head like a dog might, unsure he had heard what he had heard.

'I can only imagine what you are going through, dear.' His smile was limp, questioning: *Don't you know who I am?*

She was already onto the next person, her hand reaching out, but her mind now retreating from the line of people, all of them keen to demonstrate their support in her time of grief. All of them leaning on ceremony yet shying away from reality, grateful they weren't in her shoes. At this thought she looked down at her feet.

Size three Louboutins.

She had had a great time choosing them. Never thought that when she was handing over her credit card they'd be on her feet at Thomas's funeral.

Next in line was a couple in their seventies who looked like they'd been eating nothing but watery soup for the last thirty years – their faces stripped down to nothing but skin and sinew. And they looked so alike. Were they brother and sister? 'Thomas will be missed,' said the man.

'First you lose your only son,' said the woman. 'How can one person take all that grief...?' She was silenced by a look from her husband. Paula decided they must be married. Who else but a spouse would look at you that way?

Already, she missed that way of looking. That *knowing*.

She ignored the comment from the woman. Pushed it to the back of her mind. That was seven years ago. Almost to the day.

That grief she wore like an old friend. A welcome reminder that Christopher had been in her life. This one was a new wound. Fresh. Gaping. A pain that plucked the air from her lungs.

Anyway, who were all these people? she wondered. And who decided we should line up like this at the end of a funeral service? Whoever they were, they were sick in the head. Without the chemicals soothing the barb and bite of her loss, this would have been enough to send her to the nearest psychiatric ward.

She'd always seen herself as part of a couple. A pair. Her identity was wrapped up in that idea. She loved being married. That it was Thomas was mostly a good thing, but the state of marriage was what really gave her satisfaction.

Even after thirty years she loved saying to salesmen, 'I'll have to speak to my husband first.'

Now she was in the singular.

Flying solo.

Well, not flying so much as drifting.

Adrift.

And heavy with regret that in the latter years she hadn't made more of an effort.

One more person and she was at the end of the line. Thank the good Lord, the line was running out of the sympathetic and suitably morose.

A young woman stepped forwards. Wide-brimmed hat, large sunglasses, thin nose, plump lips. A chin that almost came to a point. She offered an embrace. Confused, Paula leaned into it, finding that suddenly, surprisingly, human contact was needed. The woman, a girl really, touched her lips to the side of Paula's face.

The woman spoke in a whisper and Paula felt something being slid into the pocket of her jacket. What did she say? Paula heard her clearly, but the words were so out of context in the situation that she struggled to make sense of them.

She looked down to her pocket as if she was trying to work out what had just happened. She raised her eyes to question the girl, but she was already walking away as if desperate not to be stopped. Through the throng all Paula could see was a back view of her black hat and a fan of long, straight, blonde hair across her shoulders.

'Who...' she turned to the man at her side, her husband's elder brother, Bill.

'That was tough, eh?' he asked, his hand light on her arm, his smile distorting his face. Then he turned away without waiting for her answer. Which figured. She'd always felt that Bill had little interest in her, and just over thirty years of knowing each other – twenty-nine of them in a marriage with his brother – had done nothing to soften that feeling. He must be pleased, Paula thought. At last he had a reason to ignore her.

Oh, get over yourself, Paula. Thomas always said she read way too much into things. The man was grieving as well, wasn't he?

The woman's voice echoed in her mind, but through the medication she couldn't make sense of her words – their incongruity. People were here to tell her how much they loved and admired Thomas, surely?

She craned her neck and looked around the milling mourners for the hat and the blonde hair, but she saw no sign of them. It was probably some young woman who had a fancy for Thomas – he was a handsome man after all and he did attract lots of admiring glances. As far as she was aware he never did anything to encourage them, though.

Whatever his faults, he was a one-woman man ... wasn't he?

Her knees gave, just a little, but she managed to right herself, managed not to fall to the floor in a heap. A wave of bone-aching loss crashed down on her and she allowed her hand to drop away from the pocket. If it was a note, she should simply crumple it up and throw it away, unread. Whatever it was, it was surely just a cruel joke.

Thomas. My Thomas. She recalled the moment – was it really just a few breaths ago when the curtains slid shut, hiding his...? She couldn't bring herself to even think the word coffin.

She turned again to try and find the young woman. There was no sign of her, but her words repeated in Paula's mind.

'You need to know who your husband really was.'

2

Father Joe, Thomas's younger brother, took her by the elbow.

'We need to go, Paula. The car's waiting.'

Again, she saw the curtains closing, imagined the fires lighting up, flames engulfing the coffin, and a sob burst from her mouth, for a moment clearing the drug mist in her mind. She stumbled, but Joe was there, helped her gather strength.

She looked into Joe's face, searching for signs of Thomas; saw them in the cast of his eyes, the line of his nose. But where his brother could, in recent times anyway, be withdrawn, she only ever sensed warmth from Joe; an openness to living and life.

'Waste of a good man,' she said, leaning into him.

'Yes. Far too young to be taken,' Joe answered.

'I'm talking about you, Father Joe.'

Joe snorted. This was an old conversation. 'By serving God I try to make lots of people happy.' And that was an old response.

'You and your organised religion,' she sighed, but she was aware she was dissembling. Perhaps if she focussed on something else, someone else, even for a moment, it would take away some of this pain.

'C'mon,' Joe said and pulled her into his side in half a hug. 'Sometime next week, I'll bring over a bottle of gin, we'll watch the sunset from your rooftop garden and we'll debate life in all its flavours.'

'Rooftop garden,' Paula said dismissively. 'It's a balcony with some potted plants.'

'That was always a surprise to me. How Tommy took to gardening,' Joe said with a sad smile.

'Helped him to think,' Paula said. 'It was a release from all the decisions he had to make every day.' Then the stray thought: who would make all those decisions now?

◆

The funeral 'purvey' was being held at a city-centre hotel; a big shiny tribute to ambition at the side of the M8 as it shot through the city.

'Hate this place,' said Paula as the limousine drew up at the hotel entrance.

'Why choose it then?' asked Joe.

Paula shrugged. 'It seemed like a good idea at the time.'

'Think they might have vol-au-vents?' he asked, a smile laced through the question. He was remembering family get-togethers and his late mother's cooking. Pride of place at every supper was taken by vol-au-vents with creamy chicken. The rest of the world moved on to olives and Italian cold cuts, but old Mrs Gadd persisted with her vol-au-vents.

'God, I hope so,' said Paula, thankful for Joe's presence and his sense of humour. His experience was showing. He'd be going through this on a weekly basis, attending the funerals of his flock, doing his God's representative-on-earth thing. She looked out of her side of the car, towards the hotel. Steeling herself.

'Let's go,' said Joe, placing a hand on hers. 'You'll be fine.'

◆

Inside, and up the wide staircase the suite set aside for their reception was already full. At the far side of the room it was ceiling-to-floor smoked glass and a number of small round tables were positioned around the space. They were all about chest height and held platters of edibles, like a series of islands. *An archipelago of snacks*, Paula heard in her mind, and it was Thomas's voice, coloured with his trademark sarcasm.

With a stab low in her gut she turned back to face the door, as if it had really been him who'd spoken. As if he was about to enter, walk over to her with that big smile of his and start a wry monologue on the faults of everyone in the room.

The thing was, when he did behave like that people loved it. Folk gravitated to him, caught up in his glamour.

Paula could have laid bets on the first thing a stranger might say to him.

'Haven't I seen you before?'

He had that look. Success, and a confident air that intrigued.

'You sure I haven't seen you on TV?' they would ask, and Thomas would smile, laugh and shake his head, delighted at the response.

It's all smoke and mirrors, honey, he would tell her. *People see what they want to see. I have a mirror for a face, and I trail smoke out of my arse.* If he was actually here, he'd be surrounded by men and women, each of them wanting a moment with him, like he could offer some sort of benediction.

Wondering who she could talk to safely, Paula scanned the food and with a weak smile noted that there were, indeed, no vol-au-vents.

A hand on her shoulder, a chirrup in her ear. It was Daphne. Big brother Bill's wife.

'Paula. How are you, hen?' she asked.

'Oh, you know, as bad as you'd expect,' said Paula.

Paula looked at Daphne. She was in a black trouser suit and a pink blouse, of a quality she'd never seen her wear before. Usually Daphne's clothes looked like she'd thrown them on without giving it much thought. Paula recalled a time she'd offered to take Daphne shopping but was rebuffed. Her sister-in-law clearly didn't want her charity, which she understood, but Paula's view was that if you can't share your wealth with family, what was the point in having it? Yes, distance had grown between the brothers, but she was keen that the women should show the men how families behaved.

'Such a shock, hen. Such a shock,' Daphne said.

'Aye,' said Paula, as if it wasn't the ninetieth time Daphne had said that to her in the last few days. 'Here. You should try those sausage rolls. They're delicious.' As she spoke she tried to remember where the distance between the men had come from. It seemed so stupid now, in the event of Thomas's death.

'Anything we can do for you, Paula...' Bill came over to stand beside his wife. He looked like he meant it.

'Thanks, Bill,' she said, knowing the offer wasn't genuine.

It was after Christopher was killed, she remembered – that was when Bill and Thomas had grown apart. That was when they'd all grown apart. She coughed back rising emotion. Now wasn't the time for such introspection.

'When's the will being read?' Bill asked, pushing his specs back up into position. She looked at him properly, for the first time that day. He'd grown a beard and suited it. He hadn't been immune to the Gadd family handsome gene, but his tendency to look at the world as if it had let him down badly, gave his good looks an unpleasant slant.

'I ... I'm not sure, Bill. I haven't spoken to the lawyer about that yet.'

Bill raised his right eyebrow. 'I don't imagine my brother would have left us anything...' There was a tightness in his expression that made Paula think big brother Bill was praying that this was indeed what would happen. 'But I just wanted to say that whatever the will says, we won't be contesting it.'

'Well, that's ... okay then,' Paula replied and edged away from him. What was that about? Won't be contesting? Contesting what? She'd been Thomas's wife for nearly thirty years. Whatever was coming her way, she deserved.

Bill turned to the food, shrugged at Daphne as if to say, *I'm trying*, before he picked up a plate. Paula looked at her sister-in-law and read the impact of several decades in a menial job: school cleaner. Bill was a floor manager in a men's clothing store and Paula realised early on in her marriage that he was threatened by Thomas's success. He was the eldest brother, took his role seriously and didn't take the fact well that middle brother, Thomas, had won all the prizes.

If *all the money* was the prize you were after.

In the early days of that success, Paula had tried to share some of the symbols of it with Daphne – shoes, jewellery, gadgets – and, before Daphne put on all the weight, clothes. But Bill had made her return everything, saying they didn't need any of their charity.

Paula felt a grumble in her stomach. That was a novelty. She hadn't felt any hunger since the news first came through. Since the two young plods showed up at her front door, with their hats in their hands. Out of the blur of words coming from their mouths she had heard *heart attack* and *restaurant*. Followed by *dead on arrival*.

She debated now having anything to eat. Considered that it might not be hunger, but thirst she was feeling. And made for the bar at the other side of the room.

The barman smiled. He looked about nineteen, but filled his white shirt nicely across the shoulders.

'You look like you could do with a drink,' he said.

'The widow,' she said waving a hand in front of her black suit, then realising that her attempt at humour was inappropriate, she fought the heat of a blush.

She sat on a stool and placed her handbag on the bar. 'Sorry, son,' she said. 'And yes, I could do with a drink.'

'What would you like, madam?'

She read his name badge.

'Sam, I'd love a G&T. Heavy on the gin with just a smidge of tonic.'

'A large gin and tonic it is,' Sam said with a hint of a smile and turned away from her to make her drink. As she watched him work she couldn't help but compare him to Christopher. Would they have made friends if they had met? she wondered. Christopher was probably only a few years older than him when he died. Twenty-five. She held her hand to her belly as if it could contain the gut-punch of grief at all that lost potential.

This was something she did on an almost daily basis; placing Christopher into the lives of the people she encountered. Of course, it couldn't be healthy, but she was powerless against the compulsion.

When the drink arrived, she gave Sam a small nod of thanks, swivelled in her seat, placed her back against the bar and surveyed the gathering. It's me, she wanted to shout. I'm the widow. Why are you all avoiding me? Grief isn't contagious. If Thomas was here they'd all be flocking around. Magnetised by his energy.

◊

After a few drinks and more than a few clichéd expressions of support from the more conscientious 'grievers', she eased herself off her stool and made her way to the ladies.

In the toilet, she made straight for a cubicle, locked the door, and took a seat.

She'd noticed a couple just beyond the entrance to the toilets. The woman had leaned in to the man. Head on his shoulder. And he'd taken a moment from reading whatever was on his phone to kiss the top of her head. A casual intimacy. It looked like the phone was the distraction, not his partner.

It had been a long time since she and Thomas had communicated like that.

It would be nice to feel his strong arms around her tonight in bed, a thought that brought on a crushing guilt. She could have been a better wife, and now she'd never be able to make things better.

Then the tears fell.

And felt like they would never stop.

◊

Once they had subsided, she made for the sink, tossed her handbag to the side and sluiced her face with cold water. Then, she patted it dry and examined herself in the mirror.

Her eyes weren't too puffy. A little bit of make-up and no one would notice.

Once she finished touching up her mascara and dabbed some concealer onto the bags under her eyes, she rooted around her handbag, searching for her pills. Her mini-breakdown in the toilet suggested that the drugs were losing their effect.

She held the small, brown, white-capped bottle in her hand and gave it a little shake as she debated whether or not to take more. The worst of the day was over, surely? And she hated the way they'd made her feel; at a remove from everything and everyone.

The toilet door opened and she heard the clacking of a pair of high heels against the tiled floor. She looked up to see that it was Daphne.

She gave her a little smile. 'Had a wee greet?' Daphne asked.

Paula turned to face the mirror with her fingertips pressed against the skin under her eyes. 'That obvious?'

'You've looked better, hen.'

Paula smiled at Daphne's uncharacteristic honesty. She usually kept her opinions to herself.

'Why did we never get on?' Paula asked her.

'Sorry?' Daphne walked towards the sinks, her gait that of the mildly pissed.

'We married the two brothers who could marry. I've no siblings and yours are all boys. We could have been like sisters to each other,' Paula explained.

Daphne looked at Paula. Her expression one of disbelief.

'You really don't know, do you?'

'Know what?' Paula asked, mystified. Just how pissed was Daphne? Usually a Bacardi and lemonade was her limit. She must have been hitting the whisky for a change.

Daphne held her gaze for a moment as if trying to read her. Shook her head. 'Nothing, hen,' she said, turned away to face the mirror and fished in her handbag for her lipstick.

'What?' Paula felt a surge of irritation. She didn't have the strength to fight it. 'God, I tried to help you as much as I could. You always were jealous of me and Thomas.'

'Jealous?' Daphne laughed. The sound held no humour. She swallowed and crossed her arms as if that might help her contain what she had been about to say.

But Paula knew what was on her mind. The same argument that

would come up over every family get-together. Some people just wouldn't respect the fact that hard work reaped rewards; and that not every success had a trail of bodies behind it.

But before Paula could respond, Daphne spoke again. 'Time to wake up, Paula. The big man's gone. God knows what he was up to before he died...' She sniffed. '...But I'm betting a few chickens are about to come home to roost.'

With that, Daphne gathered her things and left. The door closed behind her with a solid thud.

◊

Paula fled from the reception, only managing to breathe once she got outside the hotel. She stood just beyond the door, bent over, taking great gasps as if she had just ran a marathon.

She straightened her back and paced back and forth. Thought of Daphne's twisted expression and her certainty as she threw the words at her like poisoned darts. Thought of Bill and his assertion that however Thomas had drawn up his will, there would be no contest.

To hell with them, thought Paula. Throughout her entire marriage, at every family occasion, Bill would sniff when he saw her, as if he caught the scent of a dog turd and was trying to work out who'd dragged it in on the bottom of their shoe. And Daphne had taken his lead, just staying on the right side of not being downright rude.

She turned to her right and saw the smoker's area – a covered gazebo with two potted ferns on either side of the entrance. There was one man inside; his eyes squinted behind an exhalation of smoke when he saw her enter.

'Got any spare?' she asked.

'Sure, no bother, darling,' he replied.

As he pulled a packet from one pocket and a lighter from the other, Paula studied him: bald, clean-shaven, late-fifties. His suit jacket was unbuttoned and his white shirt was just a tad too tight across his belly. She didn't recognise him, which didn't mean he hadn't been at Thomas's funeral reception; she barely knew any of her husband's friends – she corrected that: *associates*.

'Here on business?' she asked, as she took a cigarette from him. And as she did so their hands touched. A split second of connection. Human skin on hers. A moment of appreciation. A moment of awkwardness. *He was a total stranger*. She hid her momentary discomfort in the mechanics of lighting her cigarette.

'No,' he replied. Here we go, she thought. But he surprised her. 'I'm at a wedding.'

'Oh, right,' she said, grateful that he hadn't known Thomas. She held the cigarette between her lips, and took a deep breath. Coughed. Coughed some more.

'Been a while?' the man asked, the skin around his eyes crinkled in a smile.

'I've not had a cigarette in twenty years.' She inhaled again. This one settled better in her lungs and she felt the nicotine hit. She held the cigarette up in front of her face and looked at it as if wondering why she'd ever stopped.

'Hard day?' he asked.

She nodded. 'Funeral.'

'Somebody close?'

'Husband.'

'Shit.' He took a hit from his cigarette. Exhaled. 'Life can be a right bastard, eh?'

Later, when she got home, she would run through the conversation that followed and wonder at her ability to tell a total stranger everything. Well, not everything. She told him she'd met Thomas when she was sixteen. In a nightclub. She'd just started a new job as a secretary and was splashing her first wage. Thomas was a scruffy eighteen-year-old student. She remembered him sizing her up then nervously asking her for a dance. They quickly moved to smooching and had been together ever since.

'Romance of the century, eh?' Paula said with a faint smile. 'No drama. He saw. He conquered. They lived happily ever after.'

'How long were you married for?' the man asked.

'Our thirtieth anniversary is coming up in a couple of months. What should I get for that one? Pearls?'

'Thirty years? Really?' He looked at her with the expression that said, *You're in your late forties? Wow.*

She was used to it; but to be fair, she worked for it. Ate clean, barely drank, didn't smoke – usually – and exercised almost every day. So, yeah, she was used to that little look. But normally she would shrug it off. Other people's opinions weren't usually important to her. But, unaccountably, this stranger's approval gave her a little frisson of pleasure.

'Kids?' he asked.

Paula nodded. Probed at the wound, like she might push her tongue into a mouth ulcer. Felt a flare of pain, a momentary fatigue in her core, but that was fine. It was a reminder. Her Chris had lived. And, boy, how he had lived. Energy enough for five people. A mind that could grapple with any idea and an innocence that life was yet to quell – and then he died. But she couldn't tell this stranger that he too was dead. The poor guy had just come out here for a cigarette, not to have her woes heaped upon him.

'That's what it's all about, eh? Family.' The man said. 'I'm sure they'll be a great comfort to you.'

Paula just smiled. And thought of Daphne's expression in the toilet, envy wrapped up in her snarl, and her words, carefully chosen to wound:

God knows what he was up to before he died.

3

Thankfully, the taxi driver was silent as he drove her home to her townhouse in the west of the city.

Just as he parked the car, her phone rang. She really didn't want to speak to anyone, so with a sigh she fished it out of her handbag. But she didn't recognise the number on the screen. Could it be someone who couldn't make the funeral offering their condolences?

'Hello?'

There was nothing. But the connection was still live.

'Hello?' she repeated.

What was that? Breathing?

'Can I help you?'

Nothing.

'For goodness sake,' she said as she disconnected the call.

'Something wrong, missus?' asked the driver over his shoulder.

'Third time this week,' she said absently, as she read the taxi meter and fumbled through her purse for the correct money.

Getting out of the taxi, she tried to ignore the alarm bell ringing faintly in the back of her mind. She had enough to worry about; she didn't need to fret over a few prank calls.

After he drove away, she stood on the front step, the key in her hand, reluctant to enter her own home. The house Thomas worked towards – dreamed of – reached above her into a night sky turned featureless by electric light. His monument to success.

Cold and as welcoming as a mausoleum.

♦

Somehow, miraculously, she slept. Only for an hour or so, but still, better than nothing. When she woke up, the room was in darkness and she imagined Thomas beside her, on his back, hands on his chest, his breath a soft gurgle in his throat.

She tried to assess what time it was. A slice of streetlight showed through a gap in her curtains. It would probably be nearly time for him to get up and get ready for work.

After Christopher's death, work – the business – had become the channel for Thomas's grief. While she'd thrown herself into charity work, he'd spent hour upon hour working on deals. And to be fair it worked, and he was soon expanding into bigger premises and sites in London and Manchester.

Sure, she suspected that there were some dodgy dealings going on; who grows quite so rapidly in such a short space of time without blurring the lines a little? But she trusted Thomas not to get into anything too tricky. And if she was honest, she had allowed the riches it brought her to blinker her. She had developed a tremendous ability to buy *stuff* – and then, when she was bloated with all kinds of nothing, she would sell it and raise cash for charity.

The money continued to flood in. They moved to a bigger house in the city. Then an even bigger one.

All of this room – she looked around herself – a tangible representation of the emotional space that had grown between them.

She twisted on the bed and faced his side. She reached a hand out and stroked the sheet where he only recently lay. Imagined her hand resting on his naked hip; the skin there smooth and hairless in contrast to the matting of hair that covered almost everywhere else.

Once again, an image of her son popped into her head. The ache of missing him ever present.

Enough, she thought. Sat up and kicked her feet off the bed. She was being morose.

She got to her feet, picked a silk dressing gown from a chair at the side of the bed, drew it around herself and went through to the spare bedroom, where Thomas sometimes slept when he came in late from a business meeting. He always said he didn't want to disturb her, which was fine. He would only reek of cigarettes and whisky. Fumble at her as if prompted by memories of better times, and then turn onto his back and snore like a road drill was stuck in his throat. She sat on a small leather armchair that was tucked into a corner, looked over at the pristine, empty bed, and felt a shock to see that her husband wasn't there. He wasn't working late. He was never going to work late again.

Grief sucked the air from her lungs. She gasped with the pain of it. How had she managed to get through the funeral?

How was she going to get through the rest of her life?

Pulling her knees to her chest she thought about the day. All those people, and how many of them did she really know? How many of them really knew Thomas?

Then, from somewhere, an image of the young woman in the wide-brimmed hat. Her brief hug as she slipped something into her pocket.

She had been so caught up in the day she hadn't even bothered to check what the girl had given her.

Her jacket. She'd just allowed it to fall to the floor in the hall. Since when had she become so careless about her belongings? The suit had cost her more than four hundred pounds and she'd let it fall to the floor like a rag...

She got to her feet, walked down the stairs and along the hall. There was enough of a glow from the street outside for her to see what she was doing without switching on the hall light.

There, a black slump of cashmere on the carpet. She bent forwards and picked it up. Patted it down to locate the pocket then slid her hand inside and pulled out the small envelope. Tucking her jacket under her left arm, she examined the contents.

It was a small piece of unlined paper, the upper edge ragged as if it had been torn out of a notebook. And there in careful, feminine, curled handwriting, three short sentences. Sentences that could have the power to change her life.

Your husband was not the man you thought he was. Call this number. You need to know the truth.

4

It was a warm, sunny day when they brought baby Christopher home from the hospital. Despite the warmth, she'd put him in a padded blue suit that was several sizes too big, his pudgy pink face almost lost in the cushion of it.

They were terrified: this tiny human was completely reliant on them and they had no clue what to do. Thomas only admitted this later. At the time he projected confidence. It's a baby, he said. Millions are born every year. If other people can manage, so can we.

She was weepy, her body adjusting to the trauma and the blessing of childbirth, while her mind fought to come to terms with the enormity of it all. This was her baby. What if she got it all wrong?

Christopher started wailing the minute they walked in the door. Paula tried to shush him, placing a hand on the down that covered his soft skull. Already she'd forgotten everything the nurses had shown her.

'The wee soul's probably roasting inside that suit,' Thomas said with a calm that caught her in a contradiction – she felt simultaneously soothed by it, and worried. Thomas was already showing capability here; could she match it?

'And he's probably needing a wee feed, honey. You up for it?'

'But...' She'd fed him several times already, but in the hospital with a capable and caring nurse on hand.

'C'mon up to his bedroom...' And Thomas gently took her hand. With the other he was holding the baby in his car seat as if it was something he'd been doing every day for the last year.

They'd bought a huge wing-backed chair especially for the nursery. In the latter days of her pregnancy Paula had fantasised about spending dreamy afternoons there, feeding her child, a radio playing Mozart or something in the background – she'd read an article that said the sound of it could raise a child's IQ.

Now they were going to do it for real. 'What if...?'

Thomas stretched over and kissed her. 'You're going to be the best mother this little boy could ever dream of,' he smiled. 'I have no doubt in my mind of that, Mrs Gadd.'

With trembling legs she allowed herself to be guided up to the room and onto the chair. She settled herself on the inflated ring Thomas had jokingly bought her – *In case you need stitches, honey,* he'd said. Now she was hugely grateful for that moment of thoughtfulness. Thomas made for the changing table, lifted Christopher – still wailing – onto it and took him out of his padded suit.

As if any sudden movement might break something, Thomas cradled their son in the crook of his arm and made his way across the room to where Paula sat on the chair.

'Ready, honey?' he asked, and looked pointedly down at the front of her blouse.

'Oh. Right.' She looked up at him; at their red-faced child in his arms.

'If you just...' He motioned with his free hand. Following his instruction, she unbuttoned her blouse and fidgeted with her nursing bra to allow her child access to her milk.

Then he handed the baby down to her and ... it was as if she'd been doing this all her life. Christopher's hot little mouth tugging at her nipple, drinking furiously. She felt a tingling trickle as the milk flowed, and a sudden calm. Thomas crouched at her feet looking up, watching them both in wonderment, his cheeks wet with tears.

◆

Your husband was not the man you thought he was.

Exhausted, Paula fell to the floor, her mind unable to grasp what she had just read. Her husband; the man she was with for three decades was up to ... what? A young, pretty woman had given her this. Was Thomas having an affair?

Nonsense. She threw the note away from her.

Thomas was a lot of things, but a philanderer? Sure, they'd grown apart the last few years, but he was always truthful with her, or so it felt. Her Thomas? Having an affair?

The ground tilted.

But why else would that young woman go to all that trouble? Attending his funeral, slipping a note into her pocket? She tried to think of all the things those three sentences might be about, but that was all she could come up with. They'd been having an affair. That was it, surely. And then her mind began to run away from her. Perhaps she'd had a child with him?

She could see a desperate mother going through those actions at a funeral if it meant getting something for her offspring.

If only the drugs weren't cloaking everything in a heavy veil, she might be able to make sense of all of this.

In a few hours the sun would rise and the streetlights would be switched off. People would go about their day, locked into the hamster wheels of their own thoughts. Mindless people working for stuff they didn't really need but wanted with a desire that was unholy, probably viewing everything through the lens of a smartphone, because only then could it exist.

And how much she wanted to be one of them. Not to have this ache.

Nobody does anything real anymore, she thought. Strength is nothing more than a display: an act. Nobody wants to be vulnerable. Nobody wants *you* to be vulnerable. Your son and husband die and nobody *really* cares. The world shifts but stays the same and your home, your anchor, isn't where you left it.

She was still there, back against the wall, buttocks numb and cold from the wooden floor, hours later when the light shifted from artificial to natural. The world was waking up to another day and she was here, weak, exhausted, and unsure of whom and what to grieve for.

At some point Paula made it through to the sofa in her front living room. There she curled up on the soft leather, bolstered by a small mountain of fat cushions and was feeling herself drift into something approaching sleep when there was a knock at the door.

She groaned. Felt the weight of her fatigue. She considered answering it but ignored the impulse and turned to face the back of the sofa, pulling her knees up to her chest.

The knock sounded again. Firm and loud. The caller was obviously confident that she would grant them entry.

She heard the squeak of the small brass hinge of the letter box and a male voice.

'Paula? Sorry, doll. It's only me.'

Kevin Farrell. Her husband's business partner.

She sat up. Groaned again. He was the last person she wanted to see, but he was always coming round, and she was sure he'd persist until she answered the door.

Fixing her robe, she mustered up the energy to get to her feet and pad through to the hall.

'Paula?' Farrell's voice sounded from the letter box.

She paused before answering, looking in the hall mirror to check if she was decent. She was about to fluff up her hair, then thought: to hell with it, the widow does not care. She pulled the door open.

'Hey, Paula,' Farrell said, his eyes roaming. Enough of his reaction leaked into his expression, just momentarily, for Paula to see that he read the state she was in and felt sorry for her. 'How are you today, sweetheart?'

'Mmmm...' was all she could manage. She'd always found his attempts at being sociable cloying – so false in their sweetness that she could barely resist running her tongue over her teeth. He'd gone to school with Thomas, but she never could quite work out how he and her husband were friends.

His face was full and round like a football, the skin dotted with acne scars. His hair was already almost white and, regardless of how new his suit might be, he always managed to make it look like he'd just come off a twenty-hour flight.

'The kettle on?' he asked. 'Thought you might like some company.' He held up a small brown bag. 'Got some croissants from that posh place down Hyndland Road. I thought you might want a late breakfast.' He took a step inside the door and Paula felt a flare of irritation at his presumption. Then gave in. She didn't have the energy to back it up. Besides, although it was the last thing she wanted, she supposed company would be good for her.

The note she'd been reading the previous night still lay on the floor. She bent down and picked it up before he could get a look at it.

'What's that?' he asked.

'Just some kind of flyer,' she said as she tucked it into the pocket of her dressing gown.

'Always someone trying to sell something, eh?' He brushed past her and she trailed after him like a pup in its new home.

In the kitchen Kevin said, 'Ah, right, you guys got that new coffee machine. Cool.' He walked towards it. 'Easy to work, is it?' He pushed at a button and the machine whirred into life.

Paula pushed past him, lifted a mug from a cupboard and placed it in front of the spout. 'Here, let's not drown the kitchen in coffee.'

She looked at him. Squinted at a recollection. 'You weren't at the funeral yesterday, Kevin. How come?' She handed him the filled mug, not bothering to ask about milk. Today he would have to take it how he got it.

'Shit excuse, I know...' He accepted the mug and took a sip. Then he placed it back on the worktop surface before holding both of his hands out, palms up. It occurred to Paula that he looked as if he really didn't care how she might feel about his answer. 'I'm allergic. Hate funerals. I've never been to one. Not even my mother's.' Then he gave her a smile that had a whiff of apology pushed through it.

Paula often wondered if Kevin had tried to learn how to behave with other people from a book. He clearly didn't really care if Paula was upset that he hadn't been there.

"Sides, I said cheerio to Tommy in my own way.' There. A flash of sadness. A suggestion that there was a little more to this man than had met her eyes over the years.

'I'm sure you did,' said Paula, and caught Kevin glancing at the opening of her robe. 'What do you want, Kevin?' She pulled her robe tight and held it at the throat. 'I barely resemble a human this morning.'

'Just wanted to see how my wee pal was doing. Offer you my support. I'm happy to listen if you want to talk...' His face formed an expression of sympathy, like a stranger had just taken possession of his brain for a moment.

'Jesus, Kevin, did you just google how to behave around the bereaved? I prefer it when you do your remote-human thing.'

'That's harsh.' He looked offended, and Paula felt a rush of conscience.

'Please get to the point, Kev. Why are you really here?'

'A man can't check on his friend's widow?' He held his arms out. But it was there. Paula's mind wasn't too addled by grief that she couldn't see there was something other than Thomas's death that was bothering him. There was a tightness in his face, an edge to his apparent concern, and he shuffled from one foot to the other.

She put her hand in her pocket, felt the corner of the note and considered showing it to him. But she quickly decided against that. Perhaps his evident nervousness was transmitting itself to her.

'Mind if I ask you something, Kev?' She needed to ask, even though she was pretty sure he wouldn't tell her.

'Sure. Anything.' His expression was open, but there was an underlying apprehension in his tone. Farrell might be grieving, in his own way, but there was something else there.

'Was Thomas having an affair?'

5

Kevin took a big slug of coffee, as if it was his first drink of the day. He put the drink down on the work surface and tapped the brown bag containing the croissants. 'Remember to eat,' he said and walked out of the kitchen.

Paula followed him, thinking: What the hell? That was it? Why bother visiting?

Farrell reached the door, pulled it open and turned to her before stepping outside. 'Put any thoughts of Tommy having an affair out of your head, Paula. He didn't have it in him.' Then, obviously trying to look as if the question had just popped into his head, 'Had any visitors this morning?'

'Visitors?' Paula repeated and gave a small laugh. 'Nobody really knows what to say to a widow.'

He turned to her and opened his mouth as if to say something else. Then his head slumped as if he'd lost whatever battle was going on his mind. 'I'll give you a couple of days,' he said, turned and left.

She shut the door behind him and leaned against the cool of the wood.

A couple of days for what? Why had Kevin even bothered to show up here? She reviewed his behaviour from the moment she'd opened the door to him. It was as if he'd come to ask her something and then backed off before he did.

Her head throbbed. She turned, leaned forwards, placing her palms over her cheeks, and rested her forehead on the wood. She'd heard Kevin assert that Thomas wouldn't have had an affair with a sense of relief. But then, there was that note. What would drive a woman to do something like that? Who would hijack a funeral, for God's sake?

But why was she so quick to wonder about Thomas's fidelity? Yes, they'd drifted apart since Christopher died, but why would her mind instantly go there? She searched her memory for indications that Thomas might have been unfaithful over the years and came up with nothing. There were lots of time away with work, but no lipstick on his collar, no lingering perfumes on his return. She crossed her arms as if warding off any uncomfortable facts that might back up her new suspicions.

The door vibrated against her head as someone on the other side knocked.

Who could it be now? Had Kevin come back already? Her pulse was a throb at the side of her throat and she registered the worry that was now thrumming through her body.

She reached for the handle and pulled the door open, aware as she did so that her robe was gaping again.

'Hi Paula,' it was Father Joe. 'Have I...' He had the good taste not to look as Paula hastily fixed herself. 'Have I called at a bad time?'

She closed her eyes. Shook her head.

'Go away,' she said.

'But you said to come over,' Joe said. Was that a slight slur in his voice? Paula wondered. 'And I bring gifts.' He held up a bottle that was already half empty. 'Or, should I say, gift. But you've tonic in the house, right?'

'You're drunk,' Paula said, and realised as soon as the words were out of her mouth that they were redundant. It was as obvious as the dog collar around his neck.

'It's not every day your big brother dies.' Joe brought the bottle into his chest and cradled it there like it was something beyond precious. 'So, a wee drink the day after his funeral is only to be expected. In fact, some would suggest I would be a callous human being if I didn't get rat-arsed, down-in-the-gutter drunk.'

Paula looked at the bottle. It was a Tanquerey Number 10. She stepped back and he moved inside.

They hugged, her head on his shoulder, the skin of her forehead warmed by the heat of his neck and chin.

'Why's it so bloody hard, Paula?' he asked, and she could feel the deep rumble of his voice against her cheek. His arms round her back felt so solid, she didn't want to move.

Eventually, he took a step back. With false cheer he said, 'This gin isn't going to drink itself you know.'

'Does it go with croissants?' asked Paula, trying to give him a smile.

'What?'

'Must be almost noon and I still haven't had my breakfast.'

'And?' As if having breakfast on a day like this made any sense.

Paula gave up any effort at an explanation, and instead said, 'Long story.' She walked back to the kitchen.

Once there she turned to him. 'You know where the balcony is. Give me a chance to have a quick shower. I'll meet you there in ten minutes.'

◆

The shower did little to wash the fatigue from her muscles or the fog from her mind, but it did make her feel a little more human to have cleaned up and put on clothes. She chose one of Thomas's black t-shirts, which almost reached her knees, and a pair of bright-pink leggings. It was only when she was pulling the Lycra over her toes and it caught on a ragged nail that she noted the colour and wondered if it was inappropriate. She decided she didn't much care and with an extra note of defiance used an equally pink scrunchy to hold her wet hair in a ponytail. Pushing her feet into a pair of white trainers she joined Joe on the balcony.

When they'd first moved in, they'd had the kitchen extended, and the balcony created by the flat roof was accessed from a landing halfway up the stairs. The kitchen was slick and elegant, but the balcony became her favourite part of the house. Particularly when Thomas got working with his plants.

It held a small glass table with four seats on one side, and the other half was occupied by a pair of loungers and a large patio umbrella. At every corner was a cluster of three plants – some sort of miniature palm trees and ferns, Paula presumed, suddenly aware that she'd never bothered to ask.

Joe was reclining on a lounger when she stepped outside, and he'd positioned the bottle of gin, two glasses, a bucket of ice and a large bottle of tonic on a table.

Poor Joe, thought Paula as she sized up the scene. She had to remind herself she wasn't the only one who was grieving here. She surveyed him stretched out in front of her. He looked as if he was settling in for the rest of the day.

She really wasn't sure she wanted anyone's company for a whole afternoon. But she took a moment to steel herself and then unscrewed the bottle.

Joe groaned as he got to his feet, moved over to the table, then groaned again as he sat down. 'Good Lord,' he said. 'I feel like I'm about ninety.'

Paula examined his face. Even with the grey pallor of grief and fatigue he was still a handsome man. 'You don't look it,' she said.

He reached out for his glass and took a long sip. 'Bless you, Paula. You will surely get through the gates of heaven.'

Paula took a seat. 'Thanks.' She took a sip from her glass. 'But will Thomas?' She regretted the flippancy of the words as soon as they left her mouth.

Joe looked up from the table. 'What does that mean?'

She tutted. 'Just ignore me, Joe.' Paula sat back in her chair and crumpled into a slouch. 'I've just been hearing some stuff that has made me wonder what I knew about my husband.'

'What have you been hearing?' Joe had assumed his priest expression now.

'Oh, nothing.' She thought it might be best to the change the subject. 'You okay, Father Joe?' she asked.

He stared into the distance. His eyes glazed with grief. His expression that of someone who found himself seriously wanting.

The grey in his expression lifted as if by huge effort. 'I was so envious of Thomas when he brought you home. I remember it like it was yesterday. I had just turned fourteen and in walked this goddess.'

'Please...' interrupted Paula. 'I was a spotty sixteen, frightened to look out from behind my fringe and certain that my backside was the size of...' she stopped. The well of energy required to finish the attempt at a joke was dry.

'And that's what was so attractive about you. All this beauty and you weren't aware of it.' He smiled as if it cost it him to do so, and his eyes grew distant as if a display of scenes were scrolling across his memory. 'Thomas was so nervous when he brought you home.'

'He was not.' Paula murmured her disbelief.

'He most definitely was. I remember him talking about you long into the night.'

Bill, Thomas and Joe shared a bedroom in their youth. Bill, being the elder, had a single bed pushed against one wall and Thomas and Joe shared a set of bunks, with Thomas on the top.

'He was crazy about you. You know that, don't you?' Joe was suddenly serious. His eyes were focussed on hers and his tone sharp – certainty in his voice. 'You really were the only one for him. Whatever...' he waved his right hand in the air '...nonsense you heard, you were the love of his life, Paula.'

'Oh, Joe.' Paula reached out a hand and placed it on top of his. A sob escaped her throat. She cried softly for a few seconds and then wiped the tears from her face with the back of her other hand. 'I'm so ... so *bloody angry*,' she said. 'A heart attack? He was a fit man. Well, for his age and for someone who lived in this part of the world. But still, a heart attack? It just doesn't add up.'

'There has been heart disease in the family,' Joe replied. 'That's what killed our dad, remember?'

'And as for being the love of his life...' Paula was only half listening to what Joe said. 'We could have been better to each other.'

'Show me a married couple and I'll show you a relationship that occasionally fractures,' said Joe. 'Besides, sadly, we tend to save the worst of ourselves for the people who mean the most.'

'True,' said Paula. She took a sip from her drink. 'You honestly never missed being in a couple?'

'Nope. Never. What you never had you can't miss. Besides, being important to a whole congregation of people has been a compensation.' He mused over this statement. Looked as if he didn't quite like the nuance. 'That sounds a bit egotistical.'

'I think I know what you mean. My role in life was to be part of a pair. And in the main, it worked.' Hadn't it? She thought of their last row. The night before he died. It was over something and nothing. She'd taken his words and twisted them. Turned a petty statement into a major crisis. What happy couple did that?

Joe looked at her as if he was about to say something. Thought more of it and took another drink.

'What?' asked Paula.

'You were more than *just* his wife, Paula.'

She tried to make sense of the jumble in her head. A wife. Was that really what she was? Was that all? Nearly three decades and she had nothing to show for it but a marriage and a death certificate?

'Don't get me wrong,' she said. 'I enjoyed being his wife. I enjoyed having this lovely man by my side ... and when Thomas focussed on you it was like you were the only person in the world.' She ran out of the energy to speak and looked out across the Glasgow skyline as if she might find peace there.

'Why did he have to die?' she asked Joe after several minutes of silence. 'I feel so guilty, you know? I could have been a better wife. Neither of us handled Christopher's death well.'

Joe had assumed his professional, confessor expression again.

'How daft is that? The one person who can understand your loss the most and it pushes you further away from him.' Then she reined herself in. This wasn't all about her. Joe was grieving as well.

'Thomas took Christopher's death hard,' said Joe, nodding.

Paula noted that their glasses were now drained, so she offered to pour them both another.

As the ice clinked into the glasses she asked, 'What's your earliest memory of him?'

'Playing football. What else? This is Glasgow. Bill didn't want me trailing around after them, but Tommy was great. I was never a bother to him.'

'I guess that explains why you were closer to him than to Bill,' Paula said as she pushed Joe's glass across the table.

'That and the fact that Bill can be a bit of an idiot.'

She thought about Joe's relationships with his brothers. And that between Bill and Thomas. As far back as she could remember there had been some form of competition between the two of them, and as far as she was aware, Thomas always won.

'Thomas and Bill,' she said. 'When did it start – that need to best each other?'

Joe paused with his drink almost at his lips, and looked over the rim towards Paula as he answered. 'Goodness, I'm not sure. It feels as if that pattern was set up even before I was born.'

'Did it ever turn nasty?'

'Once ... that I'm aware of.' And Joe's expression betrayed the fact he was back in the past. 'A football match. Well, a wee kickaround in the park with a bunch of pals, really. I was in goal...' he smiled '... because I was rubbish. Thomas scored with an overhead kick. An absolute beauty. All the other guys were crowding round him, praising him, and the look on Bill's face – I'll never forget it. He was so jealous. Five minutes later they both went for the ball, even though they were on the same side. Bill went in far too fast and far too heavy. Broke Thomas's ankle.'

Paula gasped. 'Really?'

'But Thomas even turned that into a win.' Joe smiled faintly. 'He got his stooky signed by half the players at Partick Thistle.' Joe held his glass up in a toast to Thomas. Then he tapped his fingertips on his glass. 'It's as if Bill took the very worst traits of my parents and ran with them.' His expression slumped. 'And Tommy took the best.'

'You're talking to his wife, Joe. There's no need to sanitise his memory. I know he wasn't a saint.'

'He was a good man, Paula. One of the very best.'

Paula looked into his eyes, considered what the note said and read a 'but' in there. 'What do you know, Joe? What was Thomas up to?'

Joe looked away from her, to the sky and the huge, dark clouds sailing towards them. There was conflict in his eyes and an uncertainty.

'Tell me Joe. What do you know?'

He looked at her and forced a smile. But she saw sadness, a weight that was all but crushing him.

6

'Mum?' Cara Connolly shouted as she walked in the door of her mother's flat, a one-bedroom on the second floor of a tenement building that had seen better days, just two minutes' walk from Pollokbrae Baths. The whole area had seen better days, a deterioration that was not helped by the growth of slum landlords. Entire families, mostly immigrants and refugees, being housed in one room, with poor ventilation, ineffective heating and dangerous wiring, was depressingly common.

The newspapers were full of articles saying that the council were going to get tough on the landlords. But Cara would believe it when she saw it.

Stretching along the street, the ground-floor apartments were all shops. But there were none of the artisan coffee establishments offering sourdough bread and quinoa that had sprung up in the more gentrified areas of the city. These were mostly charity shops, pound shops, betting shops and tatty pubs, all with signage in primary colours. The sign over the shop just to the right of the entrance to her mother's building had bright-red lettering with a fluorescent yellow background, and the window was full of hand-written notices offering cigarettes and beer at 'knockdown' prices.

As she walked into the passageway that led to the stairs and her mother's flat, Cara looked up at the building, and saw dirty windows, satellite dishes, and large-leafed plants growing out of the cracks in the stained masonry. Inside the close, as she approached the stairs, she could see that it was cleaner than the last time she visited. Mum must have got the neighbours organised. But the plaster was still cracked in the corners, and a pipe was leaking just above the back door, creating a large, foul-smelling puddle they'd all have to negotiate when going out into the back green to hang out their washing.

Inside her mother's flat, the picture improved. Everything was second-hand, but it was all scrupulously clean – a result of her mother's favourite pastime. And there she was, on her knees in the kitchen, scrubbing brush in hand as if she was trying to work off the pattern in the linoleum.

'You'll not get it any cleaner, Maw.'

Helen Connolly looked up and gave Cara a half-smile. 'There's nobody will say I've got a mucky house, doll.'

'Aye, cos it's cleaner than a nun's wimple.'

Her mother narrowed her eyes. 'Is that something rude? Cos I'll no' have a daughter o' mine using nasty words.'

Cara rolled her eyes. This was all part of her mother's rehabilitation. Since she'd come off the various substances that had haunted most of her adult life she'd also taken to cleaning up her use of language. As if using more socially acceptable words would help her to sustain the habit of better behaviour.

Helen slowly and carefully got to her feet as if she was dutifully bearing a hundred-kilogram weight on her shoulders – her conscience, thought Cara. She groaned and steadied herself against the side of the fridge with one hand while she rubbed at both knees with the other. 'Old age doesn't come itself, doll, neither it does.' She looked at Cara and beamed, displaying a misshapen row of brown and yellow teeth. 'Lovely to see you, Cara. To what do I owe this pleasure?'

Cara assessed her mother's face and tone for sarcasm. She couldn't help herself. When her mother was on drugs she was the passive-aggressive queen, and Cara, prior to the last 398 days always anticipated a response of that flavour. To find that her mum had turned into this caring, pleasant, cleaning machine was a constant and welcome surprise. And her being clean for that number of days was a major achievement.

'Your hair's lovely. You had it done?' Cara asked.

It wasn't really. It was cropped close to her skull apart from a wiry brush at the top, and dyed a harsh blonde that made her mother's bony face look even paler. But still, she was continuing to make an effort and that in itself deserved praise.

Helen raised a hand to the side of her head and patted it, obviously pleased that her daughter noticed. 'You don't think it's too short? Mrs McGarrity thinks it's too short.'

'It's lovely.' And overtaken with a rush of tenderness Cara leaned forwards and kissed the papery veined skin of her mother's cheek.

'Oh, don't be doing that.' Helen stepped back, waving her arms in the air. She was still struggling to get used to being hugged. Though, judging by how pink her face had turned, she was delighted.

As Helen lowered her hands, one sleeve remained rucked up and Cara could see the scars on the inside of her mother's arm. They were long healed, Cara remembered angry raised skin, seeping with infection.

Reading her daughter's look, Helen hastily pulled the fabric down. 'Cup of tea? How about I make us a cup of tea?'

'A glass of water will do, thanks,' Cara said, in the vain hope that her mum would take a seat and relax.

'Nonsense. I'll no' have it said that my daughter came to my house and didn't even get a cup of tea. Go through to the front room and I'll get it sorted.' With that she shooed Cara out of the kitchen.

Cara always left her mother's house exhausted. She knew the constant activity was how her mother coped. For most of her life it had been drugs, but now it was the bustle and busyness of the everyday. Cara knew she cleaned for a couple of her elderly neighbours and didn't take a penny for it. 'Keeps the demons at bay, doll,' she had offered one day in a rare moment of honesty. The past was firmly in the past and nothing good would come from digging through it. That was the belief Helen had learned at the knee of her grandmother.

In the front room, which was really at the back of the building, Cara walked over to the window and looked down on what was optimistically called The Back Green. It did have grass, once upon a time, but now the communal garden space was nothing more than a communal dump. Empty beer cans, gaudily coloured plastic bags, and cigarette butts were everywhere, and Cara counted two mattresses, half a child's cot, three wheel-less bikes, a car battery and a black, inside-out golf umbrella.

'Please don't start,' Helen entered the room carrying a tray. 'I spoke to a woman at the council and they're sending a man round.' It was a common argument between them. Cara asserted that no one should have to look out on that mess, and threatened to call the council. Her mother, terrified that someone at the council offices would take against her always replied that a man was coming out.

Still, it had been worse. Cara had come to visit three months ago to find her mother out the back cleaning a lump of human faeces off Mrs Kelly's windowsill on the ground floor. 'I heard the toilet was blocked on the top floor,' her mother had explained with an apologetic look. 'They've been on to the landlord and he'll not do nothing. An' the council says it's not their job.'

'For crying out loud. You can't be living somewhere where folk throw their shite out of the window. This isn't the sixteenth century for Christ's sake.'

Furious that her mother had to perform such a task, and feeling weirdly culpable, Cara got on to environmental health, the police, the local newspaper and local radio station, and something was done. As a result Helen became sure she was a marked woman. 'Folk are different to me now, doll,' she'd said. 'So next time let us sort it out in our own way, eh?'

She'd accepted her mother's stance, knowing where it came from and that there was nothing she could do to alter it. Being in her line of work she saw it every day. It came from being born into generations of poverty and the belief that, as far as society was concerned, you were at the back of the queue. For everything. It was so deep-seated for some people it was all but passed on genetically. You were born worthless and you would die worthless: Cara was certain this was coded into her mother's DNA.

How Cara escaped it was a conundrum.

'What you got on, then, doll?' Helen asked as she poured the tea. It was only then that Cara noticed there was only one mug on the tray.

'You not having any, Mum?'

'No, I've got...' She left the room and returned seconds later with an armful of bed linen. '...Mrs Donnolly's ironing to do. The wee soul has terrible arthritis, so she has. Can't even push the plug in.'

'Mum, will you not join me and have a seat? You're making me dizzy with all this running about.'

'I'm fine, thanks, doll.' She left the room again and came back in with the ironing board and the iron. 'Just you sit there, enjoy your tea. Have a biscuit as well. You're far too skinny.' Helen's face grew pained. 'I wish you would eat better, doll.'

'Mum, I eat properly. You've nothing to worry about on that score.'

'It's all that fitness stuff you do. Makes you skinny. Men like a woman with big hips,' Helen said as she bent down to plug in the iron.

And there it was. At twenty-eight she was still single. An age when more than a few of Helen's neighbours' daughters would be on to their third child.

'Yeah, well,' Cara countered. 'I'm really not caring what men want.'

'And all that fighting stuff you do. It's not very ladylike.'

Cara exhaled and closed her eyes, fighting to maintain her patience. 'Every time, Mum. Every single time.'

'What?' Helen assumed an expression she judged would get her into heaven.

'I'm skinny. I need to get a man. I need to stop the martial arts.' Cara stared her mother down, but then felt terrible when the older woman was the first to turn away. 'Can we please move past this, Mum? I like the way I am, and I'm perfectly happy being single, okay?'

They both knew there was more to Helen's concern about the taekwondo. The seed of that lay in Helen's abject failure to protect her daughter while she spent the better part of a decade and a half face-planted in the local drug scene.

Helen had funded her habit by bringing in a long line of what Cara's brother Sean jokingly named her 'gentlemen callers'. One of them spotted a pubescent Cara and tried it on. Cara, with the help of Sean, who must only have been about ten at the time, fought him off. This became an almost nightly occurrence, until, seeing a notice at the local community centre for ladies self-defence classes, Cara joined up, found she had a facility for controlled violence, went on to join a taekwondo club and learned to fight off drug-addled men with ease. There was one man, on the evening of her English exam, upon whom she unleashed the full force of her new skills. Word got out that Nellie Connolly's daughter had serious skills and had broken a grown man's arm, and she was rarely bothered again.

'Still,' Helen said after a few moments silence, 'it would be nice to have a grandson one day.'

Cara laughed. 'What are you like?'

Helen spat on the face of the iron, heard the resultant sizzle, and placing a flowery pillow case over the board she began to run the iron over it.

'Imagine having a bedroom with that in it.' Cara made a face.

'She's got matching curtains as well,' Helen whispered, as if the owner was within earshot. Both women laughed, a free and unrestrained piece of music, and in the weaving of those notes Cara felt a rare and deep connection that she once thought she would never share with this woman. It was a shame she was going to have to spoil it.

'Mum,' she said after a long pause. 'It's about Sean.' They never spoke about her only sibling, now just over two years dead. 'I think I know who killed him.'

7

The first thing Paula noted when she woke was that she was in bed. The next thing was that she was still wearing her day clothes. She opened one eye, then the other, and realised it was dark.

How did she get into bed? Had Joe helped her? She felt a flare of embarrassment, that he'd seen her in such a state.

What time was it?

She rolled across the bed to her side. Lay still for a moment and then had the thought that the entire king-sized mattress was hers alone now. Her throat tightened. A cry escaped. She turned onto her side, brought her knees up and allowed the tears to flow.

Once they subsided she tried to work through how she had got to bed. Last thing she could remember was making some toasted cheese for her and Joe: a classic Gadd family snack, usually made in the small hours, after a rare night out. But she remembered daylight. And some staggering. It was a wonder she hadn't burned the house down.

Joe must have put her to bed. She opened her mouth to speak, but her tongue felt as if it was stuck to the roof of her mouth. 'Joe,' she croaked. 'Joe, are you there?' Managed some loudness. Nothing came back to her but silence.

Paula sat up in bed, but her head started spinning, so she lay back down again. Had another go and twisted so that her feet came off the side of the bed.

'Jesus,' she said out loud. She was old enough to know better. Last time she had that much to drink was ... wait, when? She couldn't even remember.

She stretched out and touched the iPod docking station on her bedside cabinet. A small light came on and she could read the number: 01:23.

Bloody hell, it was the middle of the night.

Getting to her feet, all she could think about was that she needed to moisten her mouth, so she crossed the thick pile of her bedroom carpet to the en-suite bathroom. Feeling the deep cushion of the carpet under her feet prompted the memory of an argument that she and Thomas had when they were in the showroom choosing it. She wanted white; Thomas had said she was clumsy and was bound to spill some nail varnish or red wine on it. She remembered his comments sparking a massive row. The saleswoman had cowered behind her desk, not knowing where to look.

She'd won the argument by reminding him of several of their early dates when he had been the one who spilled stuff. He'd grinned, stepped back and said, 'Look at you, Miss Memory Bank.' Which of course became a joke between them. She remembered *everything*, Thomas would say, while he could barely remember what he had that morning for breakfast.

Porridge. It was always porridge. Half milk, half water and a pinch of salt.

How many arguments had they had over nothing? How many days and weeks had they lost to a solid wall of silence? In the end, she'd won, got the white carpet and had managed to spill both red wine and pink nail varnish on it within the first month.

In the bathroom, she flicked on the mirror light. Then she found a tumbler, filled it with cold water and had a long drink. Filled the glass again and had another.

She drank so fast it made her breathless. She put the glass down, stepped away from the sink and sat on the edge of the corner spa bath. Where she and Thomas had make-up sex after the white-carpet argument. She slumped to the floor, sobs coming again. Every part of this house echoed with memory. How could she escape it? Did she even want to?

She lifted the t-shirt she was wearing to her nose and breathed.

There he was. Just a fragrant piece of him.

Oh, Thomas.

She pulled at the underarm, positioned it under her nose, breathing in a lungful of air with the cloth as a filter, and she could almost taste him.

He'd worn this the morning of the day he died, as he went through his daily exercise routine. As work pressures began to mount he couldn't afford to take time off to go to the gym, so he asked a personal trainer to set out a bodyweight routine for him.

She took another sniff and this time she caught Palmolive soap and sweat. And he was in the room, at the sink, shaving. She screwed her eyes shut against the vision.

For some reason she'd always been certain she'd be the one to go first and was reassured each time the thought occurred, because after the suffocating grief she had experienced after Chris died she was sure she'd never be able to survive anything like that again.

After some time on the floor, she pushed herself to her feet. She should go back to bed, set the alarm and get up at seven-thirty like a normal person.

Instead, feeling wide awake, she headed downstairs to the kitchen, half expecting to find Joe slumped in a corner somewhere, but he was nowhere to be seen. She stood by the coffee machine, with the nagging thought that she shouldn't have a coffee at this time of night.

Warm mug in hand she wandered through the house like a haunting, her footfall silent in the darkness; the only sound, the swish of cloth when her Lycra-clad thighs slid against each other. That and her breathing. Slow and heavy.

In this way, she visited Thomas in her memory. There, in front of the fireplace in the sitting room, toasting someone – she couldn't remember who – but his smile was expansive, his body language assured. The king in his castle.

Then, she moved to the dining room, walked round the large table, her fingers lightly trailing across the top of the oak veneer. It was large enough for a dozen people to be seated round it comfortably. When they first bought it they had great intentions, but it was only ever used at Christmas.

Halfway up the stairs, she stuck her head out of the door and looked out onto the balcony in case Joe was there. His seat was empty. He must have taken a taxi home. She carried on up the stairs and into her study. It had two large desks: his and hers. One for Thomas on the off chance he ever did any work at home. It was almost bare. A black leather folder and a fountain pen sat in the middle as if waiting for the owner to use them. She opened the folder in case Thomas had left her something: a note perhaps? But the pad of lined paper inside was pristine. A torn ridge at the top did show that he had used it though, but whatever was on the ripped-out paper was lost to her.

On the left side of the folder was a zipped pocket. She opened it and pulled out a chequebook and – she looked at the date – an expired cheque card. She opened the chequebook and looked at the last stub to be used. Miller's Garden Centre, and it was dated two years previously. Whenever she could face it, she really should dispose of these.

Her desk, in comparison was an essay in organised chaos. She knew exactly where anything she might need might be in each pile and resisted her cleaner's efforts at tidying. In fact, she was expressly forbidden to do anything in this room in case she messed up Paula's system.

Paula sat down, lifted the lid of her laptop and the light from it was sufficient to show her phone sitting to her right. She put a hand on it as if preparing to read any messages or texts, but she couldn't face anyone's sympathy right now and pushed it away from her. But as she did, she awoke the screen and noticed that one of the many text notifications was from one of her oldest friends, Shelley Collins. She shook off the notion of speaking to Shelley. She couldn't face her, or anyone for that matter.

The laptop opened at the documents she'd last been working on. What day might that have been? She shook her head, struggling to recall. Recent days were a blur of painful breaths and sympathetic faces.

The document was from the crematorium. She'd had to fill it in, print it off, and hand it back to them.

Sentences popped out at her again: *The container and the body shall be placed in a cremator and cremation commenced no later than seventy-two hours after the service of committal.*

With louring curiosity she continued reading.

Cremation of a dead body is carried out at a temperature ranging between 1,400 and 1,800 degrees Fahrenheit. The intense heat helps reduce the body to its basic elements and dried bone fragments.

Then:

The remains will automatically be strewn in the Garden of Remembrance four weeks from the day of cremation. However, if you wish to be present at the dispersal please tick the RETAIN *option, which will ensure the remains are not scattered and instead can be collected by the family.*

Her heart thumped. Her breath quickened. For heaven's sake, she'd completed this in the days after Thomas died. What had she indicated she wanted done? How on earth did they expect people to give a considered response to these things at a time like this? Had she said she wanted them scattered? For the life of her she couldn't remember. And how many days did she have to collect them?

She didn't even know what day this was.

Bloody hell.

She sat back in the chair. Did she want the ashes home with her? Or should she take them somewhere that was significant to them both and scatter them there.

But where?

When Christopher died, Thomas wanted a burial. He couldn't articulate why, just that was what he was sure Christopher would have wanted. Paula had agreed, mainly because she didn't have the strength to argue her case. Anyway, what did it matter? A slow decomposition or rapid incineration? Either way, the inescapable fact remained: Thomas was gone: snuffed out with the bone-crushing pain of seized heart muscle.

She searched her mind for happy memories.

When they were three.

In those days they had little cash – everything was invested back into the business – and had always gone on modest holidays: long weekends to a caravan at Lochgoilhead, Butlin's down in Ayr, or their favourite place, a bed and breakfast near Ettrick Bay on Bute. At that thought she recalled Christopher on the beach there. His face smudged with a mixture of sand and chocolate, tongue sticking out of the side of his mouth as he concentrated on building a small wall of sand for his little fort on the beach.

She sighed, and tucked the memory away, like placing a photo back in a well-thumbed album.

Then, after Chris died and Thomas lost himself in work, the cash flooded in and he would take her to far-flung places; the Caribbean, the Cote D'Azur, Bali.

They were all lovely, Paula thought, she would go there, enjoy it, but miss the simplicity and familiarity of those beauty spots they'd enjoyed and explored when they were still a family.

Bute was gorgeous. She always felt a lightening when their car drove off that ferry. But the money went to their heads and they took holidays that other people recommended rather than the ones that had always made them happy.

Her mind slipped to the woman from the funeral – whoever she was – and that note she'd slipped into her pocket. 'I'm not having it,' she shouted into the room. When would Thomas ever have the time to have an affair? There was nothing she needed to learn about her husband.

She started crying. The tears came from nowhere. One second she was shouting defiance into the world. The next she was hunched over the desk, wheezing with grief – the switch in emotion a seamless transition.

She wiped at her cheek with the pad of her right hand, then, as if to get away from her thoughts, she turned and looked out of the room, across the landing and into their bedroom. From where she was sitting she could see past an open door that led to Thomas's section of their large walk-in-wardrobe, and the beginning of a row of beautiful suits.

This prompted a memory of Thomas in one of them. Navy, three-piece, worn with a white shirt and a gold-and-blue tie. He was sporting a trim beard, grey hair spiking through the dark, matching the silvering tint at his temples.

His handsome face was tight with anger. Then, like a row of index cards sliding through her mind in order, the facts presented themselves. They were out at a dinner celebrating an anniversary. He had been withdrawn all evening, his mood worsening as each course arrived. She'd challenged him.

'I'm fine,' he'd stated.

'Well, tell your face that,' she replied.

Without another word he jumped to his feet and all but fled from the room.

She gave him a couple of minutes, then throwing her napkin onto the table, she apologised to her fellow diners and followed him.

He was at the door to the gents', towering over a young man, giving him the hair-dryer treatment. At first she thought he might be one of the waiters, but he was wearing jeans and a dark t-shirt. Who was he? Rather than charging in, which was what she would have normally done, something made her stop before she got too close. The poor guy was terrified, all but melting under her husband's fury.

Paula took a step back, retreated just around the corner, and listened. It was difficult to make out exactly what was being said. The young man said, 'Don't shoot the messenger.' Or something like that. He said he was sorry, over and over again, like he hoped it might be a good luck charm. But with each 'sorry', Thomas appeared more and more angry. Finally, Paula heard, 'Do it, or you're fucking dead, son.' And then a noise as if someone had fallen.

Without thought, she rounded the corner asking, 'What the hell is going on here?'

The kid, because now she was closer she could see he was no more than a boy, scrambled to his feet, turned and fled.

'Mind your own business, wife,' Thomas replied.

'Wife?' Paula got in his face. 'Wife? Who do you think you're talking to?' This was so out of character it was like a department-store Santa spitting into the face of a child. Thomas was often short with her, but being this dismissive made her feel like another man had taken over his body.

'Leave me the fuck alone,' he shouted, turned, pushed the door open and walked into the gents'.

Paula considered joining him, but decided not to. Whatever was stewing in his mind obviously needed release.

When he came back out of the toilet about ten minutes later, he was back to normal. She made several attempts to discuss what had gone on, but he rebuffed each of them. His good cheer now so hard and forced, it was difficult for Paula to speak.

'The boy spilled soup on my suit,' he said. 'It's sorted. Stop going on about it.'

From the distance of time, Paula now reviewed that evening. Was it anything more than a bad day? For the life of her she couldn't remember any spill that evening. What had really happened? Her memory was fogged, but she would never forget the raw look of fear on that boy's face.

She slumped till her head fell onto her desk. The wood cool and smooth, and a solid reminder that she was still in the world.

That moment in the restaurant was so remote from his normal behaviour. What had prompted the memory now? A stranger's assertion that she didn't really know her husband?

Paula located her mobile, then all but ran through to her bedroom, found her dressing gown on the floor beside her bed, rummaged for the pocket and found the note. She read the number and dialled as she trod back through to the study. As she sat down in front of her laptop the phone was answered.

'Yes?' A young woman said, wariness a low note in a voice worn with sleep.

'It's Paula Gadd here.'

'Right.' She was awake now. And even in that single syllable Paula heard hesitancy warring with ... what? Relief?

'Okay. I'll hear you out. I want to know what you've got to say. Could you come to my house?'

And suddenly the need to find out surged up through Paula's chest. The need to see this woman face to face; hear what she had to say. Watch her as she said it.

'Now, please?'

'But it's the middle of the...'

Fair enough, thought Paula. She was being unreasonable. 'First thing in the morning then? Eight?'

She gave the address, then cut the connection without saying another word. Worry was a cold coiling through her stomach reaching up towards her heart. Thomas was a good man. A loyal man. The alternative was too ugly to contemplate.

Shaking her head against her ruminations a movement across her computer screen drew her attention.

The mouse arrow was moving as if of its own accord. She looked down. She hadn't touched anything, but it was definitely moving to programmes on the main screen. She watched open-mouthed. What on earth was happening here?

Microsoft Word, spreadsheets, and then her internet connection were being opened. Google filled her screen. One bank after another filled the search bar. Then it settled for the Bank of Scotland, as if it recognised a regular connection.

What on earth...?

The shock of this realisation pulled her from her inertia. She must be being hacked remotely as she watched. Who could even do that? And why?

She closed the lid. Then realised that wouldn't be enough to stop whoever it was. Panicked, she turned the laptop on its side. Fiddling with the catches, her fingers refusing to obey her quickly enough, she finally managed to pop the battery out of its bed. She stared at the laptop for a moment, realising she was panting and that her heart was racing.

Her phone rang out loud into the room. She jumped. As her heartbeat thumped in her ears she answered it without even checking who it was.

'Hello?' she said, trying to keep her voice level.

Nothing. There was no response.

Wait. There. The slight sound of someone breathing.

'Go away,' she screamed into the phone. With trembling fingers she cut the connection.

What in God's name was happening?

8

Cara Connolly took a deep breath. Paused, as if she was about to change her mind, and then climbed the last step up to the Glasgow townhouse. The door was impressive. A centre panel of smoked glass inserted into an oak frame. If the door was representative of what was behind it, this was going to be some house. She was more used to shabby tenements or the ambitiously entitled 'maisonettes' in the concrete towers of the city's sink estates.

Even knocking on the thick wood, she could feel the quality.

Bet she's a cold-hearted bint, Cara thought as she took a step back and pushed her hands into the pockets of her denims to hide the shaking.

Nothing. No answer.

Maybe she'd lost her shot at speaking to her?

She took another step back and looked around the door's blonde sandstone lintel. Spotted a white ceramic button inside a brass ring. She pushed it and heard nothing and wondered if it was ringing somewhere far inside.

Again, no response.

She craned her head to the side and tried to look inside the giant window. The morning sunshine was hitting the glass at an angle that made it difficult to see into the room. All she could make out was the back of a cream, leather sofa and on the far wall, a giant mirror in an ornate frame. Made her think of the stately homes she'd seen in historical TV dramas.

Cold-hearted *lucky* bint, she amended her earlier thought and tried the door again, this time with the side of her hand against the door.

As she waited for a response she thought about the conversation she'd had with her mother, a conversation that had played over and over in her mind since they'd last spoken.

'I wish you'd leave that, doll,' her mother said, leaning forwards, her hands clasped on her bony knees. 'It's done. Sean's no' coming back.'

'But, Mum...'

Helen shook her head with slow care, her brown eyes leaking love. 'To bury a child is my burden. I'm no' having you on some sort of crusade that could end up with you killed as well.'

'What makes you think I could end up being killed?'

'Did they find the man who did it?' Helen demanded, suddenly losing her cool. The force of her worry made the ligaments that stretched from under her chin to her collarbone stand out starkly. 'Naw. So there's a murderer out there and if you go kicking at hornet's nests you might get stung. And that...' She bit her lip as she tailed off. 'Just leave it, honey, please?'

Leave it. A simple request. A sensible request. But Cara couldn't.

The door opened, throwing Cara from her thoughts. And she took a little cheer from the fact that the woman facing her was a mess. Her hair was all over the place, and her eyes were puffy and red. Cara took a step closer, but couldn't smell any booze, just mouthwash.

'You don't look like the girl from the funeral,' Mrs Gadd said, her eyes narrow with suspicion.

'I was wearin' a large pair of sunglasses, and a big hat.' Cara paused, gathering her determination to get to the truth. 'Can I come in?'

Without a word, Gadd turned and walked away. Cara stepped inside, closed the door behind her and followed. They walked along a long, light-flooded corridor, past the foot of a wide staircase and into a kitchen straight out of a movie set. A series of white units, a pair of Belfast sinks under the window, an island cooker and *lots* of shiny devices.

This was beautiful. Everything was so classy. And you could almost fit Cara's entire flat into this room.

'We can talk here,' the woman said. 'That's where the coffee is.' She reached a coffee machine, pressed a button and then turned and asked,

'What's your name?'

'Cara.'

'Cara what?'

'Let's settle for just Cara at the moment, please.'

'Well, Cara...' she paused as if this was costing her a lot of effort '... you should call me Paula.'

'Paula,' Cara repeated somewhat unnecessarily. The woman might be a mess and in the midst of grief, but she could detect a core of steel there and Cara suddenly felt unsure of herself.

This was something she hated about herself; that flare of feeling she got when she first met someone that people would deem her social better – that somehow she wasn't quite as worthy. It was something she fought on an almost daily basis. She looked out of the window, away from Paula Gadd, in an effort to marshal her strength and to remind herself why she was here. What she could see of the garden was pretty. A trim lawn, plants of various sizes along the borders, plant pots bursting with reds, yellows and blues, and some rattan furniture under a large umbrella.

'My husband loves the garden,' Paula said as she followed Cara's gaze. 'We could have had a gardener, but he was determined to do all that stuff himself.' The machine made some gurgling noises and Paula lifted a pair of mugs from a cupboard. 'What do you take in your coffee?' she asked and for a moment Cara caught a glimpse of how difficult it was for this woman to hold it all together.

She felt a knot of uncertainty. What was she doing here? She resisted the impulse to leave, the muscles of her back suddenly aching as if someone was pushing her out of there.

'Tea, actually,' she said. 'I'm no' a fan of coffee.' Then reminded herself of society's expectation. Regardless that she was here to stick it to this woman, she had to be polite. She added a defiant, 'Please.'

Paula nodded as if in recognition of her tone.

'Don't have tea in this house. Nobody drinks it, so it's coffee, milk or...' she looked over her shoulder in the direction of a massive fridge-freezer '...I might have some bottled water?'

'Water's fine, ta.' And she added another 'please' for good measure.

Paula walked over to the fridge, pulled out a green bottle with a tear-shaped bottom, which to Cara's estimation probably cost more than a box of teabags. Then she reached into a cupboard, pulled out a tall glass and handed both items to Cara.

Cara accepted the bottle and glass with a nod of thanks. She had to admire the woman. If someone had gone through this with her she'd have probably chucked them at her.

Paula took a seat on a stool at the end of the island and Cara took another, pulling it away from the older woman to give her more space.

'What age are you, Cara?' Paula asked and then took a sip of her coffee. She made a face at the taste and Cara thought she saw a look of confusion pass over her face.

'Twenty-six...' she answered, allowing her tone to say, *why are you asking?*

'A bit young to be leaving cryptic messages in people's pockets,' observed Paula. Then she paused as if another, more worrying question had occurred to her. 'What do you know about hacking into computers?'

'What?' asked Cara, mystified.

'Nothing,' Paula shook her head, then she gave a pained smile. 'Okay. Please. Rip off the plaster. What do you want to tell me?'

Now that the moment was here, Cara was again unsure of herself. Besides, where to start?

'As I said in the note, there's more to your husband than...'

Paula took another sip of her coffee. Then made a face and stood up. 'Needs milk. Who forgets to put milk into their coffee? I swear my head is all over the place these days.' She walked over to the fridge and pulled out a carton of milk.

Cara watched as she poured, seeing this for what it was – a delaying tactic – and again questioned what she hoped to achieve here. The woman looked tiny. Out of it. A blast of air from an electric fan would be enough to push her over.

Cara stood up. 'This is a mistake, Paula. I should go.'

'After you've gone to all this trouble?' She turned, visibly steeling herself. 'Let's just get this over with, please.'

'You're sure?' Now that the moment had come, Cara wished she was anywhere but here, in this woman's kitchen, about to pile more bad news on her head. She looked around herself. Used the obvious wealth around her as fuel. How could this woman not know who and what her husband was?

'Just ... tell me,' answered Paula.

'You should have a seat.'

With a sigh, Paula moved back to the stool and sat down. 'There,' she said. 'I'm sitting.'

'Okay. This is a lot to take in, but...' Cara looked around herself again '...it seems to me you've been well compensated for having to put up with that man all these years.'

'Just tell me, will you?' Then as if realising her tone was a bit too sharp, she added a quiet 'please'.

'Your son was killed in a hit-and-run seven years ago, yes?'

Paula sat up and looked over at her as if she was finally seeing Cara.

'He was hit by a red car. A Ford Focus.' She paused and steeled herself to force the words out. For this was *her* shame. 'My brother, Sean, was drivin' it. He was seventeen. A doped-up nut job. But I think he was paid to do the hit.'

'What?' Paula blinked rapidly, as if that might help her to digest the words.

Cara took a deep breath. 'I think he was paid to kill your son in some sort of gangland payback for your husband. And in revenge, your husband tortured and killed my brother...'

9

Paula jumped up from her stool and moved over to the younger woman. 'What on earth? Are you some sort of delusional...' She put a hand to the side of her face as if she had just been slapped. 'You need to leave. You need to leave right now.' She'd barely slept after catching someone hacking into her computer, and then receiving yet another silent phone call. And now this outrageous statement. It was as if all around her the world was going mad.

Cara stepped away from her. 'Listen, I know this isn't an easy thing to hear...'

'An easy thing to hear?' Thomas a murderer? 'I've never heard anything so ridiculous in my life.' She tightened her robe around her waist and wished she was properly dressed. And that she had her make-up on. She was never without it. Concealer, foundation, blush, mascara and lipstick. And if she was meeting an actual person, eyeshadow and a further layer of mascara. But now she had nothing. No defence.

In just a few words, this young woman had thrown the shreds of her life in the air. Not only had she accused her husband of torture and murder, but she'd given her a version of Christopher's death that ripped at her heart. Her baby was targeted? He'd been driven at deliberately?

Oh my God. She placed a trembling hand over her mouth. What had she just heard? The implications, if this was true were staggering. She imagined Christopher lying there, broken, at the side of the road. She screwed her eyes tight against the mental image. The police told her he'd died almost instantly. That was pretty much all they'd told her – their investigation had yielded little in the way of facts. No witnesses. Nothing to tell other than it was a hit-and-run; no description of the car or the drivers. Just that her boy had died when his head hit the kerb.

Paula gathered herself together. Or tried to. Her head was hurting. No, it was way more than that. Her skull was fractured. Her brain was reduced to mush. The bone between her eyes held a deep ache, a strong sense of *wrong*.

She looked at Cara properly for the first time. Quite tall for a girl ... five eight or something? Long blonde hair pulled back in a ponytail. She was wearing tight, black jeans; she was curvy but athletic and her sleeveless top displayed good muscle tone in her upper arms. She was an attractive young woman. Would Thomas have found her mix of vulnerability, looks and strength impossible to resist? Was all of this nonsense about Thomas and Christopher a weak and nasty ploy from a spurned lover? Did Thomas promise her all sorts of things, but his death now meant she came away from their affair with absolutely nothing?

Cara's eyes held hers and she could read a mix of confidence and uncertainty.

Who was this girl? And why was she saying this stuff? And why now?

'You have two minutes to get out of my house. Because that's how long it will take me to find my...' she cast her eyes around the room as if her mobile would just appear '...bloody phone and call the police.'

'Mrs Gadd...'

'You need to leave my house and you need to leave now.'

'Paula, I'm telling you the truth. My brother stole a red Ford Focus and ... God help me, but he ran over your son Chris, and then legged it.'

'No, Cara, no.'

'Then your husband caught up with him and made him pay.'

'Cara, no. Please. Get out.' Paula was on her feet, right arm rigid, pointing in the direction of the front door.

A chime rang out. Cara looked at her and Paula read a sense of real fear there.

'Who's that?' Cara asked, immediately getting to her feet in a stance suggesting she was happy either to fight or flee.

'I have no idea,' Paula said and trudged in the direction of the front door. 'But I'll show you out while I'm at it,' she aimed over her shoulder.

But when she reached the door she realised she was on her own. Cara hadn't followed. She pulled it open to see a pair of elderly women, both of them as prim as a stack of freshly printed bibles. They were each wearing sensible coats and sensible skirts and their faces were geared to show their certainty in what they were doing.

'May we interest you in the word of The Lord,' one of them said while holding out a small piece of bright-yellow paper. Paula took it. Read the headline: *God Chose Jesus To Rule the World.* Paula handed it back to her.

'Very nice,' she said. And shut the door. She made sure the snib was in the locked position and then walked swiftly back down the hall to the kitchen. Cara was at the back door as if she was about to run. She opened her mouth to speak, but Paula beat her to it.

'Right, what's really going on here?' She forced herself to calm down a little, while cursing the women who'd been at her door. She'd been working up a good head of steam, but somehow the interruption had dissipated the urge to throw the young woman out. And that had been replaced with a drive to know ... and an unfathomable dread.

'Our Sean,' Cara began, then took a seat back up on the stool. '...You sure you don't want to go and get some clothes on?'

'I'm sure,' Paula answered. 'I'm sure I can be excused relaxing my standards for now.' She waved a hand. 'Carry on. You were saying...'

'He died a couple of years ago. It took your husband a good while to track him down.' Cara paused. Bit her lip. 'Sean was doing well. Getting his life back on track.' She looked at Paula, eyes pleading for understanding.

Paula gave her nothing back; she had nothing to give.

'So, you claim this is when my husband, Thomas Gadd, tortured and killed him?' Paula snorted, allowing a little of her fear and anger to leak through. 'Don't you hear how ridiculous that sounds? This isn't some tawdry television crime series.'

'No, it's real life, Mrs Gadd,' Cara retorted. Then, as if realising that showing attitude would not win her over, she dropped her shoulders and lowered her voice. 'There's stuff going on in this city that would frighten you.'

Paula crossed her arms, realising how defensive it looked. She leaned back against the worktop and said nothing, hoping her expression said 'convince me', but she feared instead it betrayed the sick terror of what she might hear.

'Did anything happen in your life around two years ago? Did anything change? Did your husband start to act a little more strangely?' Cara asked.

Paula's lips tightened as the words hit. She felt a hiccup at her throat as if she was releasing a bubble of grief.

'Can you think of something? Anything?' asked Cara.

'Something that would make him go and murder someone?' Paula demanded, after taking a moment to get her emotions under control. 'No. Absolutely not.'

'Were you guys happy at that point?'

Paula drew herself up, tightening her arms around her. 'Why on earth would I discuss my relationship with my husband with you?'

'I met a guy.' Cara looked at Paula and paused as if calculating how best to carry on.

'You met a guy?'

'I'm an advocacy worker. I support people ... in one o' the roughest parts of the city.' She looked around herself. 'Compared to here, it might as well be on the moon, as opposed to just a couple of miles down the road. Anyway. This guy. His weans were in trouble at school. His wife was refusin' him access and unlike a lot o' the wasters around there, he was actually keen to spend time with them.'

'What has any of that got to do with Thomas? Or with me?'

Cara made a face, as if she was thinking, *What a self-centred bitch*. But then, to Paula's surprise, she held out her hand. 'Please, I'm getting there. But I have to put it into context or you won't believe me.'

Paula slumped in her seat and shook her head, overtaken by

weakness. 'Okay. Sorry. Please, go on...'

This appeared to mollify Cara somewhat and she offered Paula a smile of truce before continuing. 'When this guy heard my surname – Connolly – he got all funny. Asked me if I was Sean's sister. Said he could see the resemblance.' She bit her lip, as if forcing down a surge of emotion. 'Then I remembered him, but the drugs had changed him so much I couldn't match up the man with the boy in my head, you know? Anyway, he told me how it went down. He ran about wi' Sean for ages. Was in the car that night Chris was run down. And he was there the night Sean was eventually tracked down by Tosh Gadd.'

Paula started at the name: Tosh.

Despite herself, she murmured, 'His brother called Tom 'Tosh' when I first met him.' She was almost speaking to herself. 'Apparently that's what they called him when they were kids.'

She looked up, to see Cara's eyebrows were raised, her mouth turned down.

But Paula couldn't have it. 'Oh, for goodness sake,' she said, rebelling. 'What rubbish. An old name, a crackhead and you're convinced about this unbelievable story? He probably told you all of that to try and win you over, so you'd help him.'

'He told me all of that *after* I helped him. I already got him visits with his kids. There was nothing in it for him by then. He was telling me the truth, Mrs Gadd.'

10

'Bless me Father, for I have sinned.'

'Paula, there's no need for you to come to the confessional box.' She heard the smile in Father Joe's voice. 'I'll do you a home visit.'

'I'll have to get one of them voice modifier things so you don't recognise me next time.' Then, because this was a regular thing between them, 'And, anyway, I'm not sure I'd ever get used to confessing to you face to face.'

'Voice modifier? You'll sound like that scientist fella, Stephen Hawkeye.'

'Hawking.'

'Who's the Hawkeye guy then?'

'Isn't he in those Marvel movies?'

'Is his first name Stephen?'

Paula smiled despite herself. She knew he was joking. Knew this was Joe trying to help her – to tell her they could still play, that they didn't have to change their relationship because Thomas was gone. But it all felt like a huge effort to her.

She felt her knees ache on the hard wood of the knee stool. Trust the Catholic Church to make confession physically, as well as mentally, uncomfortable, she thought. She shifted slightly and leaned back to look at the crucifix on the wall above the meshed window through which she and Father Joe were talking.

The silence lengthened between them as Paula wondered what to say. How to say it. She replayed the knowing look on Cara's face – the one that said, *You know something was wrong back then, don't you?* And should she tell him about the phone calls and the computer-hacking incident? She discounted doing that. He had enough on his plate.

'Too soon?' Father Joe asked, his voice heavy with sympathy. From his tone, it was as if he wanted nothing more than to move across to her side of the cubicle, rest his chin on the top of her head, allow her to burrow into his chest and share a soothing hug.

'For humour?' answered Paula. 'That was always how you Gadd boys said you loved each other. A round of comedy and cutting insults. I might not be strong enough right now to keep up with the jokes, Joe, but if I ever lose my funny bone, please just put me in a box and tip it into a big hole.'

'Want anything in the box with you?'

'A bottle of that fine gin you brought over the other day, and a straw.'

'The straw will come in handy, you know, when the oxygen starts to be depleted.'

Paula started to cry. Leaned forwards and pressed her forehead against the knuckles of her clasped hands. Through the mesh she heard Joe join her.

'It's tough, eh?' she managed to say.

A sniff. A cough. And then through a tight throat, Joe managed to say, 'Aye.' One syllable that wore several octaves.

'Is it bad that I hate him, Joe? Is it awful that I'm so bloody tired of crying all the time?'

'Do you hate him, or are you angry with him?'

'A little of both,' Paula said without thinking. 'I'm furious at him for dying. For leaving me here. How silly is that? But there's something else ... something I could hate him for ... I heard something today that makes me think my marriage might have been, well, not what I thought it was.' And Paula was back in the kitchen with Cara, listening to the girl speak, unwilling to take it all in, but nevertheless hearing the truth in the girl's tone and seeing it in the cast of her eyes, the shape her body made as she spoke. Quick words. Clipped. Each with the power to wound.

'My husband wasn't a saint.' Paula had said to Cara. 'But that doesn't make him a gangster.'

'No, that's where the intimidation and murder come in.'

Paula read it in the young woman's eyes: Thomas had killed her brother; she was convinced of it.

'Don't listen to gossip, Paula.' Joe's voice interrupted her thoughts. 'That way madness lies.'

'Maybe I have to get through the madness before I can deal with all of this,' she replied.

'Do you want a side of Hail Marys to go with the insanity thing?'

'Throw in a couple of Our Fathers and it's a deal.'

And they were both back on a temporary even keel.

Paula stood up and the stool protested at the movement.

'Hey,' said Joe. 'I've got a very large frozen pizza that I need to share with someone. Want to join me? Or are you rushing off?'

'Thanks, Joe, sounds like an offer a lady shouldn't refuse, but there's something I need to do.' She needed to be on her own to consider Cara's words, and work out if there was any truth in them. The young woman believed them. That certainty was stamped through everything she said. And she hadn't been accusatory, attacking or bitter. She had been firm and controlled. Genuine. It had moved Paula in a way that vicious words wouldn't have.

She left the cubicle and walked to the church foyer, her footsteps ringing in the hallowed air like an announcement. Here she comes. Here she comes. Refusing to face the truth.

Other footsteps joined the echo of hers. More rapid. Heavier.

Joe reached her at the door and placed a hand on her arm.

'Is that it?' His eyes searched hers. 'You came all this way to confess you're angry with Tommy?'

Paula managed to meet his gaze, and thought, you're far too clever for your own good, Joe Gadd. She debated telling him what she'd learned, but he looked like he needed a few days under his duvet. Or a few weeks. His skin was grey; his eyes looked as if just opening them caused them to ache.

Instead of saying anything more she reached up onto her tiptoes. He read her movement and leaned down, she pressed her lips against the scratch of his cheek.

'You give yourself a day off, Father Joe,' she said. Then she shrugged his hand off, pulled the main door open and walked outside to the chill air, blare of traffic and the ache and low drone of her conscience.

He followed her out. 'Paula,' he shouted, and caught her before she reached her car. 'Hey,' he said, 'talk to me.'

She rubbed her eyes. 'If you knew Thomas had been up to no good would you tell me?'

He took a step back towards the church, buried his hands deep in the pockets of his black trousers.

'Joe?' she demanded.

'What?' he forced himself to look at her.

'Would you tell me?'

'I loved my brother, Paula, but I'd be lying if I said he was a saint.'

11

An hour later and Paula was on her knees again. This time she was waist deep among Thomas's suits, trousers and jackets on the floor of his walk-in closet. She touched the material slowly, lovingly, as if his energy would transmit from them through the whorls of her fingertips, up through the veins of her arms, and take residence in her heart. There. A blue tie with a little yellow fleur-de-lys design, repeated at random intervals. They'd bought it together for a charity event they were attending weeks before Christopher died. Thomas had stood in the changing cubicle wearing suit trousers that were too big, like a little boy waiting for his mother's approval. She remembered placing the tie against the middle of his chest, judging the light blue of his shirt, tutting that the waist of his trousers was too loose, and catching him rolling his eyes at the salesman, while clearly appreciating her attention.

She ran her forefinger and thumb along the length of the tie, stopping at a worn patch that must have been the top part of the knot that would rest under Thomas's chin, where his stubble had rubbed the silk.

Oh Thomas, she thought. *You were not the man that Cara described to me.*

Thinking about the young woman's claims about him was why Paula was in this closet, among his clothes. She was curious as to what she might find among his stuff. She'd been with him all her life: did she really know him?

And then Father Joe.

I'd be lying if I said he was a saint. What the hell did that mean? He'd refused to expand, spun away from her as if he regretted every syllable and left her there by the kerbside, in silent confusion.

For hours she had tried to stop herself from going down that rabbit-hole. All she had to go on was that crazy woman's word.

But, what if?

There was that time in the restaurant where Thomas had the poor waiter terrified. The poor wee guy had all but wet himself. Paula had never seen Thomas quite that angry in all her life.

After Christopher's death, after the funeral, the formal grieving, the time away from work, when family had stopped arriving every day, when it was just her and Thomas, Paula was determined that they would act like a normal couple. Do normal couple things. Honour Christopher's life in the banal. She had planned to visit the zoo, go to the cinema, go for a walk along the beach at Ettrick Bay in Bute. They had the odd meal, and otherwise Thomas was too busy.

He was always too busy, but that didn't make him a criminal.

All that hard work – to bring them all these riches. But what else? She heard a laugh. Realised it was coming from her. And this was before she got at the gin. She felt a hit of emotion, and fought it off. She wasn't going to start crying again. Nope. Not today. She was exhausted by her tears. Surely there were none left.

Thomas and his money. How did he do it? The hard way, with decency and scruples? Or did he bend a few rules? Which to be fair, Paula was prepared to accept.

But her Thomas behaving like – what? A gangster? No, she wouldn't accept that, not for a moment.

She reached up from her kneeling position and pulled another suit from its hanger. This one was dark grey, with a faint pinstripe, three-piece. The waistcoat had those wee lapels she always felt looked smart; it meant he could take his jacket off if he felt too warm and still look dapper.

Her handsome man.

Before she knew it, she was holding the fine cloth to her face, breathing deeply.

Nothing.

With a note of disappointment, she tried the waistcoat pockets. Nothing. And nothing in the trousers, either. In the jacket pockets were a pen, some paper clips and a couple of paper hankies.

She got to her feet and pulled more suits and trousers down from their hangers and went through them one by one, until she was almost hip deep in expensive tailoring. With no idea of what she was looking for, she kept searching.

Stuck in a kneeling position for so long, her back started to ache, so she moved into a seated position, with her back against the wardrobe wall. Her chin dropped towards her chest. Tired. So tired. She could just sit here, hide from the world and sleep among Thomas's suits, the clothes his body had inhabited, until this nightmare was over.

She shifted position again; the ache was in her back. The heat from Thomas's hands would be a great relief right now. She often kidded him that he had his own internal furnace, his skin gave off that much heat. And he made good use of that when she was pregnant. She just needed to make a little face when she was hurting and Thomas would oblige. Rubbing gently the areas that she felt needed his ministrations.

Mind full of him, and imagining the pressure and warmth of his hands on her back, she idly lifted another jacket and mechanically now explored each pocket. In the inside of the jacket, she reached into one of those small pockets, where a businessman might store some cards.

She felt a little resistance. The slick of a slip of paper. She recognised the feel of it; the kind that was used for receipts that were printed off on those little automatic printers.

She pulled it out. The light was restricted where she was kneeling, so she got onto her knees again and edged closer to the door and held it up to the daylight coming in through the large bay window.

She heard a noise.

Paula got to her feet. What day was this? Could it be the cleaner? 'Lynn?' she called as she walked to her bedroom door. 'Is that you, Lynny?' This was Tuesday. What was her cleaner doing here on a Tuesday? She listened for the direction of the sound. Her study. That was where it was coming from.

Who the hell was in there?

Fearful now, she wondered if she should close and lock her bedroom door. No, it had to be Lynn. She'd forgotten the day.

She stomped out of her bedroom, across the landing and pulled open the door to see Kevin Farrell, pulling at the drawers of her husband's desk.

'Kevin,' she said. 'What the hell...?'

He looked up at her, his eyes wild, then turned away and went back to his search.

'Kevin!' Paula said, raising her voice and walking over to him. She caught a whiff of whisky from his breath. Or perhaps from his crumpled jacket. She stepped back.

Was he drunk?

'Kevin,' she tried a patient tone.

He ignored her and kept on searching.

'Kevin?' Same result.

'Kevin! What are you doing?' Her phone was on her desk; she picked it up and held it in the air. Even doing that cost her energy. She was way too tired and way too emotional for any of this. 'Right, either you stop what you're doing right now, or I call the police.'

That got his attention. He turned to her. Ran the stumpy fingers of his right hand through the grease of his hair. 'Where is it, Paula?'

'Where's what, Kevin?' She caught a good look at his face for the first time and noticed that the right side was red and swollen. His bottom lip was cut.

'Oh my God, Kevin, what's happened to you?' Regretting her tone, she held a hand to his face as if her touch might heal him. He stepped back. Swallowed as if a pebble was stuck in the back of his throat.

'Where's the money, hen? We're in serious fucking shit here.' His voice was shaking.

'Where's what money, Kevin?' Pause. 'And how did you get in?'

He looked at her as if seeing her properly for the first time. His eyes narrowed. 'You know fine well what I'm talking about. You two were as thick as thieves. You expect me to believe Tommy kept it all a secret?'

'Kept what a secret?' Her heart jumped in her chest. 'For God's sake, Kevin, you're not making any sense.'

He didn't reply, but studied her, the smell of booze and body odour drifting off him like his own personal fog.

She felt the crumple of paper in her hand and tightened her fist, she wasn't sure why but something told her she had to keep it a secret from him. She still couldn't make sense of what it was for. Crossing her arms, she tucked her right hand under her left armpit, as if that might offer some support and strength.

'I think it's time you left, Kevin. By all means come back again when you're sober...' *And after you've had a good wash.* 'We'll talk about whatever it is you think I know.' She tried to inject steel into her voice. 'But I'm serious. If you don't leave now, I'll phone the police, say you were harassing me and you'll spend the night in the cells.'

'That might be an idea,' Kevin mumbled and to Paula's relief moved towards the door. 'You'll tell me everything?' he asked, and looked almost pathetic as he waited for her answer. 'We really don't have a lot of time.'

'I'll tell you everything I know, Kevin. Which really doesn't amount to much. In the meantime, please, go and have a shower and a sleep.'

She escorted him down the stairs and along the corridor to the front door. He paused at the threshold and turned to her, his expression tight. He'd clearly taken the time to try and gather himself together. He looked frayed at the edges; his eyes held an appeal and Paula felt herself respond to his worry. She shrugged it off, reaching for the door handle. Why on earth would she be concerned about him? She was in far too difficult a place herself right now and he had come into her home uninvited.

A thought. She held her other hand out. 'Give it to me.'

'What?'

'I'm assuming, for whatever reason, Thomas gave you a key. Or had a spare you knew about? I'll take it back, thanks.'

Kevin reached into his trouser pocket, retrieved the key and dropped it onto her upturned hand. Immediately, she was struck by the warmth coming off the small piece of metal. It was as if the heat of his worry had transferred onto the key.

'That daft wee bitch Cara Connolly? Don't believe a word she says by the way.'

He was off and down the stairs before the surprise of what he had said lifted enough for Paula to consider it properly.

'What do you mean?' she shouted after him. 'Have you been watching me?'

She received no answer but the leaden echo of his retreating footsteps.

Paula slammed the door shut. What the hell was going on here? She made straight for the kitchen and the bottle of gin. Poured herself a generous measure, sat at a stool and sipped.

Her mind swam. Had he been watching her? How did he know about Cara? And he had looked genuinely worried. No, not worried.

Scared.

What on earth did he think she knew about Thomas's business that he didn't? She snorted a laugh at the notion, and felt some of the alcohol trickle down her nose. Wiped at it with the back of her hand and then remembered she was still holding the slip of paper.

She placed it on the worktop and smoothed it out. Yes, it was a receipt.

It read 'Loch and Quay' in bold along the top. The ink was blurred where the street was detailed, but the town was clear enough: Gourock. The price was £15.30. The name of the place made her think of some sort of marina. What could you buy at a marina for that? A couple of drinks? Loch and Quay ... did that sound like a bar?

She made her way back up to the office, sat in front of her laptop and brought up the search engine. When she typed in the words, she was presented with the details for a locksmith.

She looked back at the receipt and found the date. Just a week before Thomas had died.

What was Thomas up to in those moments? Was this important, or was she just allowing that Cara girl, Joe's comments and now Kevin's behaviour to spook her? She closed her eyes and concentrated as if attempting to summon her dead husband. None of this was making any sense to her. *Please, if you're there, Thomas, send me a sign. Something. Let me know what was going on?*

She shook her head at her own actions. That was what desperate people did, wasn't it? Prayed to the dead, believed that the veil between the land of the living and the land of the dead was really a thing. That it could be breached with nothing more than a thought.

On the top right-hand corner she noticed a small series of numbers: *0246.*

She studied them. Rather than a receipt, might this be some sort of docket to prove he'd requested a key to be cut and this was proof?

What was Thomas doing in Gourock, at a locksmith's? The only time they ever went to Gourock was to pass through it on the way to the ferry terminal for Bute, and they hadn't done that for years.

A memory. A blink, and she was there in the car with them. Christopher singing something in the backseat, waving a toy ninja turtle through the air. They were on their way to the ferry for another weekend on Bute. Their special, family place.

'Mum, can I get some ice cream from that place at the big beach?'

'Ask your dad.'

'Dad, can I get some ice cream from that place?'

'The one at the big beach?' Thomas asked.

'Yes,' Christopher answered then added when he remembered his manners. 'Yes, please.'

'Ask your mum.'

'But she...'

And then the three of them were laughing.

The music of that noise played in her mind and then transformed into a discordant wail – when she couldn't stop herself from crying.

Reliving memory was a sweet-bitter pastime. The resultant ache was a cold slab of granite pressing down against her head, shoulders and chest. Her two men were now dead. How would she ever get over this?

12

Cara Connolly looked at the woman sitting on the hard, plastic bucket chair in front of her. Her crossed arms and the tilt of her head all asked her not to waste her time. She also noted the dark swellings under each eye and the fatigue in the tight jut of her shoulders – as if she was frightened to let go of whatever energy was sustaining her, in case she fell to the floor in a puddle. Paula was holding a giant, black – probably designer – handbag on her lap like it was bolstering her strength.

Cara damped down the resultant empathy. Swallowed it like it was a lump of charcoal. She couldn't afford to let this woman get to her.

'Why am I at your office?' Paula asked as she looked around. Cara considered what she might be seeing. The pale-blue walls and seating, the dark-blue carpet tiles on the floor, signs everywhere, and screens between the various work stations. Just like a thousand other offices in the city.

Out of the small barred window, a wedge of bruised sky and a sixties tower block that was scheduled for demolition.

'Thank you for coming,' Cara answered, her tone quieter than the other woman's in the hope she would get the hint and lower hers. She didn't want to draw too much attention from her colleagues. Nor did she want the older woman's reluctance to be here to be too obvious.

'It's important that people see us together in a kind of official capacity,' she said in a near whisper. 'If we tell people we're trying to solve a murder they'll think we're nuts.' Then she spoke a little louder. 'We are incredibly proud of the work we do here at Independent Advocacy Scotland. We don't need to raise money per se, but our mental-health partners in our outreach programme will greatly appreciate your help.'

Paula glanced about and then back to Cara. Gave her a tight smile.

She understood, but the flare of irritation in her eyes let Cara know she needed to get to the point. Fast.

'A murder?' Paula said in a harsh whisper. 'Frankly I'm getting very tired of all this murder stuff.'

'You're going to help me find out the truth about my brother, and your son.' Then louder, 'And the money we raise will be a boon to the local community.' She gave a couple of sideways looks, to see if any of her colleagues were listening in. None were. They were understaffed, overworked and exhausted. Cara knew from her own experience – you clocked in at 8:45 a.m., made sure you got your tea breaks in, for, you know, sanity, sacrificed your lunch hour by munching your limp lettuce and paper-thin ham sandwiches at your desk. Even having this meeting was going to cost her a lost Saturday morning as she'd need to catch up with her paperwork, but it had to be done.

Paula lifted her handbag and placed it between her feet. 'Perhaps you could explain what the money could be used for?'

Cara relaxed a little. Good. The woman was going to play along for now.

'Oh, a number of things,' she added breeze to her voice. 'The basics, really. Our young mothers need help with nappies, sterilising bottles ... stuff like that. And we're thinking of running some sort of education programme for them, you know? Creative writing perhaps? The local library closed down, but we got their computers. So, we're thinking of also teaching office skills. Help people write a CV. Help them apply for jobs.' Cara leaned back in her seat. 'Most employers expect applicants to have access to technology, and to be able to find their way round a computer. That's not so easy around here.'

'Sounds like you are doing important work,' said Paula, her tone softening as she cast her eyes around the room again. Cara followed her gaze and saw a couple of busy colleagues, Lesley and Alison, each sitting with a young woman; girls really, each holding a baby.

'And every day is different, so we—' Cara stopped speaking. Paula was suddenly on her feet. Her eyes were heavy, her face long with the weight of her grief.

'Is there a...' Paula managed to say.

'The toilet is over there,' Cara said, and pointed behind Paula.

She turned, picked her handbag up and all but ran to the loo.

Cara debated joining her to make sure she was okay. One of her colleagues sitting at a desk to her left sent her a questioning look.

Her husband just died, Cara mouthed. She remembered for months after her brother's funeral, grief would hit her at random moments, slamming into her with the power of a truck. She could be watching the news on TV, standing in a queue at her local supermarket, or even on one occasion she was at the dojo, practising a grab movement, when a bubble of grief burst and she fell sobbing onto the mat.

Minutes later, and a pale Paula rejoined Cara at her desk.

'It just hits you, you know,' Paula said as she took her seat. And Cara's attitude to her softened a little as she noted the older woman's conflict: she shouldn't have to apologise for her mini-breakdown, but at the same time wanted to apologise for apologising. Then, 'Sorry,' Paula said. Bit on her lower lip and took a deep breath. 'Won't happen again.' A weak smile. 'Where were we?'

'I was telling you—'

'Actually,' Paula got to her feet, shaking her head. 'I really can't do this.' And she turned and left the room.

Cara waited a moment and then followed her.

She finally caught her in the car park as Paula was about to get into her car. It was a dark-blue Range Rover – probably cost more than she'd earned in the last two years.

Paula turned to face her half defiant and half apologetic. 'I'm not quite used to ... people just yet,' she said.

Cara walked round to the passenger side and climbed in. 'Nice,' she said as she sat down, wondering how many people had been harmed to pay for this vehicle.

Paula said, 'It was Thomas's. I've got a wee Toyota Yaris, easier to park in this city. But I'm using this because...' She turned, suddenly irritated at herself. 'Why do I feel the need to justify myself to you?'

'What...?'

'Whatever you think you know, Cara, you're wrong. And please stop looking at me as if you're judging me. Say what you've got to say and then we can go our separate ways.'

Cara looked at Paula for a long moment. Searched her expression for duplicity. Saw nothing but a tired and sorrowful woman. She slumped back into the soft leather seating and acknowledged her own bias. Cara was surrounded by grinding poverty every day and couldn't help but see the money that cushioned this woman's life. And hate her for it.

But then there was the clear and heavy weight she was carrying, and it was as burdensome as her own. Cash might be feathering Paula's nest, but it was no help whatsoever with the sense of loss the woman was feeling. Perhaps that was the way to connect with her.

'You're right,' Cara said and looked Paula in the eye. 'I see all this...' she gestured to the dashboard with all its lights and gadgets '...and can't help but compare it with the lack in the lives of the people I meet every day. Every. Single. Day.' She tried to bite down on her resentment but failed. 'You people and your...' She shook her head as if that might get her back on track. Then she spotted movement to her right. Pointed.

'See her?'

Paula made a sighing sound and turned in the direction Cara was pointing. A woman was walking past the car park entrance. She was rake thin, dark hair pulled back in a ponytail wearing a thin sweat top and grey, baggy jogging pants, though Cara doubted since the woman left school she'd walked faster than the exhausted pace she was currently setting.

'We've tried endless times to get her to leave her husband. He loves her, she tells us. Loves her that much he forces their two wee boys to kick and punch her every now and again. It toughens them up for life in the scheme, she says. And once they tire of hitting her she's got to get to her feet and make them their tea.

'While that shit's going on, people on your side of the tracks get to sip moccachino and eat olives. And your husband and the other gangsters running drugs in this town milk every last penny from these poor bastards...' She tailed off. Looked away. So much for getting back on track.

'For God's sake,' said Paula. 'You invited me. I came. If all you're going to do is insult me I'll just leave.' She turned the engine on. 'Please get out of my car.'

Cara screwed her eyes shut and exhaled sharply, as if she might expel some of her bad feeling towards this woman and her family and manage to have a proper conversation with her without being such a bitch.

'I'm sorry,' Cara said. 'I really am. And I really do need your help. Hear me out, please?'

Paula looked to the side and followed the slow movement of the woman Cara had just pointed out to her.

'Start again?' Paula offered as she turned to face Cara. 'But one disparaging remark about my husband or "my people", and I'm leaving. Okay?'

'Okay,' Cara said and hated herself for sounding like a scolded child.

'When you called to invite me here, you said you wanted to meet this guy, Danny. The one who ... well ... So, what's his story?'

Cara saw the small boy with the gap-toothed smile and the blond hair that was almost permanently gelled, and compared it to the haunted, almost skeletal young man who told her he was there the night Sean was killed.

'Him and Sean were best mates. Lived in each other's pockets, you know? Even for a poor area like this, Danny's story is just riddled with tragedy. His old man was killed in a street brawl when he was only about nine or ten. One punch and his dad went down. Hit his head on the pavement and he was gone.'

'Dear God,' said Paula.

'Aye, then his maw turned to the booze – she's straight now, like, but when Danny was a boy she was a proper mess.'

'What chance did he have?' Paula asked with evident sadness. But then, as if her need for answers was asserting itself, she asked, 'You said something about helping him get access to his kids?'

'Yeah, well, that's gone a bit tits-up of late,' Cara answered. 'I swear some people are like bad-luck magnets.'

'Why, what happened?' Cara looked across at the older woman. She thought she saw genuine concern.

'The access thing was predicated on him getting off the street and into his own place, aye? But the housing the council gave him was in a notorious block of flats. Full of dealers and their clients. And most of these people don't have jobs or any prospect of getting one, so they party late...' Cara paused, picturing Danny sitting hunched in a chair, grimacing with pain every time he moved, facing her in her office as he told her what happened.

In her mind, she heard him speaking, as if he was still there sitting in front of her: 'So, I'm pure ragin',' he'd said. 'I've to get up and collect the wee yin in the morning and take her to playgroup. She pure loves that by the way. Playin' wi' all the other weans.' His smile was just like any other doting father, except it was on a face marked with serious bruising. 'But these pricks up the stairs...' he ducked his head in apology when he realised he'd used a rude word '...were having a party. Yet again. Givin' it all that *boom, boom, boom* music. I went up there, aye? And telt them to keep it down. Got a fist in my face for my bother.' He pointed at his left cheek. 'Then for good measure, when I finally got to sleep, they kicked my door in and gave me a doin'.' He eased himself to the side and lifted up his shirt to show the discolouring on his skin. 'Cracked a couple of my ribs, the bastards.'

Cara brought herself back into the present and tried to paint the interview for Paula as best she could, not sure she was really doing the sadness of the situation justice. But Paula listened, quietly nodding.

'When the mother of his child heard about the violence she refused to allow him to have the little girl on his own,' Cara continued. 'He could take her to the park for an hour or so, but that was it. To make matters worse the council refused to re-home him because of his dog. And eventually things got so bad the mother's trust in his rehabilitation was destroyed.'

'He has a dog? What's that got to do with anything?'

'Apparently one of the council guys said they could re-home Danny but he'd need to get rid of his dog, give it to someone or get it put down.'

'Really? Get it put down? They said that? The dog is probably the only real friend he has. For someone in that position that's no choice at all.'

Cara nodded, pleased Paula was taking in the story to such an extent she was defending Danny. 'It got worse. Another client was in the office when he was telling me his story. She overheard everything and went straight onto Twitter to try and shame the council. From the information she put online they managed to work out who it was...'

'That's good,' said Paula. 'Did he get a new place?'

'Well, that's it. We don't know what they said to him when they went to visit, but he ended up back out on the street, so it couldn't have been good.'

'Poor guy,' said Paula. 'What on earth could the council worker have said that ended up with him homeless again?'

'My guess? The council got a bit of a kicking online, and someone isn't too happy about it. I'm sure they delivered a put-up or fuck off message to the poor guy.'

'My God, that's heartless.' Paula looked out of the window.

'Welcome to my life,' said Cara. 'I deal with local-authority staff all the time. Most of them are brilliant, genuinely trying to do their best with miniscule funds and increasing numbers of clients, but some of them are...' she fought for the right words '...almost as brutalised by the system as their clients. They see them as an item in their inbox that needs to be in their outbox – not as a living, breathing human being existing in the most trying of circumstances.'

The two women sat in silence for a moment, as if the power of Cara's convictions was too much for them to bear in that small space.

At last Paula gave a nervous cough. 'And we're meeting Danny when?'

'Shit,' Cara looked at the clock on the dashboard. 'Fifteen minutes ago. I hope nothing's happened to him.'

13

So much for the Connolly girl's attempt to get her to speak to Danny, Paula thought ruefully as she drove with Joe along the M8 on her way to Wemyss Bay for the ferry to Bute. It had been a complete waste of her time. Whoever Danny was, and whatever Connolly hoped he was going to say, he hadn't even bothered to show up. Hopefully that was the last of the girl's nonsense. But she sensed that was a vain hope. Each day seemed to bring some new mystery – her whole body felt tensed for the next shock.

She took the turning into Gourock. She'd pocketed the docket for the locksmith on her way out of the house that morning. She was keen to have this one last connection with Thomas – and she also wanted to know what the docket might be for. She knew she could take a short detour and pop into the shop on the way to the ferry. Surely if she had found the docket, that meant Thomas never got around to collecting whatever it was for?

'Why are we stopping here?' Joe asked from the passenger seat, craning his neck to look at the row of small shops beyond the parking space she'd just driven into.

'Just need to pick something up,' she answered, injecting a neutral tone into her voice, hoping Joe wouldn't read anything from it, wouldn't pick up on her concerns today.

He leaned back into his seat with a worn sigh. 'We don't have long, or we'll miss this boat.'

'Won't be more than a minute.' She reached across and patted the back of his hand. 'And then we can get on with this.'

This was the small thing of the disposal of her husband's ashes. Gathering up all her strength, she'd picked them up the day before, on the way home from Cara's office. She was gratified to find out that, even in her haze, she had in fact notified the mortuary office that she did intend to claim them, and there they were, on the backseat of the car. She'd almost belted them in, giving Joe a small smile as she made as if to perform the action.

'Nutter,' he muttered, but he managed a smile back, and Paula counted that as a small victory – she was out of the house. It felt like she was off the floor at least, not about to burst into tears every other second.

But, bracing herself as she left the car and walked towards the shop, she felt trepidation and a sense of remoteness. As if someone else was operating her mind and body. Why was she scared? This was just for a key or something. She forced a slow breath. Whatever Kevin had been overreacting to, she wasn't going to take it on.

Inside the shop, in front of a wall of hanging key templates, shoelaces and door signs stood a young, bearded man in a mauve uniform. He looked up from his phone, pocketed it and asked, 'Can I help you?'

'I need to pick this up, please.' Paula answered and heard the quaver in her voice. If the shop assistant noticed, he gave no sign. He simply took the small piece of paper from her, read it and stepped to the right. He opened a drawer, thumbed through a number of items, and picked out a small brown envelope about two inches square.

'Here you go,' he said and dropped it into her hand. She stood there, momentarily frozen. This was real. Thomas had performed this little action not long before he died. Was it significant? She opened the envelope and peered inside to see two small house keys. Why would Thomas be getting a key cut? She normally took care of such tasks.

'Can I get you something else?' The assistant had his hand back in his pocket as if desperate to get back to whatever was on his phone screen.

'Sorry,' Paula replied, worried that she must look odd. She offered him a smile. 'I can't remember who I got this done for...' Now she must be looking deranged. 'I run errands for some old people. Sheltered housing kinda place,' she improvised. 'Did I leave any instructions with this?'

The young man looked like he was keen to get her out of his shop. 'You just gave us the key, missus. We cut from the original. Job done,' he said with a shrug.

'Of course,' she replied and made a face of self-mockery. 'I'll just need to go on my rounds and ask.'

Discomfited by her awkwardness, the young man retreated to the world of his phone, signalling he couldn't do anything else to help her and hoping she would just go away before her behaviour got any weirder.

◆

On the ferry, Joe brought her attention back to the present.

'You okay?' he asked. 'Ready for this?'

She didn't answer. Leaning against the railings, from the houses that clustered on the hill behind the ferry building and down to Skelmorlie, she turned to face open water. Down to the right she could just make out the stretch of houses that made up Innellen, before the ferry pulled alongside the point at Toward. Wind whipped hair in front of her eyes and she pulled it back and tucked it behind her ear before pulling her jacket tight against the cold and crossing her arms.

She turned back to face Joe who'd been mostly silent since they'd left the city. Leaning into him, she nudged him with an elbow.

'And you? Are you okay, Padre?'

He grunted. Pulled his eyes from the scenery, blinked and looked down at her.

'You've made this a whole lot easier, you know?' he said. 'Thank you.'

She bit her lower lip and whispered, 'Don't know if I could have done it without you, Joe.'

'Aye. Well. I spend all my time helping others. It's a damn sight harder when it's...' His voice tailed off into the wind as he twisted away from her. Then he turned back and looked down at the bundle she was carrying. Adding some energy to his voice, he said, 'You might have found a better carrier bag than that.'

Paula raised the thin, blue carrier bag in which she was carrying the plain urn that held the remains of her husband. She shrugged. 'What would you rather I have? One from one of the supermarkets? A bag for life?'

Joe laughed. Made a face at their irreverence.

'What are the rules for this kind of thing? The etiquette?' Paula asked.

'Etiquette might have meant asking Bill and Daphne if they wanted to come,' Joe said with raised eyebrows. Paula read the admonishment in his voice and replied by averting her eyes.

'Pair o' fannies,' she said, and gave a weak laugh. 'That's what Thomas called them.'

'You're incorrigible, Paula Gadd,' Joe said, and hunkered into the heavy wool of his navy pea coat.

She let loose a heavy sigh. 'I really have tried, Joe. I'm sorry but I can't be doing be with Bill and Daphne. They barely bothered with me while Thomas was still alive. Besides, they're probably busy balancing their tea bags. Making sure they've got enough to do them if the weather turns and that massive snowfall the *Mail* predicts every year is actually going to happen this winter.'

Joe snorted. 'You saying my oldest brother and his wife are boring?'

'So, where do we do it then?' Paula asked. 'And can we hurry up and make a decision? I'm cold.'

'We could drop a ladleful here, a ladleful in the bay...'

'Away and don't talk nonsense, Joe.' She chuckled, sending a silent thank-you to him; there were times when she thought she'd never be able to laugh again. Then she felt guilty for laughing and sobered. 'Does that make us bad people? Laughing at a time like this?'

'My guess is that Tommy's looking down and having a chuckle himself.'

'That's a nice thought.' She thought for a moment and came to a decision. 'I think when it comes to disposal, one big empty is called for.'

Paula scanned the people around them and felt a stab of envy that they were just going on with their lives while she was … She stopped that thought. Would they think it strange if she leaned over the railing of the ship and tipped the ashes out into the wind and sea? She caught the eye of someone. A man, tall with red hair. She held his gaze until he turned away. It may just have been her imagination, but she read his final look as if he was telling her he was giving in. This time.

She wrapped her arms tighter around the urn as if protecting it. She was used to men looking, assessing, before the braver ones would move closer and deliver some weak chat-up line. But this guy's interest wasn't sexual. His eyes held none of that hunger. It was more like he was measuring her for a coffin.

Paula shuddered, turned away, leaned against the railing and looked down into the grey-blue depths. She was being silly. Allowing Kevin's fear to affect her.

'See the tall guy with the red hair?' she asked Joe out of the corner of her mouth. 'Does he strike you as a bit odd?'

'What tall guy?'

Paula looked up. He was gone. She turned her head into the wind so her hair would be blown back off her face. 'Och, just ignore me. Getting strange notions in my old age.' Ever since that evening when she'd found Kevin in her house she'd been imagining all kinds of nasty things.

'Want to go below and get a coffee or something?' Joe asked.

She looked out into the Firth, judged the distance to the landing at Rothesay ferry terminal. 'Yes. That sounds like a good idea. I'm freezing up here.'

🜂

Down in the café with a cup of coffee in her hands, Paula scanned the other passengers to see if she could see the tall redhead.

'You alright?' Joe asked.

'It's hard to believe we're here to scatter my husband's ashes.'

'Too soon. Way too soon,' said Joe, falling into platitudes as his eyes sparked with tears.

Paula studied his face. Grieving brother aside, she wondered if there was something else playing on his mind.

She raised her eyebrows at him and leaned back in her seat. 'Why aren't you wearing your dog collar today?'

Joe's eyes clouded briefly. 'Today I'm Joseph Gadd, brother of Tommy. Father Joe can have some time off.' He held his cup to his mouth and blew over the top of it before taking a drink. 'Where are we going to do this, then?'

Paula looked to her right, out of the window, saw the buildings being pulled in by the journey of the ship and felt a twist in her stomach at the thought of saying goodbye to Thomas. And then she pictured the road out to her favourite spot on her favourite island.

'Ettrick Bay?' She felt a twinge of pain at the memories threatening to break the surface. Her chest ached, as if a band was squeezing at her ribs, but for once, she went with it; perhaps this was the price for thinking of happier, simpler times.

'I remember going out there once with you guys,' Joe said then made a dismissive sound. 'It rained nonstop for three days.'

'We had some amazing times. Do you remember the old fishing boat beached there? At high tide there would be kids climbing all over it. The thing was a death trap, but we didn't think anything of it back then. The kids were having so much fun.'

There was a small bowl on the table filled with thin fingers of paper-wrapped sugar. Paula reached out and began to divide them into brown and white. A deep breath took her unawares. She saw Christopher climbing up on the boat, shouting, *Dad, watch me,* keen for Thomas to see how brave he was, how clever. He was so lean in this memory. Ten, maybe eleven? Wearing nothing but a pair of blue sports shorts; hard muscle under fresh skin showing how active he was. She blinked back a tear. Breathed out. Saw Christopher jump from the deck and sail through the air into his father's arms. The force of his movement enough to knock Tommy onto his backside.

'For goodness sake, Christopher,' she'd remonstrated with him, but both boys, for that was what they both were in that moment, laughed at the sheer joy and release of it. That was where they stated their love for each other. In the boisterous ... in the abandonment that pure fun allowed. While she stood clucking over them like their private health and safety officer, seeing nothing but the potential for broken bones and torn flesh. Imagining squeals of delight turning into cries of pain. Worrying over the two most important people in her life.

She smiled at her younger self, as a tightening crept into her jaw. She exhaled hard as if that might release the emotion.

'There was this wee ruined cottage, just up the road. We used to fantasise about renovating it and spending the whole summer there. Thomas could commute to the city every day. Chris and I could wander the beach...' She shook her head. 'Where did we go wrong, Joe?'

'We're human. We go wrong. Then we pick ourselves up and start again.'

She looked out at the sand and sea and sky, thinking about what Joe just said. She and Thomas were definitely flawed, definitely human. After Christopher died they had each withdrawn, unable to handle the grief of the other as well as their own.

'The surprise was,' she thought aloud, 'having someone to share the grief with was kind of a blessing and a curse. The blessing is that you have someone who *really* understands how much it hurts. But a curse because on so many days it's all you can do to help yourself survive let alone someone else. Shutting down and shutting each other out became like a defence, you know?'

Joe reached across the table to her, and the warmth from the palm of his hand on the back of hers said everything that needed to be said in that moment.

Paula tested her coffee, and realised that the heat had mostly leached from it. She took a big gulp then asked. 'Were you always so sagacious?'

'Ooh, get you with the big words.' There was lightness in his tone, but again Paula could see Joe wasn't quite himself, distant.

'What's up, Joe?' Paula asked.

He studied her. 'Aside from the fact that we're about to scatter my brother's earthly remains?' His voice was edging into aggression.

'It's just that...' Paula said. Then began again. 'It strikes me there's something other than the final farewell that's bothering you today. But if you don't want to talk...'

'Sorry, Paula. I'm an old grump.' Joe wiped a hand across his forehead. 'Ignore me. I'll be fine.'

'It's like that old Streisand song: "Who sings for songbird?" Who does the listener go to when he needs to be heard?' Paula chose her words carefully. She was annoyed that Joe had responded to her previous question with some bite, but now was not the time to delve, or confront. Whatever was eating at him she would get to the bottom of, but not yet. If he was in the anger part of his grief cycle she wasn't going to respond in kind. They'd just end up falling out, and now, more than ever, they needed to be friends.

'Were *you* always so sagacious, Paula?' Joe asked, his energy levels popping back to where she would expect them. 'We have our confessors, you know.' His eyes grew distant. 'Tommy and I used to tell each other everything. He knew more about me than anyone alive.'

The stress Joe placed on the words *used to* gave Paula a moment's pause.

'When did that stop?' Paula asked. She tried to hide her need to know with what she hoped was an indifferent expression. Her husband had changed in the last few years. He was always an ambitious man, but he became a workaholic almost overnight. And of course that time away from her heightened the degree of separateness, and gave them less chance to reconnect.

That night they argued in the restaurant; the Thomas Gadd she knew and loved would never have spoken to a waiter in that manner. She'd never seen such anger in his eyes. But did he look like he was capable of terrible violence? Shivering, she refused to consider that.

Her mind returned to what Cara had said.

Did he change enough to torture and murder someone?

A horn sounded and a voice on the tannoy requested all drivers and their passengers make their way to the car deck.

People around them were gathering their belongings. Joe stood.

'Better go back to the car, eh?' he asked.

Relieved that she was saved from entering dark territory, Paula put her cup to her mouth, tipped her head back and drank the rest of her coffee while also feeling a little regret that Joe hadn't answered her question. When did Thomas stop talking to Joe? Was it around the same time?

They walked over to the stairs that took them down to the car deck, Joe stepping back to allow Paula to walk down the narrow stairway first. As she made her way down Paula thought about their conversation. Why was the answer to her last question to Joe so important? Just as the words left her mouth she realised she was all but holding her breath while waiting on the answer.

She thought back to what Cara had told her and her subsequent response and how she veered between flat-out denying the possibility that anything Cara said was remotely true, and hearing the belief in Cara's voice. *She* certainly believed it.

Did she need to know?

Did she want to know?

Who was her husband really?

Thomas was dead, so what did it matter now?

A series of faces in her mind: Cara. Kevin. That man with the red hair. Joe. Thomas. Always back to Thomas. She shook herself, muttering, 'Oh for God's sake.' She needed to get out of her own head.

'What's that?' Joe asked.

'Nothing,' she said over her shoulder and took the last step onto the car deck. She turned to the right, remembering where her car was lined up in the queue, then edged through the space between a Ford and a Peugeot, noting as she did so that her knee hit the bumper of the Ford and there would be a big dirty smudge on her jeans. Just a few weeks ago that would have had her charging over to her car, searching for wet wipes in the glove compartment and assiduously wiping her clothes clean. Today, she couldn't be bothered. Her right knee was dirty ... had she changed that much?

As she neared her car she began to rummage in her coat pocket for her keys and remembered again that this was purely a reflex action. The Rover came with keyless entry, she told herself and she reached for the handle. But then something stopped her. Something in her peripheral vision.

She turned her head.

The man with the red hair was climbing into a blue car two vehicles behind them. She felt his eyes on her like a burning.

'Who...' Paula felt a cold surge of fear in her gut. She climbed inside. Closed the door and when Joe got in she pressed the door lock, relaxing slightly when she heard the click.

'What's wrong?' Joe asked looking over at her. 'You look like you've seen a ghost.'

'It's nothing, Joe,' she answered with a fake smile, while fighting to curb a shiver. 'Nothing at all.'

14

The cars in front of her began to move up the ramp and onto the quayside. Paula handed the urn to Joe and started the car. As soon as she was able, she moved in time with the queue off the ship.

And they were on dry land, on her favourite place in the world. This small island on the Firth of Clyde, just thirty-three miles as the seagulls fly from the vast human spread of the city. A paltry distance really, but it was like a different world. Palm trees on a stretch of cultured lawn, a long line of Victorian villas, and hills in almost every direction covered in fir and heather.

On the short drive to the main road they passed a long, low building on their right, the fancy Victorian loo that Thomas took great delight in visiting every time they were on the island.

'They knew how to build things to last in those days,' he said every time he used it. And now, Paula had a quick look at the door, almost expecting to see him walk out and wave at her.

She sought the easing she normally felt whenever she drove off that ferry. And it was there, but muted. Thoughts of the man staring at her on the ferry were holding it off. Men stared at her all the time. Why was this one so unsettling?

When the traffic allowed, she took a right onto the main road.

The silent phone calls, the computer hacking, Kevin and his panic – all this was colouring everything, unsettling her. She should just relax and allow the island's usual magic to work on her. She shouldn't permit all of that to affect her day. The guy on the ferry was just a guy, doing the usual stuff she'd experienced most of her life from men. It was nothing unusual.

She momentarily took her eyes off the road and looked in her rear-view mirror, searching for the man's blue car. She saw one she thought might be it, as it took a left. Her eyes returned to the road in front of her and she released a breath.

She was being silly ... wasn't she?

A loud noise came from behind. She almost jumped out of her seat. A car horn. She realised she was dawdling and looked in her rear-view mirror again to see the driver behind gesticulating. His mouth moving as if he was cursing. He beeped his horn again.

Paula looked ahead and saw that there was a parking space just beyond the Victoria Hotel. She waved an apology to the angry guy behind her, feeling a blush at her inconsiderate driving, indicated and drove into the parking space.

Parked safely, she pulled on the handbrake and turned to Joe.

'I'd better tell you why I stopped at that locksmith,' she began. And she told Joe about the docket, and then went on to Kevin's unwelcome appearance and how terrified he'd been.

'What the hell's happening here, Joe?' she pleaded. An image of Kevin Farrell appeared again in her mind. His face a frozen mask of fear. 'He asked if I knew about some money. He was scared and desperate. Any idea what he might have been talking about?'

Joe snorted. 'I wouldn't put any stock in anything Kevin Farrell has to say,' he said, but his eyes were heavy with something she couldn't define.

'You didn't see him the other night. He was bloody terrified. There's more to all of this. Much more. First Thomas dies and then Kevin's acting as if some Mexican cartel is after him.'

Joe made another dismissive sound. 'More to all of what? What are you actually saying, Paula? You think Farrell and Tommy were involved in something that ... what? ... got Tommy killed? You think the medics got it wrong? It wasn't a heart attack?' Joe's voice was sharp. 'That's ridiculous. It's too much like a conspiracy from a movie. And forgive me for being unkind, but Kevin Farrell can barely open a fridge door without instructions.'

'I didn't say Thomas was killed, Joe.' She crossed her arms. Perhaps this was all part of the denial stage: Thomas was too good, too fit to die a natural death, so it had to be something out of the ordinary, because only then would it make sense. She knew she was being ridiculous, but she couldn't help it. Sure it was like something out of a movie, but these things happened in real life, didn't they? What if the police had it wrong? What if the disbelief she'd felt when they turned up at her door to tell her the news was based on something real?

'But you didn't see the state of Kevin,' she continued. 'The man was really scared. And anyway, why did Tommy keep him around all these years?'

'I often wondered that myself. Maybe Tommy felt sorry for him.'

'Thomas was a good businessman, he wouldn't keep someone around he felt sorry for.' She exhaled and stared out of the window at the quaintly titled Winter Palace. It was a squat round building, one storey, with four pagoda-style towers boxing it in, its gently sloping circular roof a landing and roosting point for a multitude of large gulls. The grass around the building was neatly clipped and was still, judging by the little wooden flags placed at intervals across it, being used as a putting green. In her mind she heard a whoop from Christopher as he magically produced a hole-in-one – Thomas picking him up and proudly swinging him in the air.

The image was so sharp it stole her breath. Paula shook her head as if trying to dislodge it. This island was too full of memories. Was it a mistake coming here?

No. It wasn't. It was the perfect spot – their happy place, and she felt that certainty as if it was pinning her to her seat along with the seatbelt.

She replayed Joe's previous question and noted the mockery in his voice. Was denial about Thomas's death now so strong, that she'd taken his heart attack, linked it with whatever he and Kevin and been up to, and the story Cara Connolly had told her and concocted some elaborate conspiracy?

Feeling foolish, she also told Joe about the man who was staring at her on the ferry.

'Now you're putting two and two together and coming up with the plot of a bad movie, Paula.'

She looked out of the window again, trying not to get annoyed at the dismissive tone in his voice. 'Isn't it all just a bit strange? And the timing of it all?'

'Supposing there was a man on the ferry staring at you. Other than for the fact you are a good-looking woman, and men stare at you all the time...'

'Don't patronise me, Joe.' She turned back to him and gave him a stare. He had the decency to look abashed.

'Right, supposing he was there for some nefarious purpose, how did he know you would be on that ferry? Did he follow us? Or did you tell someone we were coming over here today?'

'Who would I tell?' Her voice grew quiet. 'Thomas always said I had more acquaintances than friends. He was worried that since Christopher died I'd cut myself off from people.'

Which was true. At first it was a gradual slide away from company, until the thought of other people became unbearable. They had lives she didn't. They had children. Happiness. And the impulse constantly to compare and contrast became the mental prism through which she considered every moment she spent with another human. It had been best to just withdraw. If you don't let people in you don't get hurt, right?

And that became the new normal for her. That and what her counsellor called 'suicide ideation'. Each time she drove across the Erskine Bridge she'd wonder what it would be like to park at the side of the road, climb the fence and jump. Each time a bus drove past her she would wonder what it would be like to step in front of it. Each time she popped one of her pills, she wondered what it would be like to take the whole lot. It was only the idea of the mess that other people would have to clean up that stopped her. Besides, as she explained to the counsellor, it wasn't that she really wanted to kill herself, she just didn't want to be alive. To her mind, that was an important distinction.

They sat in silence, Paula struggling with a melee of memory. And the additional complication that she'd been given: a horrifying reason behind Christopher's death.

'There will be an explanation for all of this that doesn't involve anything strange or illegal.' Joe said, backing up her change in thought. 'The man giving you the eye on the ferry was just a man giving you the eye. And Tommy died from a heart attack. It was tragic but natural.' Joe turned in his seat to face the front and crossed his arms. 'Can we go now, while we still have daylight?'

Checking the traffic in her wing mirror, Paula judged the space and pulled out. Images from the past continuing to jostle each other in her mind, she drove along the coast to Port Bannatyne, where she took a left and joined the narrow road that cut across the island to the beach at Ettrick Bay.

Before she knew it she was there, in the car park, with the flat roof of the tearoom off to the side, mouth dry, pulse hard in her ear, staring out to the expanse of sand, stretch of water and, beyond that, the hills of Arran breaking the horizon.

Silence.

Joe was the first to speak. 'One of my favourite views.'

'This is perfect, Joe. Perfect.' She looked at him, tears welling in her eyes, certainty fuelling her. 'We really couldn't do this anywhere else.' She climbed out of the car and took a step towards the sand, paused. Thinking, where do we do this? How do we do this? Then she thanked God that Joe was with her. He was a veteran of this kind of thing. How many times must he have gone through similar with his parishioners? She reached a hand out to the side, expecting Joe to be there. Nothing. She turned. He was still in the car. Through the windscreen she could see the look of trepidation on his face.

She walked back to the car and pulled his door open.

'Right. Get your backside out here.' Forced cheer into her voice. 'These ashes aren't going to scatter themselves.'

Joe offered her a smile. 'What are you like?' He got out of the car and held up the blue bag with the urn. 'Want to take these?'

She accepted the ashes with a nod, then she took a small step towards him, took his arm in hers. 'Let's go for a walk, Father Joe.'

He leaned forwards and kissed the top of her head. 'Let's.'

They walked in silence. Words were insignificant in that moment. Nothing but a meaningless jumble of syllables waiting to be given noise. All Paula had was a mind soaked in emotion and breath being pushed out in a fog in the cold air. A foot on the sand. The pull of muscle to lift and replace and move forward. The chill nipping at the exposed skin on her face and neck.

And nature. Sand, rock, sky, a chill breeze and blue-grey water.

And ash.

In unison they walked, towards the sea line as if obeying the timeless pull of the tide. Once there, with the water licking at the toe of her boot, Paula unwrapped the urn, took off the lid and with the sharp movement of the hammer thrower, she spun on her heel, arms out and offered Thomas's remains to the unfeeling brine and breeze.

Then, she paused, closed her eyes and imagined Thomas, a profile in dust, walking away into the distance, on top of the water until, just before he faded into the indistinct horizon a hand went up in a wave. She snorted at the silliness of the notion, but decided she liked it anyway. And feeling the cold slide of a tear on her cheek, she turned to Joe.

'Right,' she said, took his arm, turned and began to walk back to the car park. As they walked, he said. 'Shouldn't we have said something?'

She snuggled up to him. 'Nah. We loved him. We didn't need to tell his ashes that.' Then, 'Coffee?'

Joe nodded. 'That would be perfect. I'm freezing my arse off.'

'Father Joe,' Paula made a mock shocked tone. 'You're incorrigible.'

'I'm having the day off from being intractable.'

♦

In the tearoom, they sat on either side of a small table, each of them with a mug of coffee in their hand. Paula looked out into the wide bay.

'Heaven,' she said. And smiled. 'And memories.'

'Mum and Dad used to bring us out here as well. That's probably where Thomas got the urge.' Joe gave what looked like his first genuine smile that day. 'Always seemed to rain. Lots of our neighbours were going abroad, but Dad was adamant we should holiday in our own country, like he had done as a boy.' He laughed. 'He'd pile up all his beach paraphernalia in the car, get the ferry, drive over here, pitch his striped windbreaker into the sand and lie there on his blanket, wearing shorts and a simmit, regardless of the weather.'

Paula laughed at Joe's automatic use of the old Scottish word for vest. *Simmit*. 'You never see them anymore. Windbreakers. I'm sure Thomas inherited your dad's.'

'That's cos none of the rest of us wanted it.' He paused. 'Right enough, it must have been nearly in tatters. It saw a fair bit of service over the years.'

Paula saw three wooden poles, about waist high, linked with cloth coloured in red, yellow, blue and green stripes that Thomas would hammer into the sand. Then she and Thomas would huddle behind it sheltering from the cool July wind while Christopher ran yelling to the sea-line.

She saw Thomas pull up his t-shirt exposing the skin on his trim stomach with its coating of dark hair. Then the bump and curve of chest muscle, shoulders and bicep. He'd emerge smiling as he pulled the cloth over his head, his hair a mess. He'd do a Tarzan yell and race after Christopher. Vitality. Strength. Press-ups and burpees in their massive bathroom. Freshly prepared food at every meal. His lifelong pursuit of health.

'No way Thomas had a heart attack,' she said with feeling.

Joe grimaced an apology. 'That's what it said on the death certificate.'

'He was a fit man, Joe. Looked after himself. It just doesn't add up.' Paula slammed a hand on the table.

'Death doesn't add up, Paula. It sneaks up too often and—'

'Don't, Joe. Just don't. I'm not one of your weak-minded parishioners desperate for a soothing word from the local priest.' She tried to bite back on her irritation but nonetheless even she could hear it in her voice.

'That's unfair, Paula,' he said, and she heard Joe's voice rise in response to the anger in her words.

'I know death sneaks up, Joe. I know it. I've lived it. I do not need you to tell me that.' She clipped off each word.

'I just—'

'Explain it to me then, oh holy one,' Paula demanded, part of her aware that the serenity she'd found on the beach was quickly dissipating and she was returning to the anger part of her grieving. But she didn't care. She didn't care if she was offending Joe. Something was wrong here. *Very* wrong. Why was she the only one who could see it?

'No need to be nasty, Paula.' Joe's eyes were cold. The priest was retreating and the grieving brother taking centre stage.

'Your fit and healthy brother, not quite fifty years old, died of a heart attack?'

'It happens. This is Scotland after all. The land of sugar and processed fat.'

'Thomas never had pie and chips in his life.' Paula crossed her arms, feeling her hands in fists tucked into her oxters. Nails pressing into the flesh of each palm. She pushed her fists in there for fear she might punch something. 'He was totally healthy.'

'Sadly we can't control what kind of people get what kind of illness.'

'Oh for goodness sake, Joe, stop it. Don't retreat into sanctimony. Not with me.'

'I'm not.' He looked stung, but Paula was past caring.

'You bloody are. You're not wearing your dog collar today, Joe. Be a man, not a religious cypher. There's something distinctly suspect going on here, and all you can do is spout nonsense about processed fat.'

'Paula, you're overwrought. You're...'

Paula shot to her feet. 'I'm seeing clearly for the first time in a long while, Joe Gadd.' She stabbed a finger at the table-top. 'Go find a sand dune to bury your head in, but I'm going to find the truth.' With that, she turned, fled from the tearoom, all but blinded with tears and fury, and ran out towards the water's edge hoping to find peace, and possible answers in the spot where Thomas had been borne onto the wind.

She got there, panting, after several minutes of running. Guilt at how she'd spoken to Joe now acted like the tip of a knife pressing against her conscience, and she questioned her reaction. Was she overwrought? Was she taking two and two and turning it into murder, in a weak attempt to make sense of all the recent random occurrences?

She checked the sand at her feet for signs of Thomas's remains. Any change in colour? She closed her eyes and saw the arc of ash, then opened them again and tried to work out where it might have landed. She ran along the water's edge to her left. Stopped. Searched the sand for signs of him.

Nothing.

She fell to her knees as a wave approached, feeling the chill of the sea water bite at her knees and shins. Her head fell forwards and she gave in to the emotion, shoulders shaking, each juddering breath driving home the nails of her grief.

Oh, Thomas. *Thomas.*

This time out loud. A shout. His name an accusation. 'Thomas.'

At last, she got to her feet, and brushed the wet sand from her jeans. How must she look?

But glancing around she noticed she was on her own, apart from one person over to her far left, their jacket a red smudge against the sand. She read the man's height and his gait. Hope surged in her gut. Thomas? She quashed the thought. Where would Thomas get a dog, she questioned when she noted a large yellow Labrador at the man's side, its tail a wagging blur of content.

Content.

That was a long time gone.

Would it ever return?

She kicked into the sand. Jesus, she needed to get out of her own head. That was where Joe was usually a good choice of companion. A careful mix of empathy and laughs. At the thought of him she felt another prod of conscience. She shouldn't have talked to him in that way. He didn't deserve any of that.

She turned and faced the tearoom just as a car drew up in the car park. A taxi? A man left the café and walked towards it. Before he got in he turned, his face scanning seawards. Even from this distance Paula could see the apology in Joe's body language before he ducked into the car.

Another mark in the out-of-character column for Joe Gadd today, she thought. There was no way that he'd leave her here on her own in normal circumstances.

Then she tapped her forehead with the fingertips of her right hand. Joe was grieving as well. The usual behaviours get pushed aside. She should cut him some slack. Let him go away.

Leaving her on her own. Adrift. She thought of what she'd said to Joe earlier. That Thomas had worried she didn't have enough friends. She'd poo-pooed him at the time. And look at her now, the only friend she had in the world was a priest.

Her phone buzzed from her pocket.

She plucked it out and read a message from him:

Thanks for bringing me along. It meant a lot. Need to be on my own for now. Getting next ferry home. Talk soon please?

She thumbed out a reply: *Sure. Hug. X*

She thought some more. Typed out something else: *Sorry for acting the bitch. Peace and out.*

A moment.

Then his reply: *Peace and love, ya gallus besum.*

She laughed with relief. She still had Joe on her side. And that was an expression Thomas used from time to time when talking about her. Some used it as a put-down but he used it with a wink and a grin, telling her that *gallus* meant bold. He enjoyed it when she was strong.

That was the line of women she came from, she told him. Bold and brazen. No men were going to silence them. That was as true then as it was now.

Phone back in her pocket she turned to the sea. *Oh, Thomas, what should I do? Tell me what to do?*

She began to walk along the water's edge, further away from the car park and the tearoom. Best to give Joe his space. If she went back to the car now, chances were they'd end up on the same ferry going back to Wemyss Bay.

She felt the breeze against her forehead as she walked, chill and probing, and imagined it pushing the worries from her mind, leaving only a solid resolution. There was something going on here. Her husband was not the man she thought he was and it might have killed him. It might have been what killed their son.

Sometime later, head down, she could see – and hear from the sound of her tread – that she was reaching the end of the beach. The sand making way for stones, pebbles and grit, some of it coated in brown seaweed and egg wrack. Watching her footing, she turned slightly and made her way to grass and soil, then with a gasp realised where she had been heading all along.

Looking up and to her right, just within a small copse of trees she could see the dark bulk of the cottage she and Thomas had dreamed of renovating all those years ago.

She increased her pace, stepped beyond the trees and with a brief flare of happiness saw that the cottage no longer resembled the partly roofed, broken-windowed wreck she remembered.

Some lucky person had shared their ambition ... and beat them to it.

See, Thomas, I told you, she thought. There was a home to be had here.

Moving closer she studied the small house. The thick walls were painted white. The door, made from good solid oak, was stained a similar colour to the one back at her home in Glasgow. The guttering and roof had been replaced, the windows double-glazed.

She clapped her hands. How wonderful. This was great. Something nice on this day of all days.

Then she had a thought that someone might be inside, looking out at this strange woman staring in, and was about to phone the police. She craned her head to the side, looking towards the far side of the house to see if there was any car parked.

The parking bay was empty.

Could the house also be empty? Could she risk an investigation? Wouldn't it be great to see what someone had made of 'her' wee house? She stepped onto the gravel path and took the six steps to the door. Read the 'Welcome' on the doormat and moved to the side to peer in the window, all the while expecting someone to tap her on the shoulder and ask her what the hell she was doing.

Forehead pressed against the glass she looked into a cosy living room – low ceilinged, with a door on the far wall, possibly into a kitchen. On the wall to the right a small log-burner set into a large fireplace, with a mirror over the mantelpiece. One cream leather armchair to the side, with a matching two-seater sofa. With a pleased sigh, she realised it looked just like something she might have put together.

Something on the inside of the windowsill caught her eye. A gold-coloured photo frame containing the image of a family. The thought of witnessing a happy moment that belonged in someone else's life almost stopped her, but something perverse in her made her look. She saw a handsome, healthy man, woman and child. All tan and teeth and windblown hair, with the sands of Ettrick Bay behind them. She took a closer look and her heart all but stopped.

The woman was her. The man, Thomas, and between them, with a gap-toothed smile, Christopher.

She knew that photo. Could remember it being taken out here on this beach.

What the hell?

Hand to her mouth she stepped back.

And while her mind spun, attempting to make sense of what she'd just seen, her body was acting on remote. Her hand was in her pocket and her fingers were locating one of the keys she'd picked up from the locksmith.

She stepped across to the door, the pop of gravel echoing, and placed the key in the lock.

She turned it. The door opened and she stepped inside.

15

Feeling that someone had temporarily taken control of her body, Paula closed the door behind her and stood in the hush of that small space, as if in a cathedral. So accustomed had she become to the breeze and occasional cry of a gull that silence rang in her ear like a sullen bell.

Stunned, she stood there and scanned the room. Stifled a sob.

Thomas.

What were you thinking?

Hope surged, stealing breath. Could he still be alive? After all, she was too drugged to face going to view the body so Joe went in her stead. Could he have been convinced by the wrong dead man?

A number of scenarios coursed through her mind. In all of them, rather than having a heart attack in a restaurant, Thomas avoided death in some accident, put his wallet in the pocket of a faceless man beside him in a car ... then walked off into the distance.

She told herself to get a grip, then looked around.

The living room spread out to her right and there were two doors, both painted a crisp white. The white-stippled ceiling was only about a foot above her head; Thomas would have to walk about in here with slight stoop, she thought.

Trembling, she fumbled her way into the room, edged past the sofa and took a seat in the armchair. Eyes smarting with tears she breathed out low and hard. Breathed in. She had to pull herself together. There was a reasonable explanation here.

Could he be alive?

Could he?

She became aware of herself – her hands were pressed together as if in prayer. She stuffed them into the pockets of her jacket. Looking down at the black, cast-iron wood-burning stove and the dried flower arrangement off to the side, she noted that was just what she would have picked.

You knew me, Thomas. You knew me.

She bit her lip. Heard a sob escape into the room. Felt a tear slide down her cheek. Shook her head. *He's dead, Paula. Dead. Don't you go there.*

She stood and walked over to what she guessed would be the door to the kitchen and pushed it open. White walls and ceiling, a blue marbled work surface, pale cupboard doors with a blue wash on her left, split by a chrome oven – facing her a half-glass back door, to the right of that a large picture window over a Belfast sink. To her right a small pine table with three chairs and a large aluminium fridge-freezer.

She walked over to the cupboards and opened them, looking for clues, but there was nothing but the usual cups, plates, cooking utensils and cutlery. Everything had the shine of the new and unused.

Stepping across the room to the fridge she noticed with a smile that it displayed one magnet, with a picture of Rothesay Castle. Christopher had loved their sole visit there. He had been particularly taken with the thought that a Viking King, Haakon Something, had taken the castle in the thirteenth century. Vikings were cool, he'd announced. And he shyly asked for a toy axe.

Hand on the cool chrome handle of the fridge, she pulled it open. It was empty apart from a carton of milk. She plucked it out of the shelf, held it to her nose and sniffed. It was fresh. Hope surged again.

No, she was being ridiculous.

She replaced the milk and closed the door. Then she turned and walked over to the sink and, with a start, noticed that there was a single mug in there, stained with two rings of dried coffee.

Paula picked the mug up and held it to her lips, imagining Thomas's had been pressed there just moments earlier.

She let the mug drop into the sink and heard the clatter of china breaking.

Ignoring her impulse to clean up the breakage, she looked out of the window. Despite the theories that were colliding in her mind, she couldn't help but appreciate the view. It was like someone had stood in this spot and shouted to someone outside to clear just enough shrub, branch and tree to frame the perfect scene.

Had Thomas been here to oversee the work, just before he died, or was this after his supposed death and funeral? She imagined him standing at this window, scanning the beach for her, waving as she approached from the sea.

She slapped her palm down hard on the sink. Enough. More clues; she needed more clues. What was real was the cottage. The photo on the windowsill. The key. Thomas had died and she had the death certificate to prove it.

This was surely her gift from him. His way to bring them both back together. And it would have worked.

It would have worked, you lovely, stupid man.

Paula left the kitchen and walked across to the other door. Turned the handle and pushed it open. This room was about the same size as the living room; it had one door off it – a bathroom? – and was crowded with a king-sized pine sleigh bed, the exact same as the one at home, with matching bedside cabinets, and against the far wall a wardrobe. Even the wallpaper, bedding and curtains were the same as her bedroom at home. But everything felt crowded and too busy in this much smaller space.

She quashed the urge to have any note of complaint spoil the moment. That Thomas had gone to this much time and trouble was adorable and deserved more from her.

She walked over to the other door, noting the plush feel underfoot and resisting the urge to climb onto the bed and smell the pillows, and pushed it open. The bathroom. A pedestal bath. She'd always wanted one of those. In the far corner a shower unit. The expected toilet and sink and, above the sink, a mirrored cabinet. She opened it, and inside saw a pair of bottles of scent. His and hers, as if on display. Oval bottles filled with an amber liquid. Obsession, by Calvin Klein. She imagined

Thomas placing them there with a small smile of pleasure at his own wit and cleverness.

Yeah, you were that clever you got a heart attack, or got yourself killed.

She took a step back out of the bathroom, closed the door and walked over to the wardrobe. Pulled it open. There was a suit inside. Hanging there, dead centre. The exact match of the one from which she'd pulled the locksmith's receipt.

'Thomas, what are you playing at?' She said the question out loud and realised that she was feeling his presence around her. Everything within these four walls had been chosen by Thomas, with her in mind. The daft big soft lump. She hugged herself, imagining that it was his strong arms around her.

'I never did it when you were alive, buddy. Why do you suddenly think I'm going to go around checking your pockets again?'

Yet, she instantly did, trying the waistcoat pockets first. Nothing. Then the outside pockets of the jacket. Empty. Next, she pushed her hand into the inside pocket of the jacket. Nothing. Once she'd tried all of the pockets, she started at the beginning and tried them all again.

Last, she tried the trouser pockets and found a solitary toffee still in its clear wrapper, and a folded over leaflet for a will-writing service. Why would he be looking for one of them? Their wills had been updated about a year after Christopher died. What had happened in the meantime to make him think about changing it?

The front of the leaflet showed an imposing sandstone building, with a large wooden front door and gilt lettering on the arched downstairs window. She turned it over and saw the address. It was in Dumfries. A lawyer's office in Dumfries? What would Thomas be doing down there? That made no sense at all.

She stepped back and frustrated, ran a hand through her hair. She was missing something, she was sure of it. To the side, tucked in between the wall and the wardrobe she spotted a wicker laundry basket, stained the same colour as the furniture. She lifted the lid and peered inside. Sports clothes lined the bottom. A light-blue t-shirt and what she judged to be a pair of shorts. She lifted them out. Underneath was a pair of white socks and white underpants. As she lifted the pants something fell from inside them.

A small black rectangular shape.

A moleskin notebook.

She bent forwards, stretching to the bottom of the basket to pull it out. It had to be meant for her to find. Who else but a wife would go near a man's dirty underwear?

'Right, Thomas, what have you got for me here?'

Moving back to sit on the edge of the bed she opened the notebook, hoped for a message, something – a sign that all of this was him. She was sure the signals couldn't be interpreted in any other way, but she needed a solid note, a hello – *something* to help ground her in this increasingly surreal moment.

The first page was blank. The second held a series of numbers and letters. With a quiver she recognised Thomas's careful script.

But then nothing. The rest of the notebook was empty.

With a sigh she turned back and studied the numbers for some sort of meaning. She could come up with nothing.

She closed the book and moved through to the living room and took a seat on the sofa. She had another look, and noted that there were ten rows, each beginning with the number eight. Then she discerned a pattern for the first set of numbers on each row. They were clustered in sixes. The next cluster on each row held eight numbers, all of them starting with a double zero. Next came a seemingly random collection of numbers, symbols and letters. It occurred to her that each of those felt like passwords. She paused. Took a breath. Passwords. Each row ended the same, with the number one and a letter, a capital M:

1M

In her mind that signalled a total of ten million.

Money?

Was this cash?

No.

Ten million pounds? She pursed her lips and blew out a sharp breath. Utter nonsense. That's what that thought was.

In her peripheral vision she saw movement. Someone going past the window. Her heart thumped. Calm down, she told herself. It was just a walker, heading for the beach. Though why were they moving in that direction?

She jumped.

A knock at the door. Solid. Expectant.

She stood, thrust the notebook into the pocket of her jeans and moved back towards the bedroom door, out of the sightline of anyone who might look in the window.

But then whoever it was could look in the bedroom window and see her. She darted out of view, moved along the wall and into the kitchen. But she had the thought that the visitor could walk round the back of the house and look in the kitchen window. Her heart was thumping fast now.

It wasn't anything to worry about, she told herself. Not here. But her trembling hands told her different. She was in the middle of nowhere. Completely alone. And no one knew where she was in this house. There was another knock at the door. More insistent now.

She stuffed the knuckles of her right hand into her mouth to stifle the squeal that wanted to escape.

She heard the letterbox squeak open.

A voice sounded into the room. Deep and bassy.

'Mrs Gadd. Paula? There's no need for you worry. I'm friend of Tommy's. Can you let me in? I explain everything?'

The voice held a cajoling note. But it offered friendship too. And it was accented, she realised. Eastern European?

There was an explanation? Without another thought she marched to the door, twisted the lock and opened it.

There stood a large man in a red jacket. By his leg a copper-eyed, pink-tongued, yellow Lab. It was the guy she'd seen across the beach.

He pulled the hat off his head.

She recognised him instantly. It was the ginger-haired man from the ferry.

16

Paula slammed the door shut in his face, but not before the dog, wagging his tail had darted inside, walked past her and made for the kitchen.

What?

Oh my God.

That man. He was on the ferry. And the way he stared at her.

She leaned against the door, heart thumping. Drew her phone out of her pocket and held it up to see if she could get a signal. One bar. Then nothing. Shit, it could cut out while she was phoning the police.

The dog appeared at the kitchen door and sat back on its haunches, wagging its tail, mouth open, tongue out, as if it was smiling.

He'd been here before, she thought. He knew the way to the kitchen. She judged the expectant look was for water.

And if he *had* been here before? And all of this work *was* done by Thomas? And the man on the other side of the door knew Thomas...

'Paula,' the man spoke through the letterbox again. 'Please. My name is Anton Rusnak. Forgive my poor eyesight. I wasn't sure that was you on the ferry or I would have said hello.'

This gave her a little relief. If he was to be believed, he hadn't been giving her the evil eye, he was just trying to see her properly.

Silence. As if he was waiting for a response.

'I know this must be strange,' he said gently. 'Let me explain you.'

She said nothing. Tried to work all of this out. Her mind wouldn't let her.

'Could you give dog some water, please? He will expect water.' Pause. And with a smile in his voice. 'His name is Bob. He is friendly.'

Not knowing what else to do, she obeyed his request: she walked through to the kitchen, found a breakfast bowl in a cupboard, held it under the sink tap and filled it, noting the shake of her hands as the water splashed over the brim onto her fingers, as she placed it on the floor.

She caught herself and thought: *What the hell are you doing?* She should be diving out the back door and running across the bay to the car to get the hell out of here.

The dog slurped noisily at the bowl. Paused to look up at her as if to say thanks and then went back to drinking.

She heard the squeak of the letterbox opening again.

'Please. You can trust me, Paula. I was friend of Tommy's. Can I explain?'

Pause.

The dog appeared from the kitchen and stared at her. And she realised she was going to have to open the door to let it out. And this man Anton would be there.

Should she find some weapon to defend herself? Should she run out the back door? If she did would she make it back to the café before he pounced?

But then she wouldn't find out what he had to say ... and she acknowledged now that she needed to hear exactly what it was that was happening here.

She turned and unlocked the door, her body tensed, ready to escape.

'No funny business,' she said. 'I know karate and I know exactly where to aim to make you hurt.'

The man called Anton held his hands up, an expression of apology on his face. 'Do you mind if I come in?'

'No, absolutely not. Come in and tell me what the hell is going on.' She fought to disguise the trepidation in her voice, finishing with a high note of false laughter.

He entered. The dog appeared and stood by his side.

'I am builder. I helped Tommy...' the large man scanned the room '...with all of this.' Shrug. 'Then we became friends. Spent a few evenings chewing fat, as you say. Having drinks.' He laughed. 'I couldn't persuade him on Polish Vodka, but I was happy to try whisky.'

So, while she thought Thomas was away on business, he was here getting pissed with a Polish builder? Was that who this man really was? Paula studied him, remembering the look he gave her on the ferry.

Anton reached into his inside pocket and pulled out a pair of black-rimmed spectacles. He put them on and then looked at her as if seeing her for the first time. 'There,' he beamed. 'Now I can see pretty lady.' And Paula struggled to see any trace of the man she'd noticed staring at her.

He was a large-framed man, with the beginnings of a belly. He wore a weathered face, topped with a head of hair that wouldn't look out of place on an industrial brush. And his eyes, now behind frames, appeared completely benign.

'Yes, I did much of work. He did much of talking. My wife and I...' his face grew sombre '...also lost a son. Gregor. He committed suicide three years ago. My first-born. I light candle for him still, every Sunday. Tommy and me, we had much in common with such tragedy. It is nice to finally meet you, Paula. I hear so much it feels like I know you.' He pointed to the sofa as if suggesting that they should sit. Feeling her neck stiff with tension Paula nodded her agreement, but stayed standing herself, her hand on the open door, ready to flee.

Was she being silly? Overcautious? She breathed, forced herself to relax a little, then examined him for a long moment and finally closed the door and took a seat. *Thomas, I'm trusting you here*, she thought. *If you get me killed...*

'I'm alone in a house I didn't know my husband had, with a friend I never knew he had,' she said, trying to hide the slight tremble in her voice. 'Perhaps you could tell me more?' She wanted to exude confidence but knew she was failing.

'Okay,' he said as he crossed his right leg over his left, suggesting he was completely at home. Just how much time had he spent here? 'You have a wedding anniversary in a few weeks. Thirty years, yes? This...' he held his arms out in an expansive gesture '...was your present.'

Paula's hand moved to hover over her heart. Thomas *was* giving her their dream cottage. She bit her lip.

Anton's face grew sombre. 'He said he had not been great husband recently and that making up meant ... would take something big. Grand.' As he said this, Anton made a gesture with his right hand the way a head waiter might indicate a dish of which he was particularly proud. 'He was going to retire early and make you happy lady.'

'Oh my God,' said Paula, thinking that she had been right after all. 'He was?' She closed her eyes tightly. Then a thought. 'How did you know I would be on that ferry?'

'That was luck. I have business in Glasgow and I was coming home.' He made a face as if to say there was nothing more to it than that. 'The plan, if it was ever necessary, was to find you in car park of tearoom. Tommy knew you would come over to throw ash in the bay. I walk dog there every day, so is easy. He knew you would use his car.' He formed an expression of appreciation. 'Everything he say come true. He was clever man, your Tommy.'

'Yes, but that only works if he knew he was going to die. He had a heart attack, Anton, how could he know he was going to have a heart attack?' Did Thomas have some sort of premonition of his own death? Why didn't he share his fears with her? She trembled at the thought and cursed herself for being so self-obsessed. What a terrible wife she had been. How could she not know any of this?

Anton scratched his cheek. 'Yes, that is strange. He say...' He looked away and to the right as if searching for the memory and the exact wording. 'He say he had bad feeling.' At that Anton rubbed at the centre of his chest. 'He had pain, yes?' he asked as if she was sure to know. 'His parent die of heart attack, but he wouldn't go to doctor. Said they were quackers.' He made a face of apology as if the word sounded very wrong to him, but it was the best he could do. 'And he say one day, wouldn't it be strange if he died and all this was left untouched. A present you never saw.' Anton laughed. 'He was man of dreams. He wanted bow. Big red bow around the cottage and he bring you over with blind...'

'Blindfold,' Paula added helpfully.

'Yes.' Anton closed his eyes and held a big hand over them.

That was so like Thomas, she thought: few words, big gestures.

'So, he tell me one night, this is plan. Just in case.' Once again Anton held a hand over his chest and made a rubbing motion. 'In case the pain mean something and he die, there was a way for you to have your present.'

Paula sat with that. Ran Anton's words through her mind. Judged them for weight and truth. She looked at him there on the seat, belonging, happy to help, bearer of Thomas's secret will, but she had a feeling he was holding something back.

A favourite phrase of Thomas's occurred to her. If something felt too good to be true, it usually was. There was something off about this whole thing. All of this *was* Thomas, there was no doubt about that, but what was she missing? And the thing about the chest pain? If he was suffering from chest pains, why wouldn't he tell her? But if it was true...? It felt like another betrayal.

'So, what do you think?' asked Anton. 'Tommy do good job?'

'He certainly did,' replied Paula. 'This is ... just ... amazing. But why didn't the crazy bastard let me know?'

'Have you had good look around? He was proud of bedroom. He said you would love. You love?'

'I love it very much,' answered Paula and felt a little squirm of discomfort that this man was asking about her bedroom.

'Find any nice little surprises?' asked Anton.

Something tightened in her stomach. There was an intent to that question. Not prurience: something else. What was he looking for? Did he know about the notebook?

'Surprises?' asked Paula, feigning confusion. Which wasn't difficult at this moment.

'Obsession. Perfume for Mr and Mrs.' Anton thumped down on his knee. 'Tommy have good smile about that.'

'Yeah. That was clever.' Relief made her shoulders drop.

'He said cottage was his obsession, like the perfume.' He softened his tone. 'Like you. He love very much.'

The sincerity in his voice caught Paula off guard and her throat tightened in response. 'Thank you,' she managed to say. 'Thank you. And thank you for all your hard work. The place is ... very special.'

'No need to thank. I get paid,' Anton said while he nodded his huge head. 'Is work for many weeks. Now I need to find more.' He laughed. 'But there is always work for good workers, no?'

'No,' answered Paula. 'I mean yes. Good workers are always in demand.' She looked at her watch. Got to her feet. 'Listen...' she made a face of apology, '...I need to be getting back to Glasgow. If I don't go soon I'll miss the last ferry.'

'Of course.' Anton stood up, but kept his head bowed so he wouldn't hit it on the ceiling. At his movement, the dog trotted over to the front door. Paula paused to allow Anton to get their first.

He pulled open the door and stepped outside.

'Is real pleasure to meet lady who inspire all this,' Anton said.

'Thank you,' said Paula. Then a thought. 'You've been here before with the dog? On your own?' She paused wondering how to ask him. Decided just to go for it. This was her house after all. 'May I have your key, please?'

Now that they were standing in close proximity she was fully aware of his size and physicality. A light shone in Anton's eyes at her question. As if he'd just realised there was more to her than a pretty face and a dead husband's obsession. He rifled in his trouser pocket, pulled something out and handed it to her.

'Spare key.' He smiled. 'And now...' He looked down at the dog, who looked up at him and wagged. 'I must take Bob for rest of his walk.' He gave her a small bow, bending from the waist. 'One day soon we meet again. Talk old memories of Tommy.' There was an invitation in his voice, and something else. A promise? Was he flirting with her?

He held a hand out.

She accepted it and as they shook she had the thought that he could crush the bones of her hand as easily as he might snap a twig.

But then it occurred to her: for a builder the skin on his hand was very soft and smooth.

17

Cara Connelly was at the Sufferin' – the Southern General, a new super-hospital in the south of the city. Given that the locals knew their way around a nickname, it was also called the Death Star, on account of its shape. The authorities preferred that people gave it its proper name: Queen Elizabeth University Hospital. Whatever you called it, the place was huge.

She was fifteen minutes late for a hospital discharge meeting with Mr and Mrs Skelton, as was usual for any hospital visit in this city. It didn't matter how much time you allocated to get there and find a parking spot, there was some immutable law of the universe that meant you'd only find a space once you'd searched beyond the time set for your appointment.

And then you'd arrive all flustered, knowing the 'professionals' would be looking down at you – social workers, consultants and medical staff – all of whom worked on site and couldn't understand how 'you people' were always late.

Mr Skelton had suffered a massive stroke. His mind was intact, mostly, but the sideways sag of his mouth and constant dribble was the first sign that he needed ongoing care. It was Cara's job to ensure that he and his wife understood the process and to ask questions of the authorities that they didn't know they needed to ask, or were too afraid to.

When Cara first met Mr Skelton, despite having come across plenty of people in this situation, she could barely look at him, such was the devastation caused by the illness. But now, seeing him in his hospital bedroom, sat upright in the high-backed chair, clutching his bag of toiletries, and wearing his grey jogging trouser and a pair of blue slippers, her heart went out to him and his wife. She sat to the side, holding his hand, eyes full of love and fear. Could she cope with what was about to happen? Medical opinion was that he needed twenty-four-hour care. Mrs Skelton, although a few years younger than her husband, looked like a stiff breeze could blow her over. Her fine-boned face was pinched with worry. How on earth would she deal on her own with this lump of a man who couldn't feed or clean himself?

♦

After the meeting, feeling drained, but hopeful, Cara had a quick look at the diary on her phone. This was a reflex action – she knew where she was going next – but it was her way of mentally setting one file in her head to the side, and dealing with the next issue in her case load. Next up was an evening of prep work for a visit to the Welfare Court: a reformed addict, Annmarie Pitt, wanted access to her infant son now that she was clean. Cara had spent hours on the phone yesterday to Annmarie, who was really only a child herself, reminding her over and over again not to talk about what *she* wanted. The system was a child-centred one. Foremost in the minds of those present would be what was best for the child. If her client talked *me, me, me*, as she had a tendency to, the authorities would be less inclined to hear her.

So lost was she in thought that she made it back to her car completely on automatic and it was only when she sat down inside that she came back to herself. She felt an itch in the back of her mind. Had an image of throwing someone over her shoulder onto an exercise mat. That's what was required. A satisfying training session down at the dojo. Get rid of some of her work frustrations by pounding someone into the ground.

Pulling her phone from her jacket pocket, she thumbed out a text to her training partner, Dave Roberts. She judged how much work she needed to do on Annmarie's case and worked out what time she'd be free:

Up for it?

In the time it took to fire up the engine and put on her seatbelt a reply came through:

Sure. Toni has the girls tonight. Sounds like someone needs to vent?

She laughed. He knew her too well.

Cara smiled as she considered the man. A part-time single father to two preteen girls, he often came to Cara for advice, convinced these little creatures were another species.

Last Christmas she almost got a t-shirt made for him that said 'Confounds Expectations'. At first glance he was an intimidating individual. Approaching six feet tall, shaved head, a beard visible from space and a frame that warned of efficient muscle – you held your handbag tight to your body as he walked past. But the minute he spoke – and you heard his soft Highland accent – noticed the intelligent spark to his eyes, you realised there was more to this guy.

Having spent a lot of time with families who punched the dysonto functional, she considered Dave and his ex-wife, Toni, to be the poster parents for divorce. Theirs clearly was a child-centred approach and it made her warm to Dave even more.

There was no chance of romance there, even if she was tempted; it was clear that Dave was still in love with Toni and that one day he hoped for a re-match with her. Cara didn't have the heart to tell him that ship had not only sailed, it was so far over the horizon it was in a different time zone.

None of that was why she chose him for a training partner. It was his skills on that mat and the challenge he presented that attracted her. If she could learn to handle Dave, she was confident that most of the idiots she came into contact with on the city streets would be relatively easy.

She sent him a time. He confirmed, and with a satisfied feeling she slid her phone back into her pocket.

Right. She had two hours before she met Dave. What could she do in the meantime?

Perhaps she could go over to Paula Gadd's house. See what she was up to? That woman knew more than she was letting on. She mentally recounted the journey it would take to get there from here, and realised it meant going past the offices of Gadd Enterprises. Two birds with one stone? She could drive by and see what Kevin Farrell was up to. The death of his long-time business colleague was undoubtedly going to cause him problems. Maybe in his moment of stress she could face up to him and prompt him to divulge more information.

◆

Twenty minutes later she was parked outside the white three-storey building that housed the business of Thomas Gadd (deceased), burgher of this proud city. She'd sat here a number of times over the last couple of years, staring up at what she judged would be Gadd's window, wishing looks could indeed kill.

At that moment a man walked past her car. Something about him caught her attention. The way he was cradling his arm. It was in plaster. His female companion was walking ahead as if she was trying to keep upwind of him. Cara looked back to the man and realised it was Kevin Farrell himself. She noticed his grey pallor and wondered what the hell had happened to him.

Cara turned her focus back onto the woman as she watched them both approach the office door. She was wearing a black trouser suit, with a white blouse. Her dark hair was cut in a short, manageable style. Her movement, her demeanour – everything about her screamed 'competent'. She held the door open for him and stepped aside to let him in first. There was nothing in her face or body language to suggest what their relationship might be. Neither of them appeared to speak. Secretary?

Kevin mouthed something. The woman nodded. The door closed and Cara was left wondering what she should do. Stay or go?

18

When Paula drove into Port Bannatyne, instead of taking the right turn that would lead to the ferry at Rothesay, she took the left and drove down the stretch of road that would bring her to what the locals called the 'wee ferry' at Rhubodach.

The ferry was indeed 'wee' and the journey across to Colintraive was very short, little more than a stone's throw. Thomas, in a short-lived attempt to learn the Gaelic told her that *Caol an t-Snaim* – meant 'swimming narrows'. A name, Thomas told her, that came from a time when cattle were swum over from the Isle of Bute to Colintraive on their way to the cattle markets of lowland Scotland.

She heard his voice in her ear, repeating this history. He loved all that kind of thing and would tell her every time they took this route home. Depending on her mood Paula would listen, pat the back of his hand and say, 'Sure, babe.' Or if she was cold, tired and desperate to get home, she'd groan, say, 'Heard it already,' and turn up the car radio.

What she would give to say 'Heard it already' one more time.

The rest of the trip to Glasgow took on the aura of a pilgrimage. As she drove off the ferry and out of the village of Colintraive, she looked to her left, across the water and up towards the hillside road that led down into the village of Tighnabruaich. She remembered standing up there, looking down over the Kyles of Bute and hearing Thomas's laugh as he recalled reading about Magnus Barelegs, a Viking king who was given the nickname after adopting the short kilt of the Celts. Apparently Magnus bargained with the Scottish King Malcolm that he could have rule over the islands around which he could sail.

Paula could almost feel Thomas's arm over her shoulder as he pulled her close. She recalled the smile in his voice as he had told her that

Magnus had a hankering for the land of the Cowal peninsula, so he duly had his crew carry his boat overland across the isthmus at Tarbert, with him sitting at the helm as if he was still a-sail.

'That's the ingenuity you need to get on in business, sweetheart,' he said.

His voice was still thrumming in her ear when an hour later she noticed the turn-off to Lochgoilhead. It was near here that Thomas proposed all those years ago, standing over The Tinker's Heart. That was the first time she'd ever heard of the place. It was a sacred site to travellers – where the old Strachar road met the road to Hell's Glen. For centuries, as far back as the 1700s, they'd come for miles and miles, Thomas told her, to get married, christen their children or bless their dead.

X didn't mark the spot. Instead it was a heart shape formed by ancient, white quartz crystals embedded in the old track. That part of the route containing the heart was now in the middle of a field.

Thomas had parked the car, drawn her out and ignored her protests as he climbed across a fence, cajoled her over it with and into the field where that part of the old road now lay.

'See,' he said and pointed down. She was too busy worrying about the large Highland cow and its calf to be caught up in the romance of it all. Until Thomas got down on one knee.

What happened to that young man? Where did he go? His eyes were bright, his face eager, his hair flattened by the constant drizzle. At least she'd had the good sense to wear a jacket with a hood.

'Get up off your knee, you daftie,' she remembered saying, thinking his jeans would be muddy. But he refused to move until she gave him an answer. How could it be anything but a yes? She'd known they were going to be together from the moment he approached her the night they first met.

At her answer, he'd whooped, pulled her off her feet and covered her face in kisses. They'd gone from that, over the years, to a state of indifference. They said the opposite of love was hate, thought Paula. It wasn't. It was irrelevance. Feeling that the person you love actually didn't care much whether or not you were there. At least that was how it had often felt over their last few years together.

But then, the cottage ... A physical demonstration that he wasn't indifferent to her. More that they were lost in a maze of miscommunication and had forgotten their way back to each other and to their love.

Paula spotted a sign that warned of a layby. She drove there and parked with that long-ago moment filling her mind. She sagged under the thought that the two most important people ever to feature in her life were now fragments of bone and memory.

And in Thomas's case, lies.

Thomas had the cottage renovated while they were barely talking to one another. Did he really think they could rebuild their relationship like that?

She looked out of the window into the distance. The light was failing and the far-off hills were a dark smudge against a weak sky. The light from a vehicle approaching from behind lit up the interior of her car. She slumped down in her seat as if hiding. It rushed past. And Paula was alone again.

She told herself to get a grip and sat upright in her seat. People have worse, a lot worse to deal with.

The cottage.

The notebook.

She pulled it out of her bag, turned on the interior light and had another read.

Did that symbol at the end of each chain of numbers and letters really mean a million? Pounds, dollars, euros? Her head spun with possibilities and explanations.

She opened it at the one page that had been written on. Studied each line. Again she saw that the first six numbers on each were clumped together. Then eight numbers, starting with a double zero each time. Then it became random, with letters and numbers and then it ended with the 1M.

Her chequebook was at home in the study. Fewer people accepted cheques these days, so they rarely used it. An image came to her – from the last time she'd opened it. The pattern of numbers along the bottom of each cheque were similar to a section of the numbers on each line on the page of the notebook. Could these numbers be bank accounts?

Thomas, what on earth were you up to?

Bill at the funeral asking about the will.

Kevin Farrell searching through her office.

One was afraid, the other fairly confident, but they both wore an expression where hope and expectation sat.

Bill, Kevin and Thomas were an unlikely grouping. She couldn't see that working. But she couldn't un-see the faces on each of those men since the funeral. Thomas always told her she should trust her gut. Perhaps on this occasion she really should listen.

Why the secrecy?

Would she still be blithely unaware if Thomas were still alive? If this was about money, what the hell was he doing with it? All ten lines of it. That was a crazy amount of cash. If it was secret, did that mean it was illegal?

She thought of the two sides of Anton. The death stare she'd first thought he had given her on the ferry, and the familiar and affectionate tone he'd used in the cottage. Was he involved? Should she be worried about him?

Another car passed in a blur of light and sound. Instinctively she ducked down in her seat.

And sat back up again once it passed.

What was she doing? She was acting like a crazy person.

But still. This whole situation was strange. With all of the bizarre things that were happening to her recently it was no surprise she was being just that little bit more careful.

She looked at the numbers once more. Read them again. And again. It was time she put her memory – famous among those her knew her – to the test. She sat there for the next half an hour until she could recite each line correctly and completely.

Then she tested it ten times for each line. If this *was* cash she couldn't get it wrong. Equally if it was cash she couldn't go around with a notebook on her person that held this much of a secret. Then, when she was at last satisfied, she tore out the page, being careful to leave a jagged edge, making it obvious that a page was missing.

She tore the numbered page into as small pieces as she could manage, opened the window and released them into the breeze, like a brief display of confetti. Then swallowed down her concerns as she put the notebook back in her handbag.

If somebody demanded to know what she found, she had something to show them. An empty notebook with a torn-out page. In the meantime she would resist making for the first computer she could find and keying one of the lines in. If someone was watching her movements, that would be a dead giveaway.

She had a flash of self-awareness and cringed at her behaviour. She was continuing to behave and think in a very strange manner.

But if she was right, there was a huge amount of money involved.

An amount of money that people might kill for.

19

Back in the environs of Glasgow, off the Erskine Bridge and coasting along the M8, wanting nothing but the oblivion of sleep, Paula spotted a road sign for the business campus where Gadd Enterprises was based.

She looked at the clock on her dashboard. There was a chance Kevin would still be at work, and he might have some answers for her. She was tired of feeling like she was the little woman being kept in the dark. It was time she got in front of this and found out what exactly was going on.

Minutes later, she had parked, and, feeling certain in her need for answers, she walked up to the office, pulled open the door and stepped inside. She ran up the stairs, but on the second floor she paused for a moment – it wouldn't do her any favours if she confronted the man while out of breath.

She reached the door, turned the handle and opened it.

Elaine Teenan was in her usual place behind the desk at reception.

'Hello, Mrs Gadd.' She looked up from her computer terminal with some surprise. 'What can we do for you?'

Paula gazed past her. A plain, light-brown door led to Thomas's office. She remembered the wide desk, the photos of Christopher on the corner beside his phone, and sagged at the thought that he wouldn't be in there. At some point she'd have to go in and sort out his personal effects.

'Hi Elaine. Nice to see you.'

As if suddenly remembering that she hadn't seen Paula since the funeral, Elaine pinked slightly and asked her, 'How have you…?' Then, as if that was a stupid question, she stopped. 'I haven't had a chance to look through Mr Gadd's personal things,' she said as if she had just read

Paula's thoughts. 'Will I box everything up and have them couriered over to the house?'

Paula closed her eyes against the emotion that the woman's kindness aroused in her, and feeling sorry to have caused her any awkwardness, Paula gave her a little smile. 'Thank you, Elaine. That would be very kind of you ... Just whenever you have the time. I'm eh ... looking for...'

At the sound of her voice, Kevin appeared at his office door. 'Paula? Thank Christ.'

First, she noted that, if anything, he was even more harassed than when she'd seen him the other day, his tie askew, his eyes just as wild. Then she noticed that his left arm was in plaster.

She decided to set aside his rudeness for the moment. 'What on earth happened to you?' Without waiting for his answer, she walked into his office and stood by his desk.

'Great,' Kevin said as he brushed past her to close the door with his good hand. 'You've come to tell me where it is.' Not an assumption. A demand. His face sharp with the need to know, he stepped back as if aware that he was standing too close.

'Tell you where what is? I've nothing to tell you, Kevin. I'm here for answers,' she said. 'What were you and Thomas up to before he died?'

'What?' Kevin asked, his face a stew of confusion.

'You and my husband. What was going on? I need to know, Kevin.'

'Oh, shut up, you silly cow.' Kevin spat, turned and ran his good hand through his hair.

'What on earth has got into you, Kevin Farrell?' He would never have dreamed of talking to her like that if Thomas had been alive.

He moved back into her space.

She held her ground, but felt a stir of fear as she noted the cold light in his eyes.

'Thomas had something a lot of people are looking for. Don't try to tell me you know nothing. I'm not falling for that shite.' He moved closer, his eyes wild, face red, specks of saliva firing from his mouth as he spoke.

'Kevin, I have no idea...'

Before she could finish, he had her pressed against the wall, using his elbow and plastered forearm.

'Kevin, get off me.' Her fright spiked now – she couldn't move.

'Where is it?' he shouted.

Looking into his eyes, Paula could see that he had lost all reason. She was no longer Thomas Gadd's wife; she was in his way and he would do whatever it took to get what he needed.

'Kevin...' she managed to gasp out, '...you're choking me.' She didn't know what to do. Finding some strength she tried to squirm, but he held her with terrifying firmness.

'Where is it?' he repeated. His breath smelt stale. Paula turned her face away from his. But he gripped her chin with his good hand, forcing her face round.

'I will fucking kill you if I have to, you bitch.'

'Kevin ... please. You're hurting me,' she whispered, her air cut off now, her panic escalating.

'That's just for starters.' His breath was hot on her face, and the smell was so foul she fought to turn from it, but he held her too close. 'I will mess you up if you don't tell me where it is.'

She fought down the feeling of revulsion that this man was all but molesting her. She always thought he was a bit of a fool, but a harmless one. Now she was seeing a whole other, frightening, side of him.

Trying to dampen down her fear, she ignored the arm at her throat and went for the one now aimed at her breast, aiming to grab a finger and twist it, hopefully break it. He was quick to read her attempts though and shaped his hand into a fist. He pressed it under her breast into her ribs.

Her heart was fluttering in her throat. He could hurt her. Really hurt her, and she could do nothing to stop him. He was too close, his body pressing against hers. She needed to get away.

'Kevin, please,' she cried, hearing the fear in her voice. 'Stop it.'

A movement to her right. There was someone else in the office.

She tried to turn to see who it was and saw a dark flash. There was a grunt from Kevin and next thing she knew, there was cool relief at her throat and Kevin was on the floor.

He tried to get back on to his feet and was pushed back down again. 'Cara...?'

'You're welcome,' Cara replied with a tight smile, shooting Paula a look while keeping her focus on Farrell.

Once more he tried to get to his feet, placing his good hand on the floor and heaving upwards. But Cara was there, kicking his hand away, and down he fell again with a pained cry – by instinct he had used his broken limb to support himself.

'Cara,' croaked Paula, 'what are you doing here?' She turned back to her, pushing her hair from her face with a shaking hand and feeling a tremble in her thighs.

'I saw you coming in...' Cara began, but seeing that Farrell was trying to get up again she pushed him back down, having none of it. He scrabbled with his legs until his back was against the opposite wall, and looked up at Cara as if worried about what she was going to do to him next. 'As I was saying,' said Cara, 'I don't know why, but I followed you.' She reached out to Paula's face. 'That's going to be a nasty bruise in the morning. You should get some ice on it.'

Paula shrank away. She didn't want anyone touching her.

Farrell was sat on the floor now, staring at Cara, clearly daunted for the moment by this confidently aggressive woman and how easily she had forced him onto the floor.

'What was that?' Paula asked quietly, as if she didn't quite want Farrell to hear. 'Kung Fu?'

Cara groaned, looking as if she was going to give a stupid answer. 'Something like that.'

There was more movement at the door. A voice. Paula and Cara turned as one to see Elaine Teenan. She challenged Cara with a glare.

'Mr Farrell, Mrs Gadd, what on earth is going on? Should I call the police?'

'Nothing you need to concern yourself with, Elaine, thanks,' Paula answered, trying to sound calm. 'Why don't you get yourself off home? Have an early night.'

'Sorry, Mrs Gadd,' she replied, standing just beyond the doorway, 'but Mr Farrell came back from an appointment in a lot of pain and wearing a plaster cast.' She pointed. 'He needs me to drive him home.' She looked down at him. 'What are you doing on the floor, Mr Farrell?'

'He's just leaving, aren't you, Kevin?' said Paula trying to inject confidence into her tone, but still feeling shaken.

As the man got to his feet, Elaine stayed by the door, unsure about her place.

'I'm prepared to ... to put this down to whatever accident you've had,' said Paula, keen now to get him out of her sight.

'But, Paula,' he said, taking a step towards her.

'But, Paula, nothing,' said Cara stepping in between them.

'That's enough. Both of you. Please,' Paula tried to raise her voice, but her throat felt bruised. She was still trembling.

'He's harmless now,' Paula said, giving Kevin a measured look. 'Aren't you, Kevin?'

'Paula,' he said, 'there are some very—'

'Cara. Elaine,' Paula interrupted. She could see he wasn't going to leave without speaking to her. 'Would you two give us a second, please?' Feeling certain that they were on secure ground now, she pulled at Kevin's good arm and drew him further into his office, ignoring Elaine's increasingly puzzled expression and Cara's loud protests. 'And close the door, please.' She said to Elaine.

Once the door was shut, Paula led Farrell to a two-seater sofa under the window and without speaking pointed at it. He sat down. She stood over him, aware that he was cowed for now and hoping that her stance signalled she wouldn't accept any more violence from him. She hoped Cara was still just outside.

'Suppose you tell me what it is you think I have? Why you're so afraid and who you are afraid of?'

'You really don't know?' His panicked eyes searched hers.

'No, Kevin, I really don't.'

'In that case' – he rubbed at the top of his head – 'I'm fucked. We're...' He looked at Paula. 'We both are.'

'What the hell did *I* do?'

'Not you. Tommy. They're not going to believe he didn't tell you anything. And I'm not sure he didn't tell you anything either.' He studied her as if looking for a sign of duplicity.

Paula changed tack; pulled herself in and made herself small. She sat on the chair opposite him. 'So who are these people who're going to come after me?'

'It's really best you don't know,' he said and got to his feet.

Paula had a thought. 'Kevin, do you know Anton Rusnak?'

'Who?' The tone of the question was a denial. He cocked his head to the side, but there was a flicker there. He was lying, Paula was sure of it.

'Tall guy. Red hair. Goes by the name of Rusnak. Polish, I think.'

Kevin coughed, got to his feet and moved towards the door. 'I have to go.' He patted the side of his right leg as if reassuring himself his car keys were still in his trouser pocket.

At the sound of movement, a voice sounded from the other side of the door. 'You okay in there, Paula?' asked Cara.

'Yes, thanks,' Paula answered. Then she looked at Kevin's arm. 'Are you going to tell me how you broke that?'

'I fell,' he replied, with the look of someone terrified to inform on his bully.

'Is it connected with whatever you think Thomas told me about?'

Kevin took a few laboured steps closer to her. Paula shrank back automatically – was he going to try to hurt her again? But she relaxed when she read that the fight had truly left him.

'If you really don't know...' he studied her for confirmation.

'I really don't know, Kevin.'

'Then for your own protection it's best that we leave it that way.'

20

Cara followed Kevin and Elaine out of the office and down the stairs. She tossed back a 'whatever' when Paula thanked her again for helping her. Thanks that felt grudged to Cara. What the hell was wrong with that woman?

'Mr Farrell. Mr Farrell,' Cara shouted after him as he exited the main door. It was dark now, and he hurried with Elaine across the road to the car park, his body language suggesting he was almost frightened of Cara. Or was there something else he was frightened of?

'Can't you leave him alone?' Elaine asked, as she tried to support him as he walked. 'The man's in a lot of pain.'

He's not a bloody cripple, Cara wanted to say. Instead, she hopped in front of them and stood in their path.

'Leave me be, Miss Connolly,' Farrell said, and moved to get past her.

Cara stepped to the side, cutting off his progress.

'How do you know my name? Do you remember me from somewhere?' she asked.

He grimaced, holding his bad arm closer to his body with his good arm. 'You came round here spouting all kinds of shite about Tommy.'

'I was there, too,' Elaine said, and took a step closer to Cara, her eyes narrowing. 'You were very rude.'

Cara dismissed her with a glance. 'I was here, but I didn't leave my name...'

'Tommy looked into you.'

'He did? Why?'

'I said he was wasting his time. He thought you looked the type to go to the press, so he wanted to make sure he had something on you, just in case.'

'Just how close were you as business partners?' Cara asked.

'None of your business, doll,' Farrell huffed. 'Now get out of my way or I'll have you down at the local nick on assault charges.'

'Assault?' Cara asked.

Farrell held up his plastered arm. 'I'll say this was you.'

'Might as well break your other one then.' Cara moved closer, but Elaine stepped in between them.

She was a few inches shorter than Cara, but she held herself straight, ready for confrontation. 'Calm down, sweetheart. The man may be difficult, but I'm not going to let you hurt him. Now why don't you just leave us alone, eh?'

Cara studied Elaine's expression. She read the certainty there, and knew she could get her out of the way without any problem, but admired the fight in her.

'Mr Farrell, your business partner tortured and killed my brother. I got this from a good source.'

'Did ye, aye?' said Farrell, his face telling Cara he thought she was talking shite.

'And I can't believe you – his business partner – had no knowledge of the fact that Mr Gadd was one of the city's worst gangsters.'

Elaine Teenan's laugh was a mix of exasperation and disbelief. 'Listen, Miss whatever your name is, you need to leave,' she said. 'I need to get this man home to his bed. Can you not see he's in a lot of pain?'

'I'm gathering evidence. And once I do, I'm coming for you,' Cara said.

'Sure ye are, doll. Now run along and play detectives in your own time,' Farrell said, dismissing her by turning and walking away.

Cara let them go but only because she had nothing left to say. She hoped she'd rattled him, but his lack of response had her worried. Was she wrong to focus her energy on him? Paula Gadd was even less likely as a source. From the little time she had spent in her company it was quite clear the woman knew nothing about what her husband had been up to.

She turned and walked back to her car. Once inside she angled her wing mirror, watching Elaine and Kevin Farrell settle themselves in his car. She was tempted to open her window, stick out a hand and give them a finger as they passed.

Decided that was beneath her.

Instead, she buttoned into her own frustration, wondering how on earth she was going to find out the truth about what happened to her brother.

She glanced back at the office just in time to see that Paula had left the building and was making her way across the car park. Her movement was slow and purposeful – almost as if she was drunk. This confused Cara for a moment, until she realised the woman was weak with fatigue.

She suddenly felt guilty. Paula looked utterly worn down by grief, and the attack from Farrell wouldn't have helped. She recognised the line of her body and the gait – it was the same as she'd seen in her mother after Sean had died. Her mum had walked as if every step was an effort, as if the ability to plant the next foot on the ground was based on hope rather than expectation, her head bowed, back stiff from trying to hold everything together.

Feeling a sudden need to apologise, Cara thought that perhaps she should go over and offer the woman some help, but then her view was obscured when Farrell's BMW slid past. Kevin was in the passenger seat, staring straight ahead. Elaine was driving and entirely focussed on where she was going. It was only a second as they passed her, but to Cara it seemed like they were both preternaturally still. Even that brief moment was enough to see that they were both frozen in position. As if they were afraid to move.

Then, as if in slow motion – perhaps Elaine was driving deliberately slowly – the rear of the car drew level and Cara saw that there was a third person in the car. A man in the back seat. A large man.

The car sped up and they disappeared over the brow of the hill.

21

Paula barely made it back into the house before her strength gave out.

Going up to the bedroom was beyond her so she aimed for the sofa in the living room and curled up there. She had a stray thought that she should eat. This tiredness surely indicated her body needed fuel, didn't it? But that would mean having to go through to the kitchen, raking through the freezer and making a decision about what she should prepare. Such effort was beyond her. As was raising the energy to chew, to swallow.

Then she recalled she had episodes just like this after Christopher died; of feeling that she was walking on the bare bones of her heels, that her knees weren't solid enough to hold her, her mind struggling to compute everything around her.

So Cara's brother was responsible for Christopher's death? But did she really believe her? Why would the woman make something like that up? She must be aware how earth-shattering it would be for a mother. No, she clearly had an agenda against Thomas. Paula returned to her original theory that they had had an affair and this was Cara's twisted way of getting back at him. So outlandish were Cara's claims, an affair seemed preferable.

Or was the woman telling the truth?

It was too much. Too much to process. Too much to believe. She was just a middle-aged, middle-class housewife from the suburbs. Things like this didn't happen to people like her. They happened to people in movies and books.

Everywhere ached. *Everywhere.*

Maybe she had the flu.

How long she lay there she had no idea. Daylight weakened, the streetlights on the pavement outside lit her room in amber hues. It made the room around her look cold. She shivered and wrapped her arms around herself in a vain attempt to generate some heat. So cold. And somewhere ... she lost track of her thought and closed her eyes because the illumination was making her head ache. But still the light made it through the paper of her eyelids, prodding hard fingers of muted colour into her brain.

Curtains. She should close them. She should pull them shut, but that required actually moving. And finding the energy to do that from somewhere was...

Thomas. She imagined him lying on the floor just below where she lay on the sofa. His shirt pulled open to show skin shining from the electric light. A shirt that had been opened to allow the medics to work on him.

She opened her mouth, fighting to breathe. Her need for oxygen was such that she was forced to sit up. A painful sob escaped, scouring her lungs and the soft tissue of her throat as it passed. Then she was taken over by grief so hard, so solid, she was surprised it didn't sound like a siren as it forced her head backwards. She heaved air in and out of her lungs, filling her ears with the sounds of her own panic and loss. And guilt.

She should have been there with him. At the restaurant when he keeled over. In the ambulance when they tried to resuscitate him. At his side when they pronounced him dead.

'Call yourself a wife,' she sobbed, and wiped the saliva and mucus from her face with the back of her hand.

Aware of a pressure at her back, she reached round and felt the soft give of a fake fur blanket. She got a hold of it, lay back down and pulled it over her head to shut out the light.

Maybe someone would find her there in six months or a year, and they'd have another funeral. Poor Paula, they'd say, she just wasted to nothing. Because what was the point of anything now? No Christopher. No Thomas.

She slid over to the edge of the sofa and allowed herself to slip off, to fall onto the spot where she had just imagined Thomas had laid while waiting for a paramedic to save his life. She stroked the rug, trying to imagine that the fibres were the hairs on his chest. This action became a frantic tug.

Why aren't you here, Thomas? Why did you go first? It should have been me.

It should have been me.

♦

She woke to the sound of the bin men in the lane behind her garden. To her sleep-drunk mind it sounded like their footsteps were coming from inside the house. She sat up in a panic and realised she was in bed. How did she get there? Hadn't she been on the sofa downstairs?

The noise continued and she thought: Kevin again. How had he got in? It was only when her brain registered the rumble of the plastic wheels that she realised what she was hearing.

She slumped back onto her pillows and forced open her eyes. They felt so heavy it was an effort to hold them open for more than a couple of seconds. Turning on her side, she brought her knees up to her chest. There. There was nothing more to do than to just lie here and pray for the annihilation of sleep.

But sleep resisted her this time.

She sat up. Rubbed at her forehead and slipped her legs over the side of the bed. Best get up, she thought, and then fell back from her sitting position to lie across her bed.

Get up for what? The day yawned ahead of her. Nothing in her diary. No purpose. And the constant ache of missing Thomas. The lovely, beautiful, big bastard.

Purpose. That's what she needed. Something to occupy her mind.

And her thoughts turned to the matter of the string of bank accounts with, quite possibly, a huge amount of money in each of them.

Coffee. Perhaps that would help her focus on this new mystery Thomas had left behind him.

His dressing gown was hanging from a hook on the back of the bedroom door. She put it on, enjoying the warmth of it, the plush pile of it against her neck. She sniffed at the collar and found a faint note of his aftershave. She fastened the belt around her waist. There was enough fabric to go around her twice.

Down in the kitchen she made straight for the coffee machine and turned it on. Normally, she liked silence when she was in the kitchen, but today she turned on the small TV in the corner. Perhaps a voice from outside her bubble would help. The machine was a little indulgence for Thomas. When he was cooking – which was a once-a-month event – he liked to chop his vegetables with the sound of the TV for company. Thinking that perhaps watching the news would be a good idea, Paula clicked onto the news channel.

There was a serious-faced woman on screen, and a scrolling headline underneath her. Something about a murder in Glasgow. Paula cringed. That was not what she wanted to hear about. Then someone was talking about a money-laundering scheme involving shell companies that officials from a foreign country had used to steal money from their own government. There was something she couldn't quite follow about the Scottish financial system making this possible. Just another excuse for the London media to have a go at the Scottish Government, thought Paula. Then they moved on to a bombing in the Middle East, showing a grief-stricken mother holding a dead little girl, her limp body covered in grit and dust.

With a shudder she turned it off. She was barely holding it together. Why compound her troubles by watching endless misery from another part of the world?

As she waited for her drink to brew she located her mobile phone and looked to see if she had any messages.

There was an email from one of the charities she worked with, reminding her about an imminent AGM, a whole bunch of spam emails, and one from a travel company suggesting that she and her husband would enjoy a trip to Venice or Rome or Paris.

She lingered over that one for more than was healthy, before deleting it. They'd never do that again. Go on holiday. And Venice was one of those places they'd never got round to. And now...

She put the phone down as if it was hot.

She needed something to keep her busy, she told herself. Distractions would help and it came to her that there was a mountain of paperwork she had to complete. The business of grief was a paperchain, or so it seemed. Bank accounts, the deeds on the house, companies who billed them to be informed to remove Thomas from the account. And so much other stuff. The death certificate. She quailed at the thought. She leaned forwards on the blue-marble work surface, rested her forehead on a cradle she formed with the palms of both hands. Tired. She was once again so tired.

Thankfully, their finances weren't too complicated. She and Thomas had a joint will. The survivor was to get everything, and if they both died at the same time Father Joe was to put everything into a charitable foundation. As far as she knew the house was worth about half a million. And there was at least the same again in bank accounts and then whatever the business was worth.

Although now Paula wasn't sure she wanted anything to do with the business. Judging by the state of Kevin, there was something horribly wrong there.

A text pinged through. It was from Joe:

Have you seen the news?

'The news?' she asked out loud. Why was he asking about the news? And, anyway, shouldn't Joe be apologising for leaving her on her own? Then it came to her that he already had. And that was enough.

She sighed at last and pressed reply, considering what response she should send, when there was a knock at the door.

She should move to the cottage in Bute, she thought, then everyone would leave her alone. But then a series of images presented in her mind: the man on the ferry, standing in the doorway, sitting in the living room. Was he really who he said he was? Would she feel safe if she was in his company there? Alone. The cottage was fairly remote on that corner of the beach. Few people ventured that far round the bay.

The knock at the door came again. A solid rap, like a pronouncement.

With a sigh, she located the pocket of the dressing gown, dropped the phone inside and walked down the hall to the front door.

She opened it to see two people: a woman and a man, both wearing dark suits and looking incredibly official.

'Mrs Paula Gadd?' The woman said. She was pretty in a kind of stern way.

'Yes,' Paula said, automatically crossing her arms in front of herself.

'My name is DS Alessandra Rossi. This is DC Daryl Drain.' She held a card up, just long enough for Paula to see that it had a police logo on it.

Paula was instantly taken back to that moment when the police came to her door to tell her about Christopher. Then the day they came to tell her about Thomas.

Her eyes refocussed on the two people in front of her. It couldn't be Joe who was dead – because it had to be about a death, hadn't it? That was the only reason the police ever came to her door.

She felt her legs weaken and held onto the frame of the door.

'May we come in, Mrs Gadd?' asked the woman. Rossi? Was that what she said her name was?

'Sure. Sure…' Paula stood where she was as her mind continued to try to work out why they were here. Who else was there in her life that could be dead? Bill?

'Mrs Gadd?' The woman stepped forwards.

'Aye, sorry, yes,' said Paula. 'Please, come in…' She stepped to the side and let them both enter. 'The coffee is on. Would you like one…' she gave them a practised smile, aware as she did so that her cheeks ached.

'Are you OK, Mrs Gadd?' asked the man – DC Drain.

'Sorry.' Paula held a hand to her heart. 'I don't think I can take any more bad news. It's bad news, isn't it?'

'Is there somewhere we can sit?' asked Rossi.

'Yes, sorry to keep you out…' Paula rallied a little. 'The kitchen.' She turned and walked back down the corridor.

She took a seat on the stool at her kitchen island, placed her hands round her mug to stop them shaking and faced the police officers. Waited.

'You know Kevin Farrell and Elaine Teenan?'

'Yes, of course. Kevin is my husband's business partner and Elaine is their secretary. Why do you ask?' Paula found herself blinking.

There was a long pause. Then Rossi spoke: 'They were found in the early hours of this morning – in his car. I'm afraid to say both of them are dead.'

'Oh, dear God,' said Paula. For a second she thought she might slip off the stool.

Then she became aware that her mouth was hanging open. She closed it. 'Poor Elaine,' she murmured, holding a hand to her mouth. 'Oh my God.'

She looked down at the countertop for a moment and then raised her head, blushing, aware of the scrutiny of both the officers.

'And Kevin...' And then it hit her: he was terrified the previous night. An image of him popped into her mind; he was running his fingers through his hair. The skin tight on his face. Veins bulging. He had looked desperate. And what was it he had said – something about *them* – about she and him being 'fucked'.

What the hell had he and Thomas been up to?

'How...' Her throat was dry. 'How did they die?' asked Paula.

'We can't say at this point in the investigation,' said Rossi.

'My ... my husband only recently died,' she said. And then stopped herself. But why – why shouldn't she just tell them everything? What did she have to hide? Within her though, there was some kind of deep reluctance. And she thought of the codes in the notebook.

'Yes, we know about your husband,' said Drain.

'Bit of a coincidence,' said Rossi.

Paula was pulled out of her thoughts. There was an accusation in that comment.

'If you knew my husband had died, you also knew he died of a heart attack,' she said. 'So I don't see what the coincidence is.'

'Just ... two prominent businessmen – business *partners* – dying so closely together, it makes you wonder.' The way Drain said the word 'partner' made Paula think they were angling at something.

Paula shifted so that she was on the edge of the stool. 'Do you think Thomas's death *wasn't* caused by a heart attack?'

'We're not implying anything, Mrs Gadd,' said the woman as she shot her partner a look. Then the woman's eyes softened a little. Paula wondered what she saw. A small woman in a giant towelling dressing gown that must have belonged to her dead husband. Dark circles under her eyes. Hair limp and tangled from sleep.

Paula sat upright in her seat. Squared her shoulders. She would not accept anyone's pity.

'What can you tell me about how they died – Kevin and Elaine?' Paula asked.

'I'm afraid we can't tell you anything at the moment,' Drain said.

'But the news is going with a lovers' suicide pact,' Rossi added.

Paula laughed. It was involuntary. The sound shot out of her mouth before she could stop it.

Both officers were looking at her with a question in their eyes.

'I'm sorry. It's just, no way was Elaine Teenan having an affair with Kevin Farrell. She had far more respect for herself than that.'

'How well did you know them?' Rossi asked.

'I've known Kevin for years. He went to school with Thomas. Thomas was very much the public face of the company. Kevin was in the background. And I'm afraid ... well, it's just my opinion, but I've always thought he was a bit of a fool...'

Rossi raised an eyebrow and exchanged another look with her colleague. 'Did you ever socialise with him? Do you know much about his private life?' she asked.

'No. Definitely not. Thomas knew I ... let's just say I didn't like Kevin. I made it clear that I had no interest in spending any more time with him than was necessary.'

'What can you tell us about Elaine Teenan?' Drain asked after a moment.

'Not much really. I mean, I've known her all these years but I've actually no idea if she was married and even if she has kids.' Paula felt her face heat. 'But she was a good sort, from what I could see. Smart. One of those women who make themselves indispensable. But, as I say, if she was having an affair with Kevin I'd be amazed.'

She paused. They seemed to be waiting for more.

'Where are the news getting the suicide pact idea?' she asked at last.

'Information already in the public domain is that Farrell cut Ms Teenan's throat and then turned the knife on himself.'

Rossi suddenly looked tired.

Drain chewed his lip and looked out of the window.

'Somehow the press got hold of that fact that...' Rossi stopped to look at Drain as if looking for someone to blame '...Farrell drew a love heart on the inside of the windscreen using Ms Teenan's blood.'

22

The police left, having made Paula promise that she would get in touch if anything occurred to her that might help the case. Rossi placed her business card on the countertop and gave her a pointed look.

Paula went upstairs and dressed in a daze. A suicide pact. And the gruesome heart?

She shuddered and looked at herself in her long mirror. Black jeans. Dark-blue blouse. Black jacket. She hadn't even considered the clothes. It seemed being a widow had come to her without thought.

Widow. She winced at the word, ripped the black jacket off, turned to her wardrobe and put her hand on a red one. But she found she couldn't do it. She slowly pulled the black one on again. What did it matter...?

Shortly after, she was outside the manse house at Father Joe's parish church. She knocked and he opened it straight away, as if he'd been waiting for her.

Paula stepped inside.

'Aye, come in,' said Father Joe with a half-smile.

'Too early for a gin?' Paula asked, sniffing the air pointedly. She looked him over. Dog collar, black shirt, black trousers, finished off with a dark-green cardigan. She looked at his feet. Brown corduroy slippers. All topped off with a grey and harried expression.

'That's Eau de Morning after the Night Before,' answered Joe although his face seemed to strain to form a smile.

Paula gave him a quick hug. 'No judgement from me, Father. But you might want to brush your teeth before you meet one of your parishioners.'

He crossed his arms. 'I presume you've heard about Kevin Farrell?'

Joe crossed himself. 'God bless his soul.'

'I have. The police came to ask me about it this morning.'

His expression slumped. 'Really? Well I guess they have to do their job. And poor Elaine. It's all over the news.'

'Can we go and take a seat?'

'Of course. Where's my manners?' Joe smiled. 'The sitting room.'

They sat on opposite sides of the ancient seventies' three-bar electric fire set in a wooden fire-surround. Joe leaned forwards, elbows on his knees and hands clasped as if in prayer. There was a slight tremble there and Paula had the thought that this was more than a hangover.

'You okay, Joe?'

'Sure, sure,' he said and rocked back in his seat. 'Actually, no. This killing has really thrown me.'

'Killing?' Paula asked. 'You're not buying the suicide pact thing?'

Joe made a weak trumpet sound out of pursed lips. 'No way were they having an affair. Elaine Teenan was devoted to her husband and kids.' He paused and looked into the distance as if he saw nothing but a bleak future there. 'Those poor boys, growing up without their mother.' He shook his head. 'She treated Kevin like he was her feckless younger brother. Did his books. Kept his diary. Washed the egg stains off his ties.' He shook his head.

Paula sat back in her seat, crossed her legs and arms. 'You seem to know a lot about them.' And she thought about what she'd told the police – she knew nothing of Elaine's home life.

'Not really. Just an impression formed from a few random visits to the office over the years.' Joe crossed his arms too.

'Joe?' Her tone was a request for more information. What wasn't he telling her?

He stood up. 'Look, I've got Mass in fifteen minutes.'

'Doesn't Father Martin normally take the noon service?'

'Some kind of stomach bug.' Joe made a face.

'Hope you don't catch it,' Paula said as she got to her feet, but thinking this wasn't right. Was he trying to get away from her?

'I think it must be the gin keeping me disease free,' Joe said with a weak smile that was clearly an effort. 'The preservative effect. It's definitely a thing. They should look into that.' He walked to the doorway. Turned back to her. 'See yourself out?'

Paula went to the sitting room door and watched him as he walked along the long narrow corridor that led to the sacristy. His head was bowed, hands in his trouser pockets.

She was right. Something was very wrong with her brother-in-law. He was trying to give her his usual chat, but it was like he was phoning it in. Working on auto, while his real attention was focussed inward. And this was more than grief. Or, more correctly, something other than grief, because she was sure Thomas's death was something Joe would never quite come to terms with.

He said he was performing the service? She considered when she'd left her house and pulled her phone out of her jacket pocket to look at the time. It read 12:02. If Joe was giving Mass, he was going to be late.

She hesitated for a second, then followed him down the corridor. She came to a tall, unpainted door. She knocked.

There was no response.

This was the only door he could have gone through, so she knocked again.

Silence. She pressed her head to the door and heard a faint cough. She pushed the door open, calling 'Joe?' as she stepped inside.

She looked around her. It was a small room. High ceilinged with a tall, narrow window inset among wooden panels. Under the window there was a large cabinet made of the same wood as the panels. So this was the sacristy. The only women who ever entered had a duster in one hand and a brush in the other.

Bill, Thomas and Joe had all been altar boys and at family events they often talked about their antics in here while the priests were getting ready for Mass. Stealing sips of the altar wine. Putting big dollops of Brylcreem on the back of each other's heads. And one occasion when they'd arrived too early, Thomas had put on the priest's vestments and blessed his brothers, only to be caught having gotten as far as *In the name of the Father* – and was then given a slippering for his trouble –

being hit by a slipper on his bare backside by old Father McLaughlan.

A movement, and she was plucked from her reverie by the sight of Joe sitting as if folded up on a small wooden chair just beyond the vestments that were hanging off a series of hooks. He looked up at her, opened his mouth, just as Father Martin's voice boomed through the wall from the church PA system.

'Joe?' Paula said. The sympathy in her voice enough that Joe fell forwards in his seat, hands over his face and sobbed.

'Joe,' she said again and stepped across the room, kneeled before him and took his hands in hers. 'Joe, what's going on?'

He looked at her, his eyes dull with tears, imploring forgiveness. 'It's all my fault, Paula. All my fault.'

'What's all your fault?'

'Everything, Paula. Thomas's death. Kevin and Elaine's murders. Everything.'

23

Cara was in Stewart Street Police station, sitting across a desk from
two cops who had introduced themselves as DS Alessandra Rossi and
DC Daryl Drain.

'Thanks for coming forward, Cara,' said Rossi. 'Could you tell us
again what you told the desk sergeant, please?'

'Sure. So, I popped in to see Paula Gadd at her office...' At the
mention of her name the detectives looked at each other. 'And Kevin
Farrell was there with that woman who died in his car.'

When Cara saw the news that morning she had barely been able to
believe her eyes. Not least because a passerby had managed to take a
photo of the bloody heart on Farrell's windscreen, and the picture had
now gone viral and was on every newspaper's front page.

It made Cara's blood boil, how the news agencies curated what was
important to broadcast. A whiff of sex and murder and everything else
was relegated. It mattered little to them how many refugees were being
murdered overseas. The salacious won every time, thought Cara with
a shake of her head.

'You're on record as having complained about Thomas Gadd...'
Rossi pulled a notebook from her pocket. 'What did you say ... ah
... Mr Gadd had tortured and murdered your brother in retaliation
for him having done a hit-and-run on Gadd's son? And what, you're
besties with Paula now that her man has died?'

So that's why they'd taken so long to see her. They'd been catching
up. She examined the expression on the detectives' faces and considered
just getting up and walking out.

'Aren't you interested in this? I saw a man in the back seat of their
car and not long after, dead bodies are discovered.'

'Okay,' Drain sat back in his chair and crossed his arms. 'You saw this guy in the back seat. Could you describe him?'

Cara saw him in her mind's eye. Saw a moment of shadow and pale skin under neon. She cursed the quality of the light. 'He was big. Hunched forwards in the seat as if he was too tall for the roof of the car. Or...' A thought occurred to her. 'He was holding a knife to the throat of the driver.'

Drain sighed. He actually sighed. 'Got a vivid imagination, haven't we?'

Cara cursed her stupidity. Even she thought it sounded crazy now the words were issued into air. 'Given what we now know it doesn't take that much of an imagination to join the dots. He was white. He was big. Light-coloured hair...'

The two cops looked at each other. Cara read the look and felt a flare of anger. She stood up. 'Sorry I wasted your time, officers. Clearly, thinking I was being a good citizen was a mistake.'

'Sit down, please, Cara,' said Rossi. 'We do appreciate you coming in. Any leads on this will help. However, the evidence of suicide-murder is pretty strong.'

'All I know is that I saw those two together last night, and if they are lovers then it's incest, cos she was acting like she was his big sister. And there *was* a guy in the back of their car.'

Drain sat forward, planted an elbow on the table. 'What else can you tell us about him? Any distinguishing features?'

Were they now taking her seriously? Somewhat mollified, Cara sat back down, her mind going back to the moment when Farrell's car passed her. 'As I said, he was tall. Had to be, the way he was hunched over. Caucasian. No facial hair. A lean face. Looked like he was wearing a black leather jacket. His hair was a light colour. Not blond. Light brown, maybe? It was hard to tell in the dark.'

'And what were you doing at Gadd Enterprises?' asked Rossi.

'A charity thing I've got with Mrs Gadd,' Cara answered. 'But Mrs Gadd was a bit knackered so I said I'd come back and see her another time.'

'You guys are good friends now?' Drain asked with a raised eyebrow. Cara sniffed an *As if.*

'You're not besties and, yet, you're at Mrs Gadd's office to witness a strange man in the back of a car.'

Cara exhaled. She had the lie ready, but hoped it came across as genuine. 'I work with an advocacy company. We don't normally get involved in charity work, but I came across one who needed help and I thought I'd try to get her involved.' She added a shrug.

'The woman whose dead husband you accused of torturing your brother?'

Time to leak a little bit of truth into her story, Cara thought. The best lies were coated in truth. 'I didn't want her money at first. I initially contacted her after her husband died cos she had to know something, right? I was angry. Tosh Gadd dies and the truth of my brother's death dies with him. I wasn't having it, so, rashly' – she made an apologetic face – 'I got in touch to try and find out what she knew.'

'And...?' said Drain.

'Clueless. Bloody clueless.' And in the saying of it, Cara realised that this was true. However much she tried to convince herself that Paula Gadd was the devil incarnate it wasn't working. She caught an image of Paula up against the wall with Kevin Farrell's hand at her throat. There was fear in those eyes, and no little courage in the way she recovered. Either she was a brilliant actress or she was completely in the dark about what her husband had been up to.

She drooped in her chair. She might never find out what happened to her brother. She damped that thought down and sat up straight again. 'Paula Gadd was happy to take her husband's ill-earned cash and turn a completely blind eye as to how he made it. Does that make her a bad person? I'm not her judge, but if she has access to wads of cash and someone I know needs it, I'm going to take advantage.'

'Her husband's ill-earned cash?' Drain asked.

'Aye. Guy's a total crook.' She coughed. 'Was.'

'Based on what?' asked Rossi.

'Aww, come on.' Cara looked from Rossi to Drain and back again.

'You telling me Tommy Gadd wasn't on your radar?'

'Far as we know Thomas Gadd was one of the leading lights in Glasgow's Chamber of Commerce. All above board and hugely successful,' said Drain.

'Squeaky clean—' added Rossi.

'And filthy rich,' interrupted Cara. 'I mean, who gets that successful without bending the rules?'

'Bending? You're talking about butchering them,' said Rossi.

'The guy that told me was terrified. And certain Tosh Gadd was involved.' She thought back to Danny's expression as he recalled the night of her brother's murder. 'I believed him. Completely.'

'From what we hear, you made yourself a giant pain in the arse with our colleagues. Enough that Thomas Gadd was investigated,' said Drain, with a note of grudging respect.

'And...?' Cara sat forwards. This was news. Her gut gave a little twist. Hope against hope that the police had found *something*.

'And they found nothing. Mr Gadd was – as I have said – squeaky clean.'

'Clean, my arse.' She found the old hurt at her brother's passing. Her attention was like gas to a pilot flame and she felt the pain of it rise in her mind and body as if the two years since his death was a mere two days. She bit her top lip as if the pressure there would bring her back into the moment.

Sean was a good kid. Worked hard in school. Played football with his mates. Kept out of trouble. Until, like many of his disaffected peers, he got onto drugs, and the change was incredible. Made Cara think of those seventies movies about demonic possession. She held an image of him in her mind. They'd met by accident two weeks before he died. Walking on Argyle Street, just outside Marks and Spencer, she heard her name being shouted:

'Ignoring your brother, ya snooty cow,' he said. His smile was big in the thin wedge of his face. His eyes were dulled as if everything he had ever lost was recorded there, and the pallor of his skin was on the turn towards jaundice.

She fought to hide her shock at his appearance and drew him into a hug. She felt the bones of him through the thin cloth of his sweatshirt. As if he read her pity, he stepped back from her, and studied the ground at his feet. He pushed his fists into his pockets as if his worldly belongings were held there and he wanted to protect them. Eventually he lifted his head up to meet her gaze.

'How's Ma?' he asked.

'She misses her son.'

'Aye, well.'

'Go and see her,' Cara said. 'She really doesn't care what state you're in.' She recoiled from her words, knowing they were cruel but also feeling they had to be said. 'She misses her son,' she repeated and put a hand on his shoulder, hoping the physical contact would get through where words could not.

'See you around, sis.' Sean turned and walked away. When he threw a cheeky wave of his right hand back at her, she was reminded of his boyish former self, and read what he might have become as if there was a hologram hanging there. A faltering image of what his better self might have been.

That was the last time she had seen him alive.

24

Paula knelt in front of Joe, grasped his hands in hers and looked into his face. The certainty of his claim was in the shine of his eyes, the way his skin was drawn tight across the musculature of his features.

'It's all my fault,' he said again, his voice a whisper.

'Joe, what the hell are you talking about?' Paula asked. His pain was a physical thing. Whatever he was feeling was very real to him, but it sounded to Paula like the mix of gin and grief was affecting him in strange ways.

Joe rubbed at his eyes. Swallowed. Looked into the distance. 'I had ... I *have* a terrible gambling habit.'

'So, you go down to the bookies now and again? What has that got to do with people dying?'

'It's more than that, Paula. It's ... complicated.'

'Okay. Tell me...' Paula got to her feet, and sat on the chair next to his, managing to move without losing her grip on his hands. 'Go on.'

'Started off at Ladbrokes. A wee bet on the gee-gees here and there. But soon that wasn't enough. I needed bigger stakes. Bigger risks.' At the word 'risks', his head fell forwards and he sobbed. Hard.

Paula said nothing. This was a time to let the tears flow.

Joe coughed, pulled a hand away from her grip and wiped away some of his tears with the pad of his thumb. 'Sorry,' he said. Coughed again. 'Next it was the casino. But I was shite. Knew nothing. Didn't learn from my mistakes ... and I ran up a huge debt. But...' he laughed '...the guys knew I was a priest, thought I was good for it and let me carry on.'

'Oh, Joe...' She felt his pain, and matched it, the cool wet of a tear trickling down her cheek. She wiped it away as she asked, 'But what has that got to do with Thomas?'

'Just a minute. Let me, tell you the whole story...' He looked around as if searching for answers in the hushed and sacred atmosphere of the sacristy. 'Helps me make some kind of sense of it if I say it out loud, you know?'

Just then, the door Paula had come through creaked open. A footstep. A cough. She turned round to see Thomas's other brother, Bill.

'Joe,' he said. 'I thought we'd talked about this.' His tone was conciliatory. Empathic. He gave a little nod to Paula and stepped closer. 'You don't want to be laying all of this on Paula. She has enough to contend with.' Again, he offered a nod to Paula. He stepped across the room and stood over them.

He had assumed his usual floor manager in a men's store persona. Not a hair was out of place, and his dark suit was clean and pressed. In fact, if she wasn't mistaken, it was of a much better cloth than he normally wore. She looked down at his feet: a high-gloss shine reflected from his black shoes. He looked like he'd been spoiling himself.

'I'm sorry I haven't been over to see you, Paula,' Bill said. 'You know how it is.'

'That's okay, Bill,' Paula said as she searched his expression. Sympathy from Bill. Real actual sympathy. She masked her surprise. Thomas's loss was certainly bringing out a side to his big brother she hadn't seen before. 'We all get on with this in our own way.'

She looked up at him and saw Thomas in his face – almost as if they were twins. It was enough to steal her breath from her. She closed her eyes hard against the thought, and then opened them again and studied him. He'd lost weight and his hair was cut just as Thomas used to have his done, although there was a touch more grey at Bill's temples.

Bill rested a hand on her shoulder, and it didn't feel patronising. 'If anything ever happened to Daphne I don't know how I'd cope.' He gave her a small smile. 'I could have been a better support, Paula. Since the ... well, we both could have been. I'm sorry.'

Paula felt her throat tighten, making her cough.

'Thanks, Bill. That means a lot to me.' She swallowed, and repeated herself. 'Thank you.' Perhaps she'd been too harsh on him.

'You okay, bro?' Bill asked Joe. He nodded, his tight smile indicating he was anything but okay.

A chorus of voices raised in praise sounded through the wall as the Mass drew to its conclusion.

Joe stood and tucked his black shirt in at the waist, trying to mask his awkwardness, thought Paula.

'Coffee?' Joe asked looking from Bill to Paula. 'Let's go through to the house and have a warm drink, eh?'

Back in the room where Joe and Paula had sat earlier, the three of them sat facing each other, each of them nursing a hot drink and warm memories of Thomas.

'Remember that time, what was he, ten? He brought home a wee black Staffie. Called it Katy.' Bill laughed, throwing his head back. 'Said it was a compliment to Mum. She was furious. Didn't want a dog and certainly didn't want one named after her.'

Joe snorted on a mouthful of coffee. Wiped it off his mouth with the back of his sleeve. 'Mum was really not pleased. Dad found it hilarious.'

'Perhaps that added salt to the wound,' Bill grinned.

'Remember that wee park that was across the road from our house?' Joe smiled over at Paula. 'He arranged all these mad wee obstacles and told all the local kids we were having our version of the Olympics.'

'And he was furious when you beat him at the sprint,' added Bill.

'That was Tommy. Always doing something. Always planning his next thing.'

'Can see why he went into business, eh?' said Bill. 'That time he stole Dad's porno mag and charged boys ten pence a look in the school toilet.'

'He did not,' said Paula.

'He did so,' said Joe. 'It was great for me as the younger brother.

Tommy had such a reputation at school, nobody bothered bullying me. They just wanted me to tell them what Tosh Gadd's latest scheme was.'

'And he didn't mind getting stuck in when it was needed. Never walked away from a fight,' said Bill. He took a sip. Held the mug at his mouth, his eyes peering across the top, but his vision locked in memory.

Paula shifted in her seat, uncomfortable with the direction in which the conversation had turned. Thomas fighting and getting into to all sorts of dodgy things – was that an early sign of the kind of thing Cara Connolly was talking about?

Paula made a mental note: she really needed to speak to Cara Connolly.

'Don't worry, Paula,' Joe said as if he had read her discomfort. 'Nothing illegal.' He shook his head. 'And really, he didn't scrap much. He always told me you attract more flies with honey than with vinegar.'

'Tommy and his sayings,' Bill said.

Paula nodded in agreement, thinking he'd stopped that habit a long time ago. Around the time of Christopher's death. Once again she thought of Cara ... her suggestion about why Christopher had been knocked down. If she was telling the truth – and that was a big if – Thomas must have known about it. And he kept that from her? She felt the pain of that throughout her body, and crossed her arms against the crush of it. No. That would be a betrayal she could not deal with.

'He had a saying for every occasion,' continued Bill, rousing Paula from her reflections. He sent her a look as if to ask her where her mind had drifted off to. 'It was like he read a book of clichés every morning as he ate his cornflakes.'

'Don't focus on the problem...' Joe said.

'...Focus on the solution,' finished Paula, while thinking, no, Thomas couldn't have known.

They laughed.

'Jesus, he could be a fool,' said Paula.

Both brothers nodded. Sighed a yes.

'Anyway,' said Bill. 'You doing okay, Paula?'

She searched his eyes, remembering his comment about the will while they were at the funeral tea. But she saw nothing there but compassion.

Paula held her mug on her lap with both hands. 'They talk about all these stages of grief, don't they?' The men nodded. 'Denial, anger, bargaining ... can't remember the rest. I think I'm stuck on anger. Is tiredness a stage? Because I'm always worn out. Exhausted and angry. Then I get angry for being angry and that makes me...' she felt her voice breaking '...even more bloody angry.'

'I'm firmly in the denial stage,' said Joe as he stared out of the window. 'I keep expecting to see his face in the congregation at Mass. Or see him walking up the path...'

'I'm totally with Paula. Bloody furious. And I resent him for dying. How could he die, and how could it feel this bad?' Bill's eyes filled with tears. His lower lip trembled. He exhaled, low and sharp. 'And what part of that makes any sense, eh? It's not his bloody fault he died. He was my wee brother. I should go first. I should have saved him...'

'No, Bill, you can't...' Paula began, then stopped what she was about to say. She knew that the boys' father had died just as Bill was becoming a teenager. He had taken on the father's role in the family, ran with it and clearly found it difficult to cast it off even when his brothers reached manhood. 'One thing I'm learning is there are no *shoulds* when it comes to grief and loss. We all need to find our own way through it. What works for you, what works for Joe, might not work for me.'

'Aye, cos you're the sensible one in the family,' said Joe with a smile. She felt a surge of pleasure that the Joe she knew and loved was coming to the fore.

'I've lost count of the people I've counselled through bereavement,' Joe continued. 'I was too young to deal with Dad properly. Mum's passing was part of the natural order. Didn't make it any easier, though. But it made it easier to reach acceptance. But Tommy...?' He shook his head.

'I do have one *should* for you, Joe. That gin bottle should be chucked into the bin,' said Paula.

'Aye, aye,' Joe mumbled.

'Don't just say aye, brother,' said Bill, his voice falling an octave. 'Drinking your way through it just causes a whole other set of problems.'

'I said aye,' Joe bristled. 'The gin is out. In the bin. Okay?'

A beep sounded from Bill's pocket. He pulled out his phone, read the screen and then looked over his shoulder out of the window.

'Okay,' he said and got to his feet. 'That's our Daphne. She dropped me off while she went to the supermarket.'

'Ask her in,' said Joe.

Bill shook his head. 'Stuff to be getting on with, bro.' He turned to Paula. 'Walk you out?'

'Sure,' said Paula, thinking it odd that on this occasion Daphne didn't want to come in and speak to them. Or perhaps it was Bill who wanted her to keep her distance. Besides, she wasn't quite ready to go – Joe had been in the process of telling her what had been going on. But she didn't quite have the presence of mind to come up with a reasonable excuse to stay.

Maybe Bill wanted a quiet word with her about Joe.

Joe stood. Paula gave him a hug.

'Talk to you later?' she looked up into his eyes.

He nodded. Looked away.

Joe stepped to the side and moved towards Bill. The brothers hugged, clapped each other on the back and coughed. They suddenly looked unsure of themselves and Paula had a flash of insight. The lines would have to be redrawn. The surviving brothers would have to negotiate a new way of being with each other now that Thomas wasn't there in the middle.

🕯

Outside, Bill walked towards a silver Audi. Paula looked at the plate and realised it was brand new.

'Nice,' she said. 'Been treating yourself?'

Bill ignored the question, and with an expression of concern, put a hand on Paula's forearm. 'I overheard some of what Joe was saying to you. Did you make any sense of it?'

She shook her head. 'I have no clue. You?'

Bill took a step back and looked towards the house. Then away. 'He's watching. Pretend we're talking about the car.' He put a hand on the roof, said. 'Nice, eh?'

'Lovely,' Paula reached out and touched a car door, thinking how crazy this felt. 'What's going on, Bill?' her voice was almost a whisper, which was stupid because there was no way Joe would be able to hear what they were saying.

'I have no idea.' His low voice matched hers. 'But I'm going to find out. There's something far wrong there.' His head twitched to the side as if he was resisting the impulse to have a look round to Joe. 'We talked the other day. He mentioned something about gambling and then froze.' He gave a shrug.

'He says that everything is his fault,' Paula said moving closer to Bill. 'What on earth could he be talking about?'

Bill shook his head, exhaustion and worry written across his features. 'Do you think it's the booze? He's long hidden his fears at the bottom of a bottle. Do you think Tommy's death has tipped him over the edge?'

'Heaven knows,' said Paula. 'It's a worry.' She thought back to the pain scratched into Joe's expression. 'Should I go back in and see if he's wants to talk?'

Bill gave that some thought. 'It strikes me that the moment has passed. Sorry. I shouldn't have walked in or we might be closer to knowing what's going on in that boy's head.'

Boy.

The big brother was finding it difficult to step outside his role, and Paula felt a surprising surge of affection for Bill.

'Leave it with me, Paula,' Bill said with a determined nod. 'I'll give him a day or two and then I'll have a word. Maybe we'll try and get the

Church involved. They must have counsellors for their priests.'

'You'd think so...'

Before she could take the conversation further, Daphne's head appeared from out of the driver's side door, her face flushed as she wiped crumbs away from the side of her mouth. She threw Bill a look as she climbed out of the car, then softened her expression and walked towards Paula, smoothing down her pink blouse over the swell of her stomach as she drew near.

'Paula, hen. How are you? Sorry we haven't been over since the ... you know...' She held her arms out and Paula stepped into her awkward hug.

Then, as quickly as she could, she disentangled herself. 'Not a problem,' Paula answered, trying to sound as genuine as she could. 'I know how it is.'

'Managing okay?' Daphne asked. Paula read an awkwardness in her sister-in-law's concern, as if this new form of relationship was as brittle as an eggshell and she didn't know what kind of approach was required. Paula wondered if she was being a little too sensitive.

'If there's anything you need just ask,' said Daphne.

'I will,' said Paula as she studied her sister-in-law. Dark, loose trousers and a twin-set – matching top and cardigan. Marks and Spencer, she thought. 'I've got a string of pearls that would go lovely with that,' she heard herself say. Then cringed at how condescending she must sound.

'Thanks, doll,' Daphne answered, reaching out and stroking her arm.

Paula recalled the last time they'd met, feeling that Daphne's attempts at warmth then had fallen short. But this physical contact, although a little awkward, seemed to have real empathy in it. Had Paula been way off the last time in reading her sister in law? Had her belief a moment earlier that Daphne's concern was false been wrong? She vowed to do better. Joe aside, Bill and Daphne were all she had left, she should take Daphne's lead and try harder.

'Bill,' Paula said as she turned away from Daphne. 'If you want anything of Thomas's let me know, won't you?' She looked him up and down too now, mentally comparing his size with Thomas. Had he lost a bit of weight? 'Before I give them all to Oxfam, there's quite a wardrobe of suits you could choose from...'

Bill gave her a smile. 'Hello...' he laughed, and held his arms out. 'Floor manager at a menswear store?'

Paula nodded her agreement while thinking that the suits Bill usually wore were nice enough, but not quite of the same quality as Thomas's. 'Right enough. Thomas probably got them all from your shop. But if there's anything else...' It suddenly felt important to Paula that Bill take something. This was the first time in a long while she'd felt that connection with him. She missed the Bill of old. The big brother who had welcomed her into their home when she and Thomas started going out together. He had a steady gaze then, a ready smile. He was a young man who was certain of his place in the world. That gaze had long since clouded.

'There's that watch you like,' Daphne said, as if she realised how much Paula wanted this to happen. 'The TAG one?'

'The TAG one,' Bill said with a dismissive tone, which suggested to Paula that he really did want it. 'I wouldn't mind Thomas's golf clubs. He bought a brand-new set last year. Must have cost him a fortune.' Bill grinned. 'And that wee electric caddy. Did he ever get a chance to use them?'

Paula gave that some thought. 'Probably not,' she answered, but she had no idea if he'd used them or not. Hadn't even realised he'd got them. She felt a pang of sorrow. How much time they'd wasted. She forced a smile. 'Come over and get them. And anything else you want. Thomas would hate the idea of them going to waste.'

'What about Tommy's iPad?' asked Daphne. 'He always joked he was going to leave it to me in his will.' She made a face. 'I'm rubbish at computers. Tommy said the iPad was so easy to use even I would be able to work with it.'

Bill snorted. 'You and computers just don't get on, honey. But if you want one I'm sure we could afford to buy it.'

'No point in spending cash when there's one going for free,' she replied and smiled at Paula. 'Is there?'

Paula crossed her arms, suddenly aware of the chill that had crept up her legs as she'd been standing talking. She hadn't given the iPad a thought. While Thomas was alive it was never more than a hand's length away from him. She often cursed him about it, saying the device was more of a wife to him than she was.

'You know I've forgotten all about that.' Paula searched her mind for an image of it. Had she even seen it since Thomas died? 'I've no idea where it is.' She looked at Daphne. 'Sorry.'

'No worries,' she replied. 'You know there's a welcome home here if you ever find it.' Daphne's eyes clouded just for a moment as she said this. 'Anyway,' she said, 'we'd better go. I've got my man to feed. You drive,' she told Bill, and with that she threw the car key towards him. He caught it easily and walked round to the driver's side.

There was an easy flow to this negotiation between them that set off another lurch of missing in Paula's gut. How long ago was it that she had that easy rapport with Thomas?

She walked to her own car, feeling more alone that she ever had in her life. Standing at the door, she waved at Bill and Daphne as they drove off. Then she wondered if she should go back in to the house and get the rest of the story from Joe.

But when she turned, Father Joe was standing at the reception-room window watching her. He lifted a hand up to wave, and it was as if that simple movement had taken his last ounce of energy. Then he turned and moved away, leaving nothing to see but a flash of winter sunlight on the pane, and shapes in shadow beyond.

25

As Paula drove back towards home in the West End of the city, she recalled the bag of Thomas's personal effects the hospital had given her when she had gone to identify his body. All the items he had on him when he died had been thrown into a plastic carrier.

Unable to look at them, she'd dumped the bag ... but where?

In her mind, she retraced her steps. She remembered the weight of it as the man had given it to her – he'd said he'd had to double-bag it, as there was so much stuff. He'd handed her a folder with a piece of paper on top of it. It looked like a list.

'Sign at the bottom, please,' he'd said. His tone was deadpan, but his expression held a note of boredom.

She duly signed, barely registering what she was doing. Numb, she'd walked back to the car park, and unable to bear looking inside, she'd dumped the bag in the boot ... And it must still be there.

In seconds her mind made several connections.

The iPad could be there.

Thomas might have used it when accessing those bank accounts in the notebook.

Was that why Farrell had died? For the information in that machine?

Almost on automatic, she stood on the brakes and aimed the car at the kerb. This rash movement earned her a loud beep of the horn from the car behind her. She flushed and offered a conciliatory wave out of her side window as the offended driver passed.

She quickly stepped out of the car and walked round to the boot, and opened it. Sure enough, there was the large bag she'd received at the hospital. Reaching in, she pulled the bag closer. Resisting the urge to lift it up and tip everything out, she teased it open and peered inside.

At the top was Thomas's belt and wallet – a matching set that she'd bought him for his birthday about ten years ago. She felt the now familiar catch in her throat. Then she saw a light-blue shirt and dark-blue tie. She pushed them to the side and felt the soft fabric of his suit trousers and jacket. Under that was a pair of highly polished black brogues. She snatched her hand away, as if burned. This was too much, how could anyone be expected to shoulder this? She hiccupped a couple of sobs and forced herself to inhale, to slow everything down. She had to breathe, she commanded herself. This needed to be done.

With trembling hands she reached again for the bag and pushed her hands inside. Only when she was sure she'd touched everything inside could she be sure of it. There was no iPad.

With that thought came the realisation there was no phone either. If the iPad was always within arm's reached, his iPhone was permanently in his hand.

Where were they?

Paula considered what the police told her about his last moments. He'd been in a restaurant in the city centre when the heart attack happened. He was on his own, according to the staff, and no one had accompanied him to the hospital. A diner at another table happened to be a doctor and tried to resuscitate him while they waited for the paramedics. He died in the back of the ambulance before they'd even set off.

She sagged at that thought. Her knees hitting the car bumper, keeping her upright. Dying in the back of the ambulance. On his own. Yet another sob escaped the tight clutch of her throat. She forced a breath. And another. She should have been with him. She should have been there, holding his hand, reassuring him.

She was clutching his wallet. She imagined it in his broad hands, saw the light hair that grew in a clump at the base of each finger, just up from the knuckle. Those long broad fingers had...

She shook her head. She had to stop torturing herself.

She opened the wallet and looked through the slots. A couple of credit cards, coffee shop loyalty cards, his driving licence. Some cash. She flicked through the notes, counting a round hundred pounds. And there, behind them, a small, folded photograph. She pulled it out and unfolded it to see the smiling faces of her and Christopher – the stretch of sand behind them signalling it had been taken at Ettrick Bay. She'd no idea he kept this with him.

She held a finger to Christopher's cheek. He would have been about ten when this was taken. His smile sending out nothing but good cheer and promise into the world. Holding it to her nose, she tried to inhale a sense of him.

Was Cara right? Had he been targeted? And because of something his father had done? No. It couldn't be.

Her boy.

Her man.

Both dead.

It was all too much. What had she done to deserve this?

She felt her knees give again, and had to flex her thighs to stop herself falling to the ground.

Enough, she scolded herself. There would be plenty of time to feel sorry for herself. First, she had to find out what had happened – what Thomas had really been up to.

She mentally ran through each of the series of numbers she'd memorised from the notebook. It was still all there, intact in her brain. She needed to get to a computer to check it out properly. But the death of Kevin Farrell made her cautious – she wasn't going to risk using her own laptop back in the house. Because she was in danger too, he'd said.

She felt a twist of fear. Then a flare of anger. What did it matter if she died? What else did she have to lose?

A face imposed itself on her mind. Cara Connolly. What she'd been saying couldn't be ignored. It had sounded like she was reading from a poor script for a B movie; but, now, with everything else Paula had discovered – and with Kevin and Elaine's deaths – she knew she had to find out if there was any truth to it.

A piece of gravel popped and she became aware of a presence just behind her. Too close behind her. She turned. Mouth open, ready to tell whoever it was to go away. Saw a tall man wearing a black hoodie, but not much else.

A blow to the right side of her face, before the wallet was ripped from her hand and she was pushed into the boot, and lid slammed on her.

Then the sound of rapid feet fading into the distance.

A shout. A deep male voice. 'Hey!'

Pain was a dull throb in her head. Her limbs were a tangle. She scrabbled to turn herself over.

'Bastard,' she shouted, and damped down her fear. She was safe. They'd gone. And all they'd got was Thomas's wallet.

But then she gasped. The photo. That lovely wee photo in that arsehole's hands.

The car was a hatchback, so the boot was huge and thankfully the lid hadn't been fully closed. With difficulty, she clambered over from the boot into the backseat.

Pushing open the back door, she struggled out and looked up and across the road trying to track the trail of her assailant. Her adrenaline was raised. She'd chase the bastard down every back street in Glasgow if she had to.

'You okay?' she heard a man's voice just behind her, and recognised the accent. She turned to face him.

Anton Rusnak. And he was holding Thomas's wallet in his right hand.

26

'You are okay, Mrs Gadd?' Anton asked, and stepped towards her, his face full of concern.

'I'm ... I'm...' Paula didn't know how she was. She held a hand to the side of her face and opened her jaw slowly, feeling the tightness there. She was going to have a bump and bruise just shortly. 'That little ...'

'I know,' Anton's smile held a grim promise. 'I caught son of bitch. He won't attack anybody else today.'

A sharp feeling of nausea. Pressure on her throat. She turned to the side and vomited.

Pulling her hair back from her face, Paula then wiped her mouth with her sleeve. Gasped for air as she tried to ignore the taste of bile.

'Where the hell did you come from?' she asked, ignoring the weakness in her thighs. If she didn't take a seat soon she was going to fall down.

Anton moved closer, reached beyond her and opened the driver's door.

'Sit down,' he said.

Paula gratefully fell inside. She felt herself fold into the soft leather and tried to hide the tremble in her hands by holding them together between her knees.

Anton held up the wallet. Opened it and checked what was inside. 'Was there money?'

Paula nodded.

'None now. There's cards, but no money.' He stepped back and looked down the street to his right. 'I go back and get the money.'

Paula stretched out and took the wallet from him. Opening it she saw that the photograph was still inside. She shook her head. 'No need. Let the wee bastard have it. The important stuff is here.'

'You need tea. Coffee. With lots of sugar,' said Anton, as if he was making an important announcement. He looked as if he was debating something with himself for a moment. 'You safe now. Don't go anywhere. I will be back.' He turned and, judging the traffic, crossed the road. Paula felt a new surge of fear now that she was on her own again and watched as Anton walked further up the street and stepped inside a small café.

She pulled the car door closed and locked it, taking a slow, deep breath. There was a quiver in all her limbs. She exhaled slowly, and repeated this with her eyes shut.

A slight knock at her window roused her. Anton was there, holding up a cup. She could see the steam rising into the cold air.

As if on automatic, she located the armrest, the necessary switch lowered the window.

'Coffee and sugar.' Anton smiled as he handed the cup through to her. 'Probably more sugar than coffee.' Shrug. 'It will help you, Mrs Gadd.'

Shakily, she took a sip and couldn't help making a face at the sweetness.

Anton was grinning at her. 'You do fine, Mrs Gadd. Very courageous lady.'

'Very angry lady, Anton.' She took another sip and it was easier to control her shaking this time. 'I'm very grateful you were here, but ... where did you come from?'

'It's cold,' he answered as his head sunk down towards his chest and he thrust his hands into his pockets. 'You mind if I come inside car?'

'Sorry, Anton. I wasn't thinking. Of course.' She found the central locking button, pressed it, and Anton huffed into the passenger seat. He held his hands before him and blew onto them. 'Glasgow winter not quite as bad as home. But still is very cold.'

Now that he was sitting beside her, Paula was reminded of what a large man he was. Back in the cottage that size felt like a threat, but here, after her attack, she was reassured by it.

'Thanks again, Anton. I don't know what I would have done if you hadn't been there.'

'I think you would have chased him.' He gave her an appraising look. 'Takes a lot to frighten you, I think, Mrs Gadd.' His gaze held admiration. 'But foolish. He could really hurt you if you chase him.'

His words sunk in. Kevin and Elaine had been killed – she wasn't buying the murder-suicide explanation – and it had to be about the numbers she found in that notebook. Was she also in danger?

Her stomach turned over. Had the mugging been a ruse to get her to chase him? And once she was out of sight, down an alley or somewhere, what could have happened to her?

She began to shake again, and put the cup of coffee down in a holder before she spilled the hot drink over her hands. Before Anton saw that she was frightened.

'You were about to tell me how you managed to be here?' She fought to control the waver in her voice.

Anton looked down at her cup. 'The coffee? Comes from my shop.' He cocked his head to the side, in the general direction of the small shop he'd come from. 'Beans and Bites is mine. There is big Polish community in the area. Tommy suggest I open a café. Big hit,' he beamed. 'Glasgow people love our Polish doughnuts, and *sernik*...' Anton read her blank stare in reply. 'Is cheesecake from Poland. Next time, when you're not in shock you must try.'

'Sounds lovely, Anton.' She shook her head. 'So, I just happen to get attacked across the road from your shop?' Her life was getting stranger by the day.

'I know. Crazy, right?' Anton held his hands out. 'And I'm not here every day, either. Is difficult from Bute, right? So random days – I like to surprise staff – I come over once a week and check how is doing. Today I see your car. You at the trunk. I thought I must say hi and as I cross the road I saw man attack you. I chase. Get wallet back. Give him big kick for his trouble.'

'I hope you kicked him hard enough for him to land in hospital.'

'His balls will certainly hurt for long time.' Anton's laugh at this was almost loud enough to hurt her ears. Then he grew sombre. 'How are you since last time we meet? Is not easy, no? Death takes time to...'

She paused, reading the empathy in his eyes. 'It certainly does, Anton. It certainly does.'

'I had a look,' Anton made a motion of apology. 'Being nosy. Is Tommy's, no? How did *ned* manage to steal Tommy's wallet?'

Paula exhaled loudly. 'I was on my way home and I suddenly remembered I still had Thomas's things in the car. Crazy, I know. My head's been all over the place since he died. Don't know whether I'm coming or going.'

'You just stop in middle of road to check?'

Paula considered telling him the full truth. It would be good to have someone she could trust. And a relief not to be to work on her own. And Thomas clearly trusted this guy.

But something held her back. She couldn't say anything just yet. She didn't know enough. And she was afraid if she heard it all said out loud it would just sound ridiculous.

'Since ... since Thomas, I don't know what side is up, to be honest. Soon as the thought occurred to me, I had to stop and check. Remind myself of him, you know?' She was aware that her bottom lip was trembling and bit it in an attempt to hide it from him.

'I understand.' He nodded his head slowly, as if all the weight of his own loss was held in each small movement. He slapped his thigh hard as if that might increase his energy levels. Then boomed, 'Must go and watch staff. They eat all those delicious *paczki* – Polish doughnut – and leave none for customer.' He fished in his jacket pocket and pulled out a card. 'My number. You need? You call, okay?'

'Okay,' replied Paula. 'And thanks again.'

He got out, and she watched in her wing mirror as the big man walked across the road towards the coffee shop. Just before he entered, he paused, looked back at her and gave her a wave. Paula drove off thanking whatever star had directed Thomas towards Anton Rusnak.

27

Paula woke up the next morning feeling angry. Angry and sore. In front of her bathroom mirror she assessed the damage. Some swelling similar to the time she had a wisdom tooth removed, and some bruising. She should get some frozen peas on to the swelling and some concealer and foundation on the bruising.

But there wasn't a lot she could do about her anger, unless she happened to bump into the little shit who stole from her. And then it occurred to her that she had no idea what size he was, or even if it was a he. It had all happened to fast. She was struck, pushed into the boot and then he/she was off.

Thank God for Anton.

Imagine just stopping where his café was. How lucky was that? Or how weird? Her life had become increasingly strange since Thomas died.

She thought of Joe.

Kevin and Elaine's deaths.

The notebook.

And now, her mugging.

The anger she'd woken with was now quickly replaced by fear. All this couldn't be unrelated, could it? Again, Kevin's words rang in her head: *I'm fucked ... we both are.* Perhaps she wasn't being serious enough about the double killing. Was she at risk? And from more than just passing thieves? Should be taking her security a more seriously?

How would she even do that? Employ a security firm? Get her own personal guard?

She looked into her eyes in the mirror. She desperately wanted to scoff at the notion. To shake herself free of the apprehension gripping her. But she couldn't.

Two people really were dead. That she knew of. Could there be more? Was Thomas's heart attack something more?

As she pulled on a robe, holding it tight around her waist, and walking down to the kitchen, she was reminded of Cara's allegations.

Stuff paid for by Thomas's illegal acts? She looked around the kitchen. Thought about this house: warm, safe luxurious. Was all of this tainted?

She couldn't believe it. Could she? She'd found out so much these past few days.

She put her hand on the coffee machine. New, top of the range. And a pang of guilt made her turn away. She'd have a drink of water instead. But why should *she* feel guilty? She'd done nothing wrong! Surely Thomas had done nothing wrong either.

Feeling a flare of anger, she threw the glass of water into the sink. It hit the aluminium and broke into several pieces. Swearing at herself she reached in and gathered them together before throwing them into the bin. And as she did so she noticed her breathing was a little erratic. She forced herself to exhale. Long and slow. Calm, she told herself.

Calm.

But there were so many questions and no one had any answers as far as she could see.

Cara Connolly. Should she entertain her claims? Ask her to take her to the guy who made those ludicrous allegations. There was no way her Thomas would torture and kill someone.

She might at least find out how weak the accusations were.

Paula leaned on the work surface, elbows on the granite, forehead resting on her hands. This was a mess. A confusing mess.

Pushing herself upright, she tried to work out what she knew. She'd start there.

She picked up her phone, and dialled Joe's number. But when it rang through all she got was his voicemail.

'Hey, Joe...' she made an effort to inject some lightness into her tone. 'Just to say morning, and I love you, you daft big lump. Call me back, eh?'

Next number she tried was Cara's. It rang out.

She looked down at the rectangular object in her hand. It was weird that neither Thomas's phone nor his iPad had turned up. Had someone stolen them at the restaurant? Or did one of the medical staff help themselves?

She should try the restaurant and speak to the owner. There was more chance of things being stolen there. With all the confusion of someone suffering a heart attack, perhaps someone had taken advantage.

The phone in her hand rang.

It was Cara Connolly.

'Sorry, I missed your call,' Cara said.

'That's okay,' said Paula. She paused. 'In fact, I'm really not sure why I called you.'

'You've had some time to think and now you're worried your husband actually was a murderous arsehole.'

'What the—' Paula rang off. She wasn't listening to that. She rung for answers, not insults.

The phone rang again. Cara. She sighed, picking it up.

'Sorry, that was out of order,' said Cara, in a warmer, careful tone.

Paula didn't reply. She didn't trust herself not to scream.

'What did you want?' Cara asked. 'I'm happy to talk if you want.'

Paula couldn't help accepting the offer. 'This is just all so confusing ... My head is all over the place. The stuff you said about Thomas ... and then you were at the offices the night Kevin was killed? I guess you've heard about that, haven't you?'

'Yes, I have.'

What was she doing, calling this girl? thought Paula. What did *she* know? 'Sorry, I shouldn't have bothered you...'

But before Paula could cut the connection, Cara said: 'You're not buying the suicide murder thing either then?'

'Nope. The more I think about it the more ridiculous it sounds.' Paula sat down. Something about this woman's tone was persuasive. 'It would be good to talk to you. For whatever reason, you're connected to all of this. Whatever *this* is. It would be good to talk about it all to someone who is...' But she couldn't think of the right word. 'Want to meet up for lunch?'

There was silence.

'Okay,' said Cara eventually. 'Twelve-thirty. I have a meeting in the centre of town, so somewhere there would suit.'

'Right. Twelve-thirty it is. Two Fat Ladies? The restaurant?'

'I know it. See you there.' Cara hung up.

🔔

Paula took a table near the front of the restaurant so she could see everyone coming and going. She felt faintly ridiculous. Wasn't that what people in crime movies did?

Cara appeared on time, her hair combed back off her face in a severe style, and wearing tight, dark-blue jeans and a cerise top. Her smart work clothes, Paula thought.

'See anything you fancy?' asked Cara, cocking her head at the menu in Paula's hand as she took a seat.

'Nice top,' said Paula, wanting to put both of them at ease. 'Suits you.'

'Thanks,' said Cara with both a small frown and a smile.

They both studied the menu in awkward silence. The sound around them was a happy babble. The low hum of conversation, with occasional bursts of laughter, and the sound of pop jazz coming over the PA system. It was just Paula's kind of place; stylish, with clean lines and a modern feel. If she had been here in happier times she might have enjoyed it. Paula could see why Thomas might like to bring a client here.

'Wasn't this where your husband had his heart attack?' Cara asked at last, as if she'd just read Paula's mind.

'You must think I'm weird,' Paula replied as she clasped her hands in front of her. 'I had to see the place, you know? And I couldn't just be here on my own.'

Cara nodded, her expression one of genuine empathy. Paula had to turn her eyes away. And Cara changed the subject, as if she felt it was too soon to pry.

'What are you going to eat?'

'The chicken,' Paula replied.

'I'll go for the risotto.' Cara offered a grin as she caught the eye of a waitress.

'What can I get for you guys?' the young woman asked with a large smile.

With a look to Cara, Paula ordered the risotto and the chicken. 'And if I could speak to the manager, please?' she added.

The waitress's smile slipped. 'Oh, is there anything wrong?'

'No, dear,' replied Paula, struggling to give the young woman a reassuring smile. 'I'd just like a quick word ... about something I think was left here.'

She nodded an okay and walked off.

'Patronising much?' said Cara with a smile.

'What?'

'No, dear.' Cara said, in a gently mocking tone.

Paula found herself suddenly warming to Cara. Perhaps she could trust her. 'You're like an annoying little sister,' she said. 'I'm wishing I'd ordered some wine now.'

'Yeah, me too,' Cara laughed. 'But I've got some work on this afternoon. Wouldn't do to be meeting with the children's panel stinking of wine.'

'Children's panel?' Paula grew sombre. 'Bet you hear some stories.'

Cara raised her eyebrows. 'You don't know the half of it. I get to see the very worst, and the very best of people in this job.'

'What made you go into that field?' Paula asked.

The waitress arrived and they both smiled their thanks as she poured them each some water from a carafe, and then told Paula the manager was with someone but would speak to her shortly.

'I started working as admin in local government, straight out of school,' said Cara once they were alone. 'From there I got a job with an advocacy company and saw how vital it was. Did all the necessary exams and here I am.'

'A social conscience is good in the young,' Paula said, regretting it instantly.

'Patronising much,' Cara said again, with a grin.

'Oh, please,' said Paula, but couldn't help smiling too.

'I understand you're looking to speak to the manager?' A tall slim woman in a black suit and with long black hair was standing beside the table.

Paula looked up. 'Oh, yes please.'

'That's me. Anna,' the woman said. 'What can I do for you?'

'This is sort of delicate,' Paula said in a quiet voice, glancing over at Cara.

The woman bowed her head.

'My husband had a heart attack in here a couple of weeks ago and I...'

'You're Mrs Gadd,' Anna said, and then her hand went to her mouth. 'Tommy's wife.'

'You knew my husband?' Paula tried not to bristle but wasn't entirely convinced she was successful. This woman knew her husband, and Paula had no idea she even existed.

'Oh, Tommy often brought his clients in here for lunch. So much so he had an account...'

'He did?' Paula asked, and then reading the genuine distress in the woman's eyes she modified her tone. 'I had no idea that he came here, until ... after.'

Anna leaned forwards again and touched Paula's forearm. 'It was such a shock. One minute he was ... the next...' Tears filled her eyes. 'I'm so sorry for your loss, Mrs Gadd. Tommy was a real character.'

'He certainly was.' Paula responding to the sight of the woman's tears with tears of her own. She sniffed and swallowed in an attempt to control her emotions. And for a second regretted coming here. She hadn't been prepared to hear about how much of a character Thomas was from a stranger. She paused as she wondered how to ask her question, worried now that it might look strange.

She gave Cara another look, and taking strength in the calm, quiet expression on her face, decided that, if there was any time in her life when she couldn't care less about what people thought of her, it was now. 'I've been looking through my husband's things and can't find his techie stuff – his phone and iPad? I wondered if, in all the ... melee ... whether it could have been left behind?'

Anna looked down at her, lips pursed as she thought back to that day. 'Nope, no phone or iPad. Not that day. Which is a surprise really,' she added as if it had just occurred to her. 'You rarely saw him without them.'

Paula felt her face twitch. Anna really did know Thomas. Then a question formed in her mind and she asked it without thinking. 'Do you happen to know who he was dining with that day? It's just that I never found out.'

'Oh,' Anna said evidencing surprise. 'The guy was so like him, he had to be family. Maybe more grey in the hair? Did Tommy have a brother?'

'Two,' Paula managed. 'He had two brothers.'

More grey.

It had to be Bill.

So why did he never mention he was with Thomas the day he died?

28

After the manager left the table the two women sat in silence, each lost in their own thoughts. Paula pushed the food around on her plate while Cara ate with gusto. When she'd finished her meal she placed her knife and fork on the plate.

'What am I really doing here?' Cara asked as she leaned forwards. 'Am I just an excuse so you could come in and get your husband's iPad?'

'As I said...' But then Paula reined in her irritation. They'd been getting on so well. 'For whatever reason you seem to be involved in all the confusion that has surrounded me since Thomas died. I need some answers. I thought you might be able to help.'

'Can you handle it?' Cara asked. 'Really?'

Paula looked down at her plate of food, pushed at a piece of chicken with her fork and her stomach gave a small churn of nausea.

'I'm sure most of your friends are already busy sanitising Tommy's memory. That's not what you'll get from me,' Cara continued. 'What I've got ain't pretty.'

'The truth, as you call it, might be difficult,' said Paula. 'But I've had enough of lies. I need to know what's going on. Those ... deaths. They're bothering me.'

Cara's face suddenly shone as if she'd just had an important thought. 'Here, you don't think Tommy's death was suspicious, too, do you?'

'Myocardial infarction,' said Paula. 'It literally means death of heart muscle. I looked it up.' She studied Cara across the table. Looked at her empty, sauce-smeared plate. 'Unless his brother, or that waitress slipped some poison into his lunch that would mimic a heart attack, what killed him was natural.'

Cara looked like she was biting back a reply.

'What?' Paula urged.

'I was just going to say, what with Kevin Farrell getting killed, doesn't that make you the least bit suspicious?'

'Of course it does,' Paula answered. 'Thomas was a fit man for his age, but still, you don't get much more conclusive than a death certificate.' She cut off a piece of meat, forked it into her mouth and forced herself to chew and swallow, as if she was forcing down that particular truth. She felt a daub of sauce sitting just under her lower lip and dabbed at it with a napkin. 'That guy, Danny, who accused Thomas of those horrible things? What happened to him? Why didn't he show the last time? I need to talk to him.'

'Dunno what's happening there,' Cara made a face of apology. 'I haven't seen hide nor hair of him since. It's like he vanished.' Cara took a sip of her water, and Paula read that she was trying to hide her disappointment. Danny had been a big part of her attempt to convince her that Thomas had been up to no good.

And another person goes missing, thought Paula.

'That's bad for your hips,' said Paula, as Cara moved her seat away from the table enough to cross her legs.

Cara shrugged. 'Sorry, Mum.' She smiled.

'Could go for a coffee,' she said.

'Me, too,' agreed Paula, made a face at the cold food on her plate and pushed it away. 'I'm not really hungry these days.'

'You should eat. Keep your strength up,' said Cara. 'You don't want to fade away.'

'Never going to happen,' Paula replied. 'I like my food too much. Normally. You should have seen me when I was a kid. Porky Paula, that was me...'

'You were never called that surely?'

'My parents owned the baker's shop so that made me popular with the other kids. I'm sure behind my back they were calling me all sorts.'

'Wow. Your mum and dad owned a baker's. That must have been cool.'

Paula thought about her parents. Dad with his sleeves rolled up.

Mum with her hair back in a net. It almost always felt like her dad was visible only through a cloud of flour, while her mum was behind the counter, placing scones and pancakes into white paper bags as she exchanged the gossip of the day with her customers.

They worked all hours and as an only child Paula was often left to her own devices. Which meant books. Books and day-old Empire biscuits. Which was not a good fitness combination, and when a pudgy but handsome boy she fancied refused to kiss her under the mistletoe at the school disco because *she* was 'too bloody fat', she decided to bin the biscuits and take up jogging. She quickly got down to a size eight and stayed there until recently. But her trousers had been so loose when she put them on that morning, she guessed she was now about a six.

She had enough self-knowledge to be annoyed, now, that it was a boy who had given her the motivation to lose weight. But that was her teenage self. That particular impulse did still surface from time to time: be the girl that pleases those around her. She saw so little of her parents as she grew up and was so desperate for their approval, while making herself as easy on them as possible, she said yes to everything.

Be still.

Yes, Mum.

Be in bed before eight.

Yes, Dad.

Stop reading and turn that light out.

Yes, Mum.

That urge to say yes to everything, even when it was in her worst interests, took a long time to fade.

'Both my parents worked,' said Paula, waking up from her reverie. 'Hard. It kind of felt like I was an inconvenience to them. Meeting Thomas and his lot came as a bit of a shock. All the noise and energy – I used to think I'd fallen in love with Thomas's big, boisterous family as much as with him.'

'Your parents are still alive?' asked Cara.

Paula shook her head. 'Dad sold the business on his sixty-eighth birthday. Decided he wanted to see a bit of the world. Wanted to go to Disney.' She smiled with fondness. 'He died the day after he bought the tickets. Mum died a month later.'

'I can't remember my dad,' said Cara. 'He vanished. Or was thrown out. Whatever. Mum's still alive. She's a grafter. I think that's where I get it from. She had five jobs at one point ... before the drugs got a hold of her, that is...'

'Was it just you and your brother?' Paula almost hadn't asked, but Cara was so refreshingly blunt, why should her approach be any different?

'There was a baby in between us. Brenda. Me first. Then two years later Brenda turned up. Didn't survive the week. And then Sean arrived two years after that.' Her eyes grew distant. 'Mum still talks about Brenda. Constantly wonders where she would be in life if she had survived. Would she have gone to university? Would she have kids?' Cara looked at Paula. 'I think that's a dig at me, cos I don't have any yet. She's desperate for a grandchild.'

'Has one ever been a possibility?'

Cara snorted. 'Never really had a reason to trust men. My dad was a shit. Mum's subsequent boyfriends were all shits.'

'In that case, any guys you meet can only win by comparison.'

Another snort. 'Turns out I have similar taste in men as Mum.' She grew serious. 'Don't get me wrong. I have plenty of male friends who are good, decent men, it's just when my ovaries get involved everything becomes very, very messy.'

The waitress floated past. Cara attracted her attention and ordered a couple of coffees.

'What about you, Paula? Happy you stuck with the one kid?'

'I often wonder about that. If having more kids would have helped with Christopher's loss? But to answer your question, one son was what life gave me.' She closed her eyes as they began to sting with tears. 'Being an only child, I wanted a houseful. We did try for other kids, but no more came along.'

Paula ran over Cara's words in her mind. Felt the old, yet still new loss of Christopher.

'Remind me,' Paula said, despite herself. 'How did Danny describe what ... happened to my ... to Christopher?' She coughed to cover up the crack in her voice.

'They were only supposed to frighten him...' Cara's eyes were less accusatory in this re-telling, more empathic. But she held nothing back, repeating everything that she'd said before. She was clearly keen to know the whole truth and being careful would only harm her purpose. 'Then when Tosh Gadd eventually caught up with Sean...'

Paula studied Cara as she spoke and saw that she believed this story completely. And she couldn't stop the image that popped into her mind. Thomas. Her Thomas. His shirt spattered in blood as he stood over a bloody and broken young man.

And she thought back to Thomas's behaviour in the days and months after Christopher died. Yes, he was angry. Furious. But could *that* description of violence be applied to Thomas? Wasn't his anger part of his passage through grief? Or was he, as Cara was accusing, capable of torture and murder?

29

Dislocation.

The word filled her mind, each syllable crouching on her tongue, behind the bars of her teeth. She was a human being, but apart from everyone else. Alone. Who could possibly understand what was happening here?

The very idea was ridiculous.

But.

How she made it home she had no idea. But somehow she got there and even managed to get upstairs to her bedroom, where she threw herself fully clothed on the bed. Mercifully, darkness overtook her exhausted mind and she fell into a troubled sleep.

Thomas was in that restaurant. He was telling her he loved her while wearing that smile that turned her stomach to liquid. Then he faced a waiter who was in the action of placing a plate of food in front of him, picked up a knife and stabbed it through the young man's hand, pinning it to the table top.

Paula's scream was so loud it woke her up.

She sat up in bed, momentarily confused. Her breathing was loud in her ears and she was uncertain where she was. Then with the help of the streetlights –coming in between the open curtains she recognised the outline of the door into the hallway, the chair to the right of it, and Thomas's dressing gown bundled over it.

How long had she been asleep? She got home, what, around four p.m.? This was late autumn so it got dark early. It could be the middle of the night for all she knew. If she could reach her phone she could check, but she didn't have the strength to move, so she allowed herself to fall back down onto the plump pillow with a loud sigh. It felt, simultaneously that she'd been asleep for minutes and for hours. Should she get up, or should she get herself into her pyjamas and turn in for the night?

Thinking about her phone, she realised that she hadn't had a silent phone call for a few days now. Thank God that had stopped, she thought. But then she couldn't help wondering why. Would it start again? Would something else happen?

There was a crash from another part of the house.

She sat up, adrenaline sparking all over her body.

'Who's there?' she asked in a tiny voice. Every cell commanded that she find somewhere to hide. Under the bed? In the wardrobe?

Another noise. A loud bang as if something had fallen.

'Who's there?' she asked again, this time louder.

Nothing.

Her phone. If she could remember where her phone was she could call the police. It would be in her bag. Where had she dropped it when she returned home? She looked to the side of the bed and the space there was empty.

Silently, she slid off the bed and moved to the doorway, alert to every sound. There was the slight drone of a passing car outside. Then another. A child's laughter on the street outside. A father's shout of warning. Then more laughter.

Rapid footsteps inside. Just down the stairs. In the hallway?

Recalling what happened to Kevin and Elaine, her anxiety fired up. She could run to the window, open it and shout to the people she'd heard outside to call the police. But she was unable to move. She was frozen with fear.

More movement inside: drawers being opened in the kitchen.

And the chatter from the father and child faded into the distance. *No*, she felt like shouting. *Come back*. But when she opened her mouth, nothing came out.

No. This was not good enough, she told herself. This was her home. Hers and Thomas's, and if she could survive his passing she could face up to anything and anyone. All she needed was a weapon. If she had something heavy and she made a lot of noise as she went downstairs, maybe the burglar would take fright and run for it.

Frantically, she looked around the room. There was nothing but soft furnishings. She made a mental inventory of what was in the study across the hall. The only suitable thing she could think of was a silver paper knife in Thomas's desk. The blade was blunt, but the point could possibly do some damage.

She heard more drawers being opened and closed.

Right. That was enough. She grew indignant, and fed it with her fear. This was her home. How dare they, whoever they were?

With every muscle in her body charged with fear and certainty she stomped through to the study, making as much noise as she could, and picked up the knife. Inside the small room she could see that every desk and cupboard drawer had been opened. She gasped at the realisation. While she was sleeping, whoever it was had been up here, riffling through this room. She steeled herself. And as she moved, she talked loudly, pretending that she was on the phone.

'Police,' she said. 'This is Mrs Paula Gadd. I have an intruder. And if they don't leave my house this instant I won't be responsible for what happens.' Why on earth did she say that? Where had that come from?

But her strategy worked. She heard the hurried slap of shoes on the wooden floorboards in the hall corridor as someone made a run for it.

The fact that they were in retreat lent Paula strength and energy. 'Get out. Get out!' she screamed. 'How dare you come into my house? How dare you?' She charged down the stairs, fear and fury firing in all her limbs.

There was a rush of noise as her front door was pulled open. Still wielding the knife, she made it to the ground floor.

'Aye, run. And I hope you can run fast enough,' she shouted down the hallway. 'Cos the police will be after you.'

The door slammed shut.

Without thinking about what she was doing she ran for it, and pulled it open. A man was outlined in the streetlight. But Paula struggled to compute what he was doing. If he was the intruder, shouldn't he be running away? But he was moving towards her, arms wide in greeting as if he had just arrived and was surprised to see her on her doorstep.

His features were blurred by the strong light behind him. With a start she realised that she would know that shape anywhere. It populated her dreams.

'Thomas?' she asked, before she fell to the ground in a faint.

30

Paula was aware of a cushion under her head, a soft throw over her body. A male voice spoke in soothing tones.

'Paula,' he was saying. 'Are you okay? Do I need to get you a doctor?'

She opened her mouth to speak, but nothing came out. She was made mute by the crushing weight of her disappointment. She could have sworn it was Thomas at her door. Those familiar broad shoulders...

Of course it wasn't him. He was dead. What a fool she was.

'Bill,' she managed to say at last. 'I'm fine. Please don't get me a doctor.' She was on one of the sofas in her sitting room. She pushed herself up from her prone position. 'Thanks for seeing to me, but I'm fine.'

'What's going on?' Bill asked, his expression one of alarm. 'When I got here you looked like you were about to attack someone. You had a knife in your hand.'

Her certainty that she had been confronted by Thomas, and her subsequent embarrassment had completely thrown everything else out of her head.

'Oh my God,' she said. 'Yes. There was someone here.'

'What?' he asked. 'But I didn't see anyone when I arrived.'

'In the house,' she said breathlessly. 'Someone. I was in bed...' Then she had a thought. 'What are you doing over here at this time of night?'

Confused, Bill drew his head back. 'What are you talking about? This time of night? It's only just gone seven.'

'In the evening?'

Bill paused before answering. 'What happened, Paula?'

Paula held a hand to her forehead and groaned. Bill would surely think she was losing it altogether. 'I ... you know when you fall asleep and think you've been under for ages, but it's only...'

'I do that all the time,' Bill said with a note of kindness in his voice, but his face showed that he didn't really know what she was talking about.

'And yes, there was a burglar.' Not quite believing she had actually run after him she continued: 'I chased him out onto the street. Which is where I saw you and thought...' She stopped. Whoever the intruder had been, he could have killed her. What was she thinking, chasing him like that?

Bill's expression clouded over. Was he remembering that she had called him Thomas? Or perhaps he just didn't need another reminder that his brother was dead.

'I should check...' Paula got to her feet. Now the danger was over, she was shaking.

They both moved through to the kitchen and Bill watched as she went through all of the drawers. 'Nothing seems to be missing,' she said as she assessed the contents of the room.

That was odd. Nothing had been taken. What burglar enters a house and rakes through the drawers? 'What were they looking for?' she said out loud.

She gasped. It must be something to do with those numbers she memorised in the notebook.

Kevin.

She'd disturbed him going through her office days before. Perhaps whoever it was had hoped to find whatever it was he'd missed.

Bill took his phone out. 'I'll phone the police. You need to get this on record.'

'No, don't,' Paula said, not sure why.

Bill paused with his phone cradled in his hand, finger poised. 'Why ever not?'

'I...' She looked around. 'Nothing's missing. What's the point?'

'What's the point?' Bill was incredulous. 'You could have been hurt.'

'Yes, but I wasn't.' She thought through her impulse to shout him down. It was all so complicated. If the police came she'd have to tell them everything. Explain her suspicions about the murders. The money. Thomas potentially being a gangster. Christopher...

'Paula, what on earth is going on?'

'Honestly?' Paula answered as her shoulders sagged. 'I have no idea.'

'Okay,' Bill said as he took her by the shoulders and guided her to a stool. 'Have a seat and I'll make us a coffee.'

She snorted. 'Coffee? I think I deserve a very large gin.'

Bill laughed, and as he did so Paula got the impression that the noise of it surprised him. As if he hadn't laughed for an age. 'Gin it is,' he said. 'And while I get the drinks you can tell me everything that happened.'

As he moved to the correct cupboards to fetch the glasses and the gin, part of her mind wondered how he managed this without being told. But she didn't say anything and instead told him everything that had happened since she got back from her lunch with Cara Connolly.

At the mention of her name he started. 'Where have I heard that name before?'

'Thomas never mentioned her?'

He narrowed his eyes as he searched his memory, but Paula got the impression it was a fake response. She shook her head. She was reading something into everything tonight.

'Thomas and I weren't talking much of late,' Bill said, making it sound like an admission of guilt. He placed a tumbler full of gin and tonic in front of her.

'Thank you,' she said and had a sip. She recoiled from the glass. 'Jesus, did you put all of the gin in here?'

Bill smiled. 'I thought you said you deserved a large drink?'

She reached for the tonic and topped up her glass. 'Yeah, but more tonic than gin is the way I usually take it, thanks.' Then a question occurred to her. 'Not that I'm not glad to see you, Bill, but ... what are you doing here?'

'You said I should pop over and get some of Thomas's stuff? His golf equipment?' He looked small as he spoke, as if now that the moment was here he was ashamed to taking his brother's belongings.

'Of course,' Paula said as she remembered their last conversation. 'Sure, whatever you want, please take. It will just go to charity shops otherwise.' And she gave a little groan internally at the thought of that task – gathering all of Thomas's belongings, bagging them up and lifting them out of the house.

Bill read her thoughts and placed a hand on the back of hers. 'When you're ready to gather everything together, give us a shout. Me and Daphne will give you a hand.'

They sat in silence and sipped. Paula felt the alcohol warm her belly and noted that Bill wasn't drinking quite as fast as she was. But then, he was probably driving.

By the time she finished her drink, she noted that her shaking had stopped and the fear her burglar had induced was all but gone, leaving her with an oddly buoyant mood. She'd faced down fear and won. She was a super-woman. And then it occurred to her that her moods were all over the place. It was a reaction to the shock. Perhaps she should try to get a hold of herself.

'Madam would like another drink, sir,' she said to Bill, trying to sound relaxed.

'You sure that's a good idea, Paula? You just had a bit of a scare.'

'And I survived. That calls for a drink. Another one,' she corrected, hearing a slight slur in her words. 'Not so heavy on the gin this time, please.'

Bill performed the necessary task and slid a glass over the work surface to her. She sipped and groaned with the small pleasure of that initial wet chill and notes of juniper in her mouth.

'That's how we get past it, Bill. Small victories, eh?' She looked at him and tried to judge how he was coping. 'How are you anyway?' she asked.

His cheeks twitched in an almost smile. 'Been better, thanks, PG.'

PG. She'd forgotten about that. From the tea bags. That was the nickname Bill and Joe gave her when she and Thomas first got married, and she felt a warm rush of affection for her brother-in-law – something she'd not felt in a long time.

'We need to do better, eh?' She offered him a conciliatory smile aimed at asking for forgiveness for her part in their long family estrangement. 'Perhaps something good could come from Thomas's ... you know?' She couldn't quite say it. 'You, Daphne and Joe are all the family I have.' She felt her eyes spark with tears. Her throat tightened. 'Can we try, Bill?'

'Oh Jesus,' he managed after a moment. He wiped at his eyes. 'You'll get me started now.'

They both laughed. The sound was weak and tinny in the vastness of the kitchen, but laughter nonetheless.

'Hey,' Paula jumped to her feet. 'You like whisky, don't you? Thomas has this amazing whisky...'

'But I'm driving.'

'For goodness sake, Bill,' Paula threw over her shoulder as she moved to the other side of the kitchen. 'Leave the car and we'll order you a taxi.' She looked under the sink, ignoring the slight spin of her brain as she did so.

She located the box and pulled it out. It was a handsome container, grey-blue, with a ribbon, and heavy. She got to her feet and moved across the kitchen to the island and placed it on the work surface.

'Nice,' said Bill, and his expression changed as if he'd just made the decision that he could indeed leave his car and order a taxi. He wiped away some dust and grime from the top of the box and opened it, and they both instantly noticed that the seal was broken and the bottle was missing one large measure.

'Looks like my husband had a special occasion all to himself,' Paula said, while thinking that, at one time, he might have shared it with Bill. She regretted that change on Bill's behalf. On Thomas's too.

But then she frowned: if they were estranged, as she thought they were, why were they together on the day Thomas died? She opened her mouth to ask, but what Bill said next threw all of that from her mind.

'It could have been me,' Bill said, moving his eyes from the bottle to her face. 'I always thought he was a lucky bastard when I saw how much you loved him.' They fell silent as if Bill's words had pushed open a door neither of them wanted to enter. They both fixed their attention on the bottle.

'Remember that night we first met?' Bill asked. There was a plaintive sound to his voice, but Paula couldn't quite trust herself to look into his face to examine what might be going on in his mind.

'The night I first met my husband, you mean?'

'I saw you first,' Bill said in a small voice. He coughed as if clearing the memory for speech. 'I wanted to ask you to dance, but Tommy beat me to it.'

'Oh ... I...' Paula wasn't sure how to respond. She'd caught enough looks from Bill over the years to realise that he found her attractive, but to think that he might have approached her first? She crossed her arms, feeling more than a little awkward.

In fact, that night she had spotted the two boys at the bar, her eyes had initially been drawn to Bill. There was a vital energy in his wide-legged stance, and his hands were in his jacket pockets as if he was trying to contain it. And she always had had a weakness for dark-haired, dark-eyed men.

Thomas stepped in front of Bill at that point. His hands were in the air, punctuating his speech as if the words were never going to be enough. Then, he saw where Bill's eyes were being aimed. With a mischievous cant to his lips and a nervous light in his eyes he walked across the room to her. And won fair lady.

It was time to move the conversation on, thought Paula.

But Bill beat her to it. 'What a beautiful bottle,' he said. 'Johnny Walker Blue Label King George V,' he read it out as a V rather than the number. Paula laughed, grateful for the moment of light. 'And it's hiding under your kitchen sink. What the hell?'

'No idea.' Paula said. 'Sometimes he revelled in his success. Sometimes it made him uncomfortable.'

Bill lifted the bottle. Felt the weight of it in his hand. 'Shall I be father?'

'Yes. Pour, please, but not too much. I've nearly had my fill.'

Bill snorted.

'What?' Paula asked in mock indignation.

'You? Enough booze?'

'Oh, please. That teenager is a long time gone. This is a one-off.' She swiped at his arm and then let her hand rest on his sleeve. 'I'm glad you came over tonight, Bill.'

'Fresh glasses?' he asked. 'For a whisky as fine as this we should drink it out the proper receptacle.' He moved away as if her hand on his sleeve was a weight he couldn't yet bear.

Bill retrieved a pair of glasses. There was a chime as he placed the glasses on the work surface. Then he poured, and Paula wondered if there could be any more pleasing sound than liquid falling onto itself into a glass.

'Do we ruin this with ice, or water?' Bill asked.

'No idea,' Paula reached for one of the drinks at the same moment as Bill did. Their fingers touched momentarily. They sipped, each pretending the contact hadn't happened. Bill closed his eyes and groaned.

'Aw, man. Beautiful.'

Paula swallowed and felt the peaty taste linger in her mouth. Noted the warmth and smooth heaviness of it. She pushed off the kitchen island. 'Bring the bottle,' she instructed Bill. 'Let's go through to the lounge and have a comfy seat.'

In the lounge, on the sofa, she kicked off her shoes and pulled her feet up off the floor. Then she bunched a cushion over her lap and rested her drink there. Bill sat on the sofa too, but leaning against the opposite arm. He twisted in his seat so that his knees were pointing at her.

'Do you need to let Daphne know what's happening? She'll be expecting you back home by now.' As she asked this, she acknowledged that only an hour or so ago she was chasing a burglar out of her home. Perhaps she should have called the police?

Bill shook his head. 'She knows.'

'She knows you're having a drink with me?'

Bills expression shifted as if he'd read more into Paula's question than was there. 'She knows exactly where I am. That I've come to get some of Tommy's stuff...' He held up his glass. '...This other part of that might not go down well.'

'I didn't think Daphne was a jealous woman.'

'Wasn't always like that.'

Paula held the glass to her chin and spoke over the lip. 'Yeah. A woman puts on some weight and suddenly other women are a threat.' Then felt a flush of shame at her mean thoughts.

'Other *single* women.'

'Of course,' said Paula, as that nuance dawned. 'I'm technically available now.' She took a sip. 'She has never been obvious about it, but Daphne never really liked me.'

'That's not true.'

'Bill, it's late. We've a glass each of extraordinary whisky in our hands. Lying is not allowed.'

'Well ... she overheard me and Tommy argue years ago.' He smiled at the memory. 'Way before you guys even got married. Can't remember how it started, but it finished with him laughing at me when I said I nearly got you first.' He took a long drink. 'This really is delicious. Way too easy to drink.' He leaned across to the small coffee table in front of the sofa and picked up the bottle. Aimed it in her direction. 'More?'

She held out her glass. He poured a healthy measure in.

'And, let me guess, every time you have an argument she brings it up again?'

Bill nodded.

'We women forget nothing. You need to bear that in mind.'

They fell into a companionable silence, each lost in recollection, sipping and savouring almost on automatic. They slumped closer on the sofa, until their shoulders were all but touching.

Paula was aware of his nearness. His warmth. His well-clothed leg, brief showing of sock and his brown-leather brogues. She was aware of her breathing; deep and slow. The whisky on her tongue, the moisture on her lips.

He turned so that he was looking directly into her eyes. She closed hers.

'I miss him so much,' Bill said.

Paula could only nod. And that missing was the bridge to close the gap.

Breathing hard. Shifting clothes.

Nothing real but this.

Now.

She wanted love. She wanted to punish herself for not being there. For her failings as a wife, but most of all she simply wanted Thomas.

Please let this be Thomas.

He was on her. Fumbling with her clothes while she fumbled with his. Her mind intoned again, *Please let this be Thomas. It feels like Thomas. Looks like Thomas.* And there was gratitude there, like a shell around the shame of what was actually happening, because it *could* be Thomas. This could be a way of, if not denying the truth, delaying it for just one delicious, improbable moment. A moment she could carry with her into the trials of her loss.

Paula felt the weight of him. His hands rough on her skin, his breath hot in her ear. And bit on the inside of her bottom lip to stop herself from admitting the truth of the situation. The pain was sharp enough to make her gasp and Bill paused and looked into her eyes as if asking for permission to carry on. She met his gaze for a moment, before her eyes slid away to find and focus on the sense of wrongness, despite herself. The hot tang of blood on her tongue cut through the breathing, the needing, the heat between them, and the differences between the brothers couldn't have been more pronounced.

This wasn't love; this was consolation.

His cheek, wet with tears, burrowed into the crook of her neck.

'You sure?' he asked and she felt the pressure of the words on her skin, like braille.

'I'm not sure about anything, Bill.' And there it was in the air between them. He wasn't Thomas.

Never could be.

Bill slid off her and landed on the floor. Paula looked down. He looked ridiculous. Trousers and underwear round his ankles, shirt gaping open.

Bill began to laugh. A sound that quickly became high-pitched. He hid his face in his hands as the laughter bled into tears. Paula patted him on his shoulder feeling more than a little ridiculous too, and wanting to be anywhere in the world but here.

'I'm a horrible human being,' Bill was saying behind the fence of his fingers. 'Horrible. I've done some...' He paused, looking up at her as if he wanted to unburden himself, opened his mouth to do so, but then his eyes clouded and whatever he was about to say died in his throat. His mouth opened and closed a number of times as if emotion and articulacy were at war within him, as if he was closed off from his own narrative.

Paula rearranged her clothes, burying the notion of guilt and stupidity in the back of her mind for now. Throwing a cushion over Bill's lap, she sat beside him, and pulled his head onto her shoulder as his grief and its necessary display took over. If she couldn't help herself in this moment, she could help her husband's grieving brother.

'Is that the first time you've cried since Thomas died?' she asked, somewhat in awe.

'Pretty much,' he replied.

Paula got to her feet with a suddenness that made her head swim. Shame at her behaviour was a wave that was about to crash down on the feeble protections and justifications she'd tried to offer herself. This was all wrong. She needed to be on her own.

'I'm sorry. That was...' Bill began as if reading her mind. 'I shouldn't have...'

'No ... we ... neither of us....'

'Yes.' Bill's chin was so low it was almost on his chest.

'Barely happened,' Paula said, feeling a rush of embarrassment. What would Daphne say? 'Never happened?' What were they thinking? They both needed comfort, company, someone who understood what they were each going through. This was not the way to achieve that.

'I'm so sorry, Paula.' Bill nodded. Relief pale on his face. 'Never happened.'

It was only when she stood there, at her front door, watching him drive away that she realised he hadn't taken away the golf clubs, and she hadn't asked him why he'd never mentioned he had lunch with Thomas on the day he died.

31

'Bless me, Father, for I have sinned.'

'Oh, sweet Jesus,' said Joe from the other side of the curtain. 'Do we really want to go there?'

'What do you know?' Paula asked, instantly concerned.

'I know you've done something bad enough that you need to tell me through a hole in a wall.' There was a weary chuckle in his voice. 'What have you been up to?'

There was no other way to say it than to say it.

'I kinda almost had sex with Bill last night.'

Pause.

'Wait. I thought you said you kinda almost had sex with Bill.'

'The nut is in the shell.'

A moment's pause and then Paula could feel the air around her shift as the door into the adjoining cubicle was opened. Then her door was pulled open and Joe stood there, stooping forward, his face bright, mouth wide.

'How in the name of God can you kinda have sex with Bill?' His voice was a harsh whisper.

Paula waved at him furiously with her right hand, while with her left she held her large handbag in front of her like a shield. 'Get back in your cubicle. I can't talk to you about it like ... *this*.' Mentally adding, my face needs to be hidden.

Joe disappeared momentarily and reappeared in his original position.

'I'm going to take a series of long, slow, deep breaths in the hope that it brings my mind back into that still pond place. While I do that you can tell me what the hell is going on.' The last five words were spoken in a rush.

'Long, slow and deep, Joe,' said Paula grateful for the delay.

Pause.

'I'm breathing. You should be talking.'

'Oh, man,' said Paula. 'This is a mess.' In a kneeling position, she leaned forwards on her elbows, head in her hands. Felt the same need she had last night. For intimacy. The touch of another human. For Thomas.

'What were you thinking?'

'I can't make sense of it, Joe. It wasn't me. I'd never do a thing like that.' And yet it was. There was the pattern of thought and bad decisions trailing through her mind like a red silk scarf in a dirt-borne breeze.

'According to you, you kinda did. How can you kinda have sex anyway?'

'He was...' She cringed at what she was about to say. 'We were ... and then Bill started crying.'

Joe was silent for a moment. 'Bill was crying?'

'This is horrible, Joe,' said Paula. 'It's so messed up.' Then she recounted the entire episode from chasing the burglar to the moment Bill left her house, his face long with embarrassment. His last words to her. 'I'm a despicable human being.' And his expression of self-loathing stayed with her through the night. She wondered if it matched her own.

'Wait. You had a burglar?' asked Joe.

'And anyway why should he assume all the blame?' she asked, ignoring his question. She didn't want to have to justify her decision not to call the police. A decision that was now beginning to bother her. What if he came back? 'Bloody typical. I'm not some helpless little woman. I played as much a part in that scenario as he did.'

'Well, I'm pleased you're taking ownership,' said Joe. And it felt to Paula that he was fighting back his disgust and inclination to judge.

'Oh, please don't talk to me like you're some kind of Californian TV shrink, Joe.'

'Nonetheless, the sentiment applies. You made a mistake. A huge mistake. And there are mitigating factors, but you're assuming responsibility for your actions. You're not trying to blame the demon drink...'

'I was pissed, to be fair.' She paused for a moment. 'It was like it was me, but it wasn't me, if that makes sense? I knew what I was doing was wrong, but...' Paula thought again about that sense of dislocation. Being apart. Looking down the length of her body as if it belonged to someone else. And yet, feeling the ache of longing, the need for skin on skin. The search for human warmth.

'What happens now?'

'We pretend it never happened,' said Paula firmly. Paula thought about the slump of Bill's shoulders as he left, the self-loathing in his eyes. But before that they'd shared something. A moment where they'd eased each other's loss. That had to count for something, surely?

'My brother is the kind of man who hates showing weakness. You saw him at his most vulnerable last night. I'd wager Daphne's never even seen him cry.'

Paula scoffed. 'How can a wife never see her husband cry?'

'For a clever woman, you say some stupid things, Paula Gadd.'

Just then there was a rattle on Paula's door. 'Are you two reading a book in there or something?' A deep and querulous voice demanded.

'We've just been reminded that we've been in here some time, Paula. Why don't you go through to the house, put the kettle on and we'll finish once I've spoken with this gentleman.'

♦

Fifteen minutes later, Joe joined her in the lounge.

'I thought *I* talked for ages,' said Paula.

'A few more people came in, sorry.' He looked at the empty mug she was holding. 'Get you a top up?'

'Please.'

'Let's go through to the kitchen and we can continue our chat.' He studied her face as if looking to assess her mental state.

She studied him in turn then got to her feet. 'You look better.' The dark circles under his eyes weren't quite so pronounced.

'Lying is a sin,' Joe said.

'Will you hear my confession, Father?'

Joe snorted and walked out of the room. Down the corridor and in the kitchen, Joe reached for the kettle. While the water started its rush to a boil, he turned to her.

'I always thought Bill had a soft spot for you.'

'Well, last night it got a whole lot harder.'

Joe opened his mouth and made a retching sound.

'How was he when he left you?' He asked. 'He actually cried, yeah?'

'He actually cried.'

Joe spooned some coffee into a pair of mugs. 'I've never seen my big brother cry.'

'Not even when your mum and dad died?'

'Not even.' Joe poured water into the mugs.

'Wow,' said Paula. 'That's a whole level of buttoned-up I've never experienced before.'

They sat at the kitchen table and Joe pushed a mug across the table top to her.

'What now?' Joe asked.

'We scratch it from our collective memory bank and resume our in-law status.'

'And pray Bill doesn't get an attack of the guilts and tell Daphne everything.'

Paula cradled her mug, enjoying the heat on her hands. 'That could happen?'

Joe shrugged. 'They're a strange pair. They shouldn't work, but they do.' He looked into her eyes. 'She's taken him back before...'

'Noooo.'

Joe nodded. 'Not that I'm one to gossip.'

'Bill's had an affair?'

'Affairs. Plural.'

'No.' Paula sat with that for a moment. Felt a flare of humiliation that she might just be a notch on his belt. Then she pushed that thought aside as being unworthy of her. She should forget about his other women. Last night was more complicated than that.

Daphne's face imposed itself on her mind. She felt a squirm of sorrow for her. 'What a prick.' And then a thought gave Paula's stomach a lurch. 'He told her or she found out for herself?'

Joe sucked at his teeth. 'Not sure.'

'Hey, Mr Oracle, did Thomas ever have an affair?' She placed both hands on the table as if bracing herself for the reply.

'Let's not go down that rabbit hole.'

'If you knew would you tell me?'

Joe just looked at her, his face a mask. His expression shifted, softened and then recovered as if he had hit the 'inscrutable' setting.

'Right,' she said. 'Let's not go there.'

'You have much wisdom for one so young.' Joe lifted up his mug and took a sip. Groaned as the warm liquid filled his mouth. 'Who knew that listening to people unburdening themselves would make a man so thirsty?'

Then they sat in a companionable silence, each one's presence at the table enough in that moment, until she dared to breach the quiet with a question she needed an answer to.

'Last time we spoke you were about to unburden yourself, Joe.'

He nodded. 'I was, but I've since seen my confessor. I'm good now.'

Paula narrowed her eyes. 'You were saying Thomas's death was all your fault. How can confession make that alright?'

'I was talking guff, Paula.' He smiled. 'I hadn't slept in days and I was trying to fill my calorific needs with gin. None of that is fertile ground for a healthy mind.'

'Mmmm.'

'Cross my heart and hope to die,' he smiled.

'Here's another saying for you. Liar, liar, pants on fire.' She paused. 'How much did I tell you about the cottage?'

'What cottage?' Joe looked mystified.

'In Bute?'

'There's a cottage in Bute?'

Paula told him. And as she talked his mouth fell open.

'You really knew nothing?' she asked.

He shook his head. 'Wow, Tommy did that for you?' His eyes filled with tears. 'That's beautiful.'

'He was all about the grand gesture, eh?'

He sat back and placed his hands on his lap. 'Tell me more about this wondrous cottage.'

Paula thought about the cottage. The notebook she'd torn up.

And asked, 'Where's the parish computer?'

32

Cara loved this feeling. Strength in her thighs, breath light in her lungs, her cushioned feet drumming on concrete. She felt at this pace she could run forever. Or until her feet bled, whichever came first.

The music that came through the pods tucked in to her ears changed to 'Love is a Losing Game'. *Sorry, Amy*, she thought, *this ain't running music*. Reaching across with her right hand, she flicked at the screen of her iPod, which was strapped to her upper left arm.

A van drove by. The driver beeped his horn and the passenger shouted something out of the window. Wind whipped his laughter past her, truncated it to a burst of noise. She made the universal sign for wanker and dismissed the incident as unworthy of any more of her attention.

She was on the Great Western Road. A crossing was drawing near. She looked around and judged her pace to see if she could get to the other side without adjusting. There were too many cars, so she slowed, dodging an old woman and her tartan shopping trolley. Then she swerved to miss a bald man and his yellow Lab, its tail high.

A car slowed as if keeping pace with her. A long, dark-blue Ford. Mondeo? She turned to the side to see who it was, but all she could make out was the lower half of a male face. Wait. Could that be?

No. She was imagining things.

The car sped up and moved on. She shot him the finger. For a second she had thought it might have been the guy who had been in the back of Farrell's car. She gave herself a mental shake. She hadn't seen enough of him on either occasion to make a solid judgement.

She came to the crossing, thought about stopping to stretch out the niggle in her left calf, but ran on the spot instead. She only had a couple of hundred yards till she reached the entrance to her flat, so she might as well wait. Keep her heart and lungs working till the very last moment.

Minutes later, she was almost home, approaching the shop where she was going to buy her breakfast – today was cheat day, so she could eat whatever she wanted. Then, up ahead, leaning against the wall ten yards before the secure entrance to her flat she saw a tall, lean, hooded figure, a small wiry dog on a leash at his feet. She slowed to a walk as she neared him and bent her head forwards as she tried to see his face.

'Danny?' she asked. Her brother Sean's friend. 'What the hell are you doing here? How did you know…?'

'You want me to speak to Tosh Gadd's missus, aye?' His features were sharp under the hood – hollowed cheeks under cheekbones like blades. She caught the sight of his crumbling yellowed teeth as he spoke.

'Yeah,' she said with a small thrill of achievement. 'How we going to make that happen? I can never get a hold of you.'

He gave a small shake of the head in acknowledgement and looked beyond her as if checking out the cars that were parked along the road. Satisfied that whatever he was looking for wasn't there, he turned back to her.

'In the next couple of days. Has to be, cos then I'm out of here. Got some money coming to me, you know? Get word to my ma. Time and place. City centre, aye?'

'You okay, Danny?' she asked and then turned to track the movement of his head, to see what he was looking for. Then she looked down at the small dog, whose limpid eyes were fixed adoringly on her owner. Cara got down on one knee, unable to resist saying hello to the small creature.

'Cara meet Sandy,' said Danny with a note of pride in his voice.

The little dog wagged her tail and closed her eyes a little as she enjoyed Cara's touch. 'She'd talk to Old Nick this wan. Totally useless as a guard dog, ken? Loves everybody.'

Cara got back to her feet and looked into Danny's face, searching for a trace of the small boy who was never more than a shadow's length away from her brother. She found little of him. What a waste of human potential. Danny wasn't a bad lad. He'd made the wrong choices – from the very limited menu that were handed to people from their class. His decisions had all but ruined him.

Whatever this deal he had going on she really hoped it worked out for him. And then he could get to know his child, and learn how to become a good dad.

'You sure you're alright, Danny?' she asked.

'Aye. Golden, darling. I'm golden.' He looked into her eyes and she saw a haunted man. A hunted man. The light in his eyes indistinct with need.

'When was the last time you ate, Danny?' She heard him in her mind saying that he had money coming to him and read it as the lie it surely was. An addict's attempt to pretend that everything was on the turn for the better.

'Disnae matter, Cara. Just arrange it, will ye?'

She fished in the small pouch just inside the hip of her running tights and pulled out the tenner that was going to pay for her cheat-day food. She pressed it into his hand. 'Here, away and get something warm in you, eh?'

A look of shame, warring with gratitude and relief, was her thanks. Then he looked over to his right and saw something he didn't like. 'Got to go.' And head low, hands in his pockets, he rushed away from her.

Cara was tempted to follow him. Instead she looked up and down the street at the parked cars. What had spooked him? A blue Mondeo sat three cars up from where she was standing. Could that be the same car?

She moved towards it, but the indicator light flashed and before she could reach him the car took off.

33

Paula was sat at a small Formica-clad table tucked into a small recess of the main corridor that led to the staircase and the priests' sleeping quarters. Perched on the table was a small laptop, which was dwarfed by a boxy, black printer that squatted beside it.

Paula sat down and ran a finger along the top of the printer.

'You need a new cleaner,' she said.

'Our Martha's a gem so she is, but she won't come near this desk. She thinks computers are the work of Satan and just touching it will be enough to pull her down into the depths of hell.'

'Bless,' said Paula and switched the laptop on. 'I'll just check your browsing history to see if you are indeed under threat of that very thing.'

'Are you going to explain what you're up to?' asked Joe at her shoulder. An image appeared and Joe said. 'You'll need my password, or you won't get past that screen thingy.'

The screen thingy was an image of a brass smiling Buddha, with a lined-off blank rectangle across his capacious stomach where the password went. Paula placed the cursor inside the rectangle and shifted to the side so that Joe could type it in.

'Very Catholic,' Paula said nodding at the image.

'We like to be inclusive here at St Matthew's.' Then, 'Don't you watch me,' he said as he slowly pressed on a series of keys with the index finger of his right hand.

'Is that how you type?' Paula asked.

'What's wrong with my typing technique, Mrs Gadd?'

'Don't you do the Parish newsletter?'

'Indeed I do construct that wondrous message of hope and

enlightenment.' Joe had finished typing, so he pressed enter.

'Must take you all week,' Paula said as the screen came to life. She brought up the internet search engine. 'How good is your connection?'

'Connection?'

'You do have the internet?'

'Course we do. We're not living in the dark ages.' Joe rested a hand on Paula's shoulder.

'But you're living in mortal peril for your soul according to Martha.'

'I make a quick act of contrition every time I switch this machine on.'

Paula laughed, felt a surge off love, reached across and patted Joe's hand. Without looking she knew he was smiling. No words were needed. They both understood. Affection given and gratefully received.

'A series of numbers...' Paula typed. 'That I found in a notebook in the Bute cottage.' She finished. Waited for a response and was given a new screen branded with a high street bank. She paused to consider what her next step should be. 'A notebook that I destroyed after reading and memorising a chain of numbers...' She explained as she typed. This was just like her own home banking screen. Just a different bank. And entering it all was surprisingly easy.

A new screen appeared, asking for the first, third, fourth and sixth number of a security number – and the third, fifth, sixth and tenth letter of a password. She faltered. Should she be doing this? Did she want to find what might be here? Whatever it was might have led to the deaths of two people already. She felt a flutter of nerves in her stomach and took a deep breath. Whatever was going on she needed answers. She couldn't stop now.

Certain that this was part of a trail of clues that Thomas had left for her, the answer to the required parts of the security number, and the password were, she hoped, going to be straightforward. She made a leap of intuition and, using her fingers, she worked out the numbers that corresponded with Christopher's date of birth and then entered them for the security number. Then she did the same with his Christian name, typing in R ... S ... T ... E for the password.

The computer screen froze, a small circle turning in the middle, showing her that her request was being processed. She held her breath. The screen changed...

And they were in.

'Oh my God,' she said. That was almost too easy. She sent a silent thank-you heavenward to Thomas.

Joe leaned over her, his head moving nearer the screen and she could feel the heat from him on the skin of her cheek.

'Is that what I think it is?' he asked. Joe slammed down the lid of the laptop as if the detail on the screen had just burned his eyes. 'What in the good Lord's name is going on, Paula?'

'I ... I...'

'Don't tell me you don't know.'

'I don't,' she said. 'I honestly don't.'

'And how did you work out where you needed to go just from a series of numbers?'

'The numbers were written in a pattern. A series of six numbers followed by another eight. Just like the series printed on the bottom of each of my cheques.'

Joe turned and walked away. Paula reached behind the laptop, dislodged the cables, lifted the machine up, slung it under her arm and followed him.

They ended up back in the kitchen. Paula sat the laptop on the table between them. At which Joe made a small note of surprise.

'It's portable, Joe. That's why it's called a laptop.'

'Pfft. I knew that.'

He clearly hadn't even considered it.

Paula lifted the lid and the screen they'd been studying reasserted itself. It was a statement page from a major British high street bank. It showed one deposit of one million pounds paid in two years earlier. One withdrawal of one hundred thousand pounds a week before Thomas died and another for the remaining balance the day after he died.

'What are we looking at?' Joe asked, worry etched into his face. There was something else there. Something beyond the worry of Thomas and why he had a notebook that led to this bank account. He bit his lip, and Paula thought he wasn't quite ready to spill.

'That,' she said and held a finger over the top of the screen. 'What does that mean to you?'

Joe read. 'Ballogie Holdings.'

'Quite a distinctive name, eh?'

Joe looked at her and nodded. 'We grew up in a flat on King's Park Road. At the corner of Ballogie Street.' He looked completely baffled. 'Why would you have the numbers to an account in your head, an account that bears the name of a street near where I grew up?' Then his face changed as a thought occurred.

'What do you know, Joe?' Paula asked quietly.

He rubbed the skin under his nose with the length of his index finger.

'Joe?'

'I really don't know what this is all about, Paula. That was one million pounds in there. Why would Tommy have access to that sort of money?'

'There's nine other accounts. If they are all the same, that means ten million.' She heard a tremble in her voice. 'We need to go to the police,' Paula said.

'No,' shouted Joe, and closed the laptop lid again.

'Joe, I think people have been murdered because of this. There's a very serious amount of cash in here. What do you know? If you don't spill I'm leaving here and going straight to Stewart Street.'

He crossed his arms and legs and swivelled in his seat so that his knees were pointing away from her.

'Joe?'

'I can't.'

'Joe. You said to me earlier about your gambling...'

'I can't, Paula.' He looked at her with desperation.

'Let's go back to that conversation.' She leaned towards him. 'You got in too deep with gambling debts...'

'And Tommy said if he did a favour for some people they could make it go...' He put both hands on the table. 'Except...' He pointed at the laptop. 'You think Kevin and Elaine died because of all of this?'

'It's too much of a coincidence to be otherwise.'

Joe rubbed at his face, enough that Paula heard the rasp of skin over bristles. 'Dear God, what have I done?'

'You haven't done anything, Joe.' She thought about the possible sequence of events: Joe got into debt, and somehow Thomas, with his business acumen and knowledge of the financial world was brought into the picture to sort it out. There was a lot of money involved here. Could Thomas have been their target all along? Might Joe have been singled out, then manipulated to give them, whoever they were, access to Thomas? 'It looks like other people took advantage of something...'

'But if it wasn't for me...' His eyes were bright, begging. *Help me*, they were saying. *Help me make sense of this.*

He leaned back in his chair. Now he couldn't look her in the eyes. 'Who knows better than me that confession is good for the soul, eh?' He titled his head back and looked upwards as if looking for divine intervention.

Then he looked her in the eye as if permission had been granted.

'As I said the debts got crazy, and this guy turned up. Sat in that chair where you are now.' His eyes darted around the room as if the exact words he needed were eluding him. 'Said I was to call him Moscow, cos that's near where he came from.' He took a deep breath as if to acknowledge his own naivety. 'And I'm thinking, *I'm a priest. He's not going to do anything dodgy to me is he?* He said he knew I had family that could help me get rid of the debt. I got angry at that. No way did I want the guys involved. Then he explained that if Tommy provided them with a certain service, the fee for this service would equal the amount of my debt.' His eyes filled up. 'To my shame, I weakened. Called Tommy. He came round. Quickly caught on...' Joe's eyes clouded now as he looked into the distance, as if he could see and hear Tommy sitting right there in front of him. 'And between them they came up with a plan to clear it completely.'

'Just how much did you owe?'

'I don't really know,' he shrugged. 'The guys I owed would add interest and then I would go double or quits and then they would add more interest.' He closed his eyes. 'It came to hundreds...' he paused, '...of thousands.'

'Holy shit, Joe.'

'Believe me, before they started to add all that interest stuff my debt was in the low thousands. It just escalated so quickly. It was bewildering.'

'So, this plan. What was it?'

'I didn't really follow it. Tommy and, latterly Kevin, were the key parts of it.'

'Kevin?'

'Well, Tommy's business really. The idea was – I'm grasping here you understand? – The idea was that, for a certain length of time, a legitimate business held the cash – God knows where it came from – out of the reach of the authorities. And then it would be moved on.'

Paula sat with that. Then she recalled the news bulletin she'd heard the day that the two police officers came to visit her. Something about a money-laundering scheme that took advantage of the Scottish financial system.

'As I said earlier, Joe you weren't to blame for any of this,' she sought to soothe his conscience as her mind worked through the implications.

'I wasn't?'

'These people were aware of an anomaly in the Scottish system that allowed money to be moved completely legally, right?'

'Right...' Joe scratched his chin.

'And they needed someone with the legitimacy to make it work. And the acumen to know how to work it.' Paula paused to allow Joe to catch up. 'Understand?'

'I'm not thick, Paula. Just...' his smile was self-deprecating '...stupid.'

'I don't completely understand the machinations of the way the movement of the money works – you'd need a degree in accountancy to follow that – but I can see that, somehow, when your debt was sold on to the wrong people they identified you and were able to link you with Thomas.'

'Successful businessman and oh so very legitimate here in Scotland,' said Joe as his eyes lit up with understanding.'

'Yeah. You build up debt in the casino? The wrong people get to hear about it and buy it off them. You then owe them the money and they charge astronomical interest. They fabricated the extent of your debt to get to the real target.'

'Thomas?'

'They would have accepted anyone in his position, I'm sure. As I said, they needed a successful businessman to make their scheme work.' She sifted through her memory to see if she could recall any of the details about the news item she'd seen. 'Shell companies...' she said out loud. 'Wait a moment. There must be something about it online.' Paula gave herself time to recall some more detail. 'Could this be something similar to that? It would be too much of a coincidence if it wasn't. Give me a second. I was distracted when the news was on or I'd remember it better. Shell companies. Something about shell companies, whatever they are.'

'Right.'

Paula turned her attention back to the computer. Brought up a search engine and typed *shell companies ... money laundering ... Scotland.* The search engine presented a number of choices and she clicked on the first one. It was from a major Scottish newspaper and it told her she had access to four articles before she needed to register. She clicked on the more likely article and read. 'These shell companies were registered in Scotland and some fake loans were used to take about one billion dollars from the Moldovan Government.'

'What?'

'Yeah, here we go.' She pointed at the screen and read out loud. 'It talks about straw men directors – whatever that is – who own offshore companies. And as I said there's something about the Scottish system that allowed this to happen.' She shook her head. 'Most of it is beyond me to be honest.' She leaned forwards. 'Do you think this Moscow guy ... is Moldova near Moscow? Anyway, this is it. I'm sure of it. Your Moscow guy was doing something very similar with Thomas.'

Joe just looked at her wide-eyed with shame and guilt.

'I'm certain of it.' Paula said. Then she lifted the lid of the laptop and slowly and methodically worked through each of the string of numbers and passwords in her head. In all of them the same pattern was repeated. A one million deposit was made. One hundred thousand was withdrawn, and then the day after Thomas died the remainder was removed.

'Wow,' said Joe. 'You were storing all that in your head?'

'For some reason I thought that was safer than walking about with that notebook.'

'Impressive work, Mrs Gadd.'

Paula shrugged. 'Fat lot of good it does us. There's nothing left in any of those accounts.' She tapped the screen with a fingernail. 'But somewhere in that short string of transactions is a reason to commit double murder.'

34

Paula was in her car outside Bill and Daphne's flat – a little further up the street where she'd found a parking space. It was a typical Glasgow sandstone tenement building: large windows, golden-brown sandstone cladding, and one door that gave onto the communal 'close' or passageway, which then led to the landings, each with two flats.

This was just a few streets away from the boys' modest start in King's Park Road – and it was every bit as modest.

Paula felt a churn in her gut.

She hadn't spoken to Bill since the incident a few nights before. Had he told Daphne? She had to get past that. This needed to be done: she had to find out what Ballogie Holdings meant to him.

A man was standing at Bill and Daphne's entrance. Bald, black suit, shoulders almost as wide as the doorway, he looked like he should be standing outside a nightclub. The door opened. Another man came out. Slim, with floppy hair and designer stubble, he was wearing a leather jacket that could have come from Milan. He walked past bouncer guy as if he didn't exist, but he got into step behind the slim man and followed him up the short path, along the street and into a black SUV.

Paula climbed out of her car and walked up the street, her heels clacking on the pavement, like a drumbeat accompanying her discomfort. Reaching the entrance, she noted that the security system had been updated since she'd last visited. Was there a crime spree in this part of the city she wasn't aware of?

Bill and Daphne were on the first floor. The panel of buttons didn't have names only numbers. 1B. That was the button she needed. She paused; finger inches from the buzzer, stomach churning at the thought of the conversation she was about to instigate. Steeling herself, she pushed down. She had to face poor Daphne sooner or later.

Just as she reached out to press the button the door opened. A young man in a black denim jacket stepped outside.

'Sorry, missus,' he said and held the door open for her. Then he paused when he looked into her face, recognition clear in his eyes. He stepped back and out of the doorway, onto the path.

Paula was back in that restaurant watching Thomas shouting at a waiter; a young man – *this* young man.

'You knew my husband,' she said, moving forwards, bristling, an accusation in her tone. 'How?'

The young man took a step back from her. 'Just met him the once, missus.' He rubbed at the back of his head. 'Was asked to tell him something.'

'He was furious,' said Paula, intent now on getting the truth. 'Who are you? What did you tell him?'

'Jesus, I can't remember what I had for breakfast and you expect me to remember that?' He turned from her with a forced smile and walked away.

'Hey,' she shouted after him.

'Got to go, missus.' He gave her a wave and jogged to a small red Ford.

This was too odd, she thought. What was he...?

A door banged shut somewhere higher up in the building. The noise drew her from her thoughts and another, more pressing issue pushed itself into the forefront of her mind. The reason she was here: Bill and Ballogie Holdings. And Daphne. She had to try and find out if she knew anything of what happened the other night.

Walking to the back of the hallway, towards the staircase, she couldn't help but notice how clean the area was. Glasgow women had always taken pride in making sure their close was spick and span, she thought. Some things didn't change.

The stairs were clean too, and Bill and Daphne's doorway was pristine. Solid wood stained dark brown. On the frame at about shoulder height was the doorbell. A white button, sticking out from a brass ring that, just like the letterbox in the middle of the door, was almost bright enough to contain its own sun. To the side sat a little table with gold feet bearing a basket-weave plant pot with a large-leafed plant thriving inside it.

As she pressed the doorbell Paula considered the last time she was here. It was just after Christopher died. Until then they'd been regular visitors, but then the business took over and Thomas had much less time for socialising. And whatever family time they did have, was spent at their place. Thomas liked to show off his big posh house.

With the thought that she could have done better as a sister-in-law, Paula stepped back from the door as she heard a heavy footstep approaching it from inside.

The door opened and Daphne stood there wearing a black long-sleeved top bearing a large, gold-coloured Calvin Klein symbol, grey sweatpants and, if she wasn't mistaken, slippers with a heel.

'Paula?' she said with evident surprise. She smoothed down her hair and then the front of her top with a sub-conscious movement.

'Hi,' she said. 'I was...'

Daphne stood there. Hand on the door as if barring entrance.

'Mind if I come in?' Paula asked examining Daphne's face, to see if she could read any knowledge of her and Bill's infidelity there.

'Sorry. Of course, Paula. You just took me by surprise.'

Paula stepped inside and they hugged – but with as little contact as possible.

'C'mon through into the living room,' Daphne said as she moved out of the way. 'But I haven't had a chance to get my cleaning done the day...'

Paula walked along the short hallway and into the living room. She took a seat on what looked like a fairly new leather, cream sofa, which was eerily similar to her own.

Daphne came in, looked down at her as she sat. 'Give me a minute and I'll put the kettle on.' She turned and walked away. As she did so she shouted back over her shoulder. 'Bill's not in. You're lucky you got me, I was just about to go out as well.'

'Don't let me keep you then,' Paula shouted back as she got to her feet. That was a relief. It gave her an excuse to cut short this awkward encounter. Then it occurred to her that the 'about to go out as well' line was probably a white lie – Daphne was keen to keep the visit short too.

'Oh, I never pass on the excuse to have a wee cuppa,' Daphne called. 'Give me a minute.'

Paula sat on the edge of the sofa, knees tight together, and looked around the room. Despite Daphne's protests it was spotless. It was also frighteningly similar to her lounge. The large floor space had been stripped down to the boards, which had been sanded down, stained a light tan and then covered with an antique rug with the same red-and-gold pattern hers had. The walls were covered in the same white-flecked paper. The windows were framed in the same deep-red curtains, and very similar red knick-knacks – like the red photo frame – dotted the space to bring that colour into the rest of the room. The same fireplace and mirror.

The only difference was the gigantic TV in the corner.

What the hell was going on here? Should she be flattered that Daphne had mimicked her taste? No, definitely not. This was wrong. She shivered and crossed her arms against the sudden chill. Who did this? Did Bill and Daphne assume she'd never see it all?

Her eyes returned to the red photo frame and her heart gave a little lurch when she saw that Christopher was in it. He was wearing his graduation robes. She got to her feet, crossed the room and had a closer look. Without thought, she reached out and touched the glass covering his face. She sagged a little. Then gathered her strength, taking warmth from the large smile on his face.

He was standing between Bill and Daphne. Bill's arm was over his shoulder and Daphne was holding his hand. In the background the famous hall of arches and pillars in Glasgow University.

Daphne arrived with a small tray bearing two china mugs and a small jug of milk.

'We love that photo,' Daphne said. 'Bill took it really bad when Chris died. Really bad.'

Paula returned to where she had just been sitting.

Daphne put the tray down. 'Just milk, right?' she asked.

Paula nodded, not quite trusting herself to speak yet. She watched the other woman as she poured the drinks. Was she now wearing lipstick? Had she taken the chance to put a bit on while waiting for the kettle to boil?

'This is nice,' Daphne said. 'I didn't expect you.' She took her mug and sat on the armchair opposite, moving a cushion out of the way as she sat.

Both women sipped at their drinks. They talked about the weather. Paula said how nice the coffee was, and Daphne told her it came in one of these wee tins that say it's just like a real espresso, but it isn't.

Paula thought about Daphne's obvious fondness for Christopher's photo, and the talk they'd never really had: why she and Bill had never had kids. Thomas had told her the reason years ago – they'd been tested and found the problem was with Bill. His swimmers were a bit on the lazy side. *Practically catatonic*, Thomas had said. Bill had taken it hard apparently. A blow to his manhood.

Paula had wanted Thomas to tell him that any idiot could pump out active sperm. That it had nothing to do with being a man, or a father. As far as she could remember Thomas tried to say just that, but ended up getting them both drunk in The Pot Still.

She wondered if Daphne knew that she knew.

As these thoughts worked their way through her mind both women were sitting staring at their cups in silence.

Where were all her words when she needed them? What had she been thinking coming over here? She should have called ahead. She had thought: Sunday afternoon – Bill was bound to be in. She picked up her cup and had a sip. Should she mention Ballogie Holdings and ask if it meant anything to Daphne? Paula dismissed that as quickly as the notion rose in her mind. If she asked her, she'd have to tell her everything else.

'Well,' Paula began at last, 'I was just feeling out of sorts. Needed some company, you know?'

'I know, hen,' Daphne said, her expression imparting sympathy. 'Can't be easy.'

'And that time we spoke, I wasn't too nice to you, so I wanted to say sorry.'

Daphne gave a little nod. 'That's fine, honey. You were at your husband's wake, so high feelings can be excused. And I wasn't too nice myself.' At this a genuine look of contrition appeared on her face. 'So ... pals?'

'Pals,' Paula agreed. She took another drink. Looked around the room. 'I like what you've done with the place. Looks great.'

Daphne's gaze travelled the room, as if congratulating herself. 'You don't think it's too similar to yours? Bill thinks it's too similar to yours.'

'Not at all.' Paula dismissed her faux concern. 'I can see where you took your theme from...' She tried to hide how much all of this disturbed her. '...But you've done your own thing.' She laughed. 'You've made it your own.' She tried to make her smile as genuine as possible, but felt it ache a little at the edges. 'It's lovely. Must have cost a pretty penny.' And if she *had* gone to the same stores she had, it would have cost a lot of money.

'Good taste isn't cheap,' Daphne answered. 'As you well know. Bill had one of them endowment policies pay up. It did surprisingly well, so we splashed out.'

'Really? Endowment policies work? That's great,' Paula said, trying to cover up her surprise. Whenever Bill spoke about money in the past it was to eschew any prudent behaviour in favour of spending-now.

'There must be some life assurance coming your way. Have you checked out all Tommy's policies?' Daphne's eyes glinted. Paula thought she saw greed there, and envy.

Paula considered the documents Thomas kept in the filing cabinet at home. There would indeed be a handsome sum of money coming her way. Thomas had taken out joint first-death insurance to cover the mortgage. And way back when he was a struggling businessman, while

Christopher was still alive, there was one for a quarter of a million. She'd argued this was a crazy amount of money, but the salesman had been persuasive, talking about a multiple of earnings and asking how she and Christopher would manage if Thomas died.

For all she cared, the insurance policy could lie in that cabinet, unclaimed. She had no interest in cashing in on her husband's death. For all she cared she could cash it in and hand the proceeds to Bill and Daphne. Why shouldn't they be compensated for Thomas's death?

'How's Bill?' Paula asked.

Daphne crossed her legs and shifted on her chair. She looked at the floor at Paula's feet, then her eyes raised to her face. And in that moment there was a strange light in her eyes, enough that Paula was certain she knew, but then it was gone and Daphne gave a sigh.

'He's taken it hard, poor lamb. Really chewed up over it, you know? But don't you worry about Bill. I'll look after him just fine.'

Paula's stomach gave a twist at that. One second it was like Daphne knew, the next, she was blissfully ignorant. For all she'd been in this woman's company countless times, she struggled to follow her thoughts.

'I meant what I said at the hotel after Thomas's funeral, Daphne. I'd like it if we were better friends. Being among all these Gadd men isn't the easiest.'

'It's had its compensations.' Daphne's smile was faint in reply. And Paula wondered who this woman she'd known for years really was. Her personality had always been dwarfed by Bill's. Was she really happy to stand quietly in his shadow?

Paula drained her cup and stood to leave. Making her excuses, Paula had one last look at Christopher in that photograph. At the shine of his skin. The bright-eyed anticipation that life had only good in store for him. And it occurred to her with a pang that, standing there, framed by his Uncle Bill and Aunt Daphne, a stranger might look at the image and assume he was their son.

35

Just as Paula left Daphne's and was about to climb into her car, her phone sounded an alert from her handbag. It was a text from Cara:

Danny, Sean's mate, is willing to talk to you this afternoon. Before he disappears for a bit. He's got a pitch just off Buchanan St.

Then another.

Meet me at TGI Friday's corner. Buchanan St. 2pm.

Why would he need to disappear, she wondered? And what did Cara mean by a pitch?

She looked at her watch. It was just gone noon. She could go into town and perhaps force some food down before she was due for the meeting. There was no food at home, and although eating felt like the last thing she wanted to do, she knew she physically wouldn't last much longer without some nourishment inside her.

♦

Bang on two p.m., Paula was at the junction of Buchanan Street and Gordon Street, outside the burger bar. She cast a look inside, remembering some fun nights out when the place first opened. Thomas's tastes had become more cultured as the money flooded in, but he still enjoyed a burger now and again.

Just around the corner, on the Buchanan Street side of the junction, a young man with a beard halfway down his chest was strumming on his guitar.

The streets were crowded. Her ears filled with the noise of footsteps and the buzz of chatter. To her right someone's mobile phone rang out.

Looking straight ahead, Paula studied the old bank building.

When she had first come down this street as a teenager, pocket money burning a hole in her purse, it had been a rather impressive bank. Then a bookshop took it over and she'd spent many happy Saturday afternoons in there browsing books and drinking coffee. Now it was a nondescript clothing store.

Footsteps.

'Worst thing that happened to this city, when that bookshop closed down.'

It was Cara. She was in her usual black jeans and black jacket and she was wearing a little more make-up than normal. Paula smiled at the sight of her.

'Danny? Where is he?' she looked along Buchanan Street. 'Isn't this place a bit busy? What kind of pitch does Danny have? Are people allowed to just sell stuff down here?'

Cara rolled her eyes. 'He's homeless. His pitch is where he sits begging.'

'Right.' Paula gave herself a mental ticking off. Could she be any more middle class?

'First we go into Starbucks across the road and buy him a coffee and a sandwich. The poor guy is probably starving. And when I say we, I mean you.'

Cara started walking, seeming to expect Paula to follow. Starbucks was down the side of the old bank building, just at the archway that led through to Royal Exchange Square and the back of the Gallery of Modern Art.

Paula went inside while Cara stood at the door. When her turn in the queue came she ordered a black coffee and picked out a ham sandwich, and a couple of doughnuts Danny might keep for later. Then she spotted some chocolate. She could get him that as well.

Now that she was preparing to feed the young man she wanted to make sure he was looked after. If Christopher had grown up and ended up on the street, God forbid, she wanted to think another parent would come along and offer some care, even if it was only a full belly for the day.

She was aware the serving girl was staring at her. Her mouth opened. She was saying something.

Money. That was it. She wanted money.

'You awright, missus?' the girl asked.

Paula felt her cheek was wet. Without having to articulate the thought to do so, she wiped at it with her sleeve, then rummaged in her bag for her purse. She considered buying more food, to keep the guy stocked up for a few more days, while part of her mind registered that she'd been crying without even realising. Discounting the need to buy more food – she was worried she might somehow be overdoing it – she paid, dropped her purse back into her bag and picked up the cup and and the food that the young woman had placed in a brown paper bag.

When she came out carrying Danny's meal, she saw that Cara was in conversation with a *Big Issue* seller. Paula saw how thin he was and wanted to give him all the food she had on her and start again.

'I've just been asking Stu here if he knows Danny,' Cara said.

'Aye, missus. Danny sometimes sits on the stairs just round there.'

Paula gave him a smile. 'Hi, Stu,' she said, but was unsure what to say next. And she realised with a rush of guilt that she'd never spoken properly to a homeless person before, other than to say hello and hand over some cash. It shamed her to admit it, but she always felt so embarrassed that she had so much and they had so little, some money and a brief, mumbled greeting was all she could cope with. She'd made every encounter about her own discomfort.

'What's your story, son?' she asked, wondering if she was now overcompensating.

'Ach, you know,' Stu gave a small self-deprecating smile. 'Wife and I fell out. She got the house. I had nowhere to go...' He tailed off.

Paula handed him the bags with the doughnuts, knowing that as gestures go it was pathetic. 'There you go,' she said.

Cara took her arm and pulled her away, mumbling, 'I didn't ask you to feed everybody. Just Danny.' Then she looked at her. 'You been crying?'

Paula shrugged. 'Just happens sometimes. I'm barely aware of it.'

Cara considered that. Then her mouth slumped in sympathy. 'It'll get better,' she said. 'Meantime, we've a mouth to feed.' She started walking again, expecting Paula to follow.

They turned the corner and arrived at the steps. They were wide, and old enough that their edges were rounded with the passage of time and countless footsteps. Looking along the steps and studying the handfuls of people sitting there, Paula noted that everyone there looked way too healthy and clean to be homeless. Some were clearly local workers enjoying time away from their office or shop, eating lunch in the crisp winter air. A conversation to her right became clear as she stepped nearer.

'I was like, eh? And she was all, nut, not happenin' and I was like aye, totally is, babes.' It sounded like an utterly random collection of syllables but the speaker had her friends' complete attention. The art of conversation hasn't died, thought Paula, it's just become abridged.

'Can you see him?' Paula asked wishing she'd got another cardboard sleeve around the cup as her hand was about to get scalded. She swapped hands.

'Nope,' Cara said as she scanned the stairs. 'Let's try over here.' She walked beyond the stairs to the corner of the square. A couple of shops were tucked away there. One had what looked like an unused entrance and from her vantage point Paula could see a pair of booted feet sticking out, with a small dog sitting between them.

They approached the doorway and Paula saw a hooded figure, seated in a slouch under the cushion of a dark-green sleeping bag, head to the side as if in slumber.

'Hey, Danny,' said Cara as she approached. 'We've brought you some scran.'

The man didn't react.

Cara crouched down and held a hand in front of the dog's nose, allowing it to lick her fingers. 'Hey, lovely,' she said in a soothing voice. Then she returned her attention to her owner.

'Dan,' Cara prompted again as she reached him, this time nudging his boot with her hand.

Nothing.

She leaned forwards, gently touching his shoulder. 'Danny, son, wake up. We've got some food for you.'

Paula struggled to make sense of what she was seeing. The young man was still. Too still. Her stomach felt heavy with dread. A stillness surrounded the young man like an invisible shroud. There was something wrong here. Very wrong. Sounds fell away all around her. All she could hear was the thump of her own pulse in her neck.

Please, no, she thought.

Cara turned to Paula, confused. As if she was trying to compute what was in front of her. She got into a crouch, reached out tentatively and prodded the young man's shoulder again.

Nothing.

She held a hand to the side of his neck and her movement was enough to dislodge the quilt. The cushioned dark-green material slid off him in slow motion, as if reluctant to display what it had been covering.

Danny was wearing a football top. Red and yellow stripes. And there, above a pool of rich, dark-red blood in his lap, a knife handle stuck out from the centre of his chest.

36

Cara's eyes and nose felt raw from crying, but she gamely answered every question from the young policeman. As she answered them, Paula stayed by her side, holding her hand and stroking her arm. Cara knew this action was really an effort by Paula to calm her own shock, so didn't tell her to stop it.

Her first instinct was to disappear. She'd already thrust herself into the investigation of another violent death – albeit one that was recorded as a murder suicide. She now worried it wouldn't look good if she was present at another so soon after. But a split second after that thought struck, it was replaced with another: the CCTV cameras in the area would probably highlight her presence. Perhaps, even, if they were trained in the right direction at the right time, they could let the police know that she was the one who'd found him.

Poor Danny.

Then she was hit by a purely selfish thought: would she never get to know the full truth about Sean's death, now? She had needed Danny to tell Paula what he knew, for her to come clean on any knowledge she had about her husband's other life.

She couldn't close her eyes without seeing the sag of Danny's mouth and that knife sticking up from his chest. At first she half thought he was going to jump up and shout, *Gotcha*. And start laughing. Calling her an eejit for falling for it. When he was younger, Danny and Sean were always up to some kind of prank. She could see them as preteens: skint knees and smudged cheeks, egging each other on.

Last time she saw him just down from the entrance to her flat, he seemed jumpy. Did he know he was at risk? Should she tell the young cop this? And what about that blue car? Was that just an innocent driver or something more malicious?

She didn't have a good track record with the police, though; whatever she told them was dismissed. Back in Stewart Street police station, they didn't want to know. What did that detective Drain say? She had some imagination, or something. So, no way was she going to be believed. *Better to remain silent and appear dumb than to open your mouth and remove all doubt.* There was truth in that saying.

'Anything else?' the young cop asked her.

Cara looked at the acne scar on his cheek, the raised eyebrow, and wondered what he saw, what he was thinking, what he would tell his colleagues. In her imagination she heard him talking to them: *Aye, that Cara Connolly, daft bint.*

'Nothing,' she said. 'I know the family. Knew he was homeless, and my friend and I here just wanted to make sure he had some food for the day, you know?'

Paula gave a little sob, so she placed a hand over her shoulder and pulled her close.

'Can we go now? My friend here's had a terrible shock. We both have.'

The cop nodded. 'We have your details. The investigating team will be in touch just to go over things again.'

'What about the wee dog?' asked Cara.

'It's a cute wee thing, eh?' the cop said. 'Don't worry, we'll get it to a kennel or something.'

'Okay, officer. Happy to help in any way,' Paula murmured.

Cara pulled her away to the side, ready to make her escape. She mumbled, 'Don't appear too keen, eh?'

'That poor boy.' Paula was still holding the coffee and the sandwich. She looked at them and then up at Cara, as if she couldn't remember what food was for.

They retraced their steps. Cara saw that Stu was still there and indicated that Paula should hand him the food and drink.

'What was a' that aboot?' he asked as he accepted the sandwich.

'It's usually they dog-walkers that find dead bodies, innit? Not wee wifies bearing gifts.'

'Have you spoken to Danny recently?' Cara asked.

'You going all detective on me, doll?' Stu asked with a weak smile, displaying a mouthful of teeth that should have been condemned years ago. 'Terrible, eh? Danny was a good cunt. Wouldn't harm a fly but.' His attempted smile slid off his face as his expression lengthened and he coughed, as if bearing down on any emotion that might leak through.

'How well did you know him?' Paula asked. Cara heard the tremble in her tone and wondered if she sounded the same. There was too much death around her these days.

'Just enough to say hello, you know? We were ships passing through the shite of modern life.'

'Did you ever get past the hellos to something more meaningful?' she asked.

'Whit, like the weather?' Snort. 'He had bother with his pitch a few weeks back, right enough. Some other cunt tried to knuckle in on his space.' He lifted the sandwich out of the bag, held it up as if asking for permission, took a bite and continued talking as he chewed. 'A couple of the other guys stepped in. Huckled the guy.' A crumb of food flew out of his mouth and hit Cara on the cheek. She took a step back. 'Sorry, doll,' Stu said. 'This is just...' He took a look over to where the police had constructed a small white tent to hide the crime scene. 'Now that I remember it...' He took another bite. 'S'funny how a wee bit of nourishment helps the old brain cells, eh?'

Cara wanted to give him a 'get on with it' look, but softened it into a smile.

Stu indicated with a nod and a lift of his cheek that he understood her. 'Don't usually get such a willing audience when I'm out here, you know. Anyway. One of the guys that stepped in – Wee Gav? – said they took the guy up the alley back there and were about to give him a kicking...' He held a hand up when he saw the look of alarm on Paula's face. 'Nothing really damaging, you know. Just enough for a warning, doll. A few bruises an' that. But, they stopped when this guy claimed he was offered money to make life difficult for Danny.'

Cara stared at him hard now.

'People do that?' asked Paula, alarm evident on her face.

'This is the streets, darlin', Stu answered. 'Anything can happen.'

'Do you know this guy? Any idea where we could get a hold of him?' Cara asked.

'You are going all detective, aren't ye?' Stu asked, his eyebrows lifted as if he was impressed.

'You don't think this guy came back and knifed poor Danny in revenge do you?' Paula asked, looking at Cara and then Danny.

Cara considered this. Dismissed it. 'No, there's more to it than that, I'm sure of it.' She had another look over at the site of Danny's final rest. 'He's the one person that knows about our Sean and how he died. He was scared when I saw him the other day and that was more than the worry about someone stealing his pitch. I start pushing him for answers, finally get him to agree to speak to you – you know he wouldn't dream of it if your husband was still alive – and now, suddenly he's dead?'

She stared into Paula's face. She knew her accusation was hard: *You know something and you're not telling me.* Cara had allowed herself to be pulled in by this woman's performance as the grieving widow, but no longer. People were dying here.

'You sure you're not letting your imagination get away with you?' Paula asked, and there was a defensiveness there. As far as Cara could see she was still to face up to the fact that her husband had been up to no good.

'For God's sake, woman, open your eyes. Just about everywhere we go there's a trail of dead bodies. Is that all in my imagination, too?'

37

Paula turned away from Cara and walked towards Buchanan Street. She wasn't going to give that woman the satisfaction of a reaction. Over the percussion of her heels slamming on the pavement she said to herself, *I refuse to believe it. I can't believe it. I won't believe it.*

Thomas hadn't hurt anybody. Cara was mad. Totally mad. Obsessed. So caught up in this she couldn't consider anything else. Sure, Thomas had become involved in the money-laundering thing to help Joe out, but murder?

Short of someone showing her a movie of Thomas committing actual bodily harm, she was never going to believe it.

Paula reached the car park, made her way to her car, unlocked it and sat in the driver's seat.

And then she screamed, slamming down on the steering wheel with her hands. 'That crazy, stupid bitch!'

No more. That was it. Whatever happened to Cara's brother was none of Paula's business. If Cara wanted to keep digging into it, she was on her own.

Then a thought weaselled its way into her head. Was she so annoyed because she was worried there was an element of truth to all of this? If she was that certain Thomas was innocent, why was she feeling so threatened by what Cara was trying to find out?

She needed a drink. Wine, gin. Anything to get her out of her own head.

Her phone sounded an alert. She fished it from her bag and sighed. It was from Bill:

You went to see Daphne? What were you thinking? Can we talk?

She thought about replying and quickly discounted the idea.

Whatever came out of her in that moment would not be appropriate, and would surely only make matters worse.

Paula threw her phone back in her bag and started the engine. She needed to talk to someone to sort this in her own head at least, and the only person she could think of was Father Joe.

◆

When she knocked on the refectory door it was opened up by Father Declan. He was a young priest from a nearby parish, originally from Ireland, who sometimes helped out when the incumbent priests were sick or on holiday. He was so young, thought Paula, that he looked like he'd just come from some pressing machine where the very young and faithful were forced into a shape of piety.

'Father Joe about?' she asked.

'I'm afraid not,' Declan said in his Dublin lilt. 'He's disappeared. Jumped in his car and went off. We're still expecting a call from him to explain.'

'Disappeared? He never said...' Paula tailed off, feeling betrayed that Joe had gone off without saying a word to her. Then worry gnawed. This really wasn't like him.

'Yeah, the Bishop was none too happy. Last minute kinda thing, and not a word of warning.' Declan scratched his face. 'As far as we can see he didn't even pack a bag.'

Now Paula felt a surge of fear. 'Didn't pack a bag?'

'Well, his toothbrush is still there, but we haven't really checked his drawers to see what might be missing.' He blushed. 'Not that we would know...' he tailed off.

'Right,' she responded absently. This was wrong, she could feel it.

'Anything else I can do for you, Mrs Gadd?'

'If you hear...' She corrected herself. '*When* you hear from Joe, tell him to get in touch with me will you?' She turned and walked back down the path.

So focussed was she on her own thoughts, she almost bumped into someone.

'Paula?'

She heard a familiar voice and looked up from the ground. 'Bill. What are you doing here?' He was once again dressed in expensive-looking clothes: dark-grey turtleneck sweater, black trousers and a knee-length navy-blue wool coat.

'Probably the same as you,' he answered with a tight smile. He looked over her shoulder at the door she had just walked away from. 'Is he free?'

She shook her head. 'He's not there. Left without saying a thing to anybody.' She hoped wherever Joe was that he was okay. On top of everything else she now had him to worry about.

'Would have been nice if he'd let us know.'

Paula heard a mournful sound in that last sentence, as if Bill was heading to a dark place. She looked into his eyes and saw shadow there.

'You okay?' she asked and put a hand on his arm. He moved closer as if that was the signal he was looking for.

'The other night...' he began. 'I can't stop thinking about you.' His eyes were on hers. On her hair, her shoulders, then dropped to his feet. Then they moved through the whole sequence again.

Paula lifted her hand from his arm and pushed it into her coat pocket, giving a little shiver as if the cold was her excuse.

'Bill. That was a mistake. We agreed on the night – it never happened,' she said. He opened his mouth in an attempt to try to speak over her, but she wouldn't let him. Couldn't afford to. 'It never happened, Bill.' She enunciated each word. 'We were both in the wrong state of mind. We were drunk. Grief does strange things to a person. Besides...' She tried to soften her words with a smile. 'It's really not fair to do that to Daphne.'

'Daphne is...' He closed his mouth. Held the fingertips of his right hand before his mouth as if stopping himself from speaking his mind. 'I think I love you, Paula. I think I always have.' He moved closer. His eyes beseeching. As if he needed her to really hear what he was saying.

Paula took a step back, but was stopped from going much further by the low-hanging branches of a tree that stood at the head of the path to the priests' house.

'Bill, please,' she said and looked away. 'Please don't.'

'Sorry, Paula. I should have said something long before now.'

'What, instead of barely looking at me over the years? You were so distant at times, I was convinced you hated me.'

'I had to protect myself somehow. And Tommy, and Daphne. While you and he were happy I had to damp that stuff down.' He glanced at the church beyond. 'There were times it was torture. When Chris was killed ... I...'

'Please, Bill.'

'I could see how it affected you. And how you and Tommy almost drifted apart for a time.'

Paula crossed her arms and faced away from him. 'There only ever was Thomas,' she said. 'If Christopher's death put us under stress, there was never any doubt in my mind that we would find each other again.'

'What about the last year or so? I've got eyes, Paula. You guys were not in a good way.' He spoke louder than he intended, for he then apologised.

'Yeah, that's true, but we would have found a way through it. Eventually. That was who we were. We argued. We made up again.'

'He was a changed man since Chris died. Even I could see that.'

'And I never loved him any less.' Paula's feet were going numb with cold. She thought momentarily about saying goodbye and going back to her car, but decided not to. She had to be sure Bill understood the other night was a mistake, and would never be repeated. 'And besides, if you're having trouble with Daphne, don't use me as your rebound.'

'Trouble with Daphne,' he repeated. 'That's the story of my life right there.'

'Don't stay, then. Leave. One thing I've learned is that life's too short. I regret every moment I allowed petty arguments with Thomas to fester.'

'Petty arguments,' he echoed. Then laughed, the sound cruel and lifeless. 'If that was only what it was. We've done some bad...' Again, he held his fingers at his mouth. Stilled the words before they were released to sound. 'Something in that woman died when she had that miscarriage all those years ago.'

'Oh, my God,' Paula said. 'She had a miscarriage? When? Why didn't you tell us?' Then she remembered Thomas telling her about Bill's fertility issues. Jesus, life could be cruel. Their chance at a child was taken from them.

'Daphne didn't want anyone to know. Said she was ashamed.' His eyes were flat, the light in them dulled by visiting the memory.

'Good God, Bill. You can't live like that. That's what family are for – to listen, to talk with. To help the process of grieving.'

'Yeah, well.' He sighed as if there was a great weight in his lungs and nothing could shift it. He stepped closer and pulled her into a hug, holding her for longer than was comfortable, but, sensing the intensity of his need, she didn't have the heart to push away. 'Sorry,' he whispered in her ear, his breath a warm burden on her skin. 'Sorry.'

He stepped back, as if marshalling his thoughts, but he was still gripping her upper arms – a little too tightly for Paula's liking. He swallowed, looked down to the ground and back up, and in that moment he looked so like Thomas, Paula's heart gave a lurch.

'We could do this, Paula. I'll leave Daphne ... we'll run away...' He paused to watch as she shook her head, slowly and painfully.

'It wouldn't work, Bill.' His grip grew tighter. 'Let me go,' she said. Nothing happened. She said it again, this time raising her eyebrows and staring him down.

He released her and shoved his hands deep into his pockets. 'Fine,' he said, rejection turning the plea in his eyes to the cold, hard stare of anger. 'Let the cards fall where they will.'

Let the cards fall ... what on earth did that mean?

He turned round and began to walk back to his car. And as he did she remembered the other questions she had for him.

'You were with Thomas the day he died,' she called after him. 'I know you had lunch with him. Why did you never tell me?'

'I...' He turned and met her eyes briefly. Then looked away.

But then he seemed to square his shoulders. He turned back to face her. Paula could almost read his thought process. He had considered denying it, but the added detail about the lunch had made it impossible.

'Yes, we had lunch that day,' he said. 'My brother all but died in front of me.' His eyes clouded over, as if with the horror of being in that moment ... and with awareness of his own failings. As if no matter what their personal issues were, his little brother's heart stopped and he was powerless to save him. 'Talking about it isn't going to bring him back, though, is it?' With that he turned away once more and stomped towards his car.

'Bill,' she shouted. She wasn't done with him yet. She decided to change tack. 'Ballogie. Does that word mean anything to you?'

He stopped as if he'd walked into an invisible door, then slowly turned, his eyes burning into hers with an intensity that made her step back. 'It was a street just round the corner from where we grew up. Why?'

Something about the way he looked at her in that moment gave her pause. She decided not to mention the full name of the shell company. She would hold that piece of information back for now, or at least until she knew more. She groped in her mind for an answer that might satisfy him.

'I found a file in his desk. A flat for sale on that street ... Do you know if he was planning something?'

'Tommy wasn't prone to share his business dealings with me, Paula. You should know that.' The charming man of only a few minutes ago was completely gone, and in his place, a man whose disappointment, mingling with grief and anger was on the turn towards hate. Paula couldn't read whether that loathing was aimed at her or was being directed internally.

With one last look at her, he turned and walked away.

Paula felt a charge of worry. *Let the cards fall.* Was he going to do something stupid?

'Bill?' she shouted after him. 'Bill!'

But he was in his car and without looking at her, he started the car engine.

Paula moved back and away from his car as if distancing herself from the cloud that hung over him. Her own grief was more than she could bear, how could she possibly help him handle his? She felt something brush her ankle. Looked down at the ground and saw a pile of leaves had been swept there. Hundreds of them. Each leaf not that much larger than a fifty-pence piece. They had settled there underneath the tree like a drift of crisp and tiny amber hands, curled at the edges. Plaintive. Needy.

As Bill drove past her, she studied his face and considered the swift changes she'd seen in it these past few minutes; so much emotional movement in only a few thoughts – his apology, grief for Thomas, pleading for her to recognise they could have something together, then struggling with her rejection.

She followed his passage back down the street and couldn't help but worry he was going to do something that men do when the terror of dying no longer exceeds the pain of living.

38

Paula was still there a good ten minutes after Bill drove off. How can someone be lost while standing in the same position? she asked herself. What should she do? Who could she talk to? Thoughts whizzed through her mind like a crowd of angry wasps.

Should she have chased after Bill?

Did he know something about the shell companies after all? There was a definite reaction to her mention of Ballogie. And what on earth did he mean about the cards falling as they will?

There was something wrong there, but she recognised that as he spoke, her mind was drifting away from him, protecting her from him and his worries. She simply didn't have the emotional energy to take on his concerns as well as her own.

A cry sounded from the small copse across the road from the church. A large brown bird – a buzzard? – lifted from a branch with a sweep of its powerful wings. Then two small black shapes shot after it. Then a third. Crows. The three birds were each about two-thirds of the size of the raptor, but they crowded it, harassed it far into the sky as if pushing it away from their nests. Two of them then dropped their speed and wheeled off in an arc, but the third, smaller crow continued to harry the buzzard, swooping in from the rear as if picking at the larger bird's tail feathers.

Paula heard a shoe scuff at the pavement behind her.

'Are you okay, Mrs Gadd?' Father Declan leaned towards her, bending from the waist. 'Would you care to come in for a little heat and a warm drink?'

'Sorry, Father,' she replied. Feeling a moment's absurdity at giving this young man who could barely grow a beard such a title. 'I'm fine, thanks.' She looked into his eyes and wondered about unloading on him. And just as quickly she dismissed the notion. The poor man wouldn't be able to handle what she had to say. 'Very kind of you to offer, all the same.' She gave a little nod and walked off the path and towards her car. Aware that as she did, his eyes followed her, and she sensed how unsettled he was that he couldn't help her.

◊

Where was she going? she asked herself, as she drove along the Great Western Road. How had she even got here? She looked at the clock on the dashboard. That was half an hour she'd lost. Had she just been driving around? She must have just described a large circle. Hadn't she passed this road end already?

She adjusted her course and at the next junction turned right into Hyndlands Road. Further along she remembered it had been the route she'd taken the day she'd been mugged. The day Anton saved her.

His café came into view. Beans and Bites. She indicated and pulled in further down the road, where she spotted a space. He'd been the one person who had been any help in this whole situation. Perhaps she should go into the café, buy a coffee and lay off all her worries on him.

The only person apart from Joe, of course. She should phone or text him. Make sure he was alright. Talking to Bill, hearing his revelation, had pushed her concerns about Joe out of her mind. She retrieved her phone from her bag, found his number and pressed call. It dialled out and went to voicemail, so she cut the connection and sent him a text instead. He rarely listened to his voicemails. Texting was always the best way to get Joe's attention.

Here to talk if you need me. Let me know when you get home?

Then she pushed the door open and clambered out of the car. She crossed the road, but was so lost in thought she didn't judge her progress properly. A horn blared. Tyres squealed on the tarmac. She looked up to see a hot-faced woman, mouth open as she flung a torrent of abuse at her through the windscreen.

Paula ducked her head and jogged the rest of the way to the pavement, throwing a wave of apology over her shoulder at the woman she had forced to brake.

The shop she remembered Anton going into had a simple sign – which looked temporary – over the top quarter of the floor-to-ceiling plate-glass window. A small wooden table that looked unable to withstand a stiff breeze, with two matching chairs sat outside.

Inside, the space was just as simple. A handful of tables and chairs dotted around the room, the wooden slats of the chairs protected with some cushions in primary colours. The counter was a wide glass chiller cabinet, filled with two rows of cakes and pastries. Behind it, against the wall sat a massive Gaggia coffee machine.

Paula assessed the cakes as she remembered Anton's comments about having Polish specialties. There were croissants, apple Danish, cheesecake, a couple of tray-bakes and a large Victoria sponge. Nothing that looked particularly Polish, she thought.

Apart from an old man at one table, reading his newspaper, and a suited woman, a red coat draped over her chair, studying a mobile phone, the place was empty.

To the right of the counter there was a small doorway, presumably to the staff area. A hand pushed through a bead curtain, and then a small, chunky, bald man emerged. He was wearing a white long-sleeved shirt, a pair of black denims and a small black apron. It occurred to Paula that he looked more Indian than Polish.

'Can I help you, doll?' he asked, his accent pure Glasgow.

'Is Anton about?' she asked.

'Anton?' The waiter made a face. 'There's just me here, doll. My sister helps out now and again, but mostly...' he pointed at his chest. 'It's just me.'

'Anton, the owner? Big guy. Polish? He's a builder too. His name's...'

'Aye. Anton. You said that already.' He offered her a big smile to show he was only joking. 'Ain't nobody here but us chickens. Nae Anton the Pole. Just me. Amit, the wee Bengali guy from Shettleston.'

'So, this...' Mystified, Paula looked around. She stared out of the window down the street towards her car, as if the sight of it might add some concrete detail and place her firmly, for once, at the centre of her own life. 'He came over here ... saved me from ... got me a...' What the hell was going on? She felt dizzy.

'Here, missus,' Amit reached out, took Paula's arm and led her to a seat. 'You look like you're about to take a funny turn. Can I get you a wee glass of water?'

As politely as she could, Paula shrugged off his concern.

'Sorry, Amit. I'm not myself today. I've had some bad ... And I thought this was where Anton worked. I'll just get out of your hair...' She looked at the shine on his scalp. 'I better go.'

She walked out the door and along the street towards her car, her mind a whirl. It was on this street she'd been mugged. It was that café Anton claimed to own. She knew this city. She wasn't about to get confused over a street so easily, regardless of how grief was addling her brain. *That* was definitely the place he claimed was his.

Anton Rusnak, she thought, *who the hell are you?*

39

Cara was on the mat in the dojo, facing off against Dave Roberts. Her fringe was plastered to her forehead. She was breathing hard, but felt a reserve of strength in her thighs. With some satisfaction, she noted that Dave was in a similar state. At least she was making him graft. He answered her look with a grin.

'C'mon on then, hen. What you waitin' on?' He knew she hated it when people called her hen.

Grinning in return, she rolled her shoulders, stretched off a pain in her upper arm and adopted the stance necessary to receive his attack and deliver her counter. This was perfect. A good workout was just what she needed to try and sweat off some of her anguish and guilt at Danny's death. She couldn't shake off the feeling that she was somehow responsible – that if she hadn't pushed him into agreeing to talk to Paula Gadd he might well be alive right now.

And with his demise, her last hope of getting Paula to face up to the kind of man her husband had been was evaporating. Not that she expected it to achieve all that much. The police refused to listen. The case was long closed as far as they were concerned, but she had hoped at least to find some kind of acknowledgement of Sean's murder.

Dave slid in. His bare feet a sharp squeak on the mat. She quickly prepared for the attack. Read his movement. Countered. He overbalanced, fell and rolled back onto his feet in one fluid motion.

He faced her and bowed.

'Nice.' Grin. 'And now I need to hit the showers. Got the girls tonight. I've promised them a *Teenage Ninja Turtles* marathon.'

'Ha,' Cara laughed. 'Serves you right.'

'Hey. Don't diss the turtles. Better that than *My Little Pony*.'

They walked over to the changing area. Dave paused before he entered the men's locker room. 'You okay, Cara? I sensed a wee bit more anger in you tonight.'

Cara looked into Dave's eyes, surprised yet again at how well he could read her mood. She considered how much she could safely tell him.

'An old pal of our Sean's got killed the other day.'

A sharp breath came from Dave. 'Man, that's shit.' He put a hand on her shoulder. 'Did you know him well?'

'Not really.' She shrugged. 'But when he and Sean were kids they were inseparable, so I can't think of Danny without thinking of Sean.' She felt the high from her activity fade and her mood fall. 'Listen, you go on and get out of here.' She took a step back towards the gym. 'I'm going to get a good session in with a skipping rope.' That had always been Cara's reaction to stress. Exercise the feeling away.

Dave pushed the door that led to the gent's changing rooms open, but then turned to Cara, as if he'd just received a sudden insight.

'Don't overdo it, eh? The guy being killed is bound to bring back old emotions. You need to give them space, deal with them, not fight them off.'

Good advice, thought Cara, but no way was she going to follow it.

'Thank you for your wisdom, Sensei.' She bowed. 'Now piss off and see to your girls.'

Dave gave his warm boom of a laugh, pulled her to him and kissed her forehead. 'I hope when they grow up they listen to me more than you do.'

🔴

Sometime later, dripping with sweat, Cara made her way to the changing rooms and had a long soak in the shower. As the hot water cascaded over her head and shoulders, she thought about Danny. About Sean. Compared their guileless preteen grins with the haunted young men they'd become. A life of addiction stretching before them until both their chaotic lives were brought to a sharp and brutal end.

She slumped to the base of the shower, head on her knees, felt their pain as hers and gave in to her tears.

♦

Later still. Dressed, hair damp, she heard her phone ping an alert from her locker. She pulled it out and read a message from Danny's sister:

Mum's holding a vigil thing for Danny tonight at hers. Would b nice if u came. X

Cara sat on a bench staring at her phone and read the message over and over again. Could she face the family? Would they blame her?

All the more reason to go, she thought. Actions have consequences.

Face yours.

40

When Paula arrived home from her visit to the café and pushed open her front door, she registered that a rather large bundle of mail was building up behind it. She closed the door behind her and stared at the pile of envelopes on the floor, as if doing so might magically sort them into separate piles – those she should pay attention to and those she should bin.

She was tempted to just pick the lot up and throw it away. Trouble was, she often received mail regarding the charities she was attached to so she would have to keep it and look through it. But some other time.

She nudged the nearest one with her boot. It displayed the logo of a well-known optician on the front. She couldn't even be bothered to bend down and pick them all up.

Gin.

That was the medicine that was required.

In the kitchen she threw her bag and her phone on top of the island. Then she found a glass, got some ice from the dispenser at the front of the giant black fridge-freezer that used to tickle Thomas so much. Ice clinking, she located the bottle and poured herself a generous measure, added some tonic and sipped.

Getting up onto a stool she hunched forwards over the glass of gin, momentarily overwhelmed by a weight of loneliness. She looked around the kitchen. So much space. This room had been her pride and joy when they first moved in. Now, looking around it all left her with was dull ache and souring in her jaw as if she'd eaten something that had gone off.

She took another sip of her gin.

She hadn't turned to drink when Christopher died and it certainly wasn't going to happen now. But still.

Another sip.

Remembering that she had still to hear back from Joe, she picked up her phone. Nothing.

Placing the phone beside her glass, she contemplated topping her drink up. But then she heard herself asking Joe about his drinking when they were last in the sacristy, and pushed the glass away from her. She climbed off the stool, made her way over to the coffee machine and switched it on.

She looked at the clock on the oven. It read 20:15 in blue light. If she drank coffee at this time, she'd be up all night. She'd be up all night anyway.

A full cup of coffee warming her hand, she made her way through to the lounge, switched on the TV and curled up against one end of the sofa. A thought of what had happened the last time she'd been in here hit her – an image of Bill half naked. She cringed away from it. Thomas's brother, naked and aroused. What was she thinking? It would be too easy to blame the booze and she hated it when other people shunned responsibility for their actions. It was simple: she shouldn't have let it happen.

She ran over that evening with Bill and what happened afterwards. Was there anything she could have done to stop it? Who was her big brother-in-law anyway? Was his talk of always fancying her just a line? Did he want the notch on his mental bedpost? Some sort of sick 'I slept with my brother's wife' thing? He had been rude and dismissive to her all these years, after all. Did he really love her, or was he just being an idiot? Whatever he was, the thought of being alone with him ever again made her feel decidedly uneasy.

Shame made her retreat from her thoughts and she studied what was happening on the TV as if that might scour her brain. Someone was singing. Well, trying to. They did manage to hit a few of the notes to be fair. People behind a desk looked on in judgement.

She turned it over to the news. Hate crimes were up. A woman in a headscarf was recounting how she was abused almost every time she left the house.

Turning the TV off, she stared out of the window. It wouldn't matter what she looked at in this mood. She was beyond distraction.

Her phone rang in the background. Joe? It had to be. He was the only person who would call her at this time of night. He must be phoning to tell her that he was okay. Just the ringing tone was good enough for her – the effort required in going through to the kitchen for her phone was temporarily beyond her.

The phone stopped ringing. She sighed with relief.

But then it started again. So it wasn't Joe, she thought, he was always able to take no for an answer.

'Oh, bugger off,' she shouted through to it. 'Whoever you are, bugger off.'

It stopped.

And started up again.

'Oh, for pity's sake.' She pushed herself to her feet and stumbled through to the kitchen. By the time she arrived it had stopped again.

Then it bleeped a text alert. With a sharp shock, she saw it was from Daphne. She grimaced:

Need to talk to you about Bill. I'm REALLY worried. Come over to mine now? PLEASE?

Oh, Christ, she thought. Could this be anything to do with their brief moment of...?

She thought about just going to bed, but if she did that this text would haunt her through the night. What did Daphne know? Had Bill told her? What kind of state was he in now?

Actions had consequences, she thought. It was time to acknowledge hers.

41

Every time Cara came to this part of the city, it gave her pause. Possilburn had a bit of a reputation – much of it exaggerated, some of it justified. It was said that it had become one of the most deprived areas of the city and that had led to all sorts of social problems.

And she acknowledged that having a third of the population classed as underprivileged couldn't be the healthiest of environments in any sense. When you have wholesale neglect of people by those in authority the results were inevitable in her opinion.

She thought about a young woman she'd had sitting across from her desk that very morning. The poor woman was in her late twenties, had psychological issues and the mental age of a twelve year-old. In an effort to show willing she'd signed up for a week of work experience in a charity shop. When she got there the charity shop staff said they didn't need her. The Department of Social Security sanctioned her to the tune of four months of her benefit, as if her subsequent no-shows were her own fault. The poor woman could barely stop crying long enough to explain her situation to Cara.

'How am I going to eat? How can I...' In her distress she pulled at her dirty blonde hair with fingers whose nails were bitten down to the quick. 'I can't even pay the bus fare to go see my mum.' Her mother was in a local hospice in the terminal stages of a long illness.

Consciously callous, that's what the system was, and the people who set it up had a chunk of concrete where their hearts should be, thought Cara. She'd love to get a politician down into one of these areas and get them to live under this system and see how they felt then.

Enough, she thought. Normally she was able to close off that part of her mind when she wasn't in work, but something about that poor woman really got to her.

She drew up at Danny's mother's house and noted that a group of young men had collected at the end of the path. The only one not in a baseball cap was wearing a hoodie. She got out of the car and walked towards them, informing her posture with confidence, knowing they would respond to that with respect. The law of this jungle: show fear and become a victim.

As she drew nearer she realised her assessment of the group had been harsh. They were a mix of ages, from late teens to late twenties. There was even one man who looked like he could have been in his forties. He was the one in the hoodie.

One of them looked over at her as she approached. She offered him a small smile. He nodded and said. 'You here for Danny's thing?'

'Aye,' she replied.

'You've just to go in,' another boy said. 'You've no' to bother knockin'.'

'Right,' she said and went to move past them as they opened up a space for her.

'Tragic, innit?' The youth said to her. 'Danny was a good cunt. Didnae deserve that.'

The rest of them nodded and gave a low rumble of agreement.

She felt a hand on her shoulder just as she stepped into the middle of them and thought, *Here we go.*

'You Sean's sister?' The young man asked.

'Yeah,' she replied, searching his face to see if she recognised him.

'Stan,' he replied holding his hand out. He was slim, sharp-eyed, clean-shaven and smiling.

'Nice to meet you, Stan. How did you know our Sean?' she asked, after she shook his hand, and moved her own to protect her handbag. He pretended not to notice her movement.

'He was a couple of years above me at school. A good footballer.' Grin. 'No' as good looking as his sister, right enough.'

The rest of his mates hooted in laughter.

'Mate, your patter's pure rubbish,' one said.

Cara walked up the path to the house as they all began to compare their best efforts at chatting up girls.

Just as she reached the door she heard one of them say, 'Wait, wait, here's mine. Was your body made at McDonalds, hen? Cos I'm lovin' it.'

This received more hoots of derision.

Another said. 'Here's one to use at a wedding. Know what this kilt is made of, darlin'? Boyfriend material.'

That was Glasgow typified in one short conversation. Observe the reality of the situation, and then go right back to ripping the pish out of each other. She smiled.

Reaching the door she forced the boys' banter from her mind. It really wouldn't do to walk into this house with a smile on her face.

She could hear chatter through the door, as she stood on the doorstep, fist up, poised to signal her arrival. With a twist low in her gut she asked herself whether she really wanted to be here.

She knocked and waited. It didn't feel right to just walk in.

The door opened and a young woman with long blonde hair stood there. She had on a pair of dark jeans and a pale-blue V-neck sweater.

'Ah told those wasters to tell folk just to come in,' she said to Cara. 'Men, eh?' She stepped back to allow Cara to enter. 'Just go through,' she added. 'Everyone's in the living room.'

Everyone was indeed in the living room. All of the seats were filled and there was little standing room. Danny's mother was sitting in an armchair, with a young woman on each arm and one crouched at her feet. They were all focussed on her, offering support with a gentle touch and low words.

Cara looked around the room, sensing the community here. They were all women. All concerned about the death of yet another young man. She doubted that there would be one of them who hadn't been touched by a similar tragedy – either in their close family or in the circle of their friends. Suicide, drugs or violence – they were all marked by these things.

Cara noted a small display that had been set up on the mantelpiece. The centrepiece was an A4 image of Danny in a dark wooden frame. In front of it was a single candle.

She looked at the photo. His hair was slicked back and he was wearing the red tie and sweatshirt of his secondary school – the same one she and Sean had worn. She smiled at his gap-toothed grin. A memory came to her – Danny and Sean sharing a bike with no seat. He'd stolen it from the railings at a nearby train station, the owner thinking that if he took the seat away with him on the train it would deter thieves. No such luck with Sean and Danny. It became more of a challenge. They wanted to see if they could both ride it without. Of course, disaster struck. Danny sat on the handlebars, and Sean was peddling but couldn't see past Danny when he took a right turn. He hit a kerb and Danny fell and smashed his face on the ground. His face healed but the tooth was missing for a few years until he could afford to get a decent falsie.

Cara felt a hand on her arm.

'Look at him with that daft, big grin.' She turned to see Danny's mother at her side. 'He refused to get a cheapo from the NHS. Wanted one that looked good, you know?' She gave Cara a hug. 'How you doing, darling? Thanks for coming.'

'Wouldn't have missed it, Heather.'

'C'mon over, hen,' Heather took her by the hand. 'Meet the girls.'

Heather pulled her across the room to her chair and, while still on her feet, announced to the assembly, 'This is Cara. She was a good sort to our Danny. Helped him out of a tricky situation with that cow of an ex-wife of his when nobody else gave a shit.'

A chorus of 'Hi Cara' rang through the room.

'Can I get you a wee cuppa?' asked Heather, looking at one of the other women. 'Get Cara a cuppa will you, honey?' Then she turned to Cara again. 'Or would you prefer something stronger?'

'Coffee with just milk will be lovely, thanks,' Cara said.

They sat, with Heather in the chair and Cara on the arm, holding each other's hand. And Cara could see that Heather was straining to hold the emotion back. The black hound was straining at its leash. She could see that she took some warmth from the presence of all the people in the room, while simultaneously wanting to scream at them all to leave.

Heather gripped Cara's hand tight, closing her eyes as if against whatever thought and emotion warred in her mind. She weakened her grip and then tightened it again as if she'd come to a decision.

Finally, looking up at Cara, her eyes showing a struggle for the peace she thought would forever evade her, she asked, 'You were the person who found our Danny, weren't you? You need to tell me everything. Everything, doll, and don't hold back. I can take it.'

42

Paula sat in her car just down the road from Bill and Daphne's, listening to the rain as it beat on the roof of the car and washed down the windows, turning the world outside into a smear of light and dark. Stupidly, she hadn't thought to bring her coat or umbrella. She'd get drenched after five seconds, so she decided to wait until it eased.

But she knew she was really only delaying the inevitable, and felt guilt grip and snarl in her stomach as she imagined the expression on Daphne's face after she found out the truth.

What did the woman have without Bill? She'd be devastated.

Would she have wanted to know if Thomas had an affair? she thought. Yes. Absolutely. So why should she deny Daphne that same thing. But then could you really describe her and Bill's drunken, grief-fuelled fumble as an affair? It was over almost as it begun. Perhaps this was one situation where the lie could be, if not white, a smudged vanilla?

Then her earlier unease at being alone again with Bill returned. She became aware of movement. Someone was walking along the street towards her car. Who'd be out walking at this time of night, in this rain unless they were up to no good? She locked the car doors.

Why was she so jittery? But it occurred to her that she had good reason to be nervous. Joe and Thomas had been dealing with dodgy characters and very possibly as a result of that people were being killed.

She was on her own, in the dark, and apart from Daphne, no one knew where she was. If something happened to her who would know? She should let someone know where she was, just in case.

But whom? Joe had been out of reach the last couple of days. Not even young Father Declan knew where he was. Was he away on some retreat or was he...? She had an image of Joe slumped on a chair with a bottle of pills in one hand and a tumbler of whisky in the other. She shook her head violently to disperse it.

If something happened to Joe as well...

Who could she call? If Joe wasn't available, who was? It was a testament to her life. There was no one who would miss her? The weight of her grief pushed down on her. It was a solid thing, its pressure stealing her breath, removing all her energy. She could just sit here. Let the world do its own thing.

But, Bill. She owed it to her husband's brother to check that he was okay. It must be bad if Daphne was calling her.

She filled her lungs, admonished herself to just get out of the car, put one foot in front of the other. At least she wasn't homeless and murdered like that poor kid, Danny. She saw him again in that doorway, and flinched from the memory. Saw herself facing Cara and arguing about Thomas's involvement moments after.

And now, thinking about that dead boy, another mother's son, she acknowledged that she'd never given a thought to Cara's grief over her brother. All she had room for in her own head was for her own losses, but here other people were suffering as well.

Sean.

Christopher.

Two young men with their lives ahead of them, now dead. For all the differences that fate and life had presented to them, they were both now nothing but bone and memory.

She'd overreacted. She should apologise to Cara. And while she was apologising she could tell Cara where she was. The woman would think she was nuts but who else did she have?

Before she could talk herself out of doing it, Paula pulled out her mobile and pressed out a text.

Sorry I was a bit crabbit today. Seeing that poor boy like that got to me.

She read it over. That didn't seem too way out there. Then she thumbed out some more.

Now at my in-laws. Hope you're having a more exciting evening.

There. Was it too needy? Should she add a little emoticon? Something to show how she was not looking forward to spending time with Bill and Daphne?

Enough.

She pressed the send button.

The noise of the rain hitting the car eased a little and without giving it another thought, Paula threw her phone into her handbag, climbed out of the car, and ran along the pavement towards Bill and Daphne's door.

As she reached it, she saw it was slightly open. Then she noticed it had been propped ajar with a half-brick. She turned and looked up and down the street to see if perhaps one of the neighbours had propped it open while they went out to their car. But there was no one about. Whoever had walked past her car before had disappeared. She pressed the buzzer, so that Daphne would know she was there, and ducked just inside the close, out of the rain, urging Daphne to hurry up and answer – she was spooked down here in the dark.

Seconds later, a voice sounded over the intercom.

'Come in,' said Daphne. Paula hurried towards the stairs, thinking about the tenor of those two words, trying to find clues as to the woman's state of mind, but she got nothing. Daphne had been entirely neutral.

When she arrived at Bill and Daphne's landing, she noticed that the door to the flat opposite was open. A sliver of light from the hall inside sliced across the doormat. That was weird. Maybe the owner had gone down to the bins in the court at the back door? She'd never met the new owner. For years it had been old Mrs Paterson who lived there. But she'd died a couple of years back and she'd never heard from either Bill or Daphne who'd bought it.

She turned to Daphne's door, expecting it to be open but it was firmly closed. She knocked and waited.

Nothing.

She knocked again louder now, but still there was no response.

This was strange. Daphne had just answered the intercom.

She pressed the side of her head against the door and listened for movement, but there was nothing. The space inside seemed silent.

A noise from behind her, somewhat similar to the cry of an urban fox. It sounded again. That wasn't a fox; it was a woman. And it was coming from the flat opposite Bill and Daphne's place.

Heart thumping, Paula made her way across to the other door, placing her feet lightly on the floor, ready to run at any second.

Another cry, then: 'No, Bill. No.'

That was Daphne. Definitely Daphne, and without further thought Paula pushed the door open and stepped inside.

'Daphne? Bill?' she shouted into the flat. It had the same layout to the one at the other side of the building: a large square hall, this one with bare unstained floorboards, as if the owner had not long ago pulled up the carpet – and off the hall four doors that must lead to the kitchen, sitting room and two bedrooms, all of them closed and even in the weak light Paula could see that they all needed a coat of paint.

'Daphne?' Paula shouted again.

And there – weeping. It sounded as if it was coming from behind the sitting-room door. She felt a flurry of worry. Bill. What was happening to him? She pushed open the door and stepped inside.

And nothing made sense.

All the lights were switched off, so it took a few moments for Paula to work out what she was seeing.

She reached out with a hand to the wall beyond the door where a light switch should be, and fumbled about for a moment before she found it. She pushed it up. Nothing happened.

'What...?'

All she had to go on was the electric light coming in from the streetlights outside, but there on two chairs, upright, hands behind their backs sat Bill and Daphne. Both were staring at her with a look of fear and warning.

There was a noise, a chuckle, and then behind them, emerging from the shadow, was Anton Rusnak.

'You took your time, Mrs Gadd. Care to have a seat?' His accent was much less pronounced than she'd heard during previous conversations.

'What...?'

He pulled a seat from somewhere and placed it in a position that formed a rough triangle with Bill and Daphne.

'Sit.' It was a command. And then, with a chill, she saw he was holding his right hand up, and there was the glint of a long blade.

She sat, and looking over at Bill and Daphne, saw them properly for the first time. Bill had a swollen right eye, bruising down one side of his face and a cut on his lip. Daphne's blouse was torn open, exposing one large bra-clad breast.

'You okay? Bill? Daphne?' She looked up at Rusnak, trying to ignore the fear that was now pulsing through her body. 'What are you doing?'

'You can stop pretending now, Mrs Gadd. We know you weren't the little lady who only did lunch. Time to tell the truth.'

'What the hell are you on about?'

In two steps Anton was looming over her. His hand shot out. A slap sounded into the room. Pain sparked across her cheek.

Paula fought back a cry.

'I have no time for lies, Mrs Gadd.' His voice was deep, quiet and unnerving. 'I have already killed three people and I won't hesitate to kill another three.'

Three?

Kevin, Elaine and Danny. So not Thomas. Not Joe. She tried to take in the scene, while working out what this all meant.

Daphne gave a little whimper, disrupting her thoughts.

'Just tell him, Paula. Tell him, please?' she begged.

'Tell him what? What am I supposed to know? I've no idea what's going on.'

Rusnak snorted. 'You know everything, Paula. Tommy and I shared plenty of drunken evenings. He adored you. No way would he keep all of this to himself.'

'You killed poor Kevin?' she said, as if she was hearing his words on delay. 'And Elaine? What the hell did she do to deserve that?' Her pulse boomed in her neck now. Dear God, this was horrible.

'It deflected the police from what was really going on. We all benefit from that.'

'We all what?' She studied him, trying to find the man who had helped her when she'd been mugged. Unless...

His arm shot out again. Paula's head rocked back, pain exploding down the right side of her face.

'Tell him, Paula, or he'll kill us,' Bill begged.

'I don't bloody know anything, Bill. Aren't you people listening?'

Rusnak took a step outside the triangle, moved behind Bill and pressed the tip of his knife against the side of his neck. Even in the weak light Paula could see a trickle of blood run from where the point was pressed against Bill's skin.

'Okay,' said Rusnak, staring into Paula's face. She'd never seen a pair of eyes so dark, so lacking in anything that could be considered human. 'Let's play your game for a moment. Bill here will explain what has been going on.'

But Bill's head slumped onto his chest as if that was beyond him. As if he didn't want Paula to hear about his folly. Rusnak grabbed a hold of his hair and pulled his head up.

'Speak,' he commanded.

Bill jerked up and shot him a look of loathing, a look that promised if he wasn't tied up Rusnak wouldn't be getting it all his own way. Then he looked over at Paula.

'So sorry, Paula,' he shook his head. 'I'm so sorry for everything,' he said.

'Just tell her,' Daphne screamed suddenly, as if she was about to lose control.

Bill lifted his head up as if it was taking all of his energy. As if he was resigned to whatever was going to happen next.

'I know Joe told you about how he got into debt, how the casino sold his debt on and the loan sharks added a ridiculous amount of interest.' He swallowed and his voice changed. 'Anton and his crew helped him out...' Was that guilt she heard in his tone? Was Bill responsible for introducing Joe to Anton? If he did, how on earth would Bill know someone like that?

'What does that have to do...' Paula was shaking with fear but determined this man wouldn't notice.

'Stop playing the fool, Mrs Gadd,' Anton said. 'It doesn't suit you.'

Then, his eyes remaining on Paula, he spoke to Bill. 'Carry on, William.'

'These guys needed a legit business, so the deal was that Thomas was to open some weird account things. All legit, like, using some kind of legal loophole. There was one million pounds in each of them.'

Paula pretended to be surprised. 'Wait. One million pounds? In how many accounts?'

'Don't bother, Mrs Gadd,' Anton said with a quiet certainty. 'We *know* you know.'

'Yeah, one million in ten separate accounts,' continued Bill. 'And if Thomas complied they'd write off Joe's debt.'

Paula thought this through. She'd been right. She could see Thomas coming through for Joe. He wouldn't think twice to help him.

'And if he didn't?'

'If he didn't,' Rusnak chimed in, 'Father Joe would be lying in some nice piece of consecrated ground.'

'You'd kill a man of the cloth?' Paula asked with real shock.

'Is only man like the rest of us. The people I work for demand results, Mrs Gadd.' As Rusnak spoke he stepped back into the shadows till all she could make out in the gloom of the room was his large, louring outline. 'I don't get results, then my family pay terrible price.'

'There's one piece of jigsaw we need you to complete for us, Mrs Gadd. Before your husband's heart attack he withdrew one hundred thousand pounds from each of these ten accounts and hid it from us. He told Bill this was their commission, isn't that right, Bill?'

Bill nodded.

The mention of Thomas's heart attack reminded Paula that she hadn't ever had an answer to the question of Bill's presence when

Thomas died.

'You were with him, Bill,' Paula said quietly. 'At the end. Why didn't you tell me?'

Bill looked across at her, his expression difficult to read in the darkness, but she imagined she could see shame. 'I could have been a better brother to you, Paula.'

Daphne snorted.

'Enough,' shouted Anton.

'It would have helped to know that you were there,' Paula said.

Anton put his blade to Bill's throat. 'Enough.'

'What about Joe?' Paula asked Rusnak. 'What have you done with Joe?' She looked at Bill. 'The young priest said it wasn't like him to leave without saying. He said he hadn't even packed his toothbrush.'

'Joe's fine,' Bill said and there was certainty there. 'He must be away on a retreat or something.'

'Now if we've sorted the family out, could we concentrate on the matter of a lot of money, please?' Anton said with heavy sarcasm, stepping towards her, and shouting: 'One million pounds, to be precise!'

'I don't know anything about the money,' Paula said rearing away from his sudden outburst. 'Honestly.'

Paula thought through the transactions she'd seen on the screen, and then became aware of Anton's scrutiny.

'It's strange. Sometimes experts do get it right,' he said with unnerving calm. 'You looked up and right, Mrs Gadd, which means a visually remembered image.' He moved closer to her, pointing the knife. 'You saw my bank accounts. And I need to know where that missing million is.'

'I told you, I don't bloody know.' She kept her eyes on Anton, looking straight ahead, wondering how else she might be betraying herself. As she did so she tried to assess the distance to the door. Could she get there before he did? But if she did get away, what would he do with Bill and Daphne? Would that put them at more risk?

As if he could read her mind he said. 'Don't think about running.

That will only make me angry. I do crazy things when angry.'

Paula looked around, desperately trying to think of something that might get her out of this situation – get them all out alive. The room was almost bare, displaying nothing that suggested anyone might be living here. A long table rested against the far wall. At one end there was a chair that matched the ones they were all sitting on. Before that there was a laptop, printer and what looked like a large roll of duct tape. Underneath the table she could see that the floor was lined with boxes of various sizes.

Anton watched her sizing the place up and grinned. 'What do you see, Paula? Tommy always said you were smart lady.'

'Don't patronise me,' Paula said, hearing a tremor in her voice. She tried to swallow her fear and anger, to inject strength in her voice. Men like this respected courage didn't they? 'You're wasting your time here. Why don't you let us all go and we'll pretend it never happened?'

Anton looked up to the ceiling as if he was considering this, then made a buzzer sound. 'How about this? You tell me where the money is and I let you all go?'

'Anton, please,' Paula said. 'I don't know where it is. Really.' She heard a little girl in her voice and hated him for making her sound like that.

'I think you do, Mrs Gadd. And I need you to tell me where it is.'

That was the second time he'd said the word 'need', rather than 'want'. And she thought there was a hint of desperation there each time he said it. This was a lot of money. Could it be part of something bigger? Might he have been fleecing a larger operation and it had gone awry? She remembered the article about the Moldovan Government she'd told Joe about. Was this a similar type of operation?

He'd also said if he didn't get results his family would suffer. What exactly did he mean by that? If he was in a corner, that would make him even more dangerous.

At that thought Paula blanched. If this was part of something bigger they were all in trouble.

Rusnak read her face as she processed all of this, and as if he'd guessed where her mental journey had taken her he nodded. 'I think you are understanding the severity of this situation.' He smiled. 'Let me impress that upon you further.' He moved across to her and pulled her to her feet. 'Would you like some Polish meat? Where Bill refused, I won't and he would have been nicer.' He tutted, and his expression froze the blood in her heart. He leaned down and sniffed at her neck. Licked it.

She recoiled with a jerk, but the chair behind her stopped her from moving any further away.

And then she thought: *Where Bill refused?* What did he mean?

Anton gripped her arm with one hand and touched her face with the other. It was still smarting there from when he had slapped her and she grimaced. The evidence of her pain drew a cold smile from him, his eyes suggesting he was keeping himself on the leash, and warning that if he let himself go the result would be terrifying.

'Please, Anton, please,' she begged. 'I don't know anything.' She had no idea how she was still on her feet her legs were trembling so much.

He leaned down, cocked his head to the side and pressed his mouth against hers, pushing his tongue inside just for a moment. She choked, gasping in disgust, her knees gave out and she fell back onto the seat.

'That's enough,' Paula heard Bill say. And again. 'That's enough. You were just supposed to scare her a little. She clearly doesn't know anything.'

What?

Paula moved her head to the side and looked beyond Anton. Bill was on his feet, glowering at the big Pole. There was something in his eyes that took Paula completely by surprise, and judging by the way Daphne was looking up at him, she saw it, too.

Partnership.

Whatever was going on here? Whatever *this* was, he saw himself as Anton's equal.

43

'Do you think our Danny suffered?' Heather asked Cara, her eyes like a haunting.

Cara had carefully told Heather about how she'd arranged to meet Danny with Paula Gadd – the woman whose husband Cara held responsible for Sean's death. 'I wanted her to know what kind of man he was,' Cara had said, sadly.

Then she went on to tell the older woman how, when she and Paula had found her son, he was already dead. She decided to miss out the part about the knife sticking out of him, the pool of congealing blood in his lap.

Cara shook her head in answer to Heather's question, then coughed to clear her throat of emotion. 'No.' And the word was barely audible, so she said it again. 'The police said it would have been very quick.' She paused. 'Mind if we go in the kitchen?' she asked her, having a look around the room at the crowd of women, and suddenly feeling self-conscious.

'Sure, doll,' Heather said with a tight smile. She climbed to her feet as if it was costing her the last reserves of her energy. 'C'mon.'

In the kitchen, there was no room for any chairs, so they leaned against the cabinets and watched the kettle while it boiled. The space was narrow enough to stand in the middle of the floor and put a hand on the cabinets on either side. Eyes drawn to the ceiling, Cara noticed there was a large hole.

Heather noted where her eyes had gone and explained. 'I had a leak and the plumber had to get to the pipe.' She gave a pained smile. 'Danny was supposed to fix it ages ago. Said all it needed was some plywood. Wouldn't let me get a man in to fix it ... said it was his job.'

She turned away from Cara to face the kettle that had reached the boil. 'What was it you wanted, hen?'

'I'll just have a glass of water, if you don't mind. I'm kinda coffee'd out today.'

'I know exactly what you mean,' Heather said with a small glint in her eye as if she'd just located her sense of humour. Then it immediately faded as the tears welled up. 'Water?' Heather asked as if stirring herself and finding some energy. She reached up into a cupboard. 'There's some glasses. Help yourself.'

Cara reached up and pulled one out, then filled it at the tap. She leaned her back against the sink and faced Danny's mother.

'He had his up and downs, you know?' Heather was staring at the wall. 'He talked about mibbe coming into some money, just a week or so ago. I said, aye so you will. He was always full of big talk. But he was getting there. It was all that two steps forwards and one step back sorta thing. He'd do well – and I have to thank you for helping him getting to see his weans. He was made up about that, so he was. And then...' she shook her head '...there would be a cheap score and he would ... Stupid boy. Stupid, stupid boy.' Her head fell forwards so that her chin was on her breast bone as she gave in to her weeping.

Cara could do nothing but wait until it passed. After a few moments she felt she had to say something.

'It's nice that everyone turned up tonight. Really nice.' She reached across and stroked the other woman's arm.

Heather roused herself a little at the touch. 'Aye, hen, it was. We've a great wee community here. A great wee community. They slag us off. Say we're no-hopers, but the people here care, you know? They really care.' She dabbed at the damp of her cheek as if barely aware she was doing so. 'What did you want to talk to Danny about? I know you already told me, but I'm not listening so well...' She tailed off by way of an apology.

'Our Sean,' Cara replied, not wanting to go back through all of that after all. It would only increase her despondency. 'As I said, I wanted the Gadd woman to know what kind of man she'd been married to.'

'Oh, God,' said Heather her mouth open. 'I should've thought. You've been through all of this with Sean. How could I be so selfish?'

'Hey,' said Cara, 'that was some time ago. Yours is much more recent.'

'It never fades though, eh?'

They stood in silence for a moment, each nursing their own loss.

Heather broke the silence. 'Our Danny felt awful about what happened to Sean. Said it was a total accident what happened to that Christopher, but the Gadd fella refused to believe it. He was certain there was something else going on, apparently, and wanted Sean to suffer every broken bone that Christopher did.'

Cara winced.

'Sorry, love. But you know all that, eh? Danny would have told you.'

'He didn't tell me much really. He left that wee detail out, to be honest.'

'Was probably trying to save you any more hurt, love. That was our Danny over the back.' She crossed her arms as if that simple act would bolster her strength. 'The whole thing haunted him. He'd get drunk or be on something and talk about it for hours.'

'I only wish he had talked to the cops at the time and Tommy Gadd would have had his heart attack behind bars.'

'Aye, well, he was scared, eh? And he wasn't a grass.' Heather scratched at the side of her face, and Cara could see that her fingernails were all chewed to the quick. 'Just as well.' Heather continued. 'Or it would have been the wrong man behind bars.'

'Wait. Wrong man? What are you talking about?' In an instant Cara's heart had turned to a block of lead, her insides solid.

'Oh, sorry, love, did Danny not tell you that bit?'

'What bit?'

'He was round the other day. On the cadge, until this big wedge of cash came his way.' She rolled her eyes at the notion. 'But you know ... tough love. I'd done so much for him. I thought...' Her eyes filled again and she rocked back and forth with the force of her emotion. Cara watched in an agony. How could she interrupt and beg the woman to tell her what she knew? 'Would he still be alive if I'd given him...?'

'Oh, Heather,' Cara pulled her close. 'You can't torture yourself. I've seen it a thousand times. His life was chaotic.' How to say this. 'Something was bound to happen...'

Heather shuddered. Visibly pulled herself together. 'You're right, hen. But it doesn't really help. I let my boy down and I'll have to live with that.' She wiped at her cheek with a delicateness that surprised. As if she was imagining touching the face of her son. Then she looked at Cara. 'What were we saying?'

'Danny had the wrong guy?' And it was all Cara could do not to take her by the shoulders and give her a good shake until she told her everything she knew.

'Right. Aye. So he said he was sure it was Tommy Gadd cos the guy was behaving like it was his son that had died, but then a few days after Tommy's death was in the papers, Danny was up the town and saw the guy that had given Sean a doing.' Heather looked at Cara, a question in her eyes. 'Danny said he was so like the other guy he thought he'd seen a ghost. Did this Gadd fella have a brother? A twin or something?'

44

Bill squared up to Anton. 'I said that's enough.'

Now that he was on his feet it occurred to Paula that when she'd come in he'd had his hands behind his back as if they were tied. But now he had nothing around his wrists but his shirt sleeves.

'Will somebody tell me what the hell's going on?' she demanded.

'Sit down, Bill.' Daphne's voice barely concealed panic. She was looking from Bill to Anton and her face suggested she was worried about what Anton was capable of.

'Yes, sit down, Bill,' Anton said as he bared his teeth.

'No. I've had enough. Time after time I've listened to you, and time after time you've gone too far. I want out. I've had enough of you and your threats.'

'I don't threaten, Billy, I act.' He held the knife up. 'Now unless you want this, you'll sit down right now.'

But Bill stayed on his feet and stared at Anton as if considering making a challenge. If he did that someone was going to get hurt, thought Paula. Probably Bill.

Desperate to try and diffuse the situation she said, 'Will someone please tell me what is going on here? Daphne? Bill?'

Daphne sat as if shrinking into herself, her face tight with fear. Bill examined Paula as if he was wondering how he could say what he needed to say.

There was a look of grim satisfaction on Anton's face, as if all of his plans were about to come to terrible fruition.

'Will you tell her, or will I?' Anton asked Bill.

'Don't you...' Bill began, but Anton held up the knife to silence him.

Then he turned to Paula. 'Mr Gadd and I have been in business together for some time. Quite a few years actually. Selling a bit of this and a bit of that. Then he began to sample too much of the merchandise...'

'Hey...' Bill protested.

'I will use this,' Anton shouted, brandishing the knife again. 'Sit. Now.'

Bill looked both furious and wary. Whatever had been in the script had not included this.

Anton waited, but Bill remained standing, almost daring Anton to use the knife. What did sampling too much of the merchandise mean? Drugs? Prostitution? Paula stared from Bill to Anton. Bill blinked first and sat down.

'I thought you worked in that menswear shop,' Paula said in a low voice.

Bill looked over at her. 'Work it out, Paula for Christ's sake. You always were the smart one.'

She studied Bill as if this was the first time she'd laid eyes on him. Didn't he work in a men's shop at all? Or was that just a front so people wouldn't ask where the money was coming from? If it was drugs he was involved in she hadn't seen any signs. Certainly, since Christopher died, Bill and Daphne had been less and less in their lives, but even so, how on earth did she miss all of this? With a turn of her stomach, she wondered just how much Thomas had been involved.

'Your husband was mister goody two boots,' Anton said, mangling the phrase. 'He had no clue about drugs, but I worked out he was good prospect for helping me move big money for my clients, and then Father Joe made a mess of his gambles ... it was like a gift.' He gave her a nasty smile.

'You mean you didn't help Thomas rebuild the cottage?'

Anton threw his head back and laughed, as if this was the funniest thing he'd ever heard. 'I don't know what way to use screwdriver. No way can I build house.'

Open-mouthed, Paula shook her head. Could she have been any

more naïve? She'd have to process that fact later. If there was a later. She turned to Bill. 'So, if Anton hadn't already met you, Joe would never have got involved. You're happy for your brother to believe he was responsible for all of this mess? How do you sleep at night, Bill Gadd?' Her tone was scathing.

'Hey,' Daphne sat forward in her chair. 'Your Tommy was no bloody saint. So get off Bill's back, you little tart.'

Paula looked at Daphne as if she was a stranger. In this situation, why was she having a go at her? She struggled for something to say. All she could manage was, 'Don't talk to me like that.'

'Oh, please.' Daphne adopted a whiney tone. '*Don't talk to me like that.*' She laughed bitterly. 'You were about to shag my husband.'

'Wait ... what?' Daphne knew?

'And if that isn't a kicker.' Daphne's eyes were full of loathing. 'If you knew what he'd gone through for you...'

'Daphne,' Bill shouted. 'Enough.'

Daphne looked up at her husband, shifted on her seat and swallowed what it was she was about to say. Then went with. 'Whatever, precious Paula. Know this. Tommy was no saint. He stole a million pounds from those accounts. And if we don't get it back we could all die.'

At the mention of the missing money both men returned their attention to Paula. And from Anton's expression his previous attempt at assault was about to be resumed.

Squirming in her chair, Paula thought about everything Anton had done so far. Her death, should he go that far, wasn't going to be more than the weight of a feather on his conscience.

She needed to give him an answer.

But where could Thomas have hidden the money? And in this moment of danger she found she wasn't that bothered about herself. If she died, she died. All she wanted was that it might be painless. But his next stop after her was bound to be Joe, and she'd fight to protect him. She needed to give Anton a place to search.

'I check the cottage. Very thoroughly,' Anton shrugged. 'Nothing there.'

'Please believe me. I'll get down on my knees if it makes any difference, but I know nothing about this million pounds. I had no idea you people were involved in that much money.'

'Then I have to show my bosses something or they kill me – after they rape my wife and daughter in front of my eyes. Better you than me and mine.' He stepped towards her.

'Wait. Wait,' Paula shouted, putting her hands up in front of her. She was trembling so hard it was a wonder she could speak. 'If you kill me you have no chance of finding the money.'

'Go on,' said Anton and took a step back. And another step back, moving until he was standing between the seated Daphne and Bill.

'I knew Thomas best, right? I'm sure if given enough time I can work out where he hid the money. Please. I just need some time to think this through. Let's all go and I'll...'

'I have no time, Mrs Gadd. My bosses need money now, or they need a body. That body cannot be mine.'

'Oh, Jesus. How am I supposed to think about this right now?' She was shaking so badly the words barely sounded in the room.

'Perhaps you need a little help?' asked Anton with a mild tone.

'Yes. Help. I need some help.'

Anton smiled. 'Then I hope this works for you.'

Without pausing, Anton swung to the right, hard and so fast his arm blurred as he buried his knife into Bill's chest.

45

'He said what?' Cara couldn't believe her ears.

'Yeah,' said Heather. 'He had the wrong guy all along.'

'But how could he...? How could...?'

'You know, I'm not comfortable talking about all this drug stuff. It totally turned our Danny's head and probably cost him his life. So, if you don't mind I'd rather not. Not now, hen. I can't handle it.'

'But, Heather...' Cara began, but reading the pain in the other woman's face she couldn't push her any further. 'It's just, for our Sean's sake I need to know what's going on,' she finished, but heard the strength in her voice fade as she spoke.

'Listen, doll. There's a bunch of guys out the front. Speak to them. I really didn't want some of them here at all.' She shook her head. 'What they do turns my stomach, but everybody needs to grieve, right? And maybe some of them will see what happened to Danny and take it as a warning.'

Heather looked into the near distance, drifting off. Cara steered her back to where her thought had been going. 'The guys out front?'

'Yeah. One of them, guy called Stan. He's well in with all that crowd. Maybe he knows something? He's got that cheeky-chappy thing going on. He probably tried to chat you up as you came in.' She made a face of apology. 'Have a word wi' him.' With that, she walked out of the kitchen and back to the group solicitation she'd been receiving before Cara came in.

⚶

Outside, Cara approached the group of men and youths, looking for the one who Heather referred to as Stan. When she reached them, the men split apart to let her through. She got a couple of smiles, nods and somebody asked how Danny's ma was.

Unsure who she should answer, she spoke to them all, looking around at their faces. 'Poor woman's in a bad way.'

She got several low and gruff 'ayes' in response.

When she got through the other side and reached the pavement beyond the gathering, she had another look to see if Stan was there and with a sinking feeling realised he had gone. Looking at a couple of young men at the outskirts of the group, she picked one who looked most friendly.

'Hey, mate,' she said. 'Do you know Stan?'

'Sorry, missus,' he said and shook his head. 'Don't know him.'

His friend looked at her and said, 'Stan the Man?'

'Yeah,' said Cara hopefully.

'Never heard of him,' the man said. Then the two of them burst out laughing.

'Very funny,' Cara said, made a face at them and turned and walked away. Then she heard a shout. She turned; it was Stan making his way through the crowd.

'You're never leaving without saying cheerio?' he said to her. 'Just went inside for a ... the loo and I come out and you're about to leg it.' He was holding both his arms out and Cara could see he was playing to the gallery, and realised that was also how she could get to him.

She gave him a stare and then turned and walked away.

He caught up to her and held her arm. 'Did I say something to offend you?' His smile was large, but she read a faint worry in his eyes that she might leave him with egg dripping from the tip of his nose. He wanted to impress the gang and was concerned she wouldn't play along.

She took a couple more steps, allowing him to judge her pace, then dropped her head a little and said quietly, 'It brought it all back you know?' She allowed a little of her genuine sorrow to leak into her voice. 'Seeing Heather in there. Talking about Danny...'

'Sorry, darling, and here I'm acting all Jack the lad.' He put an arm over her shoulders. And she allowed it, granted him that little prize ... for a moment, and then quietly said, 'Move your arm or I'll mash your nuts.'

He moved his arm.

'You knew our Sean, eh?' She swung round to face him. 'How?'

'We did the odd job, here and there, you know?' He was standing back from her now.

'For the Gadds?'

His face changed. A wariness appeared in his eyes.

'Don't worry. I'm not going to tell anyone. Sean died working for those bastards and Danny was my last hope to find out the truth.' She allowed a little tear and inched closer to him.

'That wasn't what happened,' Stan said. 'Who told you that?'

'It's what I heard...'

'No, I was there as well, doll, and I can tell you that was most definitely not what happened.'

'Oh, Jesus,' she said softly. 'I don't know who to believe.' She gave a little sob, exaggerating it a little. 'This is, like, old news. I mean who cares, right? Our Sean's dead. Now Danny...' She tailed off, allowing more of her genuine feelings to show.

Stan looked around as if assessing who was nearby. Then he stepped closer, put a hand on her shoulder, but with real tenderness now. 'Listen, I'll tell you what I know, but you can't tell anyone. I mean anyone, or I'm toast. There's some dangerous people involved here.'

'Okay,' she said making her eyes large. She put a hand on his lower arm. 'What can you tell me?'

'Go to the polis with this and I'll deny everything.'

She snorted. 'To the polis I'm the crazy sister with a different theory every month. I've given up on the polis ever being any help on this.'

'Right,' said Stan making his mind up once and for all. 'Not here. That car there...' He nodded in the direction of a white Vauxhall Astra just two cars up.

Cara gave him a dead-eyed look.

'Nae funny business, doll.' He held his hands up. Cara pretended to weigh what he was offering.

'Give me your car keys?' She held out a hand.

'Nice wee car, innit?' And the cheeky chappy was back. 'Want to go for a ride?' He said the last few words louder. Got a cheer from his mates.

If he gave her what she wanted, Cara thought, he deserved that little victory. As he pulled the keys from his pocket she shot out her hand and grabbed them. His eyebrows went up.

'Impressive reflexes you've got there. You some kind of secret ninja or something?'

She ignored his question, turned and walked towards his car, aimed the remote and pressed a button. Sitting in the passenger side, she kept hold of the car keys.

'Aww, you not fancy a wee drive?'

'Thanks for the offer, Stan, but would you mind if we just talked?' She'd keep up the little woman act for as long as it took, although she was close to grabbing one of his fingers and snapping it if he didn't get on with it.

'And that's the story of my love life right there, darling.'

'How well did you know our Sean?' she asked.

He smiled. 'We did a few runs together...' He paused as he judged her expression. 'But the least said about that the better. He was a cheery wee guy, that's what I remember most. Was always the sparkiest person in the room. Him and Danny were a riot when they got together. A proper double act.' His smile softened. 'Poor bastard.' He twisted in his seat to face her. 'And the polis never listened to you? That must have been murder, darling. Pun intended.'

'It was hellish and my name's Cara.' She turned in her seat to meet his gaze, her expression a request for him to start talking.

He took the hint. 'Right. Stan.' He pointed at himself. Studied her. 'You sure you want to hear this, Cara? It wisnae nice.'

'I think I've heard the worse of it already, Stan. Please. Just tell me what you know.'

'Right.' He faced ahead and looked out of the window as if he was gathering his recollections into some kind of order. 'We didn't work for the Gadds. We worked for another mob – best if I don't mention any names – who are in competition with those boys. Sean was paid to run young Christopher off the road in retaliation for something Gadd did. Just a warning, you know? But, with Sean and Danny, you got one, you got both. Sean was driving but. And they were just supposed to break the boy's leg or something, not kill him.' He grimaced. 'Poor bastard's head hit the kerb and he clocked out.'

Cara thought about Paula, thought about the Gadds, and wondered how much she really knew about all of this. She felt a sudden pang of sympathy for her.

'For yonks nobody knew nuthin,' Stan went on. 'It was officially a hit-and-run – and Sean thought he was free and clear, you know. For *ages*. Then he started talking about it. The eejit even said to one of his mates – when he was stoned, to be fair – that he'd got away with murder.'

'Christ,' said Cara, closing her eyes against his stupidity.

'We heard Bill went totally off the rails after Chris died. He was still dealing, like, but apparently he had a strong case of the guilts cos he loved that boy as if he was his own. Found some peace on the pills and in the bottle. Then, eventually, the truth made it back to him.' He winced. 'And the rest is history.'

'So, Danny was there when Sean was beaten?'

'Aye.'

'But why wait till now to kill Danny? Why not do them both at the same time?' Cara couldn't believe she'd asked such a question. As if gang murder was a regular part of her life.

'Bill's missus – a bit of a porker by all accounts – she wanted them both killed...'

'Daphne Gadd was there – when Bill beat up Sean?'

'Danny said she was going mental. She was totally egging Bill on. Shouting stuff like...' Stan adopted a falsetto '..."I want every bone on his body broke. I want every injury our Chris had on his bones." Danny said she was very nearly frothing at the mouth.'

'How did Danny get away?'

'The way he tells it ... sorry, told it. It was as if Bill sickened himself on poor Sean. Couldn't handle it anymore and just walked away.'

'But why kill Danny now?' Cara repeated.

'I saw Danny-boy up the town, might have been the week before he was killed. He was out of his nut. He'd been doing well, ken? But something set him back onto the nasties.' His eyes grew distant as if he was accessing a memory.

'What?'

'He said he saw Bill Gadd a few days after the brother died. And Bill Gadd saw him,' he said the last part with the tone a judge might pass a death sentence.

'And why was that important? If he didn't have the stomach for it then, what changed?'

'Danny and his big gub. He approached Bill and his missus. Told them he'd go to the polis and tell them everything he knew about Sean's death, and all it would take to keep him quiet was ten grand.'

Ten grand. Cara heard Danny's mother's voice. *Something about a wedge of cash*. And Danny had said something too the last time she'd seen him alive. He really thought they'd stump up.

'Well, anyway...' Stan paused. He looked ahead out of the window and for a moment seemed like a different person. Like someone carrying a great weight and purpose, and he didn't much care who got hurt in the exercise of that purpose. Then his expression lifted and he was Stan the Man again. In that second Cara felt like she got a glimpse into who he really was. Asking more questions might be like drawing a polar bear's attention to your presence, but she couldn't help herself.

'What are you hiding?' she asked him.

He snorted. Held his hands out. 'What you see is what you get, darling.'

'Aye, so you do. You know more about all of this than you're letting on. What can you tell me, Stan? I've been fighting Sean's corner for years now, on my own. And I was almost getting somewhere. What can you tell me?'

Stan crossed his arms and judging by the tightness in his jaw there was an internal debate being waged. 'All I'm saying is with Danny they've gone too far this time. The people I work with are on it.'

'Aye, I know the story: the people you work with will sort it and no one will ever hear of it. But I want the truth to be known. The Gadds were up to all sorts and my brother was murdered because of it.' As she spoke she read his expression, convinced now he was teetering on the edge of something. 'Please?' she added. 'What can you tell me?'

He grunted and pulled his phone from his jacket pocket. 'I'm not a grass, right? And if this ever – I mean *ever* – gets back to certain people...'

'I swear. No one will ever hear anything from me.'

'Well, that will not do,' he grinned as if a new approach had just occurred to him, one with greater impact for the people he wanted to hurt. 'You know what? I've changed my mind. You can go to the polis. If that's what it takes, that's what it takes.' His thumbs flashed over the surface. 'What's your number?' She told him and he keyed it in to his phone. 'Right, there you go.' He smiled and his look was grim. 'Danny didn't deserve to die in a doorway like that. You've got a day to get your sense of justice. After that justice goes to the street.'

Cara plucked her phone out of her pocket to access the file that Stan had sent her, and as he kept talking she noticed that she'd missed a text from Paula. She could read it later. This was more important. And now that Stan had released himself from his code of silence, it seemed he couldn't shut up.

'The guy in this photo I just sent you? You need to watch him. He's connected to some big criminal outfit in Eastern Europe. Word is there was a lot of money involved and he was getting help from the Gadds to move it.'

The phone pinged that a message had been received. She opened the message and looked at the picture on her screen.

She knew this guy.

How did she know this guy?

'Danny said he saw him following him in a big Ford, a Mondeo or something. Danny was bricking it. Said as soon as he got the cash from Bill Gadd, he was going to leg it. Go somewhere warm.'

It was the mention of the car that did it. Cara did know this guy. He was in the backseat of the car that drove past her with Kevin Farrell and Elaine Teenan. And she was sure he was the guy outside her flat in the blue Mondeo who scared Danny off.

'You get that to the polis, Cara,' said Stan. 'And you watch yourself. This guy is in with some Eastern European criminal outfit. He's Polish, I think. Some kind of enforcer for hire, is what I hear. Whatever he is, he's a whole new kind of dangerous.'

46

Paula was stunned into immobility. Not believing her eyes. What had she just witnessed? This was real life, not some crime drama on the TV. People didn't just stab other people. Not in front of their wife, their sister-in-law. Was this a game? Were they using some kind of trick knife?

But the look of surprise and agony on Bill's face was all too real. His slump to the side and then off the chair did not have the look of a careful rehearsal.

And then the blood.

Paula felt a scream escape her throat.

Daphne's face was frozen in a silent O. Anton was now looking at Paula almost casually, as if to say he was just getting started. Daphne fell forwards on her seat, hands over her face.

Paula's breathing was coming at her hard as if her lungs were unable to cope with what she'd just witnessed. She wanted to go to Bill but couldn't make herself move.

'Oh my God. Oh my God. Oh my God.' This hadn't really happened, had it? 'Oh my God,' she repeated. She couldn't control herself, her thoughts.

Anton straddled Bill and pulled the knife out, and this made a sticky, sucking sound.

'Jesus,' she said as shock and fear flooded through her system. 'Jesus.'

'Be quiet, woman,' Anton shouted at her. He wiped the blade on his trousers. 'You will be next.'

Daphne was still silent, head in her hands. Then, she looked up, face long, eyes showing a morass of emotion, until it settled on a final one.

Fury.

She looked at Anton, her features rigid. 'What the hell was that? You said we'd wait till later.'

Paula gasped. 'Later?' She looked from Daphne to Anton, trying to read what was going on here, but it felt as if she'd lost all knowledge of how humans communicated.

Daphne stood up. Like Bill she had no restraints around her wrists. Both of them sitting with hands behind their back had just been a pose. She ignored Paula and punched Anton on the chest. 'You said you'd wait till later,' she said again.

Anton shrugged. 'The moment was right.'

Daphne turned to look down at Bill, her face now neutral, eyes as cold and glinting. 'Twenty-six years,' she said. 'What a waste.' She turned to Paula, her body tight with hate. 'It was always you. From the moment he met you he was besotted. And he was sick that Thomas got in there first...'

'What are you talking about?' Paula demanded, her voice cracking.

'I lost my first baby.' Daphne's eyes were vacant. Her mind lost in the past, as if she was counting up her grievances. 'And Bill was over at yours. You called. The light in your boiler went out and Tommy was away on business. And of course Bill couldn't wait to be the knight in shining armour.'

'But...' Paula tried to recall something of that time, anything that would give context to what Daphne was saying.

'My second baby – the foetus wasn't even a month old when I miscarried. Bill showed nothing. Said it wasn't real for him. All he could talk about was how you bloomed in your pregnancy. I should be more like you, rather than losing all of these children.'

'Bill said that?' Was he really that heartless?

'I've hated him from that moment. Hated him. Seeing him lying there...' she looked over towards where Bill lay, her face a study in disgust '...is like a relief.'

Paula shook her head. Hard. As if that motion would remove her from the twilight zone she'd found herself in. But of course when she refocussed, they were all still there: Daphne, Anton and the very still form of Bill Gadd.

Supposing she got out of this alive, what would she tell Joe?

Now Daphne hit Anton again. 'This wasn't the right time!' She might as well have been slamming a fist against the door. Anton took her punishment, then with a tenderness that belied his stature he cupped his enormous left hand against the side of Daphne's head.

'We will sort this, my love. First we get money, then we run and get a better life, no?'

Daphne simply looked up at him as he spoke.

'He had to go...' He jutted his chin in Bill's direction. 'You said so. I just took chance when it came.'

Paula felt numb, removed from everything around her. That woman who was having trouble breathing – it was her. She knew this, but it still felt like it was someone else. She heard a low wail and realised that was her as well.

'Will somebody check Bill to see how he is,' she shouted, the words coming from another mouth.

'Oh, for God's sake. Shut the dumb bitch up,' Daphne said.

Anton reached her in two strides. His hand shot out and her face rocked to the side. Pain burst across her face. The wailing stopped, but her breath was still coming in short, panicked gasps.

Daphne squared off to Paula, standing in front of her, feet shoulder width apart as if she was about to take her on and was relishing the prospect.

'Time to talk, honey,' Daphne said. 'Where did Tommy hide the money?'

'I told you ... I don't ... I don't know where it is.'

'As you said, you knew your husband best, so you have the best chance of working out where it is. Thing is...' Daphne cocked her head to the side, 'you don't have long to get your thinking cap on, hen.'

Paula's mind was working hard. How was she going to survive this? The situation was desperate. She needed to focus, and she would perhaps get out of this alive.

'Is this all because you know about me and Bill the other night?' Paula asked as her opening salvo. If she could use Daphne's jealousy against her, she might improve her chances of surviving. 'It was nothing. Too much drink and a whole lot of grief. We made a horrible mistake. I don't love Bill. Never even fancied him to be honest. He was just...' Paula searched for the right word. 'There. He was just there. And I took him.'

'Jesus, you are clueless, you sad bitch. I know the other night was nothing. It was me who asked him to do you.'

'Do me?' Paula was stunned. 'What?' She repeated her question. 'Do me?'

'Aye,' said Daphne, her face an ugly sneer. 'Do you. Give you a seeing-to. Get his leg over. Play hide the sausage...'

'Shut up,' said Paula, looking from Bill to Daphne. 'You're disgusting. What kind of people are you?'

'But Bill came over all chivalrous on us.' Daphne continued. 'Pulled out, quite literally at the last second. He couldn't be so conniving with precious Paula.'

'You people are...' Paula ran out of words. She didn't have the vocabulary for this. Then another thought dropped into her mind. The break-in a few nights before. The person running out of the house. Bill at the door. *He* was her burglar. He probably had a key. And when he was disturbed he pretended to flee before doing an about-turn to act like he'd just arrived. That was why she didn't see anyone running away.

What a devious ... At least he'd had some shred of decency during that whole situation, not to force himself on her.

'Whatever,' said Daphne wearing her pleasure at Paula's discomfort as if it were a crown. She looked across to Anton. 'Tie her up and then get the iPad and his phone, will you?'

He nodded, taking instruction from Daphne as if that was the real pattern of their relationship. He walked over to the table, tucked the knife into the waistband of his trousers, picked up the duct tape and attached each of Paula's arms to the chair. His grip on her was so strong she was like an infant in comparison. The tape was tight around her wrists and she felt her fingers throb as the blood flow was reduced. As he worked his face was inches from hers and his breath was like a foul scalding on her skin.

When he finished Anton handed Daphne the knife, saying, 'Just in case.' And in a few long strides he was out of the room.

Paula looked at Daphne. iPad? Then it occurred to her. Thomas would have had it with him at that last meal with Bill. And while his brother was dying, Bill had been callous enough to spot the opportunity. She looked down at his corpse.

Who were these people she'd known most of her life? How could she have not seen their true nature for all these years?

She strained her arms, trying to lift them from their binding. But movement was impossible. Her breathing was too quick, her pulse hammering in her throat as panic threatened to overcome her. Desperately she looked around herself for something, anything, that might help her.

'We can go now, Daphne, now that Anton's out of the room.' Paula asked, trying to keep the fear out of her voice. 'I know you're just trying to keep him happy so he won't kill you.'

'Right,' Daphne shook her head, and her eyes gleamed with the possibility of using the knife. 'You really are a dumb bitch.'

'Well, go on, tell me what I've missed. If you guys are going to kill me anyway why not send me to the grave knowing what you've done?'

At the words 'kill me anyway' she saw Daphne half smile as if that was indeed part of the plan. Something loosened in her core and she felt heat and liquid fill her underwear and the crotch of her jeans. Humiliation burned up her neck and face as she heard the urine drip onto the floorboards. *Don't cry, Paula*, she told herself. *Don't let this woman think she's won.*

Daphne screwed her nose up at the sharp tang of urine. 'Oh, Christ you've only gone and pissed yourself.'

'Every mother's curse is a loose bladder.' Paula tucked that shame away for later. 'But you'd know that if you ever managed to have children.'

Daphne reared back. That stung. Just as Paula had intended. She narrowed her eyes. 'I might not have carried Chris but I was more of a mother to him than you ever were.'

'Oh for God's sake. You took him on the odd holiday, how on earth is that being more of a mother.'

Daphne stepped closer and bent down so that her face was level with Paula's. 'We got the guy who killed Chris and he went to his grave in the same agony Chris did. We looked after the family. We got it done while you sobbed in the shower, and tried to raise money for people with head injuries.' She said this last sentence with a sneer, and, looking into her eyes Paula could see nothing of the woman she'd known all these years. There was a calculation there that was barely human, and it was this that chilled her more than anything.

Then Daphne went silent and placed her mouth close to Paula's ear. Her breath was warm on Paula's skin and it was all she could do not to rear back. The woman disgusted her and scared her in equal measure.

Daphne breathed.

Then again a little louder.

'Recognise that?' she asked, and Paula could hear the pleasure in her voice.

'What are you...?' Paula shivered and tried to turn away, but Daphne held her head fast.

Daphne breathed again. Heavy. The air was coming out of her mouth as if it held its own echo. 'Does that ring any bells?'

'What is wrong with...?' And then the realisation hit: the silent phone calls.

Daphne's eyes shone. 'I've been playing with you all this time.' She made a fake sad face. 'My husband died. Poor little me.'

'You're sick,' Paula said trembling. 'Sick...' She paused. 'And hacking into my computer? Was that you as well?'

Daphne stepped away and shrugged. 'Wasn't me, hen. Must've been Kevin. He's the only one I know who's good enough with all that interweb stuff.' She stopped to think for a moment. 'But the "mugging" at the side of the road?' She made speech marks in the air when she said the word. 'You're so dim you made it easy for us. All of it was my idea. Clever, eh?' She all but hugged herself with delight. 'You see, the plan was to keep you distracted. Unsettled. So you'd make a mistake and lead us to the money.' Her face darkened. 'Which we still don't have...'

'Oh my God,' Paula said with a gasp. The deviousness. Who did that? She'd been around Daphne and Bill for years and had no idea what they were really capable of. She looked again into Daphne's eyes. What she saw there chilled her to the core. She was nothing but a bug to this woman. No, worse than that, she had everything Daphne ever wanted: a child; success. Bill's love. And for that she was going to die. There was no other way she could see this situation resolving itself. Other than with her death.

Paula resorted to the one thing she could think of. The only defence she had in that situation. She could not, would not, go down quietly. People would know she was in trouble, so she opened her mouth, filled her lungs and screamed as loudly as she could.

47

Cara was sitting outside Paula Gadd's townhouse. Just over twenty minutes' drive from Heather's house in Possilburn and the difference in surroundings was so striking it might as well have been in a different time zone.

She looked along the row of cars ahead of her. They were all expensive and new or fairly new. She felt her disgust at the unfairness of life sour in her mouth. All of these massive, striking homes with only a handful of people getting to benefit from them.

Taking her key from the ignition, she thought, just for a moment, of walking along the street and keying the paint from all the cars in the row.

As if that would fix anything. Life was unfair. She needed to get over it.

What did she think she was doing here anyway? Paula wouldn't thank her for turning up at this time of night.

But she did need to know the truth – that Bill, with the encouragement of Daphne, had killed Sean. That truth burned, but Paula needed to know it. The woman could quite easily go into old age and her grave in ignorance. She'd just spend her cash on expensive baubles and ease her conscience with charity work. And as far as Cara was concerned that wouldn't be fair.

She compared the lives and deaths of the two young men. They had been about the same age when they died. Both died in an act of violence, but one of them had loving parents and all the opportunities that life could offer. While her Sean had battled through his short life against the chaff of poverty ... the huge material disadvantage and crushing self-doubt it forced on people.

Short lives. Massively different potential in each. And death bringing it all to an abrupt end. An end that continues to stab and wound and tear at the people in these young men's lives, all these days and months and years later.

Cara's phone sounded an alert. She picked it out of her pocket, and saw that it was a work email. She dismissed it. She could read that in the morning. Then she remembered that she still hadn't read the text from Paula. She swiped to her messages.

She gave a little nod as she read. At least Paula was apologising.

Damn. Just when she convinced herself to dislike the woman again, she weaselled her way back in.

The line about her current whereabouts was a bit odd, though. Why would she want, or even need to tell Cara that?

She read it again. It felt conversational. Fair enough. But that wasn't their relationship so far. They were never really chatty with each other. It was all about passing on information.

Cara could hear Dave telling her that she read too much into things. But then he applied that action to all women of his acquaintance. She gave a mental shrug of acknowledgement; it was certainly accurate as far as she was concerned. But it normally served her well.

So, why was Paula really telling her where she was? Was she worried about something? Uneasy?

Why?

Because, as she'd said herself, people were being killed.

It struck Cara then that Paula seemed to have lots of people she knew, but, as far as she could see, no real friends – apart from the priest. The nub of sympathy for Paula grew a little. She tried to quash it. The woman was nicely compensated to be fair. Cara looked over at Paula's front door. Saw the large windows, black spaces reflecting back streetlight and dark skies, with nothing behind them but *things* that would offer nothing to ease the loneliness.

She compared it with the house she'd just come from, which was tiny and basic in comparison, but it was filled with people who clearly cared about Heather and her devastating loss. Paula's loss seemed to have driven people away. Despite all her wealth, what did Mrs Gadd really have in her life? Who did she have in her life?

Cara attempted to dim her growing sense of care for the woman. Then she read the message again.

Damn.

She had followed Tommy Gadd over there more than a few times over the years, so she knew exactly where it was. And it was only a little detour.

In fact it was a massive detour, but her gut was telling her events were coming to a conclusion. There was a build-up of bodies; she knew a hell of a lot more than she ever had. This was all coming to a head.

She was sure of it.

48

Over at King's Park, Cara had to drive up and down a few streets before abandoning her car on a corner of a street one back from where Bill Gadd lived.

The security door was open. Unusual. Should she be concerned? Taking a step back she looked up at the first-floor windows. Both were in darkness. That was odd. She looked back down the street. Left and right. There. She squinted. That was Paula's Range Rover, so she was here.

Then why were the lights off? The layout of these houses were similar to many tenement flats throughout the city. The front-facing rooms were living rooms and bedrooms. Kitchens looked out over communal backyards. Might they be chatting in the kitchen, after all that's where the best parties always ended up? The wording of Paula's text, however, suggested this would not be much of a party.

Something in Cara's gut turned over – a warning. She'd leaned on her instincts many times over the years and they were rarely wrong. This was definitely iffy.

Hand on the door, she pushed it open, stuck her head inside and listened. Nothing. Her breathing seemed to echo in the stone-clad space.

Then a scream.

A fist-clenching, hair-raising, face-slap of a scream.

And she was sure it was coming from Paula Gadd's lungs.

Without a thought, she made for the stairs, ran up them two at a time and on the first-floor landing came face to face with the man from the Mondeo.

He smiled in recognition. A smile that promised much in the way of pain. 'You,' he said. His body was relaxed, expansive. He was king of this particular castle. 'They should put you in Bond movie and call you Miss Badpenny.' At Cara's lack of response he gave a little grimace. 'I never understand you Scots and your sense of humour.' He set his feet as if getting ready to attack. 'No worries. I was coming for you anyway.'

Cara stood loose. He would be strong and those massive hands could cause real damage.

He reached for her as if expecting her to stand in place and take her punishment.

She danced out of his reach.

He made a low noise of appreciation, twitched his head.

The landing area was small so there was little space to manoeuvre, which would work to his advantage. She didn't want to reveal too much to him too soon, so she pretended to be even more scared than she really was.

'Please,' she said, hands up. 'I just want to speak to Paula.'

He tried to rush her again, but she ducked and moved to her left, almost getting pinned against the banister, but moving out of his space just in time. She felt a surge of adrenaline. And fear. That was close.

'Come on, little girl. Why you dance away from me?'

'Just let me go, mate,' Cara said. 'I'm a nobody. I'm no risk to you.' She considered her options. She was used to fighting a bigger, stronger opponent, but that was in a dojo under accepted rules of engagement. Sure, she'd been in tricky situations where she'd had to be able to look after herself, but never before with someone who looked like they wanted to kill her.

She pushed that thought to the back of her mind. A scared mind was a beaten mind, and she couldn't afford to let this man win.

But while she was thinking this through, he rushed her again. She darted to the side, but his right hand caught her shoulder and sent her spinning towards the Gadd's front door.

She was in completely the wrong place to get out of here. He was now between her and freedom. And what about Paula? What state was she in that made her scream like that?

'Stand still, little girl and this will all soon be over. I will be gentle on you,' he said.

It was time to give him something to think about.

She sprang within his reach. Aimed a punch at his throat. But he swung and caught her a glancing blow to the side of the head.

Ear ringing, she ducked back and then realised just before it was too late, that she was right at the top of the stairs she had ran up just moments earlier. She had to get this over with soon. His superior size and strength could cause her a lot of damage.

But it could also be his weakness...

She feinted, and he closed in to grab her. She allowed his movement, sacrificing her safe space with a prayer that what she was about to do would work. She fell onto her back, grabbed his jacket, planted her right foot in his midriff, and his momentum and weight meant he went flying over her head.

He tumbled down the stairs, grunting his surprise, heels over his head, as if in slow motion.

Cara jumped to her feet, hoping he'd broken something important. She was disappointed to hear him groan. This was far from over. The minute his head cleared he'd be back up those stairs, furious he'd been thrown by a woman. She had to do something decisive.

Cara leapt down to his side, picked up his foot, placed it on the bottom step and, telling herself she had no choice, jumped on his knee.

His scream of agony echoed in the hall.

'Stay down,' she told him.

She ran back up the stairs, shouting Paula's name.

The door at the top of the stairs was open. From inside she heard a crash and a muffled scream. Without worrying who else might be about, she ran inside. Saw movement to her right and entered the living room.

She saw one man motionless on the floor, one woman on a chair hands behind her back as if they were tied there. Judging by the size of her this would be Daphne and judging by the lack of movement from the man, and the large stain on the floor beside him, he was dead.

Paula was also on the floor, tied to a chair that had been upended, a stretch of duct tape over her mouth.

'Oh, thank God you came,' Daphne cried from her chair. 'That man was going to kill us all.'

Cara ignored her and made for Paula. Bending down she grabbed the chair and pulled it up onto its four feet so that Paula was upright. Then she set about releasing Paula from the tape.

'Can't find the end of this,' she said, anxiously feeling for a rough edge. Paula mumbled from behind the tape, becoming bug-eyed and bucking in the seat.

She heard a creak of floorboard, sensed someone move behind her and spun away from her position. As she did so, she had the presence of mind to bring a block into play. And there she saw Daphne, a long blade jutting from her hand.

With her right forearm, Cara kept the knife at bay, and brought her left fist up in a swing into the woman's gut. It seemed to go in forever and felt like hitting a cushion, but judging by the squeal that came from her mouth, Daphne felt it.

And then Cara reached back with her right and struck again.

Daphne tumbled, as she did so she dropped the knife.

Cara lunged to pick it up, and seeing Daphne groan on the floor, hand over her face, she realised the threat was over.

49

Paula looked out of the window, across the wide bow and curve of the beach to the Ettrick Bay Tearoom, to see if her expected arrivals might be early. She didn't really have a good vantage point from there to see who was coming along the road, but she looked anyway.

After about four months on her own in the cottage she was about to have some visitors. And although she'd spoken to them both on the phone and by text, numerous times, she was feeling a little nervous.

The small clock on the oven told her she had half an hour before the ferry got in, once she made allowances for the one-hour error. She still didn't know how to change the thing to account for the clocks going back.

Did she have time to shower and change? She looked down at the t-shirt, cardigan and loose sweatpants she was wearing. They could take her as they found her, she thought.

In bare feet, she made her way through to her bathroom and examined her hair in the mirror above the sink. How could a woman live in a house with so few mirrors? What had Thomas been thinking?

She placed fingers on both cheeks, eased the skin back and down, temporarily removing the bags. Had she aged? Or was her skin dried and windblown after all those long walks? She turned her attention to her hair. She could at least tug some of the knots out. Noticing the grey hair coming in at her temples and threading through her middle parting she wondered at the woman she'd become. Big pants and grey hair. What would Thomas make of her?

After she'd yanked at her head and patted her hair down into something resembling a style, she went back to the bedroom and checked the time on the small clock on her bedside cabinet. They'd be here in forty-five minutes. She spotted the novel at the side of the clock. There was enough time to finish another chapter.

The wee bookshop and the library in Rothesay had become her refuges. Access to other lives through books helped her make sense of her own. As the winter storms battered the bay beyond her window, these volumes had become her friends and respite.

But now the real world was about to come knocking – in the shape of the only two people left in the world who cared whether or not she was still a part of it. Father Joe and, somewhat surprisingly, Cara Connolly. Who'd have thought that after that inauspicious meeting they'd have gone on to become friends.

Amazing what facing down a pair of pathological murderers could do for a friendship.

Of course the papers had been full of the death of Bill Gadd. Daphne and her Polish lover had been painted as the demon couple, which wasn't that far from the truth, but you'd think there had been no other crime committed throughout the history of Glasgow given the glee with which the media reported it.

The similarities to the Moldovan financial scandal gave the newspapers licence to attack the Scottish Government for allowing another such crime to happen. With the addition of sex and murder, the press had a field day.

Rusnak had disappeared, a feat that Cara said she found impressive, given the damage she'd done to his knee. It turned out his name wasn't Anton Rusnak at all. His car registration as recorded by Cara's phone led to an address in the Gorbals where a passport in the name of one Jan Kowalski was found. The photo inside matched the man Paula had seen murder Bill Gadd.

It was a moment that visited her regularly as she slept.

The police detective, Rossi, assured her that without a passport he couldn't leave the country and the people he would have normally turned to for help in getting over to the continent were the people he'd been fleecing. Rossi was convinced he was currently feeding whatever creatures inhabited the bed of the River Clyde.

Paula wasn't so sure. The thought that he might be alive and kicking had almost kept her away from the cottage, but then she considered that if he was still intent on doing her damage, it wouldn't much matter where she was living, he'd find a way to do just that.

Thankfully, Daphne had pleaded guilty to all charges – complicity to murder, drug dealing and money laundering. So there had been no trial, and her jail sentence was pleasingly hefty. Suffice to say, by the time she got out, should she outlive it, she'd be heading for an old folks' home. An image of Daphne, blue rinse, zimmer at the ready, surrounded by other very old people, their collective milky-white stare focussed on a giant TV screen showing nothing but an endless run of *Pointless Celebrities*, cheered Paula no end.

◊

Bang on time, she heard a knock at the front door. Without waiting for her to answer, Father Joe walked in, followed by a smiling Cara Connolly and a waft of cold, sharp air.

'Quick, come in,' Paula said, and pointed to the sofa. 'Have a seat.' Now that they were here, she was feeling weirdly nervous. But that was soon washed away with the good cheer and hugs both of her visitors shared with her.

'You look well,' said Joe as he sat down.

'Aye, you were a bit of a skinny bitch before,' agreed Cara. 'A wee bit of podge suits you.'

'A wee bit of podge,' Paula repeated, arranging herself on the armchair, pretending to be outraged, while thinking that her face might split in two, her smile was so big at seeing these two.

'Aye, and if that means you need to get rid of some of your designer gear, I'm your woman.'

Paula snorted. 'Those clothes are going nowhere, darling. Soon as I'm back in the city, I'm on the quinoa and lettuce.'

'Right,' said Joe. 'When did you ever have a diet that included lettuce?'

Paula reached across from her seat and patted Joe on the knee in lieu of another long hug. 'It's so good to see you both.' She stood up. 'Coffee?'

They both smiled at the offer.

'And some scones?'

'You made scones?' Joe asked, mouth long. He turned to Cara. 'She made scones.'

'Quick, send for the Women's Institute. We need to make sure these scones measure up,' said Cara.

'Oy, shut up, the pair of you,' Paula got to her feet and made her way towards the kitchen. 'Or I'll spit in your clotted cream.'

Joe laughed, and Paula revelled in the sound of it. They'd had lots of late-night phone conversations since Bill's death. One brother dying was bad enough, but two? There was a week or so when Paula was really worried that he might not recover. And he'd apologised endlessly for being posted missing in her hour of need.

'Not sure what you would have been able to do,' Paula had replied during one midnight call, trying to stave off his guilt. 'You would have probably ended up dead as well.'

'But still. I disappeared and...'

'Why go so suddenly? I was sure something had happened to you.'

'Everything just became so suffocating. Everyone felt suffocating...'

'Sorry for caring.' Paula tried to joke, but even to her ears it felt huffy.

'I don't know how to accept help, Paula. I can't deal with people's sympathy.'

'Would you rather nobody cared?'

'Course not. Anyway, don't remember how it happened. I was in my car, just driving. Hours later, I was in Inverness and I found a wee bed and breakfast. Bought some clean pants from M&S, and did nothing but walk and sleep for a few days.' She then heard another note of apology in his voice, 'While you were...'

Cara got to her feet, thrusting Paula back into the present. 'I'll give you a hand. And make sure that the scones are spit free,' she threw back at Joe as she walked towards the kitchen.

He laughed a hearty response.

In the kitchen in front of the kettle, Cara gave Paula another hug, holding her for a long moment.

'What was that for?' Paula asked when they separated.

'Just because,' Cara answered. A kind stranger had offered to pay for a headstone for Danny's grave when they heard his mother couldn't afford one. This was obviously Cara letting Paula know that she realised it was her.

'So, how are you? Really?' Cara asked.

'Och, you know...' Paula looked out of the window. 'I still find myself looking down that beach, expecting to see Thomas walk along it.' She gave a small laugh. Shook her head. 'I even have this wee fantasy that he faked his death, you know? That he'll turn up with a huge bouquet of roses. Beg my forgiveness and kiss my feet, carry me through to the bed and give me a good seeing-to.'

'Nutter,' laughed Cara.

'You don't know the half of it. I've got this whole scenario worked out. He faked his death because he couldn't think of any other way of getting away from the big Pole.'

'Right. So whose body did you cremate in this wee scenario?' Cara leaned against the work surface and crossed her arms.

'He paid somebody at the morgue for the body of some poor homeless guy.'

Cara made a face.

'Hey, at least in my scenario the wee homeless guy got a good send-off.'

Cara laughed. 'I repeat my earlier assertion. Crazy.'

Paula looked at the younger woman and felt her eyes tear up. 'I don't know what I would have done without you these last few months.' The two women had spoken often, as the ramifications of that evening hit home.

'The island life suits you, Paula,' Cara said eyeing her up and down, batting off Paula's thanks by ignoring it.

'Is that a nice way of saying I need to lose weight?'

'No, it's a nice way of saying you're looking well.' She grinned and looked at her hair. 'Mind you, I don't recall seeing a hedge in the garden.'

'It's out the back, darling. I drag myself through it every morning before elevenses.'

'You have elevenses?'

'Hence the scones.'

They laughed, then had a moment's silence while Paula lifted scones from the oven and put them on a tray. Cara made herself busy arranging mugs and instant coffee.

'It's like we're a wee team,' Cara said.

Paula eyed her with what she hoped was a mysterious look.

'What?' asked Cara.

'All in good time,' Paula answered with a smile.

The kettle came to the boil and in the moment's silence after, Paula heard an intake of breath from Cara as if she was going to say something. But nothing came. She looked over at her.

'What?'

Cara walked over to the sink, looked out of the window, turned and leaned her back against it, crossing her feet at the ankles.

'I don't get it,' she said. 'How do you reconcile the man who stole all that money, and the man who left you this?' She held her hands out and let them fall to slap against the side of her legs.

'I don't get it either, Cara. And, believe me, that's been on my mind these last few weeks. The cottage? Guilty conscience, or did he really want to heal our relationship?'

'It is a grand gesture right enough. Would you have fallen for it?'

'Dunno. The money thing, I get.' Paula shrugged. 'He'd do anything for his brother. And I bet he didn't trust that the Rusnak and his people would wipe out Joe's debt. Bill said that Thomas taking ten per cent and hiding it was his commission. I'm certain it was his attempt at getting some sort of insurance. He would have returned it when he had confirmation that Joe's debt was indeed written off.'

'Makes sense,' Cara offered. 'Clever in fact.'

'He was a clever man. Even in a situation like that, he found a way.'

There was a pause.

'I don't believe for a second he had any involvement in Bill and Daphne's wee drug empire.' Paula challenged Cara's view on this with a look. She said nothing, but gave a little nod to show her agreement.

'Do you think he ever found out the truth about Christopher's death?' Cara asked.

Paula shook her head. 'That, he wouldn't have been able to hide from me.' She felt a fresh stab of pain at the thought of Christopher being hit by the car. 'He'd have told me if he knew.'

A shout from the front room.

'Where's my scone?' asked Joe. 'If you heard that rumble it wasn't a passing truck, it was my stomach.'

🍷

In the living room, having eaten their scones and drank their coffee, Joe sat back with a satisfied look on his face.

'I shall be expecting this on a regular basis,' he said.

'That might well happen,' replied Paula looking at them both. 'If you agree with my plan.'

They both sat forwards with questions in their eyes.

'Now, it all depends whether or not the money is available to us. Or whether you guys think we should give it back.'

Joe and Cara looked at each other. Then back at Paula.

'Oh,' said Cara, where Paula was going with this clearly dawning on her.

'What are you talking about?' asked Joe.

'The missing million,' answered Paula. 'I found out where it is.'

Joe's mouth fell open.

The figure of nine million was what the media reported and it had been recovered. No one was talking about the missing one million. Those who knew, outside of the three in Paula's living room, were conveniently unavailable for comment.

On the morning after that fateful night before, Paula came home after what felt like days talking to a variety of policemen, slept for twenty-two hours and then, needing to distract herself, had decided to tackle the mini mountain of mail behind her front door.

Most of it, happily, she could bin. Some was for her charities, others were bills, but one piqued her curiosity. The envelope was handwritten – so rare these days – and was stamped and franked by a firm called Bloxwich, Paterson and Wright, based in Dumfries.

She had recalled the leaflet in Thomas's suit pocket at the cottage. The clues were all there. And at that she felt a pang of guilt. If she had opened the lawyer's letter just a day earlier, she would have known what Anton demanded from her. Would Bill still be alive today?

Then she remembered the comments between Daphne and Rusnak. Bill's days were numbered regardless of what happened to the money. As were hers, so any guilt she might feel was a waste of energy.

The letter explained that a certain Thomas Gadd had opened an account with the sum of one million pounds and in the event of his death his wife, Mrs Paula Gadd, should be made aware of the account and the funds therein.

Paula was certain Thomas had used the same method that the crooks had asked him to use to launder their money. And she felt a quiet sense of satisfaction as that idea struck her. Using their own plan against them had a certain kind of Thomas Gadd cleverness to it.

Theretofore – the letter was filled with all kinds of strange words – Mr Gadd's instructions were that a charitable organisation would be set up, to be called The Ettrick Enterprise Initiative, and the money should be used to encourage disadvantaged young Scots to get into business for themselves.

Now, with a mounting sense of excitement Paula explained all of this to Joe and Cara. And said how she had to drive down to Dumfries to speak to the partners and ask them to prepare the necessary papers.

Paula searched their faces as she spoke. She had a slight wiggle of worry that one of them would want the money to go to the authorities, given how it was obtained and how many people died because of it. When rehearsing what she was going to say to them she'd decided she would go with the consensus, but now the moment had come she wanted more than ever for this to happen. It would be the perfect way to honour Thomas's memory.

As she told them all of this, they listened open-mouthed. She finished by saying, 'And I would like each of you to be trustees in the charity with me. But...' she held her hands out '...if you think the money should go to the authorities, I'll get in touch with the police straight away.'

'None of us can benefit from any of this money,' said Cara.

'I like using Ettrick in the name of the charity. Our family has a long connection with this place.' Joe piped in.

'So, you're saying yes?' asked Paula.

'I'm saying yes,' answered Joe.

'It's too late for the likes of Danny, but I've already thought of people we could spend it on,' answered Cara with a giant grin.

𓆙

The sea was sliding into Ettrick Bay as if on slow rollers. The breeze was a cold salty nip on her nose, cheeks and chin. The sun wintered low, as sharp in her eyes as a torch beam when she faced it, the sky a galactic arch of blue with only the occasional butter-knife smear of cloud. In the distance, the mountains of Arran looked close enough to touch. Paula would never tire of this view, no matter how often she walked the bay.

Her mind strayed to her visitors, to their immediate assent to her plan, and their excitement at something good coming from all that evil.

She had made her way to the far end of the bay, and stopped to begin her walk back. She paused at the water's edge, allowing the slow creep of the sea to lick at her boots. Looking out towards the distant horizon, she felt a churn of hunger. She could reheat one of the scones in the oven, and imagined the butter on top melting into a golden smudge. At this thought she patted her stomach, she must have put on at least a stone in the last two months.

Thomas would barely recognise the woman she'd become. She smiled at the thought of him watching her baking, asking what had happened to the anti-sugar brigade. They'd been replaced with the 'everything in moderation' mob, she'd say.

She did that a lot still. Held a conversation in her head with him.

Further along, she noticed a woman walking a centre line from the tearoom to the water's edge. She was wearing a tan-coloured puffer jacket, a red scarf and her long black hair was streaming back from her like ribbons in the stiff breeze. There was a stateliness about her movement, as if she was performing to a ceremony of her own devising.

Paula judged that at this pace, their paths would cross, and she wondered whether or not she should alter her course. But she did nothing, curious as to how this might, or might not develop. Since Thomas had died, talking to strangers was always easier than talking to friends. No expectations. No fumbled apologies. No awkward silences.

The woman was holding a large bag. A colour match for her coat. She reached into it, and, as if feeling Paula's presence, she paused. Looking over, their eyes met and the woman lifted her empty hand from the bag and stuffed it into her pocket.

Paula would have been willing to bet that the bag held an urn. She read the loss in the woman's eyes, in the waxen slump of her expression, and increased her pace so she could get past her and give the woman the time and space she needed.

But as she drew near, she couldn't help but reach out, to offer the small easing that comes with a shared human experience. With a light touch on the woman's arm, she opened her mouth as if to speak, then realised communication in this moment couldn't be carried in vowels and consonants. Instead her offering was a smile and in that smile a promise; it may not ever ease, but it will get easier.

Acknowledgements

My huge thanks and appreciation go to...

Elaine Teenan for her generous donation to The Scarlett Fund in return for me using her name in this book. I hope you like what I've done with "you", Elaine.

Sharon Bairden and her colleagues at Ceartas Advocacy in Kirkintilloch for their patience in describing their work to me. Any mistakes in the depiction of this valuable work in our society are entirely mine. (Certain changes may have been made to suit the characters and the action of the story – it's a novel, innit.)

My first readers, Mike Craven and Douglas Skelton.

The OUTSTANDING editorial team of Karen Sullivan and West Camel.

Team Orenda – you guys rock!

And finally, to all the reviewers, bloggers, booksellers, book-festival schedulers, and most importantly, readers: none of this scribbling would be worth it without you. From the bottom of my heart, thank you!